SNOW WARS

for sweets

∞

Published by Westworld International Limited
London, England
020 8788 2455

westworldinternational.com

A CIP catalogue record for this book is available from the British Library. ISBN 0-9529215-5-3

Printed and bound by Mackays of Chatham, Kent
Cover design by TigerDesigns 020 8788 1978
Distributed by Central Books 020 8986 4854
Authors photograph by Diney Horsting

Snow Wars author J.M. Rumfitt was trekking in Morocco's High Atlas Mountains when he came across the plantation. Row upon row of terraced bushes stretching as far as the eye could see.

It looked like tea. But was it?

Days later in a bar in Marrakech a tourist was offered a **line of snow**

"It's good" boasted the Arab. "It's locally grown."

The tourist rolled a fifty Dirham note and inhaled. It was as good as the best he'd ever had. "Locally grown?" He shook his head.

"Nobody grows cocaine outside of South America."

"Why not?" smiled the Arab. "If the climate and soil conditions are right?"

"The Colombians wouldn't like it. The Cartels would close the operation down. It could get very messy."

At dawn the next morning the Arab was dumped in the middle of *Djeema el Fna*, his throat slit from ear to ear.

Snow Wars had claimed it's first victim.

1

"So what's the big deal?"

"Step outside, I'll show you." Ben Ambrose opened the terrace doors and a blast of hot air hit him in the face.

"Wow! That's quite a view." Willowby looked across the bay at the great limestone Rock of Gibraltar and down at the teeming port of Algeciras immediately below. A mere twelve miles away across the Strait the mountains of North Africa could be clearly seen.

"Here," said Ambrose, handing Willowby the binoculars. "That's Ceuta, right there."

Willowby adjusted the focus and the ancient walled city sprang to view.

"What do you see?" said Ambrose

"The world's biggest cannabis producer?"

"Aside from that."

"A small port in Morocco?"

"Spain."

"Spain? Like Gibraltar belongs to the Brits?"

"More so. Ceuta is part of Spain. Gibraltar's just a colony. There's another enclave, Melilla, about two hundred miles east of here, but Ceuta is the better bet. It's closer. It's big enough to get lost in. About five square miles, twice the size of Gib. Seventy-five thousand population. There's a five-mile land frontier with Morocco and a wall the whole length of the border, patrolled by *Guardia Civil*. Getting over, under or around the wall isn't a problem and there are two thousand illegal immigrants rotting in squalid camps. So the supply of mules is virtually unlimited. Maybe we should buy the customs post. It would take money, big money. But all I really need is some local help. Some one who knows the ground. They're both problems I can solve."

"Sounds great." said Willowby. "When do you start?"

"Already did."

***

Ben Ambrose had rented the apartment just off the *Plaza Maior* on the edge of the old town. What drew him to the place was the view of the bustling port of Algeciras just below the terrace. The Rock of Gibraltar was directly across the bay and, a mere twelve miles away across the Strait, the mountains of North Africa seemed close enough to touch. With the binoculars he kept on a table just inside the terrace doors Ambrose could pick out the individual buildings of the ancient walled city of Ceuta, and spot one of the high-powered launches when it was about half way across the Straight. Sometimes a launch would turn up the coast to Malaga or Valencia, but often they would come straight into Algeciras and he would watch them unload cargo. There was no supervision, no customs, between two parts of the same country.

Algeciras is the main ferry port between North Africa and Spain and there are constant shipping movements to and fro, between it and the North African ports of Tangier, Ceuta and Melilla. Tangier is in Morocco. But what fascinated Ambrose was that Ceuta and Melilla, though on the Continent of Africa, are in fact a part of Spain. Like the British possession of Gibraltar on the Spanish mainland, they are historical leftovers from an earlier colonial time. Ceuta and Melilla, both integral parts of Spain, have land frontiers with Morocco. Customs clearance happens on the African continent. Between Ceuta and mainland Spain there are no formalities at all.

Of the two enclaves it was Ceuta that interested Ambrose most. It was so close. Contraband and piracy had been its only significant activities for centuries and the culture of corruption, of kickbacks, was deeply rooted. Buying the customs post shouldn't be a problem. Ambrose had researched the lifestyle of Juan Muñoz, Head of Customs in Ceuta. He had just the right exploitable flaws of venality and greed. On what must have been a very modest salary Muñoz frequented some of the most expensive private clubs and gambling joints on the Coast and holidayed in exotic resorts? He might cost ten thousand dollars, maybe more. But money was not an obstacle; the potential rewards were so great. There it was, the world's biggest producer of Mary Jane, right across the water. Ambrose's only problem was his own lack of local knowledge. He didn't know the language and didn't know the ground. But Ambrose already had the solution a handpicked man with experience on both sides of the tracks.

Ambrose raised the binoculars, adjusted the focus, and watched the aircraft taxi for position on the Gibraltar runway.

***

Alex Bowman sat in an aisle seat on British Airways flight 384, while the pilot waited for clearance to take off. Bowman was close to forty, just over six feet tall, with a prominent jaw and thick brown close-cropped hair. His skin was weathered and lined, eyes light blue, hands large and clumsy. He wore jeans, trainers and a dark blue sweatshirt. In the compartment overhead he had placed his loose-fitting bomber jacket and the overnight bag that contained his one remaining suit, carefully folded. Bowman liked things tidy, everything in its proper place so if he needed something in a hurry he wouldn't have to waste time looking for it.

The BAC 1-11 is a small plane by anybody's standards but for Bowman its cramped conditions were torture. He hated flying at the best of times but the 1-11 was the plane he hated most. He'd had a problem with tight spaces ever since his time in jail, but worse was the slow juddering ascent to cruising height. Anxiety turned to panic as the plane suddenly surged forward, thrusting to get airborne before it reached the water at the end of the short runway. Bowman felt his stomach drop as the aircraft lifted off and forced himself to look out of the window as the Bay of Algeciras swung into view below. Briefly he glimpsed the narrow mouth of the Straits and the mountains of North Africa rising steeply from the ocean, when the plane banked sharply and circled the great limestone Rock of Gibraltar. The two underpowered Rolls-Royce engines hauled fifty-five tonnes of metal, kerosene and flesh into the sky and he wondered, as he always did, if they were going to make it.

The plane climbed through turbulence. Bowman braced himself in his seat and squeezed the armrests with his hands. He began to sweat and wanted to loosen his collar but his hands would not let go of the armrests, so he closed his eyes and listened to the note of the engines, afraid they might suddenly stall. Gradually the plane ascended and the juddering faded. The tightness in his stomach and chest subsided and he found he could move in his seat without rocking the plane. He released the armrests. They were going to make it after all.

"Can I buy you a drink? I've never seen anyone so nervous." Melanie Drake sat across the aisle from him, smiling. He had noticed her boarding. She might have been thirty but she moved like a young girl, a dancer. Auburn haired, with a fiery complexion, and probably the temperament to go with it. She wore jeans and a blouse that hid her figure and Bowman guessed she had a good enough body to justify the precaution. Her eyes were chestnut and she wore librarian's glasses with tortoiseshell frames. If she was wearing make-up it didn't show. She looked as fresh as if she had just stepped out of the shower.

"Thanks," said Bowman, forcing a smile. "I'll have a gin and tonic." They were at cruising height now, but he wasn't in the mood to talk, not even to an attractive woman. But a drink was something he could really use.

"Better make it two." She smiled up at the stewardess and opened the book she had brought for the journey, *Garcia Lorca*, the *Obras Completas,* with a parallel translation. Her Spanish wasn't good enough to read poetry unaided. She didn't want him to think she was trying to pick him up. It was just that he seemed so nervous. She almost felt she should take his hand and tell him it was going to be all right. She knew who he was, remembered the trial, but couldn't think of his name. He could be just the subject she needed. Good material was hard to find and the best place to look for it was in real life.

Bowman poured both of the miniatures and a little of the tonic over the ice and half emptied the glass at a throw. He smiled his thanks at the woman, but she was reading now and he didn't want to disturb her. He closed his eyes and replayed Faraday's phone call in his mind. He hadn't seen or heard from Faraday for years, not since the trial. Faraday had defended him. Unsuccessfully.

The slow descent at Heathrow was a nightmare. The turbulence started soon after they left cruising height and got worse when they entered the cloud. There was no feeling of forward motion, just the sensation of being buffeted from side to side like a small boat on an angry ocean. He breathed deeply, and waited for the worst to happen.

But suddenly the sky cleared and Bowman rejoiced to see they were a few thousand feet above the Thames at Chiswick, on a westerly approach to the airport, running parallel to the motorway. They would be on the ground in minutes. No time now for anything to go seriously wrong. The wheels hit the runway, the plane bounced once then made contact a final time, as the pilot put the engines into reverse thrust.

"That wasn't too bad, was it?" Melanie Drake closed her book and began to gather her things.

"Not if you have a death wish, I suppose." Bowman grinned. He stood to help her get her hand luggage from the overhead compartment and blocked the aisle behind her so she could exit the plane unhindered. Then he stood aside for the rest of the passengers to go ahead of him.

He saw her again in the baggage hall, loading two matching cases onto a trolley.

He thought of taking a taxi into town so he could offer her a lift but the chances of a woman that attractive being free, on the one night he planned to spend in the city, were too remote. So he headed for the tube instead, cursing himself as he went. "God! Bowman, you are a wimp! Ask her for a date! If she says no, you won't die, for God sake!"

She watched him disappear along the crowded concourse. She wasn't sure what made him so attractive. He wasn't particularly handsome. His face was narrow and his nose too large. It must have to do with his spirit she thought, the fact they hadn't been able to break him.

Five years behind bars would destroy any other man she could think of. But innocent or guilty Alex Bowman had kept his self-esteem intact. For a moment she thought of catching him up. A car and driver were waiting for her outside. But she decided against it. She had returned to

London to close a chapter, not open a new one. "Dinner with a girl friend, I suppose. Pity. Shame to waste him."

***

2

Daisy stood in a doorway on the north side of Berkeley Square, waiting for the rain to stop. It was torrential, driving hard onto the pavement and bouncing back a couple of feet into the air, like shattered crystal, slowing the late night traffic to a crawl.

A woman entered his field of vision from the right and stood peering at him through the rain. He lit a cigarette, the brief glow from the match illuminating his face. She gasped and looked away. He threw the match into the gutter and exhaled. She moved on hurriedly, glancing back at him as she went.

Suddenly the rain was over, leaving the air fresh and scented. Daisy crossed the tree-lined square and made his way south to Piccadilly, turning left towards the Circus and the tube station. People recoiled as he passed, as if his innocent condition might be contagious. He didn't mind, not any more. He enjoyed being special, enjoyed intimidating them just by the way he looked. There was a time when he would have turned his coat collar up and worn a hat with a broad brim, but he was past that now. Let the vermin take a good long look if they wanted. If they dared.

He went down the steps into the tube station and did a circuit of the doughnut shaped concourse. It was deserted except for the odd late night barman or musician, and the kids who had nowhere to go. As he completed his first circuit he could feel the buzz that had preceded him. All the kids knew about Daisy. He was a myth, a legend. Stories were told about him.

The girl was young, about fifteen, her figure full, her skin unblemished. She hadn't been hooked for long. She wore a lot of artless make-up, which he liked, especially the mouth, a vivid red, full lips pouting. She was just what he wanted, a coarse beauty, a gutter lovely. She had already found her protector, a skinny acnied youth of about sixteen in a leather jacket embedded with big steel studs to make him feel like a man.

Daisy didn't waste time. He didn't speak, just took the bottle from his pocket and showed it to the pair of them, with its pure white crystals, about the size of an aspirin. They grinned at each other, then back at Daisy, eyes bright with excitement. He could tell how badly they needed it, could sense their exhilaration almost as keenly as they could themselves. He could feel his own excitement too, mounting, growing, though his need was more terrible than theirs, slower and more dangerous, but just as compelling.

They knew what he wanted. It was part of the myth, the legend. The girl led the way to the toilets while her protector stood guard by the door. She entered the first cubicle, nearest the door, and sat down to wait for him. Daisy came and stood in front of her, taking her head in his hands.

"What's your name?"

"Mandy." She wanted to vomit.

"Mandy, is it?" He closed his eyes. "Mandy. And your friend?"

"Justin."

"Justin. That's nice. Justin."

What happened next disgusted her but she had to turn five or six tricks a day to feed her habit. At least she would not get pregnant. Best of all it would be over very quickly and she would get what she wanted, what she needed.

When it was done Daisy took one of the crystals from the bottle and watched as she dropped it, trembling, into the bowl of a short-stemmed pipe and lit it. He longed to hit her, strike her blood red mouth with the back of his hand, but he held back, saving that thrill for later, saving it for the boy.

The intense high, the rush she got from the crack was immediate. She lay back, propped in the corner of the tiny cubicle, like a broken doll. She kept moaning, eyes closed, limbs akimbo, barely breathing. The high would last only seconds, minutes if she were lucky. The depression when she came down would be suicidal. She would need a shot of heroin then, just to help her through it, would have to turn a trick immediately to buy another fix. Daisy didn't plan to be there when that happened; the girl wasn't what he wanted after all.

He left her there, still high, and went to find the boy again. Justin smiled, knowing it was his turn next. Daisy stroked him soothingly on the shoulder as they climbed the stairs to look for a taxi. He couldn't resist putting a hand around the boy's neck and giving it a gentle squeeze. It was a small neck, the neck of a child. It would snap very easily.

***

The rickety old Mercedes taxi deposited its passenger in front of the terminal building at Malaga airport. Harvey Lieberman paid the driver and asked for a receipt in accented but correct Spanish. He watched the porter load the two identical suitcases onto a trolley and followed him to the Iberia desk. The check-in clerk verified the flight details on the ticket and put the Malaga/Heathrow segment inside the boarding pass. Next she tagged the two matching cases, detached the tear-off sections, and stapled them to the ticket cover. He watched her every movement like a child observing how the grown-ups did it.

Lieberman was about fifty, expensively dressed in a tailored mohair business suit, a silk shirt and hand painted tie with matching handkerchief in the top pocket of his jacket. His face was lined and deeply tanned, hair jet black, probably dyed. His stocky frame was overweight by twenty pounds or so, but this didn't soften the menace in his face one bit. The overall effect was money, new money that was made, not earned.

He walked through the security check and passport control, glancing at the eighteen carat Oyster on his wrist.

Once inside the departure lounge he made for the washroom, entered a cubicle, locked the door, and sat with his briefcase on his knees. He took out a stapler and an unused flight ticket, identical to the one he had handed to the check-in clerk. He detached the Malaga/Heathrow segment and transferred one of the baggage identification tags, attaching it to the new ticket cover with the stapler carefully aligned over the existing holes. It was something he had practised many times, so he knew he had it just right. He tore up the first ticket with the two telltale stapler marks, and the second identification tag, and watched them vanish into the sewage system.

Two and a half hours later he stood by a carousel in Terminal Two at Heathrow Airport, watching the baggage pass in front of him. The two suitcases appeared together. He grabbed the first and knew at once by its weight it wasn't the one he wanted, waited for the belt to complete a circuit, and grabbed the second, lighter case, and placed it on the trolley. He was sweating, though the air-conditioned hall was cool. He pulled the silk handkerchief from his pocket and wiped his brow and the palms of his hands. Now was the moment of maximum risk. The next ninety seconds would decide the future of the entire project.

Just then Lieberman spotted the three black youths, uniformly dressed in sawn-off denims and sleeveless sweatshirts, dreadlocks brushing their shoulders. They were the cover he needed. He moved off, a yard or so behind them, nervously pushing the trolley through the green channel. Sure enough the trio distracted the customs official and Lieberman passed unnoticed behind them, knowing that if he were questioned the identification tag on the suitcase would not match the one on his ticket.

He went outside into the freezing air and grabbed a taxi. “Jesus it’s cold!” he said to the cabbie.

“They say it’s going to snow, guv.”

“You can bet your ass on that, my friend. Matter of fact, there’ll soon be more snow in this town than anybody’s ever seen.”

The late afternoon traffic was light and they made good time to the centre. He was glad to be in London again. It was his favourite city. He much preferred it to his native New York. He felt at home here. In his business London was a province, though its potential was truly enormous. In a year or two he could make it the next Miami. A major international hub.

By the time the taxi reached the West End it was raining heavily, slowing the traffic to a crawl. Park Lane was bumper to bumper. They rounded Grosvenor Square and pulled up outside The Connaught, London's most exclusive small hotel. A uniformed doorman in brown coat and matching derby came out to the taxi with an umbrella and sheltered him from the downpour while he paid the cab. Lieberman didn't let the suitcase out of his sight, not for a single second. He checked in, using his own name, and rode in the lift with the porter who wheeled the suitcase into his room.

Alone in the room hc locked the door, bolted it, and closed the curtains. Next he unlocked the case, emptied it, and with a small silver penknife cut the lining carefully around the inside rim. He lifted out the false bottom, which concealed a gap a couple of centimetres deep, and took out a clear plastic envelope that contained precisely 100 grams of fine white powder. He put the envelope in the drawer in the bedside table, went to the bathroom and scrubbed his hands with care, washing and rinsing them several times before he was satisfied. He looked at his watch. It was an hour before the representative was due. He switched on the television to watch the early evening news and smiled. Harvey Lieberman was about to talk himself into the biggest deal of his life.

***

The knock at the door came punctually at seven. Lieberman turned down the sound on the TV and went to the door and opened it. He hadn't expected a woman. She was neatly dressed in a black tight fitting dress and a hat with a broad brim, which put her face in deep shadow, making it impossible to guess her age or see her features clearly.

She didn't speak, but stood aside for the guardian angel to enter first. The man was an albino with Negroid features and tightly curled white hair. Even his eyes had no real pigmentation, except for the whites, which were pink. He was dressed in a dark grey business suit, tailored to accommodate his massive bulk and still leave room for the holster.

Daisy didn't glance at the American but went quickly about the room in a well-practised routine, searching the larger spaces first, the wardrobe, the bathroom, even under the bed. Then he produced a detection device from his briefcase and examined everything electrical from the television to the telephone and every wall plug. In a couple of minutes he pronounced the room clean.

"Wait outside for me, Daisy" said the woman in black, and the albino took up a position in the corridor, directly opposite the door. Then she went to the TV to turn the sound back up and sat on the bed and crossed her shapely legs.

"OK mister, I don't have much time. What's your pitch?" She had a mid-Atlantic accent, just like his, but he didn't think hers was authentic. She was faking it, as a diversion or an entertainment, as if she were playing a game.

"I'm growing *Erythroxylon Coca* in the High Atlas, thirty miles south east of Marrakech. I bought a citrus farm up there. Three hundred acres of fruit trees! Right now about half has been switched to the new product. The locals think it's some kinda tea." He paused to let her grasp the enormity of what he was saying. "It hasn't been done before, not on an industrial scale. I have the perfect site, perfect climate, perfect soil conditions. I have good irrigation, an abundant labour force, and a team of trained chemists who work for me full time. I have processing capability right there in Morocco. I do the whole thing on site, from growing the stuff right on down to pure cocaine hydrochloride. I can get it into Spain easily enough and I can get it into England. You people control the UK retail market. But I guess you're having problems with supplies. One of my guys hacked into the DEA files. They've had a major success defoliating the Bolivian jungle. Five years ago production in the source zone was

950 metric tonnes. Last year it was under 800. That's good for the DEA but it's bad for you guys, drives up the price and cuts back on volume. And if my information's right, things are about to get much tougher. I think we can do business."

Lieberman had rehearsed the presentation for days. His pitch was short and to the point, not his natural style at all, but it was what these people expected. Tiffany had told him so, and Tiffany should know.

Lieberman could tell the woman was impressed. He knew she would be. All of the cocaine reaching Europe came in from South America, from Colombia and Bolivia. Bringing the stuff across three thousand miles of ocean was a risky business and the Duty Men were making it harder as the months went by and established routes became impossible to use. Seizures and arrests were rising all the time. Worst of all, the South Americans had a monopoly and that was bad for the woman and her people. It put the producers in far too strong a bargaining position. The Colombians controlled the market and fixed the price. The woman's organisation were distributors, big and powerful too, but just distributors, with no production of their own. If they could get reliable supplies in bulk from other sources, sources close to Europe, they could break the cartel's hold on the market and drive down the wholesale price, keeping a better margin for themselves.

The woman lit a cigarette. The glow from the match gave him a brief glimpse of her face. She was older than he expected, older and more attractive. She puffed smoke in rings, watching them expand and disappear. She was considering her response carefully, feigning lack of interest. But her mind was racing as she strove to grasp the implications of what he was saying. Cocaine was the champagne of the drugs trade, the premium product everybody wanted. It had a mystique, a glamour, a folklore that other drugs simply didn't possess - even a vocabulary of it's own with code words like *Stardust, Snowbird, Candy, Peruvian Lady, White Girl* and *Gangster*. When she spoke again the mid-Atlantic accent had gone. She had decided to take him seriously.

"How much can you supply on a regular basis, say monthly?"

"Up to fifty kilos of pure cocaine hydrochloride, the very best quality in the world. Delivery would be in ten-kilo drops to a UK location of your choice. Payment in advance to a numbered account in Zurich. You people have laundering facilities to do that. You're a big organisation, respected. That's why I made contact."

This was a far, far bigger deal than she had anticipated, big enough to transform the Organisation overnight into a truly world class player. Alter the whole long-term business strategy. Potentially big enough to give them decisive leverage over the Colombians. Fifty kilos of pure cocaine hydrochloride, cut, adulterated, diluted, it's weight increased at every turn, would make five hundred kilos by the time it hit the street. The ramifications were enormous. She would need time. Finance wasn't a problem but the politics would need to be thought through extremely carefully. If the Colombians got wind of a deal like this it could lead to open warfare.

"You have a sample?"

"Sure." He took the plastic envelope from the drawer and put it on the bed beside her.

It was his first careless move. One hundred grams of pure cocaine hydrochloride would have a street value of anything up to a hundred thousand pounds. Why would anybody produce an amount that large just as a sample? It was impossible he didn't know its worth.

"You understand I have to have this analysed before we can do a deal?" His move had made her nervous but her voice didn't change and her expression was fixed.

"No problem. You'll find it's better than the best you've ever seen."

"The lab only needs a few grams. Why such a big sample?" She probed.

Harvey had spotted his mistake. Giving away that much value was dumb. He didn't need to impress her. Producing the stuff on the doorstep of Europe was impressive enough. "A token." He smiled expansively. "I don't want any doubt I can deliver." He had talked big all his life. It was more than a habit. It was his trademark. His way of doing business. "Do we have a deal?"

"I have to talk it over with my partners first. I don't anticipate a problem. Not if the sample checks out. But we may not agree payment in advance, not on the first delivery. There may have to be another arrangement at the start, until we develop a basis of trust. I'm sure it will all work out." She lit another cigarette, re-crossing her legs and adjusting the line of her skirt. "How long will you be staying in London, Harvey? We'd be happy to arrange some hospitality for you, anything you like. A few days in the country perhaps? Good food, good wine, good company. We have a place in Surrey we use for entertaining."

He didn't think it was herself she was offering. He was disappointed. There was something powerfully sexy about the lady. A sense of dominance, of danger. Next time, he promised himself, next time. Money can buy anything, even a very intelligent woman. "I'll stay here at the hotel till your lab has done its tests. I can get anything I need from room service. Where can I reach you?"

"Nice try, mister." The mid-Atlantic accent was back. He wondered why she did it. She did it very well, he had to admit. She was really quite convincing. "Don't worry, I know how to get in touch."

As she reached the door she hesitated and stood with her head slightly bowed, the brim of her hat shading her eyes. When she spoke her voice was a whisper. She had finished playing games. "How is she?"

"Tiffany? Tiffany's just fine."

"Is she clean?"

He smiled and shook his head, he wanted to laugh but he didn't. "Tiffany will never be clean."

"Say hello to her for me. And thank her for putting us in touch."

***

3

Next morning Bowman rose early. He had hardly slept. He showered, shaved and dressed carefully in his one remaining suit and checked his appearance in the long mirror. He smiled. He wore the suit no more than once or twice a year. He looked like a businessman on his way to an interview for a new job. As he looked at his reflection, the image of the woman on the plane flashed across his mind and he realised that letting her go was a mistake. A woman that attractive who read *Garcia Lorca* just had to be something special.

It was a bright spring morning and Bowman decided to walk the three or four miles from the King's Head, his seedy hotel in Earl's Court, to Faraday's chambers in the Temple. He made his way along crowded pavements to the Thames at Chelsea and followed the river to Westminster and along the Embankment to Waterloo Bridge.

He was sweating as he climbed the stairs to Faraday's chambers. When he reached the third floor he paused for breath and pushed open the door to a small cluttered office that smelled of dust and stale tobacco. This was the Dickensian world of the English legal profession, where the semi squalor belied the enormous sums top practitioners like Faraday could earn. The clerk showed Bowman hurriedly into Faraday's inner sanctum, too quickly Bowman thought, as if he were someone to be ashamed of. But Faraday rose when he entered, held out his hand and greeted him warmly enough.

"Alex, it's good to see you! How long has it been?" Faraday was almost as tall as Bowman but slightly built, with a pronounced stoop which had started as an affectation when he was young, to add a touch of theatre to courtroom performances.

Bowman was about to answer when he saw the other figure seated in a high backed chair near the window, back to the light. He hadn't risen. He seemed to be looking straight at Alex, but didn't smile and didn't speak. The room was dimly lit and Bowman couldn't make out what he looked like, except that he was small and not young.

"Take a seat, Alex." Faraday was saying. "There's someone here I'd like you to meet, which we'll come to shortly." He spoke quickly, anxious to get to the point, but needing to go through some preamble, which Alex presumed had to do with the stranger.

"Tell me how things are with you Alex, the sort of life you have now." Faraday looked from Alex to the seated man who watched, silent and immobile.

"What do you want to know? How I survive? How I make a living?" Alex was used to fielding questions. Sometimes it had gone on for days.

"That's right Alex, how *do* you make a living?"

"I run a security business on the Costa del Sol. Crime prevention. Security fences. Video surveillance. Armed guards. Licensed, of course. I'm well qualified, sometimes I even enjoy it." Bowman had a good reputation on the Coast. He wasn't ashamed of the work he did and took pride in doing it well. It was just that he felt he had talents that weren't being used, and that in the end the work wasn't really important, not like the job he was trained for.

"Well qualified." Faraday repeated Bowman's phrase, eying the figure in the chair. "Who are your clients, Alex? Mainly British I suppose?

"Brits, Arabs, Americans, occasionally Spanish." Alex had lived in Spain for five years now and spoke the language fluently, not true Castilian, but the clipped nasal Andaluz, with its hard vowels and truncated endings.

"You kept the same identity? Still Alex Bowman? You never thought of changing your name? Discard the past, make a new start, and even come back home. Wouldn't you like to, Alex? In a few years you'll be thinking of retirement."

"Sure I'd like to come back, but only as Alex Bowman. I'm innocent. You know that." He felt his throat tighten as he instinctively defended himself.

"Yes, I know that." Faraday glanced again at the seated figure. Bowman saw him nod. "Alex, you must excuse me now. There's some business I must attend to in another room. I'll leave the two of you together. This is Lord Berringer, by the way. Mary's father."

***

"You'll forgive me if I don't shake hands." It wasn't a question. Lord Berringer stood in the light by the window. He was a small man with a fleshy but distinguished face, high domed forehead, great bald pate and small hands. The head seemed too big for his frame and he looked like he might lose his balance. Alex recalled he was Chairman of a giant conglomerate with operations in Africa and the Far East. He hadn't appeared at the trial, hadn't wanted the publicity. After all, his daughter was only a witness, not the accused.

"I hope you'll pardon my charade." The voice was cultured and precise. "I wanted a look at you before we spoke. It's a delicate matter. I needed to be sure you were suitable." He was looking out of the window at something in the courtyard below. "I hadn't seen or heard from Mary for years when she called. That was nearly a week ago. It took that long to find you. I don't know precisely why she called. She rambled on for a long time, drunk I suppose." Berringer came and sat in the chair again, opposite Bowman. His movements were surprisingly brisk. His tone became suddenly deeper, businesslike.

"Let me start at the beginning. Last Friday evening I was at my house in Belgravia. I'm not there as a rule on Fridays. I go to my estate in the country for weekends. But I had a social engagement that kept me in town. I had dressed and was waiting for my driver to pick me up, when the phone went. It was the international operator. Would I accept a reverse charges call from Marbella? She said a name that meant nothing to me, but my number is ex-directory so I thought whomever it was must know me and took the call. When I heard the voice it was Mary's."

Berringer's voice softened as he replayed his daughter's phone call in his mind. He took a handkerchief from his pocket and mopped his cheeks and brow. He was trembling slightly. "She rambled on about all sorts of things, terrible things. Then suddenly she blurted out she'd lied at the trial. Said she'd had no choice. She sounded desperate, afraid. She said you would help her." He got up again and returned to the window, back to Bowman, while he composed himself. Without turning round he shouted an instruction, arms rigid at his sides, "You must find her for me!"

"Find her?" Why would I want to find her?" Alex went suddenly pale, the memory of her flooding his senses.

"Mary was a victim Bowman, just as you were. Maybe she didn't go to jail, but that doesn't mean she wasn't damaged." Berringer's voice hardened again as he turned to face Bowman. "You'll find her all right. For money. And to clear your name. Mary said she wanted to change her testimony. Faraday assures me if she did there would have to be a re-trial."

Bowman couldn't speak. He had a sudden sense of acute foreboding. His heart was racing and he began to sweat. The bitch had taken seven years of his life. Had cost him his job, his good name, his family. Back then he would have torn her heart out with his bare hands. Even now the thought that he might see her again filled him with rage. In the street below a police siren sounded and a car door slammed, like the door to his cell slamming shut. A vision flashed across his mind of himself tipping a bucket of excrement into a stainless steel sink and some of the dark urine splashing back onto his hands. With an effort he re-focused on the room and heard the echo of Berringer's words. "A re-trial. There would have to be a re-trial."

"You've no idea what name it was?" Alex saw Berringer hadn't followed his train of thought. "The name the operator mentioned? It meant nothing to you?"

"No, nothing I'm afraid. It wasn't a name I'd heard before."

***

Marcus Esler went to the window and looked out over the landscaped gardens. A tall distinguished man in his early sixties he had a full head of white hair and piercing blue eyes. He looked like an aging movie star. He was elegant as always. Formal clothes suited him best, though even in jeans he never lost his sense of style.

"What feedback are we getting on Lieberman, Helen?" He had his back to her, looking out beyond the terrace. "This Moroccan idea is very high risk. But it's the most original idea we've ever come across. We're losing too much product en route from South America. It's costing us a fortune. A reliable supplier close to home would be perfect. We could play one off against the other and squeeze them both on price. We need to do business in volume to sustain the Organisation. Otherwise it will implode. We have thousands of pushers out there. We must have more product to survive." Esler lit a cigarette, flicking the match into the fireplace. "We have the same problem the tobacco industry does. Our old customers die and we have to replace them constantly with new ones. That necessarily means the young. So it all comes back to price. Low margin. High volume. Big profit. It's that simple. Basic economics. Pity we can't advertise." Esler paused as a new idea took shape in his mind. "Why not get rid of Lieberman? Take over his operation? Put one of our own people in place? That would be quick and easy and cost practically nothing. That way we make all the profit! Not just the distributor's cut! The whole operation would be ours. We'd control every aspect. Make five times the pittance we're getting now."

"Slow down, Marcus" Helen frowned. "We have no management resources in Spain. Let alone Morocco. Best make Lieberman a partner, a junior partner; let him run that end of things. But we have to be sure he's capable of doing it properly. There's far too much at stake to set up a deal like that until we're sure he can deliver. Besides, the two of us alone can't make a decision this big. The boss will have to be consulted."

"You've put him in the picture?"

"I went to him immediately I'd seen Lieberman."

"How was he?"

"Fine. Considering. But he wants to be kept informed. You know how meticulous he is. And no decisions without his say-so."

"Of course. The Organisation is his baby after all." He lit another cigarette and handed Helen the pack. "Do you think Lieberman can pull it off?"

“I’m sure he can. I thought he was a clown at first. But when I’d heard his pitch I changed my mind. The man knows what he’s doing. He’s even hacked into the DEA’s computers. Now that’s impressive!”

“Did he just?”

“We’ve never done anything like that.”

“Does it give him an edge? Is he better informed than we are?”

“It’s just a different way of doing things. We get the same intelligence; we’re just not that technical about it. With a source as good as ours, we don’t need to be”

"You're still checking on Lieberman?"

"Of course. But progress is slow. He makes impressive claims, but we haven't been able to check them out. Keep hitting dead ends. Nobody seems to have the whole picture. One thing’s certain, though. The sample was first class. The lab says it's better than the Colombian product."

"What about the farm? Do we have any idea where it is?"

"Just that it's in Morocco. Somewhere in the High Atlas, south east of Marrakech. I hate to say so, but we need more time."

"Time’s not the problem, Helen." Esler hesitated. She didn't like to be given advice unless she asked for it. "We need to infiltrate his set-up. What about a woman? One of the girls from Lakeside might do. What do you think?"

"A woman would be perfect!" She remembered Harvey leering at her, thinking he could seduce her. "Not from the health farm though. It would have to be somebody new, somebody fresh and exciting. A woman with style, intelligence. And guts. Leave it to me, Marcus. I'm sure I'll find the right girl." She blew three smoke rings in the air and watched them glide across the room and disappear. "You realise the Cartel won't like this Marcus, not one bit. They have a monopoly now and they'll kill to keep it. If this thing backfires it's going to get messy. Killing's never been our thing. Daisy's good. But Daisy's not enough."

"It's a skill we'll have to learn. Or hire people who've got it. This is our territory. Not the bastard Colombians'. We can't put it at risk!"

Helen knew he was right. But she wasn't thinking about the Colombians, She was thinking about Lieberman. And how she would find him his bimbo.

***

Sean Flaherty was one of the biggest names in Fleet Street. He would retire in a couple of years, but wanted his knighthood first, while he was still in the saddle. He had worked for The Echo for the whole of his career, from messenger all the way up to Editor in Chief. He had made The Echo what it was today, the second biggest paper on the street. He had done it with tough reporting, no bums, no tits, and no vicars with their hands up little boys' trousers.

A shaft of sunlight fell across Flaherty's desk at an angle, leaving half of it in deep shadow. Melanie Drake sat opposite, her chair sideways on to avoid the glare. She admired Flaherty, always had. She owed him a great deal. She wondered if she was doing the right thing, but now it was too late. Any journalist would give an eye for the job she was walking away from, Chief Investigative Reporter. She had worked for Flaherty for six years. Now she didn't any more. Flaherty still couldn't understand why.

"For God sake Mel, you can't mean it! I need you! You've got more balls than any man on this paper!"

Melanie ran a hand through her auburn hair. "I'm serious, Sean. I quit."

"For fuck's sake! What is it, Mel? The money? Me?

"No, for fuck's sake! It isn't the bloody money, and it isn't you!" She had to trade expletives with him, otherwise he wouldn't understand. "I'm burned out, Sean. I've been doing the same job far too long. I want to do something else." Melanie had no idea what she wanted to do, but if she didn't quit she never would find out. "I've been writing about other people doing things all my adult life. I want to *do* something, *me* do something. People are living real lives out there, Sean. I want a life of my own!"

"Take a sabbatical. Full pay. Piss off to South America and lay on the fucking beach." He knew if she did a story would find her. The best stories always find the best reporters. South America was full of opportunity. Revolution. Corruption. Drugs. Everything.

"I've just had a sabbatical! It's no good, Sean. Whatever I had, I haven't got it any more. I know that and so should you."

He should have known, but where Melanie Drake was concerned he thought with his dick, always had. She was the one desirable member of his staff he hadn't slept with. He'd been trying for years, ever since she joined the paper, and everybody knew it. It was a source of deep embarrassment, a blemish on his reputation. In spite of that she had made it to the top. Her work was just too good to be ignored.

There was silence. They had run out of things to say. He picked up a pencil and began to rotate it end over end, sliding his fingers down the smooth hard surface. "You owe me a lot Mel, do you know that?"

"I owe you everything." It wasn't true but she felt she ought to say it. There could be a time when she would need Sean Flaherty again and she wanted to be sure she would still have access.

"Friends?"

"Friends!" She stood up. This was the note to end on.

Flaherty walked round the desk and took her by the wrists, bending down to kiss her on the cheek. As she leaned forward he let go of her wrists and cupped her breasts in his hands. He knew the risk he was taking but he couldn't resist. Melanie took one step back. He might have parried the blow, but let it come. It stung like hell. He hadn't felt this good for weeks.

"You sod!" she hissed "You absolute sod!" She turned her back and was gone.

***

Melanie's office was a couple of floors below, in a corner of the building overlooking the river. She sat at her desk, took a cigarette from the wooden box she kept in a locked drawer and lit it. She leaned back in her chair and inhaled deeply. This is good, she thought. This is very very good. For a while she sat there, leaning back in the chair with her eyes closed until the thought of Flaherty left her. Then she switched on the computer terminal, wired to the mainframe several floors below, logged into the archive and keyed in the words "Bowman, Alex". After a couple of seconds the screen flickered and a brief subject header appeared:

Bowman, Alex. Metropolitan Police Force
1959 Born Wandsworth, London
1978 Graduated Modern Languages, Exeter
1980 Joined Metropolitan Police (Graduate Intake)
1980-1984 Promotion to Detective Inspector
1985 Transferred Serious Crime Squad
1986 Married Alice Copthorne - one child
1987 Transferred Drug Squad
1988 Seconded National Drugs Intelligence Unit
1990 Convicted Possession/Supplying Cocaine
1991 Divorced
1994 Released Wormwood Scrubs
Present whereabouts unknown

She scanned the information in an instant and had a brief sensation she knew him, then that she didn't know him at all. What would have possessed him to do it, at the start of such a promising career? Why throw it all away? She was wondering what cross references to try when Philip Hyde pushed open the door waving a half empty bottle of scotch.

"Time for a last jar?"

"You know? Already?"

"Flaherty asked me to check you're OK."

"I'm OK! OK?"

Hyde reached into his jacket pocket and pulled out a couple of tumblers.

"Not here." she said, stubbing out the cigarette and dispersing the smoke with her hand. "Oh hell! Why not!"

"So you really did it? You resigned!" He handed her a glass of neat whisky pretending not to notice the sweet aroma that was not tobacco. "I didn't think you would."

"I'm stale Phil. I joined this bloody paper straight from University. It's the only job I've ever done! If I don't find something else to do with my life I'll end up a bored old hack."

"Like me, you mean?"

"Yes, like you Phil! Do you realise how much of your life you've given to this rag? Writing society gossip for heaven's sake! I've got to stop now, while I can still make the change." She took a sip of her drink. "You know what I think of as my defining characteristic?"

"Your defining characteristic?" Hyde winced.

"To consistently undershoot my potential." She was frowning. "Tell me something, Phil. If you could put right an injustice by something you wrote, even if it placed you in danger.........well, maybe not in danger exactly.........but put you at risk. Would you do it?"

"Me? No! I shouldn't think so. How much risk? Physical risk?"

"Physical risk. How much, I can't say."

"You've got a project, haven't you? I can tell."

"I think so." She smiled. "I had a piece of luck yesterday. You remember the Bowman case?"

"Alex Bowman, the drugs trial? Sure."

"He was on the plane. The poor man was so nervous I even bought him a drink. I almost made a pass at him, but he seemed so, well, shy, I suppose. It seems silly I know, big bloke like him, but that's the way he came across. Shy!"

"Is he the project?" Hyde smiled at her.

“He’s a possibility. If I’m going freelance I need something big to get started. Righting wrongs always makes good copy.”

“What makes you think you’d be righting a wrong? He was found guilty, after all.”

“You’re right. It’s just an angle. But at least it somewhere to start.” She reached for her glasses. “Wasn't there something about a girlfriend, her behaviour at the trial?"

"Mary Berringer."

"Berringer? The heiress? Didn't you do a piece on her once."

"Not once. Lots of times. How could I resist? Mary Berringer was perfect for me, young, rich, beautiful, privileged, and into every kind of vice you can imagine. Nothing ever got published though, nothing got past Flaherty. The old bugger said she wasn't a suitable subject but that was the purest crap.” Hyde emptied his glass, his hand trembling slightly. “He was protecting the little bitch."

"Why wasn't she suitable? Flaherty must have given you a reason, an excuse."

"You must be kidding, darling. Flaherty never explains, Flaherty instructs. Besides, they were having an affair."

"Sean Flaherty and Mary Berringer had an affair?"

"Just briefly. Before she got involved with Bowman. Didn't you know?"

"No Phil, I didn't know." Melanie reddened. "There's no reason why I should, is there?"

"No, no reason. But I should drop the whole idea if I were you. You should stay away from drugs Melanie. You know you should." Hyde's voice had gone suddenly quiet.

"Oh! Phil, really! A good catholic girl like me! All I ever do is smoke a little pot. It's nothing serious."

"Now that's something I've never understood. How do you reconcile the two, your religion and smoking pot?"

"Christ never expressed an opinion on pot!" She laughed. "And who knows what he got up to in the desert? He certainly didn't object to alcohol, even made some for his mate's wedding. So presumably he would have thought pot was OK too. Oh! Phil, don't be so serious! I've only done coke a half dozen times in my life. People do it at parties!"

"Flaherty supplied you?"

"Supplied me? No, he didn't *supply* me! He was hoping to get laid is all. It's recreational for heaven's sake!"

"So's this." Hyde waved the bottle at her. "But if I don't drink a pint of Scotch a day I can't function."

"That's the difference between you and me, Phil. I can use it or not use it. It really doesn't matter. It's just for fun.

***

4

The headquarters of Lord Berringer's group of companies were in a small Georgian building not far from the Bank of England. Alex arrived punctually at 10 a.m. the next morning and the uniformed flunkie swung the revolving door for him to walk through. He went to the desk and the security guard checked his name off on a list and asked him to take the lift to the fourth floor where he would be met by one of the assistants to a Mrs. Hetherington, Lord Berringer's personal private secretary.

A teenager was standing by the lift when the doors opened, probably fresh from college. She raised her arm and ran her fingers through her soft brown hair so Bowman could take a good look at her figure. This was a girl who was going to make it to the top. Alex followed the long legs down a short corridor to the mahogany door at the end. The girl pressed a buzzer set into the wall. Bowman turned and smiled up into the video camera. A light above the door changed from red to green and the door opened to reveal a large office, elegantly but sparsely equipped with aggressively modern furniture.

Mrs. Hetherington sat behind the desk smoking. Her manner was brusque. "Lord Berringer has gone abroad, Mr. Bowman. He asked me to agree certain arrangements with you." She was referring to some notes she had listed on a shorthand pad. She looked the very model of the efficient secretary, but she was more than that, there was an air of real authority about her. "I suggest you open a new bank account. There's a branch of the Banco de

Bilbao at the end of the street. Get yourself a credit card and a supply of Euro cheques. I am to pay you £5000 a month until further notice, plus expenses to be reimbursed separately, subject to proper documentation." She paused, looking up at him, in case proper documentation might need to be explained. "Should you need to communicate with the Chairman at any time, that will be done through me. Lord Berringer is a very busy man." She put the note pad down on the desk and placed her hand on top of it. Her mouth smiled but her eyes didn't. Alex wondered what she knew. He wondered why the mahogany door was re-enforced with steel and why a secretary's office would have bullet-proof glass in the windows.

"Do you have any questions, Mr. Bowman?" She stubbed her cigarette out in the crystal ashtray to indicate she had nothing more to say.

"I used to see a lot of Mary. I never had the impression she and her father were close. As far as I know he never had any time for her. Why does he want to find her now?"

"He's her father. Isn't that reason enough?"

"When did he see her last?"

"I've no idea, but not for quite some time. Do you have any children Mr Bowman?"

Alex looked down at his hands. "I have a daughter."

"And when did you last see her?"

"Not for quite some time."

"Then I'm sure you'll understand Lord Berringer's concern."

"When did she move to Spain?"

"Move to Spain?" She lit a cigarette. "We don't know that she did."

"She phoned from Marbella."

"So I understand. But does that mean she moved there? Couldn't she be away on a trip?"

"Yes, of course, you're right. I was making an assumption." Smart lady, Bowman thought, smart lady. "But if she hasn't moved to Spain, why me?"

"As you said, Mr Bowman, she phoned her father from Marbella. That must be as good a starting point as any."

"The name she used on the phone, it would be helpful to know what that was."

"Sorry, I can't help you there. The Chairman has no idea.........."

"A childhood name? A term of endearment? The sort of thing fathers invent for their children?" He looked down at his hands again.

“I’m just a secretary. I wasn’t around when she was growing up. Anything else I can help you with Mr Bowman?”

Alex thought for a moment. "Is there a men's room on this floor? I'd like to take a leak."

For the first time she smiled, a broad attractive smile that might have turned into a grin. Perhaps she was human after all.

***

The Lamb and Flag used to be as good as any pub in London. Real people used to drink real beer there. Tucked away up a blind alley off a back street near Covent Garden it had fallen victim to the unification of the area that had followed the demise of the market. Now it was patronised by new sub-species who wore pink and green spectacles, called one another darling, and touched each other's bottom as a form of greeting.

Detective Sergeant George Ramsay sat behind a pint of best bitter. He felt conspicuous even out of uniform. The raucous people at the bar made him feel distinctly out of place in a pub that had once felt like home. That time was gone now. Everything else had moved on except him and he was left stranded in the same place, except it wasn't the same at all, it had changed beyond recognition. His career had gone the same way. Other people, younger people, had passed him on the ladder and he was stuck with a rank he had held for years and was unlikely ever to surpass. It wasn't an outcome anyone would have predicted for him years ago when he was young and full of promise and Bowman had spotted his mastery of detail and picked him for his partner. It was as if someone had decided to stop Ramsay in his tracks, to sideline him. But at least he still had his job and his pension and his mortgage, which was more than could be said for his friend. They had left Alex with nothing, not even his good name.

Suddenly he spotted Bowman framed in the doorway and stood up to greet him, spilling some of the beer as he did so. They didn't shake hands. They just looked at one another and grinned.

"The usual, boss?" said Ramsay. "A pint of best?"

"That's right George, a pint of best." Alex couldn't resist punching him once on the shoulder, a left jab, short, sharp, and full of affection.

Ramsay put the pint down in front of Bowman who looked at it lovingly before he picked it up, admiring the deep golden colour, the good head, the way the condensation formed on the tall straight glass. "You look in pretty rotten shape, George. You should take better care of yourself." Alex didn't want to hurt his friend but maybe there was no one else close enough to tell him. Ramsay responded by pouring half a pint of beer down his throat and Alex wondered how things were for him at home. But he didn't ask.

"No luck with British Telecom, not yet anyway." Ramsay wiped the white moustache from his lips with the back of his hand and let out a quiet belch. "What's this all about anyway, boss? You didn't say much on the phone."

Alex told him the story, the phone call from Rex Faraday QC, the meeting with Lord Berringer, the reverse charges call from Marbella.

Ramsay cared deeply about Bowman. Alex had taught him everything, practically brought him up. But sometimes Alex's judgement was appalling, especially where women were concerned, and Mary Berringer was poison. The idea that she might get her claws into Alex again was frightening. “Are you sure you want to find her?”

“It’s a job, George. It isn’t what you’re thinking.”

"And you reckon the lying bitch would change her story?"

"That's what Berringer said." Bowman picked up his glass and drank deeply, holding it out in front of him before he put it down, in a gesture of respect. "There would have to be a re-trial if she did, Faraday is sure of that. He's convinced we'd win this time."

"Fuck British Telecom." said George with feeling. "Their computers are worse than their phones and Christ knows their phones are bad enough. They must keep a record of reverse charges calls, so they can send you the bloody bill. If we can trace where the call came from you'll be off to a flying start."

Alex wrote the San Roque number on a beer mat complete with the international codes. "Call me at home George, they're bound to turn up something in a couple of days. Check up on Berringer too, find out how he made his first million." The idea that he might see her again so soon was beginning to make him nervous. He knew he should hate her, he had every right, but the truth was that in spite of everything he didn't, not any more. Berringer was right. Mary was a victim, just as much as he was.

They stayed in the pub till closing time and talked about old times. Ramsay downed two pints for every one that Alex swallowed. Alex wondered how he did it, and why. He guessed that Ramsay was not a happy man, not happy at home and not happy with his career. Alex wanted to grab him by the shoulders and shake him out of his complacent daze but he knew there was only one way to do that with George Ramsay and that was to put him back to work again, give him something meaningful to do. That much at least they still had very much in common.

***

When they stepped outside it was almost raining, with that fine English drizzle that hangs in the air like a sodden blanket. At the end of the street Ramsay hailed a cab but Alex decided to walk back to the seedy hotel in Earl's Court, he was in no hurry to get there. He hadn't taken any exercise for a couple days but more than the exercise he wanted to refresh his memory, to remind himself why he used to think that what he did was so important.

He walked down Shaftesbury Avenue to the tube station at Piccadilly. The pavements were crowded with people coming out of the pubs looking for trouble. It was like the third world. The debris from the fast food stands littered the pavements and gave off a stench of rancid fat and putrefying onions. He pushed his way through the angry crowd and went down the pedestrian underpass.

It was nearly midnight and the last train had probably gone but the place was far from deserted. He saw the kids hanging round the public toilets waiting for the pushers to bring them their next dose of shit. That was the fashionable term they used, and how unerringly accurate it was. Over the years he had watched them turn to theft and prostitution, had known the girls get pregnant and sell the baby to the highest bidder, just to make enough money to feed their awful habit. Often enough the babies were born addicted too, and Christ only knew what happened to them. He saw the vacant look in their faces as they wandered aimlessly about, without purpose, without the hope of any purpose, except to get enough money together somehow, anyhow, to buy the next fix. He wasn't sorry for them any more. He was way past that. They just made him so bloody angry.

The beer had worked its way through his system now. He entered the brightly light public toilets that seemed to be empty, till he heard the muffled voices coming from the end cubicle. He stood at the urinal and peed and the relief was very great. When he turned on the tap to wash his hands two figures emerged, the first an attractive girl of about fifteen with too much make up. Her eyes were bright but lifeless and her legs unsteady as she staggered along the line of washbasins, leaning on them for support. When she reached Bowman she smiled and tried to straighten up but she couldn't make it and stood there holding on to the wall, trying to focus.

The second was an older man, conventionally dressed but not smart, in a pale grey business suit and a stained kipper tie. "Thanks Mandy." he said, his eyes on Bowman, as the girl staggered out. The pusher thought at first he had scored again but he took a second look at Bowman and knew he was mistaken.

Bowman pushed the man on the shoulder, no more than a tap, but he repeated the movement three or four times until the man had backed into a cubicle. He wasn't sure what Bowman was. He looked like the law but he was acting like a thug. Maybe he was queer and there was a buck to be made one way or another. They were both inside the cubicle now. Bowman made a short sharp movement with his right hand, driving rigid fingers into the man's abdomen. He wanted to wretch and automatically doubled over, the bile rising to his throat. He was shitless. Pale. Shaking. Sweating. Bowman grabbed him by the neck and eased his head into the bowl, holding it there with his right hand while he pulled the chain with his left. There was the sound of rushing water and the man spluttered as the mixture of shit and urine filled his nostrils. He thought he was going to drown.

Bowman wondered why he bothered. The man was nothing, a nonentity, and a piece of crap at the lowest level of a vast international pyramid. There were thousands like him working the clubs and pubs the poor dumb kids frequented. They traded openly and nobody bothered to stop them, they just weren't important enough.

Bowman climbed the stairs to the brightly lit world above where somewhere not too far away, in some fancy restaurant or private club were the fat cats, spending the money they squeezed like blood from the stupid kids below. Somewhere a uniformed flunkie was opening the door of a chauffeur driven Rolls or Bentley, touching his cap and calling the bastard Sir! Alex looked at his watch. Not yet one o'clock. Time to catch the last set at Ronnie Scott's.

Mandy stood in the shadows and watched him cross the Circus and disappear into Soho, not knowing whom he was. Then she turned and went back down below to find another punter.

***

Deputy Commissioner Peter Draycott, the most respected policeman of his generation, was chair bound. Most of the feeling down his right side was gone. He still had limited mobility; he could feed himself and perform all the bodily functions unaided, except bathe. But he couldn't walk. This seemed to trouble him surprisingly little. What did bother him was his mouth. He couldn't quite control it. The facial muscles were slack and he drooled constantly so that he was never without a cloth to wipe away the spittle. He couldn't manage with an ordinary handkerchief, he preferred something that would last the day, a dishcloth or a piece cut from an old shirt. What struck Alex most were the eyes, the moist spaniel eyes that had lost all of their fire.

Seeing him again after all this time was a shock. He had aged of course, but his physical condition had changed dramatically. Alex had known about the stroke but he wasn't prepared for the degree of change. They sat together in the bay window of the cottage, looking out across the garden to the open fields. The sun was warm but Draycott had a blanket across his useless legs, possibly to hide them. He sat erect, ramrod straight, his head held high.

Draycott spotted Alex's discomfiture. "Alex, it's so good of you to come. I haven't seen you since.................." The words weren't slurred exactly, but they had a softness at the edges, a lack of definition.

"Since before the trial, Peter. Seven years. A long time."

"A very long time. How have you been?"

"It gets better. How about you?"

"It gets worse. I no longer expect to improve."

Alex was appalled to see him like this. He had hoped for something, but now he didn't know what; help, guidance, encouragement. It had been a mistake to come. He had laid it all out in his mind on the way down, the circumstances surrounding his arrest, the trial. The feeling he had been manipulated in ways he didn't understand even now. But when he saw Draycott the shock was just too great. It had degenerated into a merely social visit, and maybe it was best to leave it like that, leave the poor man with his memories and his roses.

“You were the best Peter. My mentor. We all knew you were something special. You would have made Commissioner if you hadn’t had the stroke.”

“So might you Alex, eventually, if you hadn’t.................Maybe you shouldn’t have transferred to the drugs squad. If you’d stayed with me things would have turned out differently. But it was what you always wanted. Then your secondment to the NDIU, there seemed to be no end to your progress. There you were, you and a mere dozen others, at the centre everything, the National Drugs Intelligence Unit. That’s when we lost touch.”

“The secondment was on your recommendation, Peter. So was the transfer. You didn’t think I knew that but I did.”

“Was it, Alex? No, I don’t think so. It had nothing to do with me.”

“Yes, Peter. It was you who pulled the strings.”

“Was it Alex? I’ve quite forgotten.”

“And we never did lose touch, not really. I know you always followed my career. Kept an eye on me.”

“Did I, Alex? Yes I suppose I did. I knew there was something special about you too.” Draycott’s head rolled forward and his eyes closed for an instant.

Shortly the nurse would come from the village to bathe him, as she did each evening. He gripped the wheels of the chair in his knarled hands and manoeuvred into the dying light.

"I think I might come back to England, Peter. Something happened. There might be a chance of a re-trial."

"Why bother, Alex? What would be the point? Even if you got yourself reinstated, you don't imagine you could resume your career, do you? You'd never be trusted again. There'd always be a doubt, always. You have to accept that." The moist eyes flickered. He dabbed at his mouth with the soiled cloth.

It wasn't the advice Alex had expected. Not the advice Draycott would have given him years ago, before the stroke. "What's she like? The nurse?"

"Sister Duncan? Young. Pretty. A bit severe. It's a funny thing Alex, but I'd have preferred an old one, old and ugly. You should stay and meet her."

"I have a flight to catch." Alex was toying with his watch. He just wanted to get away. He would stop at the nearest pub for a good stiff single malt. He stood up. He realised then there was no easy way to say good-bye. He didn't want to shake the limp hand again. He thought of kissing him on the brow as he would have done his father, but they weren't close enough for that. So he placed a hand on Draycott's shoulder and the old man covered it with his own. Somehow it felt just right.

***

Bowman's taxi dropped him outside the British Airways terminal at Heathrow airport. He checked in, walked through into the departure lounge and bought an evening paper. The headline was depressing. "Serial Killer Strikes Again." The article below was long on words but short on detail. Another body of a teenage boy, high on crack, found on a rubbish dump in Clapham. Raped. Neck broken. Fingers severed. There was a picture of Ramsay and a brief quote, an apology. Police enquiries were getting nowhere. The only lead was an unidentified girl who had been seen with the boy on the night of the murder. There was an appeal for her to come forward.

He was looking up at the flight departure information on the screen when she spoke to him. "How's my nervous passenger?" It took him a moment to recognise her, he was thinking about the boy and what the severed fingers meant. They must mean something. It was the woman on the flight from Gibraltar, the one who had bought him a drink. She was wearing jeans and a tartan shirt. She looked older than he remembered, older and more appealing, but just as fresh, as if she had just stepped out of the shower.

"Sorry." Alex smiled down at her. "I didn't recognise you. You look different." He was struck by how self-assured she was. Not aggressive. Just confident. Out-going.

"Just different? Not better?" She flicked her newly cropped hair with her fingers. Her smile was infectious, like silent laughter. "So you weren't impressed the first time? I'm not sure I like that. You'd better buy me a drink while I think about it, you owe me a round anyway." His shyness was still there, just below the surface. Don’t frighten him. Captivate him.

Alex wasn't sure if she was laughing at him or laughing at herself, but he liked it either way. It felt as if she were trying to pick him up. He knew that couldn't be true, not a woman that attractive, but the idea made him feel good anyway. He had felt good for the last couple of days, ever since the meeting with Berringer. She seemed to match his mood perfectly, to be part of it. It was almost uncanny.

"Going anywhere interesting?" said Alex when they sat at the bar.

"Back to Malaga. I had to delay my return by a day and couldn't get on the Gibraltar flight. Not that it matters; they're both about the same distance from home. I have a flat at Puerto Banus."

Bowman did a lot of work around Puerto Banus, and knew the area well. About an hour's drive up the Coast from San Roque, just west of Marbella, it was the richest spot on the Costa del Sol. Most of it was owned by Arabs, rich ones who paid very well for protection. It wasn't a place he liked very much; it was full of new money, carefully laundered. He referred San Roque, perched on its hill, where people lived real lives, earning honest money from hard grinding work in the fields.

"How long have you lived out there?" said Alex.

"I don't live there, I just go out whenever I can organise a long enough break, but London will always be home."

Her eyes were on the departure screen and Alex sensed he didn't have long to make a decisive move. He wasn't sure he still remembered how.

"What do you do? For a living I mean." It was a dull question but it was all he could think of at the time.

"I'm a journalist, and as of now I'm freelance. I came to London to quit my job. I've been thinking about it for months, and finally I've done it. So now I can organise my work around my life, not the other way around." She raised her glass to toast her courage. "How about you? Don't tell me! Let me guess!" She looked him over carefully from top to bottom, leaning her elbow on the bar with her chin in the palm of her hand. "I would say you live in Spain, you don't get a tan like that in England. You look to me like the outdoors type, you probably work outdoors. You're too tall for a tennis pro and you look too fit for golf. I know, you're a sailing instructor! Yes, I like that. A sailing instructor."

"Sorry to disappoint you Miss.......?"

"Drake. Melanie Drake." She smiled, brushing her auburn hair from her freckled face. Suddenly she looked much younger.

Alex stuck out his big hand. "Alex Bowman. Bent copper. Retired." He regretted immediately he had said it. She looked disappointed, hurt, as if he had let her down. He tried to think of something else to say, something light and amusing, but nothing came into his head. He looked at the wounded expression on her face and wondered if she saw the deeper hurt in his.

"They're calling my flight." She was picking up her things. "I must go. Good to meet you Mr. Bowman, have a nice flight." She sounded like a recorded announcement.

When she had gone Bowman ordered another Balvenie, his favourite single malt. He downed the whisky and ordered another, silently wishing her *buen viaje*. She was potentially the best thing that had come his way in a long time. It was a pity to see her go.

***

5

Three days later Alex Bowman got two surprises, the first unpleasant, the second not. He had returned from his early morning swim off the beach below the converted farmhouse just outside San Roque and found the package sitting on the stone doorstep.

Bowman had bought the farmhouse four years earlier as a ruin and improved it only slightly. He had installed a new roof to stop it leaking and a pump to increase the pressure in the shower, but otherwise the place was pretty much as he had found it. He liked it just the way it was, rough and simple and totally unpretentious.

He recognised George Ramsay's writing though he hadn't seen it for years. Inside were a videotape and a note from Ramsay, hand-written and unsigned.

"You won't like the enclosed but you'd better take a look at it anyway. The phone call was made from a bar in Marbella by someone called Tiffany Wells. The bar is the Black Sombrero. Berringer made his first million trading commodities, mainly in the Far East. Call me if you need more help."

Alex went inside to the study and drew the curtains. He knew already what it was and was surprised by his own indifference. He loaded the tape into the video recorder and the television screen flickered into life. The picture quality was poor, a copy of a copy made with second-rate equipment and the soundtrack was slightly out of sinc. It was called simply "HEAT" and it starred Tiffany Wells. It was set in a villa somewhere hot, it could have been Spain but it could have been many other places, North Africa maybe. There was a story line of sorts, there always is, but he didn't try to follow it, it wasn't important. He watched it through twice, the first time for the general effect, the second for the detail. It should have sickened him but it didn't, he had seen worse on celluloid and in the flesh. It was just work, unless he thought of her as Mary Berringer, so he thought of her as Tiffany Wells instead and re-ran it for the detail. He didn't see anything that could possibly help, just men and women writhing about in a mass of contorted heaving flesh, smiling when their mouths weren't full. Hands touching, stroking, kneading, twisting, gouging, hurting. Mouths open, hungry, kissing, biting, sucking. Tongues caressing, searching, probing, licking. Words, sighs, whispers, laughter, screaming.

Tiffany was the star, the focus of everybody's attention. She was different from the other women, tall and slender and still beautiful, but above all she was young. The rest were sluts with big arses and big tits and too much make up. Tiffany was centre stage most of the time but her partners changed constantly and the things they did with her, did *to* her, changed as often. She looked straight into the camera a lot of the time as a sort of theatrical device, inviting the viewer to participate, to feel what she was feeling, to enjoy what she enjoyed. She looked unnaturally relaxed, almost happy. Alex recognised the glazed look in her unfocused eyes, the dilated pupils, the uncomprehending stare, as she gazed into the camera lens, not knowing what it was.

***

The second surprise happened late that afternoon. Alex was sitting at a table by a window just inside the shaded terrace, which overlooked the bay. The soft tones of *Blues for Pablo* were coming from his one luxury, the CD player he had bartered from the local contraband dealer. He had stripped, cleaned, and re-assembled first the Browning GP35FA and then the big Colt .44 Magnum. Alex loved and understood guns, knew their histories, the idiosyncrasies of each and every model. He loved all things that were well made, loved them for their craftsmanship and their precision. When he had nothing else to do he would take them apart, clean and re-assemble them for the tactile pleasure it gave him.

He saw the open topped Mercedes turn into his driveway from the secondary road, a cloud of dust announcing its arrival. He wasn't expecting anyone, but people called in from time to time on their way to and from the Rock now the frontier was open again, so he put a dust cover over the weapons and stepped down off the terrace to greet whoever it was.

Melanie had got out of the car by the time he reached it. She took off her sunglasses and said, "You were easy to find, I speak a little Spanish. *La casa del Inglès muy grande*. They know you in the café on the square. I hope you don't mind my coming. I wanted to apologise for rushing off like that at the airport. If you ask me in for a drink I'll know I'm forgiven. I think I deserve one. It took almost an hour to get here, the traffic on that road is absolutely lethal."

She knew a lot about him now. She had called Flaherty at the Echo and had him send her a copy of Bowman's file. She knew about the fast track career, the early promotion, the secondment to the National Drugs Intelligence Unit. She knew about the rumours, the tip-off, the suspension from duty, the cocaine they had found hidden in his flat, the trial. She had a pretty good sketch of his career but not much about his private life, his marriage and early divorce, the child, and nothing about his affair with Mary Berringer. Stick with him, Flaherty had said. The best stories always find the best reporters. She looked around the terrace and peered into the house through the open window. "This is nice," she said.

"I like it. It's just right for me."

"Yes, I can see it is. So simple. So straight forward."

Alex disappeared into the house. Melanie raised the dust cover that hid something on the table and peered underneath. "Jesus Christ!" she muttered, as Alex returned with two glasses and a chilled bottle of *Manzanilla*.

"So, Alex, what do you really do out here? You're much too young to have retired."

"I advise people about security. How to make their homes safe, shops and offices, hotels. There's a lot of petty crime on the Coast, some of it not so petty. A lot of it is drugs related. My biggest clients are the airports, Malaga and Gib. I don't do anything for the Port Authority, but I'm working on that."

“Don’t you miss doing what you used to do? Wasn’t that so much more important?”

“I miss the involvement, but I don’t miss being a copper one bit. I couldn’t handle procedure any more, going by the book. I enjoy being on the outside, doing things my own way. And every now and again something comes along that’s more worthwhile. Something that could really make a difference.”

“Like what?”

“Like undercover work mainly. Because of my background I can work both sides of the tracks. I get offers from both sides.”

She looked aghast. *Maybe he did it, maybe he really did it.* “I remember the trial. It caused a sensation when you lost. Faraday doesn't often lose. It was all to do with the girl, wasn't it? Something about her testimony?” She expected him to speak, but he didn’t. “Isn't there anything you can do to get yourself reinstated? Aren't you going to fight it? Surely there must be people who would help, people you used to work with?" Human interest, Flaherty had said, go for the human interest.

"Till last week it didn't seem as if there was a way. Now suddenly everything has changed." He told her the story of the London trip, the reversed charges call from Marbella.

Time was when she would have given her eyes for an exclusive as good as this. People had built their reputations on less. And that’s what Melanie would do.

Break into big time freelance work on the back of this one story. It wasn't going to change the world, but it could change both their lives. "So you think she's out here? Somewhere on the Coast?"

"Let's hope so. If she alters her testimony it could make all the difference. My QC says there'd have to be a re-trial."

Melanie took another sip of her drink. "I hope this isn't too personal Alex, tell me if it is and I'll shut up, but what happened to your wife and child?" She didn't want to move too fast, frighten him off, but there were facts she needed to establish.

"We have been doing our research!" Alex didn't like the direction she was taking. An interest in his professional life was fine, she was a reporter after all and had to earn a living, but his wife and child were off limits. "She went back to the States and disappeared, took our daughter with her. She came from a small town in up-State New York, near the Canadian Border. I went there to make inquiries. It was useless. They said she'd moved to the mid-West some place, but they didn't say where. Big country, America, and Alice had a five year start." He missed the kid, missed her desperately, even though he really didn't know her. If she walked into a room right now he wouldn't even know it was her. She'd be fifteen, almost a woman, and he hadn't seen her since she was ten.

"I didn't know she was American." Not everything was on the file.

“An actress, a good one, but not very successful.”

“And Mary Berringer, how did you meet her?”

“She was at the BBC, in the research department, working on a series to do with drug related crime. She came to interview me at the Yard. A man called Rutland asked me to help her. Someone I knew from working with the National Drugs Intelligence Unit. My marriage was rocky at the time. Mary was young, good looking, and genuinely interested in my work. I was flattered.”

“Rupert Rutland? The MP?”

“Junior Minister at the Home Office. You know him?

"We’ve met.”

“We were working on an important case at the time, about to bust a really big organisation, getting very close. Everyone was involved, police, customs, the NDIU. The pressure on me was tremendous. Somehow having Mary around seemed to help. I could discuss things with her. Test out my ideas. Don’t ask me how, but Mary kept me focused.”

“You had an affair? I’m sorry, if this is too personal..............” she reddened.

“She moved into my flat. It was very easy.”

“And if you find her, what then? What happens next?”

"Depends on what it is she has to say. Whether or not she plans to change her story."

"Why was her evidence so crucial?"

"It was Mary who found the coke. She turned me in."

Melanie's jaw dropped. "God! You must hate her!"

"I spent years hating her. I didn't have much else to think about in jail. But you can't go on hating forever. Hate exhausts you. It can take up the whole of your life."

"But if she denies it now she'd be admitting perjury, conspiracy. Alex, don't you see, that simply isn't going to happen!"

"It seems unlikely, but it's worth a try. Women are funny creatures, and Mary always was unpredictable. Besides, there's another interesting angle."

"Oh? And what's that?"

"That this whole thing has nothing to do with me. That Berringer has his own reasons for wanting to find his daughter, is just using me to do it for him. Why not? After all, that's how I make my living."

"And if that's the case, why does he want to find her?"

"That's the interesting part."

"Look Alex, if there's anything I can do to help, do ask. I'm used to asking questions, I'm pretty good at it too, and now I have the time, I have a whole summer to myself." Get close to him, Flaherty had said, use a little charm. Casually she took his wrist in her hand and he saw how pale her skin was against his. "Heavens Alex, is that the time? I must fly. I have a dinner date."

She was down the terrace steps in no time and had started the engine before he caught her up. He had to stand in front of the car to stop her from pulling away.

"Stop playing Cinderella will you! How do I reach you?"

She had reversed a little way so she could swing out to pass him but the hood was down. "Puerto Banus." she yelled. "The tennis club. I'm there most mornings. Or any Sunday after church."

“Church?” His mouth stayed open.

“Yes, church! Don’t look so shocked!” She was gone, in a great cloud of dust.

***

Verity Fuller replied to the advertisement the same day she saw it in the glossy magazine. She was twenty-two. At eighteen she had gone abroad for the first time and worked at a discotheque on a Greek island for a whole summer. She lost her virginity the very first week and went on losing it for the rest of the summer. Verity was tall and blond with the body of a goddess and blue eyes you could drown in, but she was lazy and none too bright. Men loved her for all these reasons. She was educated at a convent and had acquired an air of innocence there she never really lost, not even while she was earning her living.

When she returned to England Verity had graduated from discotheques to nightclub hostess, but her real ambition was the movies. She had had a small amount of success, not at getting parts exactly, but she had taken some screen tests and got very well acquainted with a number of producers.

She entered the lobby of the hotel, undaunted by its opulence. They had told her on the phone not to announce herself at the porter's desk, but to go straight up to suite 508. She knocked at the door and it was answered immediately. She gasped as she looked into his face, into his colourless hungry eyes. He was an albino. She knew the word but she didn't understand the condition, didn't know if she should feel sorry for him or not. She only knew she couldn't bear to look at him. He checked her name on a list and showed her through the lobby of the suite to the sitting room.

The curtains were closed, the room lit by a single lamp on the desk. Behind the desk sat a woman in a black dress smoking a cigarette. Verity was used to seeing a woman first before she got to the real decision maker, but this one was different. She seemed to think she really was in charge.

"Sit down, my dear. Is Verity your real name?" She sounded as though it mattered.

"Yes it is. So's Fuller." She was sure the woman had influence, she could tell. It seemed impertinent to ask her name. Verity smiled, her sweetest convent smile, and crossed one leg over the other, the hem of her skirt rising part way up her thigh. It was a planned gesture, but planned for a man. The woman hardly seemed to notice.

"You read the advertisement? You understand the kind of work involved?" The woman put her glasses to one side and crushed her cigarette in the ashtray. It was a surprisingly mannish gesture.

"Film work, isn't it? That's what the advertisement said." The advertisements always talked about film work, or the theatre, or modelling. They could hardly say slap and tickle could they?

"That's right my dear, film work. Working with an American producer. His name's Harvey Lieberman. Have you heard of him?"

Verity wanted to say yes, but she had been caught out like that before so she just looked thoughtful instead. Looking thoughtful always worked with men so maybe it would work with her as well.

"I've put together a montage of his work." The woman smiled. "Perhaps you'd better watch it on the video, it'll give you an idea of the sort of thing he does. Sit over there on the couch Verity, you'll be more comfortable there." She turned down the light, pressed the button on the remote control and watched Verity watching the porno flick.

Verity was just right, she was sure of it. Maybe she wasn’t as bright as the woman would have wished, but this could be an advantage. Things could easily get out of hand if Verity ever worked out the importance of the work she would be doing.

The woman had watched Lieberman's movies through and through and knew precisely the sort of girls he liked. He liked them tall and full bosomed but not heavy, with long slender legs. But above all he liked that look of schoolgirl innocence that Verity personified. The woman wasn't interested in what was happening on screen. She was only interested in Verity. She was delightful. As she watched, Verity took a strand of her long blond hair and twirled it round her finger tightly. Verity was blushing now. If she could blush like that on camera she could really be a star.

When the collection of clips came to an end the woman didn't turn the light back up, but came to sit next to Verity on the sofa. She didn't speak but simply sat and looked at the young innocent face. She was so pretty. At last she said, "Well Verity, what do you think? Is that the kind of work you had in mind?"

"It's not exactly what I'm looking for." Verity was blushing still. "I'm a serious actress."

"Of course you are, my dear. But I don't think Mr. Lieberman will want to put you on camera, you're much too pretty for that." She moved the cascading hair from Verity's cheek and brushed her hand against it lightly. "Much to pretty." Her hand moved to Verity's blouse and she undid the first few buttons and ran her fingers across the soft delicate skin of her cleavage. Verity didn’t resist but the colour rushed to her cheeks again making her look suddenly younger and more innocent, like the convent girl she still was deep inside. The woman thought she was wonderful, too good to waste on Harvey. Gently she lifted Verity's bosom from the silk garment she wore and took the nipple between her lips and kissed it softly, caressing it with the moist tip of her tongue. Verity's eyes fluttered and closed. She had been here before, but only with men. She wasn't shocked, men took this sort of thing for granted, it was part of the procedure, the routine. It was expected. She wondered if she would enjoy it. There was no reason why she shouldn't, the woman's touch was sure and gentle, not rough and hurried like a man's. Then the woman placed her lips on top of hers and kissed her, softly probing Verity's mouth with her tongue. Verity didn't resist but she didn't respond either, she wasn't sure how. The woman knew she was wasting her time. It was time to get back to business.

She went briskly back to the desk, turned up the light, replaced her glasses and lit another cigarette. She looked across at Verity and said, "Come over here to the light and show me you arms." She examined the inside of Verity's left arm, then the right, looking for the tell tale signs. There were none. "Communicable diseases?" then, seeing Verity hadn't followed, "Sexually transmitted diseases? Have you had any?"

"Of course not. What do you think I am, a cheap prostitute?"

"No my dear, I never for one moment thought you were cheap. You understand there will have to be a complete medical examination?" It was just possible Harvey might have her checked himself and if she wasn't clean the whole operation would be wasted.

"I suppose not, if you really think it's necessary." Verity was blushing again.

"Good. Now let me explain the job to you my dear, it's really very simple. You won't be working for Mr. Lieberman, you'll be working for me. I'll arrange an introduction to Mr. Lieberman for you, through a mutual acquaintance. You are never, *never*, to mention me to Mr. Lieberman, do you understand? Just the mutual acquaintance. If we meet again under any circumstances whatsoever you are not to acknowledge me unless I do so first. Mr. Lieberman and I are rivals, business rivals. You can think of this as industrial espionage, all the best companies do it. When you meet Mr. Lieberman he will invite you to stay at his villa. You will accept of course, but not right away. Keep him waiting a while. Once you're installed I want you to send me lists of everybody he sees, everybody who visits him. I want names, dates, time of arrival, duration of visit, everything. Whenever possible I want you to send me photographs, simple snapshots will do, even Polaroids. For the moment that's all there is to it, nothing a resourceful girl like you can't handle. I will pay you £5,000 a month in cash and I guarantee at least three months work. That's a minimum of £15,000 for doing very little. And if you're able to provide any extra little services for Mr. Lieberman personally, for which he's prepared to pay you, that's entirely your own affair. So you see, this could be a very lucrative assignment. And by the way, he really does make movies, so who knows where all this might lead. It could be the start of a whole new career."

Verity knew she had done well, she was being offered her very first part, not on camera, but in a way it was on stage, a private showing with an audience of one.

The woman stood up, to indicate the interview was over. “Be ready to travel in a couple of weeks. Mr Lieberman is in a relationship right now. But I have a feeling that’s about to end.”

When Verity left, the albino reappeared with his clipboard. "I won't bother to see any more applicants." the woman said. "Miss Fuller will do very well." She picked up her cigarettes from the desk and struck a match. "You liked her too, didn't you Daisy?" He didn't answer but she knew she was right, it was just that he didn't like to be teased. "You'll have to wait a while I'm afraid, we both will. Then we'll see." She saw he was disappointed. "Never mind, Daisy. You can drive me down to Lakeside this afternoon, perhaps you'll find somebody there."

***

Ben Ambrose knew the Englishman’s routine so he rose early, made himself a simple breakfast which he ate on the terrace overlooking the harbour, and drove down to the beach to watch Bowman swim. This was Alex’s ritual almost every day of the year, broken only if he was away on a trip. Otherwise winter and summer, rain and shine, he started his day by swimming out about a mile off shore and returning in a sort of circle, clockwise one day, anti-clockwise the next. Physical exercise was an obsession with Bowman, a reaction to the years of confinement when walking round and round on a tiny patch of earth had been a daily luxury.

When he came out of the water, his body heavy with fatigue, Alex saw the figure seated next to his discarded clothes. Silhouetted against the bright sand he couldn't make out the features, but as he drew nearer he saw a man younger than himself, expensively dressed in brightly coloured casual clothes. The man didn't stand as Bowman approached but sat looking up at him from the lotus position, back straight, legs crossed, shading his eyes with his hand. He was smiling and he was black.

"You Bowman?"

"Me Bowman! You Jane?"

The black man chuckled and shook his head. He stood up from the sand with the easy fluent movement of an athlete and offered Alex his hand. "Me Ben. Agent Benjamin Ambrose, Drug Enforcement Administration."

Alex grabbed his towel and rubbed his thick brown hair, taking his time, sizing up the American. He looked like a good middleweight boxer in the mould of the great Sugar Ray, except his face was quite unmarked. Come to think of it, so was Sugar Ray's. "A long way from home, aren't you Mr. Ambrose? I don't suppose you're here to play golf?"

"No, this is a working trip." Ambrose joined his hands and swung an imaginary club. "I could use a little help as a matter of fact. Unofficial of course. I can pay you cash. I understand you do odd jobs for cash?" The corners of his mouth turned up in a cynical smile Bowman didn't much care for.

"Glad to, as long as it's not too illegal." Alex had put on his jeans and sweatshirt. He was intrigued to know what the American had in mind. Whatever it was he could expect to be well paid, the Drug Enforcement Administration had more money than anybody knew what to do with. If they wanted to throw some of it Bowman's way that was certainly all right by him. "Come on up to the house and have some breakfast." Two jobs in one week, things were really looking up. Bowman found his car keys in his jeans. "Follow me up to San Roque. I'll keep an eye out for you in the rear view mirror."

"Don't bother, Alex." The smile again. "I know where you live."

***

"Tell me how you found me." Bowman poured the coffee.

"I know all about you Alex. It's my business to know. Let's just say you come very highly recommended. They say you used to be a real hot ticket. Till you got caught with your fingers in the pie, that is. Why d'ya do it Alex? Kicks or cash?" Ambrose took a look around the room. Bare white walls, terracotta floor, no rugs. no drapes. Place was a monastery. Wasn't for cash. Pity. "How well do you know North Africa, Alex? Morocco in particular?"

"I've been there quite a bit and toured around. Fascinating country. I've done some climbing in the Atlas and skied there once, but I haven't worked there very much, a few deliveries and pick-ups, stuff like that. Once I pitched for a security job at a big hotel in Agadir, but I didn't get it. Went to one of the major French contractors."

"You have any Arabic? Any Berber?"

"No. But Spanish is pretty useful there, and I speak good French as well." This was beginning to sound interesting. "So what's the job?"

"Penetration. Maybe. It depends how things pan out."

"Penetration eh? I like the sound of that. Penetration into what exactly?"

"I don't know for sure. That's what I want you to help me find out." Ambrose stirred his coffee. "Europe is the big new market for drugs, still under-exploited. The States is saturated, over supplied, prices in the market are soft." Serious now. Convincing. "The warehouse for Europe is here in Spain, right here on the Costa del Sol. They're growing the stuff all over North Africa. Morocco, Algeria, Tunisia, all over the goddamn place. It's coming into Spain by the boatload, but it's just the soft stuff so far, thank God, mostly Mary Jane. The world's biggest cannabis producer is right there over the water." He pointed out across the bay. "If they ever get into producing heroin or snow we're dead in the water. Growing the stuff is easy, getting it into Spain is easy, distribution out of Spain is the problem, how to get it to London, Amsterdam, the Scandinavian countries. We know distribution is organised from here, somewhere along the Coast. I'd like to make contact."

"So who's organising the distribution?"

"That's what we're trying to find out. It has to be somebody big. Someone with a substantial legitimate business, so they can launder the funds."

"Who's we?"

"The DEA and the Spanish boys. They're willing enough, but they don't have a whole lot of experience, not yet anyway, and of course they totally under estimate the problem, same way you guys do. Officially I'm here to observe and give advice. Unofficially I'd like to do something a little more positive, just to keep my hand in."

"You're a renegade, Mr. Ambrose. I like that. Tell me what the job is and I'll tell you if I want to do it."

"I've been watching the ferry movements in and out of Algeciras, not just the Tangier boats, mostly Ceuta and Melilla. Customs clearance is done at the land frontier in Africa, and my guess is the procedures there are pretty sloppy. I figure you could buy the whole goddamn customs post for a fraction of the value of a big consignment."

"So why don't the Spanish boys tighten up the border controls, send in more men and give them some proper training?"

"Come on Alex! You can do better than that! The stuff would just come in by a different route. There are dozens of fishing ports on both sides of the Strait. They'd just have to fragment the shipments, move it in smaller consignments. I don't give a shit about stopping a single shipment, that achieves absolutely nothing. I want to find the distributor and put him out of business."

"And what am I supposed to do?" said Alex.

"Buy me the customs post."

"Buy you the customs post! What the fuck are you talking about?" Alex had taken a liking to the American by now, he liked his style and he liked his unorthodox approach, but he was beginning to wonder if Benjamin Ambrose really did have all his marbles.

"Sure, Alex. It's really very simple. You take your car on the ferry to Tangier, the trip takes under two hours. You spend a couple of days in Morocco and buy yourself a few kilograms of *Kif*, it's easy enough to find in any of the *Souks*. Buy enough so it's not just for personal consumption, personal consumption is legal in Spain. It has to be enough so you're a dealer. Then you drive back via Ceuta and clear customs at the land frontier. Act nervous. Draw attention to yourself, so you get searched. When they find the stuff you offer them cash, the DEA's cash, lots of it. Make sure you get to the top man, his name's Muñoz and word is he's on the take. I'll let you know what time to cross so I can be sure you get to him. Then one of two things will happen. If he's clean he'll put you in jail, charge you with illegal possession, attempted bribery, the whole goddamn bit. If he's not clean, he'll take the money and let you walk right on through. Then the Spanish boys can pick him up and lean on him a little, find out who his regular customers are, the big ones. Then we leave Muñoz in place working for us and penetrate the organisation."

"OK Ben." Alex was trying to be patient. "Here I am in jail in a Spanish enclave in North Africa. I'm a bent copper with a drugs conviction. I've been caught smuggling dope and I tried to buy the customs post. How do you get me out?"

"No problem, Alex." The smile again. "I already thought of that. We sign an affidavit. Before you leave. We go along to the local headquarters of the Spanish Bureau up the coast in Malaga. The whole thing will be documented, official, we'll even have it notarised if you want. If Muñoz is clean someone will have to apologise to him, he could even get a promotion. If he's not, we could be on our way to Mr. Big. What do you say Alex? Do we have a deal?"

"How much?" It was time to be practical.

"$5,000 for the trip, plus expenses and stake money to buy the *Kif*, so you can make a little extra on the side. You'll be carrying another ten grand for Muñoz but his bills will be listed, so don't get his and yours mixed up. That's over $5,000 for a couple of days work Alex, more than you normally make in a month. And that's just for openers. After that who knows, if this thing goes right you could be working for me for months. Make yourself a bundle." He looked around the spartan room and the smile returned to the corners of his mouth. “Enough to furnish this place."

“I like this place the way it is, but cash is always handy.” His back was to him now. “And what’s in it for you Mr. Ambrose? Kicks or cash?”

“Just the glory Alex, old buddy. Strictly for the glory.”

The money was good and it could lead to more, but it was the idea that appealed to Alex, the idea of nailing one of the fat cats at last, the idea of doing something meaningful again. Compared to playing minder to some rich Arab's gilded mistress it was no contest. He would have to check up on Ambrose first to make sure he was legitimate, but Ramsay could do that in London. It would take two or three days to set the whole thing up, so there was time to find Tiffany Wells before he went to Morocco. "OK Ben, you're on. Give me a couple days to finish some other stuff I'm working on and I'll be ready to go."

Lunch wasn't part of Alex's normal routine but Ambrose insisted on driving down to the port at Soto Grande to eat and observe the expensive women who went there to look at the yachts and sell themselves to the yachtsmen. Every once in a while one of them would come up to Ambrose and kiss his cheek and whisper something in his ear that made him laugh. He seemed to enjoy the attention, but today at least he wasn't buying. Alex knew there was no way the DEA could ask its operatives to keep an accurate record of the way they used its cash, paying off informers was routine and receipts unheard of. But he guessed that Ambrose spent a lot of money on himself, on clothes and women and entertainment. Maybe it was all part of his cover, his legend, his way of fitting in. But after a time habits like that could become an addiction too, just like any other.

***

Frank Willowby, the DEA's chief liaison officer for Western Europe, came down the steps of the American Embassy two at a time. A tall lean athletic man in his early fifties he had crew-cut silver hair and piercing brown eyes. He wore a grey herringbone Brooks Brothers suit and blue cotton shirt, buttoned down. He crossed Grosvenor Square and entered Claridge's through the side entrance to the bar. Rupert Rutland, Junior Minister at the Home Office, sat at a corner table. He rose when he saw Willowby and they shook hands.

"Rupert, how are you?" said Willowby.

"Fine Frank, apart from this cold. I don't seem to be able to shake it." Rutland dabbed at his nose with his handkerchief.

"Jesus, Rupert!" Willowby frowned, "You had a cold the last time I saw you. That was weeks ago!"

"How about you, Frank? How was the holiday?"

"Spain was great. Golf was excellent. What can I get you to drink? The usual?" Without waiting for a reply Willowby gestured to the barman and ordered a couple of dry martinis. "We have a new agent on the Costa del Sol, so I was able to check him out *in situ*, which was useful.

He has some interesting ideas about the local marijuana trade. If anything comes up I'll be sure to pass it along to you guys at the NDIU."

"What's the new man like?" Rutland seemed uninterested.

"A maverick. Bit of a loner. Doesn't respond well to discipline. He has a good enough record, but he's not a high flyer. Otherwise I wouldn't have posted him to Spain. It's not a priority for the DEA. We need our best people in the Caribbean and South America. More cannabis comes across from Morocco into Spain that any place else in the world, but very little horse and no snow. Nobody's much interested in marijuana any more. The UK has re-classified it. Some countries have even de-criminalized the stuff. You can't make a market once it's legal."

"You can't want it made legal!" Rutland was aghast. "Marijuana maybe. Eventually. But not hard drugs!"

"Not unless you want to get rid of the problem."

"Excuse me?"

"Come on, Rupert. Everybody knows if you want to get rid of the problem you have to make it legal. If you're really serious about it, you should make drugs freely available."

"You're not serious."

“Sure I’m serious. It’ll never happen, but I can tell you right now how to get rid of the drugs problem within six months. Interested?”

“Try me.”

“OK Rupert. You asked for it. You rent a dozen large derelict spaces. The worse shape they’re in, the better. Unused churches. Suburban cinemas. You make heroin and snow freely available. Financed by the State. You provide the needles and whatever paraphernalia the dope-heads need. Let them go to it. The sky’s the limit. But you withdraw any kind of support. No medical help. And they look after their own hygiene. Place would be a shit-hole in days. Now here’s the clincher. Next you show the whole thing live on TV. Compulsory viewing in schools and universities. Within six months there’d be no market for any kind of drugs. ‘Course a few thousand junkies would probably die. But most of them don’t have much of a life anyway. And they’d be dying in a good cause. Saving generations of future dope-heads from the same fate.” Willowby finished his martini and ordered another round. “Don’t worry, Rupert. It’ll never happen. Our jobs are secure!”

“Nothing I should discuss with the NDIU?” Rutland had gone pale.

“I don’t think so, Rupert.” Willowby smiled. “I’m not ready for the funny farm just yet. Probably come to nothing. Anything happens, I’ll be sure to let you know. Can’t leave our friends at the National Drugs Intelligence Unit out of the loop, now can we?” He took a sip of his martini. “You read my paper on Plan Dignidad? We had a major success defoliating the Bolivian rain forest. Wiped out thousands and thousands of acres of coca. Really hurt the bastards."

"I saw the reports. Impressive. Got good coverage in the press, especially the Times and the Echo. So when will the effects hit the market?" Rutland took more interest now. Willowby's views were invaluable. Always worth reporting. Their informal meetings over lunch or a drink were particularly productive.

"It'll take a while, for sure. The pipeline is full. But in three or four months snow will be harder to come by. And what there is will be expensive. The Colombians will have to put Europe on rations. They're bound to give priority to their markets in the States. So the effect on availability and price will be magnified here. Should make things interesting for you guys. Expect to see some fireworks, when the distributors fight it out to secure supplies." He waved at the waiter. "What about lunch, Rupert? I'm starving. How about you?"

Rutland dabbed at his nose again. He seemed embarrassed. "I'll just have a salad, thanks. Can't taste a thing with this wretched cold."

***

6

It was midnight when Bowman found the place, too early yet to be crowded. The Black Sombrero was tucked away in the new part of town, away from the elegant shops and restaurants, in the basement of a half completed apartment block. The surrounding streets were deserted, except for the dogs. There were dogs everywhere, in packs, foraging in the garbage.

Bowman chose a spot to park the car just outside the pool of light from a street lamp, half way up the incline. He strolled down the street and stood at the head of the steps to memorise the featureless landscape. From below he could hear the pained intonation of the *canto hondo* coming from the cheap stereo. The steps were low-grade marble, heavily veined. Inside the place was mainly chrome and glass and cheap stained pine. There was a problem with the drains. It was hard to imagine Tiffany Wells in such a place, harder still to imagine Mary Berringer, but for Bowman this was home ground, the low life was his natural cover.

The place wasn't crowded, a handful of people, mainly women, none of them customers. Alex ordered a *Fundador* and a soda water in a separate glass. He sat at the bar with his back to the room, aware that the women were watching him, wondering how much he would pay. Some of the women were Spanish, some Gypsy, and some had come across from North Africa for the richer pickings on the Costa del Sol. Body odour. How did they expect to sell themselves with body odour? One or two of the women came to the bar to stand next to him, hoping he might buy them a drink, the cheap sweet house champagne, the necessary preamble before a bargain could be struck. At another time he might have, but tonight he had other things to do so he didn't even look. Normally a disregarded woman would mutter something dismissive *penco, maricon*, but when they looked at Alex that seemed unlikely so they walked away in silence, hoping no one else would succeed where they had failed. There is a fierce rivalry among the women of certain professions.

There was only one pimp in the place, a slightly built *gitano* who sat with two of the better looking women, younger than the rest, at a table he could watch the bar and the door from, without moving his head. Alex wondered where he kept the knife, in his boot most likely. A few tourists came and went without buying drinks, brought to the place by taxi drivers working on commission. It was a quiet night at the Black Sombrero. Nobody was making any money.

Alex felt the hand on his shoulder. He didn't turn but looked up at the mirror behind the bar. It was the pimp, showing his teeth. "Was the matter *gringo*? You no like my women?" He spoke with a Speedy Gonzalez accent.

"Your women, are they?" said Alex, still looking in the mirror. "Your women are fine, just not my type. I like thin women."

"You want to see a movie? Exhibition? Go some place else? Private? Members only?"

Alex gestured to the barman. "A drink for my friend." There were two possibilities. Alex could spend the rest of the night following the pimp from place to place hoping he might find her, or he could try the direct approach. The direct approach would save time and cost less money. He had the photograph in his breast pocket. It was a good likeness, but of Mary as she used to be, as he remembered her, young and bright and attractive. The Tiffany Wells who starred in the porno flick had put on flesh and her eyes were sunken and tired.

The pimp took his time looking at the picture. He knew there was money to be made, there always is when a man wants a particular woman, but he wasn't sure how to go about it. He knew who the woman was and he knew the people she frequented and if he made the wrong move they would very likely blow his brains out.

Alex watched the *gitano's* eyes and saw the flicker of recognition, but he didn't see the gesture the pimp made to the barman, who went to the storeroom at the back of the bar where the phone was.

"Why you want this one *gringo*? Many better women in Marbella, I show you." The pimp needed time. "You like two women? Sisters maybe? Twins? *Ménage à trois*? Maybe you just like to watch?"

The barman returned and nodded at the pimp. Alex saw the gesture this time. Something was going to happen. He retrieved the photograph and showed it to the barman but the barman looked away. Alex got up to go to the table where the pimp's women sat but before he was off the stool the *gitano* had touched him lightly on the forearm.

"*Gringo* you go now, no make trouble. You no like my women, you go now."

The two women watched Alex, standing now, looking down at the pimp still seated on his stool. The pimp was smiling, sweating and smiling, gold glinting in his mouth, eyes bright with excitement. His right hand hung loose, hovering about the top of his boot. The barman had come round to the customer's side of the bar, bottle in hand.

"Sure." Alex pocketed the photo. "No trouble. I go now."

The pimp flashed a bright smile at his women, to underline his victory.

Alex sat in the car and waited. He was parked a little way up the street from the Black Sombrero and could see the entrance clearly in the glow of the light from the street lamp. In a little while a large white Mercedes arrived, driven too fast, and came to a halt with a screech of tyres. Five men got out in a hurry and rushed down the steps into the bar. Nothing else happened for ten minutes or so. Then three of the men came back out and drove away slowly, leaving the other two inside.

It was an hour before anything else happened. Then one of the pimp's women, the best looking of the bunch, came up the steps with one of the men from the Mercedes. A moment later a taxi drew up, summoned by phone, and they drove away into the darkness. Alex followed. They drove to the outskirts of town to an American style motel where the rooms gave directly onto the dimly lit car park.

The place seemed deserted, only two or three of the rooms were taken.

Alex waited outside for five minutes, time for them to agree the price and maybe start on a few preliminaries, but not enough to make any irrevocable commitments. Then he braced himself against a pillar opposite the door, raised his boot and smashed the flimsy lock. In a single movement he was through into the room.

The woman was naked, on her knees in front of the man in an attitude of prayer. The man, erect but only half undressed, turned in disbelief, reaching for the other weapon in his discarded clothes. He didn't have a chance. Bowman smashed the butt of the Browning onto the man's skull. The blow was harder than he intended. Alex bent down to listen to his breathing. He would live.

The woman was on her feet, back to the wall, naked, eyes closed, gasping. She was in a state of blind panic. She had recognised Alex from the bar and knew that he was trouble. Alex picked up her bundled clothing from the floor and threw it to her. *"Veste te."* Get dressed.

"You kill him!" She pointed, eyes wide, full of panic.

"He'll be OK. He'll have a very big bump on his head, but that's all. *Un pedazo muy grande."*

"Now! Kill him now! He know you speak to me!" She was shaking, naked and pitiful.

"Veste te." Alex repeated. *"Vamanos."*

She let out a whimpering animal sound and hurried awkwardly into her clothes. Then she made a quick dash around the room in jerky freeze-frame movements, collected her things and stuffed them into her bag. Finally she came to a halt in the middle of the room and looked at Alex, waiting to be told what to do next. He knew he had to get her out of there to some place she could hide. She wouldn't talk unless she felt protected.

"*Vamanos.*" Time was being wasted.

.
"*Momento.*" She went and stood over the body of the man and crouched down beside him, her face next to his. Alex thought she wanted to check he was breathing but instead she drew in a gulp of air and spat into his face. "*Cujone! Maricon*!" She hissed. Then she rummaged in his pockets, found his wallet, and emptied it of cash.

They drove along the coast towards Malaga. It was nearly 5am, pitch black, the streets deserted. Alex had no place to hide her, he didn't want her at San Roque. The best thing was to take her to the airport and put her on a plane to Madrid or Barcelona, she could make a living there as easily as in Marbella. He had taken a good look at her body as he watched her dress. Wherever she went, she wasn't going starve.

Alex pulled off the road above a deserted beach. Dawn was about to break. He watched the sky in the east and saw the first beam of light break through the low cloud and then the blush of pink in the sky. He got out of the car to breathe the crystal air and was about to scramble down to the beach when he remembered Conchita, still sitting in the car. When she saw him turn to come back for her she got out of the car and stood leaning against it, waiting and hoping. There was just enough light now to see how pretty she was, prettier than she seemed in the sordid bar. She was part Gypsy, almond eyes, high cheekbones, full lips. Her skin was silk. Maybe seventeen. She was looking at Alex in a way that was meant to be provocative and was, but she said nothing. She knew the words but she wanted him to say them.

"The girl in the photograph, you know her?"

"Tiffany my friend. They lock her up. Maybe they kill her." The panic had gone now. She wanted to touch him, but most of all she wanted to be touched.

"Who locked her up? Where?"

"Rich people. Big house. Much money." She made a gesture with her right hand, rubbing the first two fingers and thumb against one another. They made a quiet sound in the still air.

"This house, Conchita. You know where it is?"

"Sure. I go there once. Big fucking party. Make movie. Pay good."

"Could you take me there? Show me?" He saw her hesitate. "Look Conchita, you can't go back to the Sombrero, you know that. Show me where the big house is and I'll take you to the airport, put you on a plane to anywhere you like, Madrid, Barcelona, Palma, anywhere. I'll give you five hundred dollars, American money, cash. That's all I have with me, OK? Just to drive me past the place?" She hesitated still. "Look Conchita, Tiffany needs my help, needs it badly. She's your friend isn't she?"

Conchita wanted to stay with him but she knew leaving town was the only option she had. There was no way she could compete with Tiffany. But she moved forward and pressed her body lightly against his, so she wouldn't regret later that she hadn't made the offer. Then she turned and got back in the car.

They drove back into Marbella, along the *paseo maritimo* to the *Puerta del Mar*. The sun was up now and they passed quickly through the deserted streets of the old town and took the road that climbs gently inland, at right angles to the coast. The streets were lined with huge royal palms and the lawns in front of the palatial houses were lush and green and manicured. They sparkled with the droplets from the automatic sprinkler systems, which were just now popping into life. The road climbed steeply and the properties got bigger and further apart until they were in open wooded countryside.

Ten minutes later Conchita made a sign and Alex swung the car into a narrow side road, which had only recently been surfaced. It wasn't long before they came to a high white painted wall topped with iron spikes six or eight inches high. A little further along they passed a heavy wrought iron gate beyond which the gravelled driveway took a sharp bend, hiding the rest of the property from view. A sign made of blue and white ceramic tiles set into the wall announced *La Hacienda Blanca*.

"Es aqui." said Conchita. "It's here."

Alex stopped the car and reversed back to the main road, relieved he was making no dust.

***

Two hours later Bowman parked the car out of sight off the main highway, just before the entry to the newly surfaced road. He had dropped Conchita at Malaga airport, used his new charge card to put her on a flight to Palma de Mallorca and given her all the cash he had. He would charge the flight to expenses, but he wasn't sure he could recover the cash, not without proper documentation.

He took his field glasses from the glove compartment and climbed the wooded hillside that rose on the other side of the road, away from the white wall. It was mid-morning now and hot, the sun high, blazing down on his back as he climbed. He was sweating and he was tired. There was lots of cover and he climbed steeply for half an hour and then traversed along a route parallel to the newly surfaced road. When he was directly above the property he began to descend till it came into view. From this position he could see clear beyond the wall. The house was huge, part Hollywood, part Arabian Nights, but somehow it didn't look at all out of place. He recognised it at once. It was the house they had used in the porno flick.

The heavies were in pairs, two on a flat roof overlooking the grounds and two on the terrace outside the main door. Bowman could see the shoulder holsters clearly and the dull shine on the black metal. He couldn't make out the model but it might have been the Smith & Wesson 686 Magnum.

In front of the house, below the terrace, was the turquoise jewel of the swimming pool. Alex could hear voices, occasionally raised in laughter, but he couldn't see anyone, nobody moved. Through the powerful Zeiss lenses he examined the building, trying to commit the external layout to memory. Then, as he scanned the front of the villa, a woman emerged from the house onto the terrace, shading her eyes against the light.

He recognised her immediately. She was lovely still but she had put on weight and there was a puffiness about her face he knew was drug induced. She wore the bottom half of a bikini and high-heeled shoes and around her waist was a fine gold chain, glinting in the light. She looked like a very expensive tart.

Suddenly a voice called out. "Hey Tiffany! Get your ass over here will ya! Harvey wants a blow job!" There was laughter. Alex located its source at once to a spot concealed beneath an awning by the pool. Tiffany peered about helplessly, unable to work out where the voice was coming from. It called out again and there was more laughter but still she couldn't spot where it was coming from. Then a man in a towelling robe appeared from beneath the awning. He went up to Tiffany and with an exaggerated gallantry that was meant to be offensive he took her by the hand to guide her down the steps.

Alex wanted to go down to her immediately. He could see she needed help. But as he watched her stumble round the pool he knew this wasn't the moment. Tiffany Wells was bombed out of her mind. Bowman had been up all night. He was tired, on edge. If he went down there now he would mishandle the situation in some way. The opposition looked too well placed for that and he wouldn't get a second chance. He decided to come back and watch the house and choose a moment when no one else was there, or break in after dark and find her room. He would go back to San Roque now and get some rest.

The two faxes he sent from the main post office in Marbella were brief. The first he addressed to Mrs. Hetherington at Lord Berringer's private office.

"Mary Berringer is residing at La Hacienda Blanca, off the Ronda road in the hills above Marbella. Claim for expenses to follow."

The second he sent to Ramsay at the Yard.

"The severed fingers have to do with identification - the perpetrator's, not the victim's."

***

The little girl in the woman's body sat in front of the mirror crying. She'd had a fix, she could have whatever she needed, but it wasn't working, it wasn't enough. She was frightened. More could kill her and without it she couldn't survive. She opened the drawer and looked at the photograph again, of a woman, devastatingly beautiful, holding a young child in her arms. Behind her, slightly out of focus, was a man with a fat featureless face and thinning hair. She was tired of being Tiffany. She wanted to be Mary again, a child again. She heard the noise in the corridor outside and slipped the photograph back in the draw.

He stood in the doorway, the fat man in the towelling robe. "What's the matter, bitch?" She didn't answer. He moved towards her, took her by the shoulders and shook her violently, watching her head roll forward and backward like a doll's, black tears staining her cheeks. "Who is she, damnit! Tell me who the woman is!"

"I can't tell you. I won't tell you. They'll kill me if I do."

"And I'll kill you if you don't."

"Kill me! Then who'll tell you? I'm the only one who knows! Christ Harvey, you can be so fucking stupid."

***

The next afternoon Alex drove back to *La Hacienda Blanca*. He took the infamous N340, there was no way he could avoid it. Statistically this road is the worst death trap in Europe. Every year it claims a victim for each of its seventy-five miles from Malaga to Algeciras. Traffic was heavy, it always was in the summer months, when the population nearly doubled. It was the tourists who caused the problem, the locals were used to turning left from the right hand lane.

The road clung to the coast, winding through the hideous resorts of Estepona and San Pedro with their high-rise hotels and unfinished tower blocks, craning for a glimpse of the sea. The brochures never mentioned you had to dodge traffic across a six-lane highway, just to get to the beach. Still, you could get anything you wanted here; egg and chips, homemade cottage pie, cream teas. Suburbia on heat.

At Puerto Banus he turned off the main road and headed down towards the coast. Puerto Banus was different. Puerto Banus was serious money. Puerto Banus had class. He found the tennis club set back off the road, shortly before entering the town. It was a small elegant place, built to attract rich people to buy the expensive real estate in the surrounding area. Along with the yacht harbour and the golf club, this was a place to be seen.

"Miss Drake is playing doubles on court six, Señor." The receptionist looked down at a chart of the courts and then at his watch. A fake Brit, blue blazer, grey flannels, club tie. "She'll be coming off court in half an hour. If you would like to wait in the lounge, I'll tell her you're here when she comes in."

Alex went upstairs to the bar and out onto the terrace overlooking the courts. Across to his right he could see Melanie playing a game of doubles with what looked like another English girl and a couple of Spanish-looking men. The girls were playing against the boys and it looked as if the girls were winning. Melanie looked good in her whites, nice tan, nice thighs, nice topspin backhand. Alex didn't want her to notice him watching her, so he went back inside and picked up one of the local tabloids from a table and ordered a large black coffee. He was thumbing idly through the paper when he saw it on the society page, a photograph of Mary Berringer smiling out at him. The shock was in the headline. *"TRAGIC DEATH OF COSTA HEIRESS."* The article below was brief.

"Mary Berringer, step daughter of multi-millionaire international businessman Lord Berringer and live-in lover of moviemaker Harvey Lieberman met her death last evening in a fatal motor accident on Spain's notorious death road outside Marbella. Lord Berringer, who is known to be travelling abroad, was not available for comment."

"Alex, in heaven's name what is it?" He had gone pale. Melanie Drake stood above him sweating, her damp hair matted, wondering what on earth could be the matter.

"Mel, I'm sorry, I didn't see you come in. Here, read this." An accident? Could it really be an accident?

"My God! This is her Alex, isn't it? This is awful, absolutely awful! What happens now?" She sat on the arm of his chair and re-read the article. "Step daughter? You said she was his daughter, didn't you?"

"Sorry, Mel? What's that?" Alex was still in shock.

"Nothing, it's not important. What are you going to do now, Alex?" Flaherty had been on the phone again, pressing her for details, offering her cash. He wanted an exclusive. He saw it as a feature in the Sunday edition, a double spread.

Bowman's mind was already on the Tangier trip. "Mary was the only chance I had. If she had changed her story there would have been a re-trial, Faraday was sure of that. Now there's no reason for that to happen, the whole thing is best forgotten." He took a sip of his coffee. "I have work to do here now anyway, important work, work that pays better than most honest coppers can earn." He felt the bitterness coming back and wasn't sure he had the strength to fight it.

"So you're going to give up? Waste the rest of your life out here playing minder to a bunch of petty criminals? Don't you have any pride?" She couldn't believe she had misjudged him so completely.

"I'm a realist. Mary Berringer was the only chance I had."

"I'm sorry Alex, it's really none of my business, it's your life, but it just seems such a waste, that's all."

***

7

Bowman boarded the early morning ferry to Tangier, a journey of less than two hours on a good day, through the narrow Strait to the Atlantic. The boat was packed with the unwashed of two continents. It was a zoo. He fought his way from the car deck, through the crowds that thronged the gangways, out into the open air. The sun was up and the air already warm, a stiff breeze lifting the early morning haze off the bay. A flock of gulls wheeled overhead, waiting to be fed.

Bowman took up a position above the prow and braced himself against the wind, drinking in the salt air. The boat cleared the jetty and nosed out into the mouth of the Strait. Off the stern the Rock loomed massively above the mist and to port the mountains of Africa rose steeply from the ocean, matched by their twins on the European side. The boat picked up speed and Alex leaned into the wind on the fore deck, the blown spray stinging his face. He breathed deeply, swaying with the motion of the boat, its irresistible rhythm rocking the horizon.

The crossing was slow in the rough and windy conditions. It took over two hours before Tangier came into view, climbing the hill side from the port to the ancient walled *Medina*, its battlements still intact. From the minaret of the Grand Mosque, high above the harbour, the amplified chant of the *Muezzin* was calling the faithful to midday prayer, a siren song from another world, trapped in another time.

Bowman had made the crossing a dozen times or more but the sight of Tangier from the sea never failed to thrill him. The place was totally alien, so different from Spain and the rest of Europe, and the shock of such a complete change in so short a journey amazed him still. Everything was different, the colours, the sounds, the smells, the people, especially the people, Berbers, Arabs, people of mixed race, in their *djellabas* and *caftans*, the women veiled behind their delicate *mansouriahs*. Alex felt totally alien, it was a feeling he thoroughly enjoyed, to be an alien had become his natural state.

Moving slowly through the congested streets around the port, passed the yacht club and the railway station, the little car was jostled by the crush of pedestrians. Progress was slow. People and animals were everywhere, stepping off the pavement without warning, stopping in the middle of the road, children urinating cheerfully in the gutter. At last he found his way along the sea front to the outskirts of the city and took the road southeast to Tetuan, the inland capital of the northern province.

He spotted the white Peugeot as he left the dockside in Tangier. Clear of the city on the open road it stayed well behind but with so little traffic its presence was obvious. Bowman knew he couldn't outrun it in the little Seat so he took his chance about fifteen miles out of Tangier at the crest of the Fondak Ridge, where the road suddenly plunges into the deep valley. The road made a couple of sharp hairpin bends in quick succession and Bowman took advantage of the temporary loss of visual contact to pull back off the road and watch the Peugeot cruise by. He watched it accelerate as it reached the valley floor and when it was almost out of sight he rejoined the road as it disappeared into the distance.

Two hours later Bowman checked in to a simple hotel in the European quarter of Tetuan, a short walk from the Medina. He took a shower and changed his clothes and by late afternoon he was in the *Souk*. This was a place of commerce, a place to barter, to haggle, to bid, to make deals. Nothing was worth the opening price, it wasn't expected. There were stalls selling pottery, leather goods, carpets, copper, brass, silver, and the ones that interested Bowman that specialised in herbs, spices and infusions. It didn't take long before he spotted what he wanted, a shop a little on it's own, apart from the rest. But it was the merchant who intrigued Bowman, a tattooed half cast, part Berber, part European. He wore army surplus trousers, a sleeveless "T" shirt, no shoes, and he hadn't shaved for a week.

Bowman pushed the bead curtain aside and entered the shop. At once a young boy brought him a glass of green tea on a brightly burnished copper tray. Bowman sipped the sweet liquid and the boy disappeared, leaving Alex alone. A moment later the merchant entered the shop from the street and made an elaborate gesture, inviting his visitor to sit down.

Bowman didn't want to spend any longer striking a bargain than he had to. "*Kif*." he said, looking the merchant in the eye.

The merchant looked at Bowman as if he didn't understand. Then he clapped his hands and the boy re-appeared from a room at the back of the shop. The merchant said something Bowman didn't understand and the boy went outside and stood on the far side of the bead curtain, so no one else should enter. Then the merchant turned to Bowman again and repeated the single word the Englishman had said.

"*Kif*?" His expression was quizzical. His breath was lethal.

"Two or three kilos. Cash. Dollars."

The merchant swallowed. Three kilos would be worth several thousand dollars, more than he would normally sell in a month. He had some on the premises, he always did, about half a kilo of the very best quality, but not enough to satisfy the Englishman. He would need an hour, maybe two, to put the deal together. "Come back at eight o'clock to-night. I'll see what I can do.

Bowman knew better than to come back to the Medina at night at a fixed time, carrying all that cash. "Come to my hotel, in the European quarter."

"Not the hotel, the café opposite, just across the square." The café was a compromise, neutral territory, no-man's-land.

When Bowman returned to the hotel he saw the Peugeot parked in the forecourt, two spaces away from his own little Seat. So whoever they were, they weren't such amateurs after all.

***

Just before eight o'clock that evening Bowman walked out of the hotel. The café lay across the tiny tree lined square. Half way across he turned and saw the two men follow him out of the hotel and stand in the doorway while their eyes got accustomed to the light. They were European, probably Spanish, squat and powerfully built. They wore loose fitting bomber jackets, loose enough to disguise the bulge of a shoulder holster.

When Bowman entered the café the merchant was already there, seated at a corner table deep in the interior, a glass of green mint tea in front of him. Bowman joined him and ordered coffee. "How much did you get?"

"Four kilos. In one kilo bags."

"Where is it?"

"In the leather bag, under the table."

Bowman pressed a foot against the heavy bag between the merchant's feet. He could see the two Spaniards seated by the open window, watching, the only men in the room with their jackets on. He turned back to the merchant. "You go first."

The merchant disappeared through a bead curtain, down a dark corridor, carrying the bag. A moment later Bowman followed. The stench was nauseating. When he found the merchant he was standing inside a doorless cubicle, unaware of the filthy odour, his feet either side of the hole in the ground.

"Let's see." said Bowman.

The merchant handed him the soft leather bag. Bowman unfastened it and saw the four clear plastic bundles bulging with a grey-green tea-like substance, the crushed flower heads, leaves and stems of *Cannabis Sativa*.

"I wanted resin." Grass looked unconvincing, not professional, but that was only its appearance, it was just as effective.

"Come back tomorrow and I'll get you resin."

"Never mind, this'll do." Getting caught was the only thing that mattered. Bowman chose one of the bags at random and punctured it with his thumbnail. He wetted his fingers and put a little of the grass on his tongue. It was good, Morocco Pure, the very best quality money could buy. He spat into the hole between the merchant's feet and handed him the cash. It took only a moment to count, four thousand dollars in one hundred dollar bills.

The deal done, Bowman re-entered the café and took a deep gulp of air. He didn't stop, but walked straight out across the square to the hotel, and up to his room. The Spaniards didn't follow. They just sat and watched him go, carrying the bag.

***

The next day Bowman slept late. Ambrose had told him not to reach the border till the afternoon, Muñoz never worked the morning shift. From the balcony of his room Alex could see the car park at the front of the hotel. The Peugeot was still there and across the square at a table outside the café the two Spaniards sat drinking coffee. Bowman had left his constant companion behind, the snug little Browning GP35FA, and he was beginning to wonder if he had made the right decision.

He showered and shaved, taking his time, relishing the slow start to the day. He put the four one-kilo bags of *Kif* into his canvass holdall with the rest of his things and left the merchant's bag on top of the wardrobe. At midday he went downstairs, had a light lunch of *bistila*, paid his bill and checked out. As he reversed the Seat out onto the street one of the Spaniards got up from the table and strolled across to the Peugeot, leaving the other to pay the bill.

The medieval fortress city of Ceuta, roughly twice the size and three times the population of Gibraltar, was only twenty or so miles to the north. Traffic was backed up for half a mile at the frontier, the line of trucks and cars shunting forward in irritating fits and starts, the midday sun beating down oppressively.

The Moroccan side was easy, there was no real customs check, just a quick glance at his passport and Bowman was waved through. The Spanish official took longer, examining his passport with care. Then Bowman crossed to the customs post, a low white structure in the Spanish colonial style. He parked the car in the shade of a bamboo awning and walked into the customs post, carrying the canvass bag.

He towered above the customs official but didn't look him in the eye. Outside, Bowman could see they were doing a thorough job on the car. The doors were open and one man was tapping the panelling to make sure it was hollow while another held a mirror on a metal rod and examined the underneath of the vehicle. The official watched Bowman watching the car and saw him breathe a sigh of relief as the men outside moved on to the next vehicle. Bowman couldn't resist a smile. It did the trick. The official went outside and called out to the others, gesticulating towards the Seat. Bowman couldn't hear what he said but he saw the two men go back to the Seat and go to work again on the interior. They pulled out the folding back seat.

"That's right, boys." Bowman murmured. "Now you're getting warm." A moment later they hit the jackpot. He heard one of the men call out.

"*Que buscan Muñoz*!" Get Muñoz!

***

Bowman stood in the middle of the room, stark naked. He felt unclean, humiliated. He had never been body searched before. He had seen it done to others and understood the indignity of the process but hadn't known how unclean it made you feel. They had made him strip then bend over a chair with his legs spread apart for the anal search. He clenched his fists as he heard their childlike laughter. Then they went through every item of his clothing and baggage. They didn't find the cash, thank God. If they had it would have disappeared and left him with no cards to play at all.

They gave Alex a chair to sit on, a simple wooden straight-backed chair, and stood behind him, slouching against the wall. When Muñoz entered they stiffened and stood erect on either side of the naked prisoner. Bowman sat upright too, his hands crossed over his genitals.

Muñoz was a short powerful man, well into his fifties. His uniform was clean and pressed, his nails manicured. Pink flesh bulged angrily around the rings he wore on his left hand. His eyes were steel and his smile as sincere as he could make it. He sat on the corner of the desk and looked down on the naked Englishman. He looked long and hard before he waved the guards away. Bowman listened to their footsteps. They had gone no further than just outside the door.

"Uneducated men." Muñoz made a dismissive gesture towards the door. "They speak no English." He had Bowman's passport in his hand. "You're in big trouble, Señor Bowman. Big trouble. You're a very foolish man." His tone was conciliatory. He spoke slowly, waiting to see if Bowman would respond. When he didn't, Muñoz went on. "Let me explain what happens to you now, Señor Bowman. I call the police. You are arrested. Smuggling drugs is a very serious offence in my country. You are kept in jail, here in Ceuta. It will be months before the trial, more than a year perhaps. Conditions in the jail are not good, not five star. Ten people to a cell, maybe more. Not the sort of people you associate with, Inglès. Thieves, murderers, sex offenders. Drug runners like yourself. Homosexuality is rife, rape is common. You're a big man, you can look after yourself. But be careful Inglès, don't offend these people." He paused again. "Tonight you will be given........" he was searching for the word, "a purge, a laxative. To make you shit. A common method is to swallow condoms filled with *Kif* but of course you know that, you're a professional. There are no proper sanitary facilities in the jail, you shit in the cell, in a bucket, in front of everybody. It can be quite a spectacle. Some of your cellmates will be disgusted, most will just be amused. Maybe they make bets how long it takes. You'll find they have a sense of humour."

Bowman felt the sweat trickle slowly down the side of his face and onto his neck. His pulse was throbbing. He could hear his own heartbeat. Maybe he had made a mistake. There was something about Ambrose that didn't fit, he was a maverick, a loner. This whole trip was a deniable fiction, even the affidavit could be destroyed. Beads of sweat had gathered on his chin, waiting to fall. The slightest movement would do it. Whatever happened he wasn't going to jail. Never again. He would kill first. Kill with his bare hands. He clenched his jaw. A bead of sweat dropped onto the back of his hand.

"In a few minutes I will phone the British Consul." Muñoz spoke in a whisper. "To inform him of your arrest. I will ask him to check with London to see if you are known to the police there, if you have any previous conviction. I think you were in jail before?"

"How would you know that?" Ambrose knew. But Ambrose wouldn't have told him.

"You have the look. What is the word? *Traumatizado?* Haunted? Things look bad for you, Señor Bowman. Alex."

Bowman knew the use of his first name was the cue, the invitation. He wouldn't be spending the night in jail after all. He was on his way. "Do you have a cigarette?" Alex rarely smoked but the passing of a cigarette between them would change their relationship in a subtle way, put them on more equal terms. Conspirators. Colleagues. Muñoz came back to the desk, took a fresh pack from the drawer, pulled out his lighter and held it while Alex inhaled.

"I've been very foolish." Bowman puffed smoke in Muñoz's face. "I admit it. I needed the money. How much do you think I would have made on the deal? A thousand dollars? Two maybe?"

"More than that surely! Think of the risk!" There was sincerity in Muñoz's voice that hadn't been there before. "Not less than five thousand dollars I would say."

So that was his price. Alex thought of bargaining some more, to add credibility to his performance, but he didn't want to spend more time than was needed. Muñoz picked up the phone and dialled the first two digits of a number.

"Ask your men to bring me my things." Bowman's tone was businesslike, they were equals now. Muñoz shouted an instruction and one of the guards scurried away and returned a moment later and knocked at the door.

"*Adelante.*" Muñoz nodded at the guard who placed the canvass bag and Bowman's bundled clothing on the desk. Alex dressed hurriedly, pulled on his sweatshirt and jeans, and took the bag and retrieved his camera from it. He opened the back and took out the wad of notes, counting five thousand dollars while Muñoz watched in silence. It was a good bargain, five thousand dollars plus the resale value of four kilos of *Kif*. The best small deal he had done in a week.

Bowman put the camera back in his bag and strode out of the room without word. As he crossed to the car he heard Muñoz shouting abuse at the guards, but they seemed to take it in good part. They knew they would be seeing a share of the spoils.

Bowman spotted the Peugeot parked a few spaces away, the driver and passenger watching Muñoz disappear back inside. Alex wandered over and the driver wound down his window, smiling. Alex bent low and addressed him in perfect Spanish.

"Tell Ambrose I appreciate the gesture. If you're carrying a copy of that affidavit, you'd best get rid of it now. I don't want my name getting too well known around here. Torch it." As he straightened up Alex dropped Muñoz's lighter in the man's lap and strode back to his car.

***

In Muñoz's safe they found the four kilos of Morocco Pure and the five thousand dollars in crisp new bills. They checked the serial numbers against the list Ambrose had provided. They were a perfect match. Muñoz didn't resist arrest, there was no point. They drove him the short distance to his villa so he could pack a few things before they took him back to Malaga for questioning. They didn't intend to hold him for long, just enough to squeeze all the information they could out of him and put him back in place to act as an unpaid informer.

Their mistake was to let Muñoz go upstairs alone. They should have recognised the hopelessness of his situation, the despair it would engender, the fear. Muñoz entered his bedroom and knelt briefly under the blue and white shrine of the Virgin. He closed his eyes and crossed himself repeatedly with a rapid, practised movement of the hand. His lips moved but made no sound. He was sweating.

There was only one shot. They found him in a pool of blood in the bathroom, the Berretta still in his mouth. The back of his head was liquid on the tiled wall, but the expression on his face was peaceful, eyes open, the corners of his mouth drawn back in a fixed rigid grin.

Then they went back to the customs post to question the other men, the small fry. They had all had pickings from Muñoz's take, were prepared to admit as much, but they had no information of value. The one thing they did know was the name of the big Englishman who had crossed the border that day and bought his way out of trouble. They even remembered he lived in San Roque.

Ben Ambrose was disappointed when he heard the news of Muñoz's death. It made the first part of his plan unworkable. But the second part, the part he really believed in, the part he hadn't even discussed with Bowman, was still very much intact.

***

8

Framlington is everybody's idea of a perfect English village, the sort of place that appears on calendars and postcards and the lids of biscuit boxes. The ancient stone built church of the parish of Saint Bedivere is set on a low rise in the middle of the village, surrounded by a broad green swathe dotted with beech trees of great age. The cemetery had been full now for generations and a new one opened up on a site not far from the original, but the Berringer family plot still had space available, even for its most wayward member.

George Ramsay was tending a grave that had not seen much attention for a decade or more and in a room above the pub opposite a man stood behind a camera mounted on a tripod, the tip of its telescopic lens glinting in the dappled light. It was a brilliant English summer's morning, more suited to weddings than funerals, and the mourners stood about in the sunshine unaware that their presence was being carefully recorded.

Ramsay knew some of the faces. He recognised Rupert Rutland, a junior Minister at the Home Office, said to be rising to cabinet rank. They had worked together briefly in the old days, Bowman and Rutland and Ramsay, on some sub-committee of the National Drugs Intelligence Unit. There were people from television and the media, colleagues of Mary when she worked at the BBC. Sean Flaherty stood talking to a group of people from industry and the city some of whom Ramsay recognised from newspaper photographs. There were diplomats, mainly from South American countries, and members of the minor aristocracy who hoped to have their pictures taken, and their names mentioned in the gossip columns. They thought of funerals the same way they thought of weddings, race meetings and polo, except that they wore different clothes. Their pictures of course were being taken and their names noted down. Ramsay would put the lot through the police computer, looking for any hidden community of interest among them, the unseen links that bound them together.

Lord Berringer was there, attended by his personal private secretary, the Mrs. Hetherington Alex had made his business arrangements with. His lordship was clearly distraught. There was no colour in his cheeks and his movements as he entered the church were uncertain and halting. He was supported by a young man Ramsay took to be a manservant of some kind, a valet or a major-domo.

The service was brief and beautiful. Mary Berringer couldn't have had a more touching send off if she had spent her life in a nunnery. Outside the sun was still shining and the congregation was reluctant to leave as the sense of social occasion took over from the show of grief. Ramsay was still weeding the best-kept grave in the churchyard. He looked up at the window above the pub and saw the dull shine on the end of the telescopic lens. It was time for a pint.

In the darkened room upstairs the police photographer was peering down the telescopic lens, trying to identify whoever it was the Minister was talking to. "Take a look at this, George. Anybody you know?"

Ramsay wiped the white moustache from his upper lip and looked through the viewfinder at the distinguished white haired figure. "That's Marcus Esler, Sir Marcus Esler, but he never uses the title. Retired early from the diplomatic corps a couple of years ago to run his family's shipping business when his older brother died. His last posting was Ambassador to one of the Central American countries, I forget which one. He runs a mission in the East End, helping drug addicted kids. The dark haired bloke is Miguel Torres, second secretary at the Colombian Embassy. I don't recognise the woman though. Did you get a good shot of her face?"

"Sorry, George. From this angle I can't get below the rim of her hat." He picked up the pint George had brought him from below and took a long pull. He liked George. George was a good guy, old school. Not much imagination, but he made up for that by hard work and attention to detail.

"Any luck with the serial murders, George? 'Bout time that one was cracked, the press has been appalling. Did you see that article in Tuesday's Echo?"

"Sod the press." George emptied his glass and gave out a satisfying belch. "And sod the Echo. We've had a bit of luck at last, though. We may have found the girl, the one who was seen with the last victim, the night he died. Christ knows we need a breakthrough. Half the kids haven't even been identified."

"All boys?"

"All boys. Buggered. Neck broken. Fingers all chopped off. Done with skill too, but then he's had a lot of practice."

***

One by one the chauffeur driven Rolls and Bentleys departed, not in convoy as they had arrived, but one at a time in random order. Helen was among the first to leave. She was alone, except for her driver, and they rode in silence as befitted the occasion.

No one noticed the switch, not even Ramsay. The driver was the one who brought her, but the Daimler was Berringer's, identical to her own. The streets were free of traffic and they made good time through the village, along the edge of the common, and over the hump backed bridge. The river was full for the time of year and there was flooding at intervals along the bank.

The chauffeur turned into the driveway, past the massive wrought iron gates and the keeper's lodge, through the wooded parkland and along the edge of the artificial lake, up to the portals of the great house, probably the finest of its period in the whole of southern England. It was a listed National Monument, one of the very few still in private hands.

The albino came down the steps to open the passenger door. Then he went to the boot, took out the heavy black case, and followed Helen inside in silence. She crossed the galleried Great Hall and went into the library, which she used as her office, and sat down at the desk to wait. The room was large and bright, panelled in unstained oak. The leaded windows stretched from the floor to the beautifully moulded ceiling. She loved this room, she loved this house, owning it was one of her achievements, a goal she had set herself all those years ago.

Esler was late. He had no conception of time. They had been partners now for a decade or more, since she first returned from the States. They had built the business to its present size, the largest of its kind in Europe. They employed close to a thousand people, most of them on the street, but at the top the organisation was very tight. Three of them took all the big decisions. She heard the crunch of tyres on the gravelled driveway and a moment later Daisy showed Esler into the library.

"God, how I hate funerals!" Helen lit a cigarette, her hands trembling slightly. She was more upset than she wanted him to know.

Esler looked at her in amazement. How could she be so detached, so indifferent? It wasn't as if she and Mary Berringer were strangers, far from it, they were as close as two human beings could be. He looked at his watch. "Is the boss coming?"

"No, he isn't up to it today."

"And our South American friend?"

"He should be here in a little while. He has a foreign driver. Thank God Lieberman stayed away today! Can you imagine, if he'd started chatting to Torres! It doesn't bare thinking about!"

“What did Lieberman say, when you asked him not to come?”

“He was fine about it. He understands we can’t be seen together in public.”

The black Mercedes was coming up the drive. The engine made no sound at all, just the crunch of tyres on the gravel. When it came to rest the chauffeur went to the rear door and the elegantly suited passenger alighted onto the terrace. A moment later there was a knock and Daisy opened the door, followed him into the room, and went to stand behind the woman’s chair and slightly to the right, as he always did when there were outsiders present. The man stood by the high backed chair. He had a swarthy dark complexion, olive skin, tightly curled black hair, a more or less permanent smile, and perfect manners. When she made the appropriate gesture he sat down.

"My condolences." The smile faded but didn't disappear.

Helen didn't answer but lit another cigarette instead. She inhaled deeply, closing her eyes to concentrate on the burning sensation deep inside her lungs. Then she made a sign to the albino who placed the heavy black case embossed with the letter B on top of the desk and opened it. It surprised him still that half a million pounds in used fifties could be contained is a space that small.

“What news of the next delivery?" Helen exhaled.

"I'm expecting twenty kilos in a week or so. Part of that’s for you. Some’s for our distributor in the north. There shouldn't be any problem." His English was Boston

Brahmin, the mark of an expensive education in his country. The smile returned to full flame to mitigate the bad news he had to tell them. "This will be the last shipment at the current price. I had word from Medellin by courier. The European market is expanding too fast, outstripping supply. Medellin wants to dampen down demand, keep the price high. We're looking at a twenty percent hike, as of your next consignment. But you won't be getting that for quite a while. Not for a couple of months. We're cutting back on shipments to Europe, so we can maintain our markets in the States. The DEA has wiped out entire crops in the Andes. Sprayed millions of acres with Agent Orange. We're going through a time of crisis. You'll have to share some of the pain."

The woman glanced across at Esler, but he didn't speak. "We'd like to keep the price low Miguel, go for the volume market. We're expanding our organisation, recruiting new people all the time. We have an army of pushers, disciplined people, well trained, young. We need volume to keep the organisation intact."

"Medellin won't buy that, I'm afraid. From our perspective what would be the point? We can't produce enough to satisfy demand as it is. And now we have this problem with the DEA. So why lower the price? It makes no sense. You people should take a course in basic economics. This is a producer's market." The smile was bright now, to show he didn't mean to be insulting. The Brits were in a bind. They had no place else to go.

Helen glanced again at Esler, but still he didn't speak. "We're determined to go for the mass market Miguel, whether Medellin likes it or not. It's part of our overall strategy. We've put a big organisation in place, given them proper training. We have to have volume to sustain it, otherwise it will implode." The cigarette was down to a stub now. She could feel it burning her fingers.

"Medellin won't allow you to set your own strategy, Helen. You're just distributors after all."

"Allow? What do you mean, allow? We're free to do business any way we choose. Besides, we plan to become producers ourselves. We can't rely on a single source any more, the Atlantic is too risky." She was running way ahead of herself, they had no such plan, not yet. She looked again at Esler. He spoke at last.

"'Helen's right, Miguel. You need us as much as we need you. Without our distribution Medellin has no presence in the UK market. No presence at all."

"You're our biggest customer, for sure, by far. But not the only one. If we let you set your own price, what happens with the rest of the market? We can't have people like you deciding important issues, fixing the price." The smile was not quite gone, a smouldering ember. "You think you're big and powerful and in your own country. It's true, you are. But in the world you are nothing. *Nada*." He made a gesture with the forefinger and thumb of his right hand, to show how small they really were. Small and crazy. The idea they could become producers was laughable. "Look Helen, you want the product, or you don't want the product. The price is the price. It's that simple. If you don't like it we'll cut you off completely. Help one of the other players develop a position. There's lots of eager people out there, just waiting for the chance. But that way you go out of business completely." Torres stood up and snapped the locks on the half million pound case. "You're in no position to bargain."

"You're right, Miguel." said Helen. "We're in no position to bargain." She wanted to add "not yet" but she didn't.

***

Marcus Esler stood at the window and watched the Mercedes move off down the drive. When it had disappeared he turned to Helen and said, "What did you make of that."

"Pretty conclusive, I'd say. Torres just made the best possible case for going ahead with Lieberman. Harvey couldn't have done it any better himself."

"Get Lieberman to send us a trial shipment. Make sure everything goes OK. If he can make a delivery without hitches we'll start using him on a regular basis. Then in a couple of months we can talk to him about a partnership."

"Sounds good to me." said Helen. "I'll clear it with the boss tonight. If he agrees I'll call Harvey on the secure line tomorrow morning and arrange for a trial run."

***

As Torres chauffeur driven car made its way back to the main road his smile disappeared completely. He didn't understand their reaction to his news at all. The price was going up and volume reduced to a fraction of what they were used to. Yet they accepted the new situation apparently without concern. It was as if they had another supplier in place to take up the slack. It couldn't be one of the other cartels. That was impossible. There were formal agreements about who got which piece of the European market. But what other explanation was there? He would have to monitor the street price carefully. If it didn't begin to rise quite soon then something was very, very wrong. "Let's hope I'm mistaken." He thought to himself. "*Detesto la violencia!*"

***

At eleven thirty that night Mandy stood with a group of friends outside the brightly lit record shop at the corner of Regent Street and Piccadilly. There were four of them, two boys and two girls, in their early or middle teens, dressed in cheap leather jackets. The girls' skirts barely covered their pelvis. Business was slow. Between them they had only turned a couple of tricks all evening.

It was one of the boys who spotted the car. The vehicle itself was nondescript but he could tell it was cruising by the way it rounded the corner and slowed again after it went through the light. He made eye contact with the driver as he pulled over to the curb a little further up the street. The boy walked the few yard to the car and leaned down to look the driver in the eye. The trick was to let the punter do the talking.

"Hey, Mand. Bloke here wants you." The boy called to the group of friends.

Mandy tottered up the street, unsteady from her last joint and not yet used to the high-heeled shoes.

"You want business?" she said, leaning on the roof of the car.

"In the back." said the driver. The man in the rear passenger seat was about fifty. His hair was thinning and his gut drooped over the top of his trousers. Mandy could smell the beer as she stuck her head inside the car to get a better look at him, trying to assess the risk.

"You want business?" she repeated. She needed a fix pretty quickly now and there was a slight edginess to her voice. "You want head? Both of you? That'll be fifty quid."

"Get in."

As Mandy settled into the back seat the car sped north towards Oxford Circus, turned left into Burlington Street and came to a halt at the corner of Savile Row, opposite West End Central police station.

"'Ere, where you takin' me?" Mandy whined. "I ain't done nothing."

"We won't keep you long." said Ramsay. He walked round to the pavement to help her get out of the car, took her by the arm and escorted her inside.

The desk sergeant nodded to Ramsay as they walked through to the rear office, but he didn't so much as glance at the girl. Ramsay sat at the desk, opened a drawer, and took out a buff folder. He motioned to Mandy to sit down, opened the folder and spread the photographs on top of the desk. He had chosen only a few, not the most horrific, but the ones that gave the clearest view of the boy's features. The face was bruised around the mouth, but only slightly. He might have been sleeping.

"Friend of yours?" said Ramsay.

"Never seen 'im." Mandy looked hard at the photographs. She knew from the telly his neck had been broken, but she couldn't tell, except maybe there was something odd about the angle of the head.

"What was his name?"

"I said I never seen 'im."

"We need to know his movements. And why he went to Clapham Common. You were seen together on the night of the murder, at the tube station in Piccadilly. Before that you were seen together a lot of the time, going back six weeks or so."

"Not me. Honest. It must've been somebody else." She could lie quite easily, she didn't even blush, but she had to keep the image of Daisy out of her mind. She was scared of Daisy. Everybody was.

"He's done it before. Seven times. He'll do it again." There was no sign of shock in the young face. "The boy was buggered. Raped. It could be you next time."

"He only does boys. That's what they said on the telly."

Ramsay had two options. He could keep her over night and question her again in the morning when she'd be desperate for a fix. But anything she said then would be disallowed as evidence so there wasn't any point. Or he could let her go and have one of the plain-clothes women officers keep an eye on her. He decided to let her go.

"What about my fifty quid?" Mandy stood glancing down at the seedy looking copper. Poor old sod looked like he could do with a little bit of fun.

Ramsay took her by the arm and eased her toward the door.

"If you decide to remember anything useful stop by and have a word with the desk sergeant over there. Tell him to pass a message to George Ramsay."

"Any use?" said the sergeant as he watched the girl totter down the steps to the street outside.

"None." said Ramsay. "Either she's the wrong one, or she's the coolest damned kid I ever came across!"

***

Mandy didn't go back to Piccadilly. She was too scared. She knew the police would keep an eye on her, but it wasn't them she was afraid of, it was Daisy. If he ever found out what had happened he would kill her for sure. So she walked north up Regent Street to Oxford Circus and took the tube to Kings Cross. Kings Cross was rough trade but it was better than having your neck squeezed on some deserted rubbish dump. She couldn't charge the same rates she got at Piccadilly but there were always lots of punters and she could make out very nicely till Ramsay finally did his job and put Daisy away for life.

As she sat on the tube her mind was totally clear, a feeling she hadn't had for weeks. She felt scared and really alone. She'd been in London for nearly a year now and the one friend she'd made was dead. Now Daisy would be looking for her. As the train sped through the darkness she could see her reflection in the glass opposite. What she saw there terrified her even more. She saw the waste, the degradation, the total absence of hope. She wanted to live and she wanted, desperately, to be clean.

That was the night she first set eyes on Gabriel. He was standing under a streetlight at the corner of one of the alleys that penetrated the goods yards at the rear of the station where the kids took the punters. She didn't speak to him that night, nor for the first several times she saw him. He was so beautiful she just stood in the shadows and stared at him. He was quite tall and very slim with blond hair and pale blue eyes. There was a stillness about him that made him seem quite special. She imagined his voice would be very soft.

Over a period of several days she watched him in awe. He seemed to know a lot of the kids by name. Often he would talk to them at length, take them off and buy them coffee in one of the late night fast food joints. He wasn't using drugs and he wasn't using any of the kids. He wasn't a punter and he wasn't a holy roller. For a long time Mandy couldn't work him out at all.

9

Everything went just as the woman said it would. Verity turned up at *La Hacienda Blanca* one morning and introduced herself to Harvey. She mentioned the name of whoever it was the woman and he knew in common and he invited her in for coffee. Verity looked ravishing in a simple white dress that set off her light tan to perfection. She had that wonderful air of innocence Harvey Lieberman liked so much. She looked bridal, even virginal. Verity knew that nothing was so corrupting as innocence, nothing as exciting as the pure, the unsoiled, and she modelled her appearance accordingly. Harvey took her out to dinner that evening and tried to seduce her. Verity was shocked, appalled, she said he could never see her again. Harvey begged forgiveness and Verity forgave. It was something she had learned from the nuns. Harvey took her to dinner again the next night and the next and slowly, gradually, Verity began to weaken. She allowed him to kiss her and then to touch, revealing little by little the great treasures she possessed. Within a week Verity had lost her virginity yet again. Harvey was very proud of himself, he thought he had seduced her.

Verity told him how expensive her hotel was, and Harvey suggested she move into the villa. She resisted, and told him how expensive everything else was. Dresses were expensive, jewellery was expensive, eating was expensive, even the hairdresser was expensive. How could a girl possibly survive out here on the Coast? There was nothing for it, she would have to return to England and marry that boring accountant. Eventually Harvey understood and started to give her money to buy things with. He never saw any of the things she bought, but every time they slept together she would think of something else she needed. Harvey kept thinking of the way the hotel bill was mounting up and eventually he got mad and told her point blank to pack her bag. By this time he was absolutely crazy about her.

Life at the villa was perfect for someone of Verity's temperament. She lay in the sun a lot of the time and Harvey was always there to rub her back and shoulders with lotion, and there were servants to bring her drinks and prepare her meals. Even screwing Harvey was pleasant enough, once she had taught him how. He would never be a great lover, he was too coarse, too hurried, too selfish, but great lovers were hard to find, especially for a working girl, so she taught him where and how to touch, how to caress and kiss and excite her, to hold back, to take his time, to wait for her. She found it best if she rode him. That way she had control of the rhythm, the timing. Otherwise he would always come too soon like a young boy, before she was ready, leaving her unfulfilled, suspended. It didn't always work. Often Harvey would simply lose control and she would have to fake it, rolling her eyes and making those little moaning sounds that always seemed to fool him. He wanted badly to be fooled. "Oh! Harvey!" she would sigh, feeling him soften, knowing it was over. "That was wonderful Harvey! Wonderful!" But Harvey was willing to learn, he wanted desperately to please her, and given time and patience and careful tuition his performance was improving very nicely. Sometimes her orgasm was quite genuine.

***

Bowman slept lightly. It was a habit he had acquired in jail. He heard the crunch of tyres at the top of the driveway and then the quiet sound of the doors closing, but no voices.

His first thought was to get dressed, he had discarded his sweatshirt and jeans on the floor next to the bed. He didn't need to put on the light, he knew the layout of every stick of furniture in the house. He found his way in the darkness to the electrical switch box and cut off the mains supply. It was several moments before he heard the next sound, the crack of a twig at the foot of the terrace steps. Next he heard voices on the far side of the house by the kitchen entrance. Both exits covered. The odds were too long for a shoot out but he stuck the Browning in his belt anyway, partly out of habit, partly for the comfort it gave him. The short-barrelled GP35FA was his favourite weapon for use in confined spaces.

None of the doors were locked, they never were, there was nothing in the house worth stealing. Bowman took up a position in a corner of the living room, back to the wall, facing towards the door. When it opened a shaft of moonlight flooded the room, silhouetting the first intruder, catching the barrel of the sawn-off shotgun. A weapon for maiming, not killing. Bowman heard the click of the light switch and the muttered "Shit." This one at least was English.

The intruder moved forward into the room, followed by a second man, and bumped into a table. That made four, two here and two at the back of the house. If these two moved away from the doorway he could make a run for it. But that way he wouldn't find out who they were, who had sent them and why.

"Put that gun down or I'll blast your head off." Bowman spoke rapidly and in a whisper.

The first intruder spun, unseeing, towards the corner where Alex stood. Bowman fired a single shot just above his head, close enough for him to think he was hit. The shotgun fell to the ground with a clatter followed by a scurrying of feet at the back of the house.

"Get over here! Fast!" Bowman hissed. "Move! I won't aim high a second time."

The man was shorter than Bowman but powerfully built. Bowman grabbed his collar and pressed the nozzle of the Browning against his temple, searing his skin with its heat. Now there were three figures crowded in the doorway, peering into the dark room. Alex pushed the man into the shaft of light, the Browning clearly visible. "Now. Before I blow your pal's head off, why don't you tell me what this is all about."

"We have to take you in." This one was Spanish, his English heavily accented. A big man, almost as big as Bowman. A livid scar ran from the right side of his mouth almost to his ear. "The boss he want to talk to you. I think he want to make you a proposition."

"Who's the boss?"

"You'll see. He want to geeve you a surprise."

"OK. Put your hands on the wall all of you, take a pace backwards and spread your legs, you know the routine. Any false move and this one gets it." He frisked each one of them in turn, surprised to find they were clean. So it was true, they hadn't come to kill him. He picked up the shotgun, emptied it onto the floor and handed it back, leaving the Browning on the table.

"OK, lets go. Whoever he is, I'd hate to keep him waiting."

They walked to the end of the driveway where the van was parked, pulled back off the road. There were no windows in the rear compartment. Two of the men got in the front and Alex bundled himself into the back with the other two, sitting on the floor. It was a cramped, uncomfortable ride. Alex couldn't see the road but he knew they were heading east, towards Marbella. After a time they left the coast and began to climb. Eventually they came to a halt and the driver gave three blasts on the horn, one long and two short. Alex heard the sound of a heavy metal gate being drawn back and closed again behind them as the van moved forward once more. After another fifty yards or so they came to a final halt.

One of the men threw a *bandana* across at Alex. It was José, the one with the thick Spanish accent who seemed to be in charge. "Put that on. It'll save me an explanation."

Alex put the *bandana* over his eyes and tied it tight, knowing what was coming next.

"Now I have to tie your hands."

Alex sat on the tailboard of the van and put his hands behind his back. He could feel the leather thong biting into his wrists as José tied it tight. The blow came from behind. Bowman heard it before he felt it, but too late to duck. He blanked out.

***

They bundled him up the steps, counting them off for him as they went, and steered him inside the building. His legs were butter. One of the men took his arm and supported him through a couple of rooms till they came to a halt in the glare of a bright light, piercing the *bandana*. Alex felt a chair being pushed against the back of his legs.

The voice was not new but he couldn't place it. "Sit down, Alex." and then in a gruffer tone, "Take that stupid thing off him will ya for Christsake. Whadaya think this is José, a goddamn movie set?" Alex sat down and the *bandana* was taken off and his hands untied. He was still groggy from the blow and the light was blinding. His head was only now beginning to clear. Then it came back to him. *"Hey Tiffany, get your ass over here, Harvey wants a blow job."* It was the man by the pool, who had guided Tiffany down the steps. He was in *La Hacienda Blanca*.

The man got up from behind the light and offered Alex his hand. "Harvey Lieberman's the name, moviemaker *extraordinaire*. I couldn't resist putting on this little show.

I hope the boys didn't rough you up too much, I told them not to."

Lieberman was older than Bowman, close to fifty, with thick black hair that was probably dyed and a tan he obviously worked on. Harvey took a lot of trouble with his appearance but he carried more weight than he should have, and his stomach bulged over the buckle of his belt. A large gold medallion hung on his matted chest, his silk shirt open almost to the waist. He leaned over Alex and slapped him once or twice about the face. “Wakey wakey, Alex. Time to talk to uncle Harvey. What’ll ya have to drink?”

"Brandy. I’ll have a brandy."

Lieberman went to a cabinet and poured two large glasses of *Lepanto* while Alex took in the rest of the room. It was large and expensively furnished in very bad taste, the furniture heavy and dark. The pictures on the walls were new copies of old masters, thick with varnish to make them look antique.

"Come over here will ya, Alex." Lieberman held the glass out in his hand. "There's something I want to talk to you about?" Alex took the glass and sat opposite Lieberman to listen to his pitch.

"So, you’re an investigator? I’ve been doing a little investigating of my own. I heard about your problem at the Ceuta border Alex, news like that travels fast. So Muñoz topped himself? Just as well, I’d’ve topped the poor bastard myself. That guy knew stuff! Anyway Alex, I've been making a few enquiries about you. I didn't even know you were down here on the Coast till I heard about the incident at Ceuta. They tell me you have a nice little business, make just enough money to get by. Life must be tough for you my friend. You've just about hit rock bottom. Let's face it Bowman, nobody likes a dishonest cop. Nobody much likes an honest one, come to that." He raised his glass and took a little sip.

Alex was about to speak but Lieberman put up his hand to stop him.

"OK Alex. So you're innocent! Everybody's always innocent! Meanwhile the judge and jury think otherwise so what's the goddamn difference. You served your time. Now you have to start over, make some bucks for yourself. Face facts Alex! Life's a bitch and then you die!" He took another sip of his drink. "Like I say, I made a few enquiries. You're a small time hood. Bowman. You make a living, sure. But small time. You haven't really got yourself established. You're wasting your talents, Alex. Think of your knowledge, your special inside knowledge, knowledge no one else has. Knowledge like that could be worth a goddamn fortune!"

Alex swirled the *Lepanto* round in the glass and inhaled. It was good, the best in Spain. He was trying hard to look as if he didn't understand a word Lieberman was saying.

"Alex, you poor dumb bastard, you've no idea what I'm talkin' about have you? Look at you! Strong as an ox and half as smart!" Lieberman was not impressed with Alex, not impressed at all. "What were you doing the last time you held down a regular job? Narcotics! And what is the biggest cash crop the world has ever known? Narcotics!

For Christ sake Alex, you and me together we could make a goddamn fortune! Don't gimme none o'that innocent shit! I know what happened!" Lieberman went to the drinks cabinet and returned with the bottle of *Lepanto*, refilling both their glasses.

"Let me start at the beginning Alex, feed it to you a bit at a time. I made some money in the movie business. It was easy. Low capital outlay, low production costs, big margins, a schmuck like you could do it. I moved out here with my girlfriend and number one star, Tiffany Wells. I built myself a studio. 50,000 square feet of air-conditioned space. We made a bunch of very successful flicks with Tiffany in the lead role. She was brilliant Alex, did anything the directors wanted, anything at all. She enjoyed it for Christsake! I still have that business. A group of pushy young executives run it for me now. It's the perfect laundry operation. But it wasn't enough Alex, it never was enough! Five years ago I decided to muscle in on the local drugs trade. It was easy, the Spanish boys weren't organised at all back then. I had a little competition from the Brits at first, but the Brits are squeamish as you know, they don't like to kill people, which is essential in this business. I'm talkin' soft drugs now, strictly cocktail party stuff. I built myself a good business in marijuana, a business to be proud of. I got to be a major player, number one on the Coast, but I'm a big player in the minor leagues Alex, a middleman, a distributor. I want to get into the real big time! I want to be a producer!" Lieberman got up and walked around the room in silence, giving Alex time to absorb what he was saying. "I think I got the idea from Tiffany to be honest. I bought a citrus farm up in the High Atlas, south east of Marrakech. Three hundred acre spread. It cost me peanuts. I started growing *Erythroxylon Coca.* Howd'ya like that? I had to look it up, I can barely say it even now."

"You're what?" Alex was stunned. He downed his brandy at a single throw. He could hardly believe what he was hearing. Growing snow in Morocco? On Europe's doorstep? This was new! This was bigtime! "Jesus Christ, Harvey! That's brilliant!"

"I produce cocaine up there. It hasn't been done before, not on an industrial scale. Isn't that amazing? My problem is I'm under funded. I need development capital for irrigation and soil improvement, for transportation. But most of all I need security, protection. Cocaine is a very high-risk business, Alex. If the Colombians get wind of what I'm up to they'll destroy the farm and wipe me out. The place should be wired. I need guards, guns, ammunition, all of which costs money. In a couple of years I'll need an airstrip. An airstrip? Shit! I'll need a fuckin' airline!" Lieberman paused, his voice had risen and he wanted to build to the crescendo that was still to come. "When it gets that big I'll have to start paying people off. Politicians cost money, cops cost money, customs officials cost money. I'm talkin' about the top people now Alex, the ones who really matter, senior policemen, government ministers, the real decision makers, not just the little guys like your friend Muñoz. But everything costs money Alex, lots and lots of money. I make plenty but I spend plenty too, always have. My problem is I'm under resourced. I need a financial partner!"

"Don't look at me, Harvey. I'm the one who's short of cash." Alex tried to look dumb but he didn't need to. Lieberman knew all policemen were dumb anyway.

"Don't look at me, he says!" Lieberman laughed. "Don't look at me! Alex you're beautiful! Not smart, but beautiful. No Alex, for you I have another job in mind, one you're very well suited for. I want you to be my Chief Security Officer. You're a natural! Trained by the finest police force in the world, relevant experience, inside knowledge, strong as an ox. I couldn't find anybody better if I went to central casting." He leaned forward and touched Alex on the hand, to let him know he was sincere. "Alex, I want you to take charge of security up at the farm. I want you to design the systems, buy the best equipment, recruit the right people, train them. I'll pay you fifty grand a year, US Dollars, cash, no deductions. And that's just for openers Alex, later on when the business gets bigger you'll get more responsibility, so I'll pay you more, maybe even double. That's capitalism for ya Alex! The free market system!" His eyes were bright with the excitement of it all.

Alex looked doubtful, but he knew he couldn't resist. This was massive! "You said you needed a financial partner, Harvey. What if you don't find one? What if you can't raise the money?"

"Alex, I already found a partner! The ideal partner!" It was hard to contain his excitement now. This was the big piece, the bit that completed the jigsaw, that made it whole. He was only just getting used to the idea himself.

"Tiffany put me in touch with these people. That kid had contacts everywhere, family connections. I tell ya she knew everybody, absolutely everybody, lawyers, judges, politicians, you name it. Alex, I haven't told this to anybody else. I've been growing the stuff for three years now, but I've only been marketing a fraction of my production, just enough to cover my expenses. Most of it I've held back, so I can develop the market the way I want. I have a massive stash hidden away somewhere in Morocco. I could flood the UK market tomorrow if I wanted to. But I don't want to. What would be the point? The street price would collapse for sure if I brought my stuff to market in one hit. This organisation Tiffany put me in touch with, they have the retail end of the market all sewn up, have done for years. They're mega-rich Alex, MEGA-RICH!" He closed his eyes, savouring the thought. "I had a meeting with one of their top people just a week or so ago. Tiffany set it up. I gave them a sample of my stuff. They were on the phone to me a couple of days ago. They're impressed with the quality. Holy shit! Of course they'd be impressed! They want me to send them a trial shipment. Make sure everything goes OK. That I can make deliveries safely into the UK. If it does, and it will, they'll give me a six month contract. Time to prove that I'm a reliable business partner. That my deliveries come in on schedule. Over the six months they'll get to know me, we'll establish a basis of trust and gradually I'll let them know there's a funding problem. But for them it's not a problem, Alex! It's a goddamn opportunity! They can become investors! Stockholders! Partners!" He lay back in his seat, overcome by the symmetry of it all, the way all the parts meshed so neatly together. "Point is, Alex." Lieberman continued in a subdued tone "They need me as much as I need them. I don't think they realise that yet. But if my information's right, South American supplies will dry up as the Bolivian jungle burns. The DEA is winning the war in the Andes. Think about it Alex. Me and the DEA are on the same side! The DEA is working for me!"

"I hope you can trust these people, Harvey." Alex spoke in a whisper. "Who are they?"

"That's my only problem Alex. I don't fuckin' know who they are!" Harvey was subdued now. This was the only blemish on the thing of beauty he had constructed. "Only Tiffany knew, and now the bitch is dead. I don't even know how to reach them. I have to wait for them to contact me." He locked his hands in prayer and raised his eyes to heaven. "You bitch Tiffany! Why did you have to freak out, just when I needed you most?"

For an instant Harvey thought of telling Alex about the woman in black, but he held back. He just couldn't bring himself to admit that the biggest deal Harvey Lieberman had ever even dreamed of was dependent on the decision a mere woman. Besides, Alex had no need to know, and it was one of Harvey's guiding principles to keep things on a need-to-know basis.

Alex couldn't tell if the tears in Harvey's eyes were of grief or anger or just plain excitement. Whichever it was, it was a very powerful emotion. Alex reached for the bottle of *Lepanto*. He felt like getting drunk. It was as good a way as any to cement a new relationship. It was a strange bond they shared, the death of Tiffany Wells and Mary Berringer threatened the thing each of them wanted most.

***

Alex woke first. He went outside, stripped, and plunged into the pool. He hadn't taken any exercise for days and it felt good. He moved powerfully through the water with an easy over arm motion, raising his head just clear of the surface to breathe with every fourth stroke. He felt the rhythm coming back and began to concentrate on his timing, so that when the woman appeared on the terrace he didn't notice her. She was wearing a white towelling robe that reached to her ankles and her long blond hair was knotted in a simple ponytail.

Verity sat motionless in shadow on a low wall, a few feet from the edge of the pool, and watched him. He made her think of the dolphins she used to see following the boats off her Greek island. He moved through the water like one of them, as if it were his natural habitat. There was an effortless power in his movements, a gracefulness she found quite sexual.

When Alex got out of the pool he couldn't find a towel so he wiped as much water off his body as he could with his hands and stood leaning against a buttress in the white wall, eyes closed, facing into the sun so it would dry him. The sun was at a low angle and cast his shadow onto the wall behind him, giving his body an added depth as if carved out of the stone itself. The air was motionless but there were still ripples on the surface of the turquoise pool. The light glinting off the water, the white wall set against the hard blue sky, the nude male figure, had all the effect of a Hockney painting.

Verity thought he was beautiful. She took in his broad shoulders and chest, his sculpted pectorals, his hard abdomen, his manhood. She had never thought of a man as beautiful before, not in the abstract sense he was. She wanted him. She wanted to touch him and make him grow, just as he was now, like a statue, without saying a word. Verity Fuller had never wanted a man and failed to have him. Whoever he was, he wasn't going to be the first.

When Harvey came out of the house, stretching and yawning, it was Alex he saw first. "Hey Alex! How ya doin'?" He yelled from the terrace. "Put that thing away will ya, you'll make the dogs hungry." Harvey went to a cupboard built into the wall behind the awning, took out a towel, and threw it at Alex. That was when he caught sight of Verity.

"Verity baby, there you are, I wondered where you'd got to. Admiring the scenery I see." He didn't sound pleased. "What d'ya think? Ever see one like it? I guess you did, like in some circus. I suppose it's too late for formal introductions?"

"Excuse me." Alex blushed as he covered himself with the towel. "I didn't realise anyone was here."

Verity stood up, eyes down cast, modestly clasping her robe to her throat. Alex looked at her and saw that she was lovely.

"No photographs!" Harvey turned to Verity, not smiling. "Not till he puts *Godzilla* back in his pants." He went across to her and patted her behind in a proprietary way, so Alex would understand who she belonged to. "Run along now babe, put on your very best dress, today we're going to hit the town, paint the place all sorts of colours. Just give me an hour or so to discuss some business with Mr. Bowman here."

Alex stood next to Harvey as they both watched her disappear into the house. When she reached the edge of the terrace she turned and smiled at one of them, her coy, shy, virginal smile. The one she had learned from the nuns.

***

Two gorillas had followed Lieberman out of the house, José and another Bowman hadn't seen before, their holstered Smith & Wesson 686s hitched just a little too high. Drawing the weapon quickly would not be easy. The angle was too tight.

"You ready for coffee?" said Lieberman.

"Coffee would be great, Harvey."

Lieberman grunted at José who frowned and disappeared inside, returning moments later with a pot of coffee and two cups on a silver tray, which he placed on a table underneath the awning. José was not a happy man. Alex had made a fool of him last night and one day the Englishman would have to pay for that.

"Get my friend a robe." said Lieberman, and the robe was brought. Then the two gorillas moved reluctantly away, out of earshot, to the far side of the pool.

"OK Alex, you've slept on it, how d'ya like my proposition?"

Alex stirred his coffee pensively. "What if I say no?" He knew the answer, but it was worth a try.

Lieberman jumped up and yelled at the top of his voice. "José! Kill this man!"

José drew the weapon awkwardly from his shoulder holster, raised it in both hands ready to fire, but Lieberman was too quick. He took one step and interposed himself in front of the target. José lowered the weapon, the right side of his face ticking like a time bomb.

"For Christsake, José! I keep tellin' ya! Be ready all the time! You're so fuckin' slow!" Harvey resumed his seat. "You're a lucky man, Alex. If I hadn't picked José you'd be dead by now, the other guy is really fast!" He took a drink of his coffee. "Now lets get serious Alex, I talked a lot last night, you know too much already. You have two choices. Join me, or you're a dead man. Just take a look at José, Alex. He's a mean sonofabitch. He wants you so bad he can taste it."

Alex looked across at the two gorillas. Harvey was right. José didn't seem to care for him at all. "Of course I'll join you, Harvey. It's the best offer I've had in years. Besides, after Ceuta there's really nowhere else for me to go."

Harvey grinned. "You made the right decision, Alex. I promise you won't regret it, not ever. Finish your coffee now and I'll have one of the boys drive you back to San Roque to pick up your things. From now on you live at the *Hacienda Blanca*, everything first class."

"That would be a mistake Harvey, from the security point of view I mean. If I move in here everybody will know I'm on the payroll. It's best if I stay in the background, keep everything on a need-to-know basis."

Harvey's eyes narrowed. "You're a strange guy, Alex. Most of the time you seem like a pretty dumb clutz but every now and then you think of something really smart."

Alex poured them both more coffee. “So what happened to Tiffany? An accident on the N340?”

“If you can call it an accident.” said Harvey. “Tiffany was bombed out of her goddamn mind. That bitch was never sober. One hell of a good lay though, never got enough of it."

"How did it happen?"

"How did what happen? The car accident? How the fuck should I know? The bitch wasn't allowed out on her own, it was too much goddamn trouble. Tiffany just could not walk past a bar, everybody knew that. Tiffany stays home, those were my instructions. The bitch stole the goddamn car keys and took off. You know what that road is like Alex, it's a fuckin' death trap!"

“Was Tiffany on drugs?”

"Was Tiffany on drugs! Did she breathe? That kid was on everything!"

"When did she start?"

"About the time I met her I guess. She didn't get the habit from me though, I never touch the filthy stuff."

"Where did she get it from, at the very beginning I mean?"

"How the fuck should I know? The health farm maybe, a place called Lakeside she used to go to, somewhere down in Surrey. They put her on some kinda chemical shit to get her off the booze. Substitution therapy they called it. She ended up getting a bigger high from the chemicals than she did from the bottle. Anyway Bowman, what is all this? I brought you here to discuss a business proposition, not to talk about my girlfriend."

"You're right, Harvey. I was just curious." Alex lay back in his chair, his brow furrowed. "Harvey, there's one thing that bothers me a lot. This Organisation, the people in the UK she introduced you to, it seems to me they have you by the short and curlies. They know who you are, where you are, how to reach you. But you know nothing about them. Knowledge is power, Harvey. You should know at least as much about them as they do about you. From a security point of view, that's essential. I think you should let me do some snooping around back in the UK. Find out who they are." He drank his coffee. "Tell me about this executive you met in London. The one you're negotiating with. Describe him to me."

Lieberman's eyes narrowed to a slit, suddenly full of menace. His face was flushed and the veins at his temples started to throb. He glanced across at José standing ready, waiting and hoping, on the other side of the pool. "Let me explain something to you, Bowman. I call it my Philosophy of Management. I keep everything in watertight compartments. Everything. Only Harvey Lieberman knows the whole picture. You have just one area of responsibility. Security at the farm. Nothing else. Zilch. Stay out of production. Stay out of distribution. Stay out of marketing. And stay out of finance! If I ever get word you're poking you're goddamn nose around anywhere you're not supposed to, I'll have these guys use you for target practice." He gestured to the two gorillas. "Got that? From now on you go where I say, do what I tell you to do. Now get your ass out of here Bowman, take one of the cars and go back to San Roque and stay there. I'll send for you when I'm good and ready. Just make sure you're waiting when I do."

Alex strolled down to the garage and picked out a little Seat like his own. If he had turned to look back at the house he would have seen Verity leaning out from the terrace to watch him go.

***

As he turned into his driveway Alex saw the car parked at the foot of the terrace steps, a sleek red Ferrari Daytona, not new but in immaculate condition, a collectors item. At auction it would fetch a fortune but on the road it would cost a fortune too, a fortune to insure and a fortune to service and maintain. Bowman understood and loved machinery but whoever was running around in a thing like this just had to be crazy, or very very rich.

Then a figure emerged from the doorway with what looked like a cup of coffee in his hand. It was Benjamin Ambrose dressed to kill, grinning from ear to ear. He had set the trap and baited it and goddamnit the thing had worked like a dream!

Alex thought of feigning anger but he saw the funny side just as well as Ambrose did. "OK Ben, I owe you one. I walked right into it, didn't even see it coming!" He thumped Ambrose on the shoulder, not hard enough to hurt, but hard enough to let him know it was there if he needed it.

"Well, at least they didn't keep us waiting." Ambrose dusted one of the terrace steps carefully and sat down. He was wearing a suede jacket in spite of the heat, white jeans, and snakeskin cowboy boots that were probably hand made. "So who is he Alex? Who's running things 'round here?"

"His name's Lieberman, Harvey Lieberman, American. Bronx accent. You'd like him Ben, he's just your type. And guess what? He's growing coke in the High Atlas! Has a massive stash of the stuff somewhere in Morocco."

"He's what?" Ambrose's jaw stayed open.

"He's growing coke in Morocco. It hasn't been done before, not on an industrial scale." Alex what trying to be cool. "He has a theory South American supplies are drying up. Sounds far-fetched to me."

"Holy shit, Alex. This is amazing. It's brilliant." Ambrose was on his feet now, a boxer waiting for the opening bell. "And he's right about the crisis in the Andes. We've defoliated half Bolivia. Sounds to me like our man's identified a major business opportunity. Maybe I should talk to Willowby."

"Who's Willowby?

"Willowby? Great guy! DEA's top man in Europe. Works out of the London Embassy. Jesus Christ Alex! This may be too hot for me to handle on my own. But I'd really like to keep it under wraps for now. Holy shit! Growing snow in the High Atlas! Well, I'll be damned!" Willowby could go screw himself. *This one's for the glory. Strictly for the glory!*

Alex told the American the whole story. Ambrose was clearly impressed. He thought Lieberman's idea was brilliant, absolutely brilliant, the most original thing he had come across in the whole of his career. If it succeeded it could change the whole global balance of the industry. He wondered if Alex appreciated all the angles. Probably not. Brits will always be Brits. "That's fantastic, Alex! Absolutely fantastic! Do you think it can be made to work?"

"Sure, of course it can, if he gets financial backing. There's no magic to growing the stuff if the climate and the soil conditions are right. There's lots of water up there in the mountains and labour is plentiful and cheap. The people he's in contact with already have control of UK distribution. They're a powerful organisation, ruthless too. They obviously killed Tiffany to eliminate the link between them and Lieberman, but I don't think he realises that. He's convinced it really was an accident. Sure, it could succeed. Except we're here to stop him."

Ambrose was silent, turning things over in his mind, wondering how far Bowman could be trusted, what turned him on, how to control him. Money didn't seem to be the key and it wasn't power. Maybe it was pride. "It grieves me to say this Alex, but I think we should give him a hand."

"Give him a hand!" Alex was outraged. "That bastard is ruining people's lives! Young people! Innocent people!"

"People who should know better. Sure, we could pass Lieberman on to the Spanish authorities and put him out of business. At the local level he's a real big fish. But then we destroy the link to his contacts back in the Kingdom, just like they did with Tiffany. The bastards get clean away. We have a great opportunity here Alex. We may never get another one like it. You're already on the inside. You'll have to go where Lieberman sends you, Morocco or any place else, but that's OK. I can get the Spanish boys to set up surveillance here on the Coast and you can have Ramsay work the London end. It's beautiful, Alex. Perfect. There'll never be another opportunity like this if we wait a hundred years. Come on old Buddy, let's keep a little of the action for ourselves!"

“We'd be taking a huge risk.”

“Sure we would, Alex. But isn't it worth it? If we get to the really big guys?” Ambrose took hold of Bowman's shoulders and looked him in the eye. “At least allow the first shipment through? Let Lieberman get himself established? Gain some credibility? Come on, Alex! We can monitor the whole process! Set up surveillance here on the coast and put a tail on the courier! Your guy Ramsay can cover the London end.”

“Just the first shipment? We’re talking hundreds of thousands of pounds. Maybe more!” Alex frowned. “OK Ben. The first shipment. Then we’ll see what happens.” Bowman knew Ambrose was right. The organisation back in the UK was big and powerful and it had to be broken. He had read Ramsay's list of the mourners at the funeral, eminent people from every walk of life, the media, the law, politics, the city, every estate but the church itself. These were the fat cats, the moneymen, the manipulators. The ones with the clean hands. He went to the desk and took out the set of black and white photographs. "It's a long shot Ben, but see if there's anybody you recognise."

Ambrose flicked through the pile of prints. "No, there's nobody here I've come across before. Not really surprising." He passed one across to Bowman. "Who's the spic? He's out of place. Sticks out like a sore thumb."

"Miguel Torres. Second Secretary at the Colombian Embassy. The white haired man is Marcus Esler, used to be Ambassador to Venezuela. The younger one is Rupert Rutland, junior minister at the Home Office, assigned to the National Drugs Intelligence Unit. We used to work together in the old days, me and Ramsay and him."

"The Home Office? Isn't that kinda like the Ministry of the Interior?"

"Exactly. Responsible for law and order. Police. Customs. The prison service."

"Sounds like an important guy. For a minister he keeps some pretty interesting company." Ben Ambrose stood up and did a little dance. He was Sugar Ray warming up before a fight. "Come on Alex, I feel like a little celebration. Lets go have one hell of a lunch, courtesy of Uncle Sam. There's a place in Algeciras down by the railroad station that does the best paella this side of Kansas City. Then we can drive up the coast in the old jalopy and find us a couple of broads for some afternoon delight. Come on you limey bastard, whadaya say?"

“Sounds good to me.” said Alex, as an image of Verity flashed across his mind. “Sounds very good to me.”

Ambrose revved the powerful engine and watched Bowman coming down the terrace steps, taking them three at a time. He had changed out of his jeans and sweatshirt into another identical outfit, except this one was fresh and clean. He looked like he had just stepped out of a cigarette commercial.

When Alex was sitting beside him Ambrose patted the complex looking dashboard with its array of instruments. "Howd'ya like my new baby, Alex? Isn't she something?"

"Very discreet." said Alex, not smiling, fastening his seat belt.

"Come on Alex! Relax will ya! Enjoy! Have a little fun for Christsake!"

"The car is great Ben. I love it. But it's not exactly what you'd call inconspicuous, is it?" Getting noticed was bad professional practice.

"Shit Alex, gimme a break will ya! How could I possibly be inconspicuous? How many goddamn Yankee niggers do you think there are, shacked up in a hick town like Algeciras? If the Willowby had wanted inconspicuous he'd have sent a goddamn honky, maybe even Hispanic if he'd had his head on straight. But he didn't, did he? And do you know why? Because I'm an effective sonofabitch, Alex. I get results. Not orthodox maybe. Not inconspicuous. But I *do* get results." He revved the engine hard, crashing the gears as he pulled away up the drive.

Alex chuckled. Ambrose was right, of course he was right, it was just that they had different styles. There was no reason Ben's approach wouldn't work just as well as his own, in some ways it could work even better. Alex took the wad of notes from his pocket and handed it to Ben.

"What's this?" Ambrose calmed down as he joined the main road and concentrated on his driving.

"$5,000 in listed notes. Muñoz gave me a discount." Alex saw Ambrose hadn't followed. "I only gave him half the cash Ben, he settled for $5,000."

"Keep it." Ambrose waived the wad away, not even looking at it.

"$5,000? You must be kidding!" It was more than Alex normally earned in a month.

"Think of it as a bonus, Alex. Why not? You did a good job. Gimme a break, for Christsake will ya! You want me to keep accurate accounts? What the fuck am I, a friggin' bookkeeper?" Ambrose pressed the accelerator to the floor to put more space between him and the white Mercedes.

Alex winced as Ambrose crashed the gears again. He hadn't met an American yet who knew how to handle a stick shift. And then, a little to his own surprise, he pocketed the cash.

Ambrose smiled to himself. He liked a man who knew the value of money.

***

Alex parked the car in the narrow strip of shade at the side of the white church. He was early, so he got out of the car to stretch his legs and strolled over to the café on the far side of the square and ordered coffee. A large white Mercedes entered the square and came to a halt in front of the church. Alex could see himself reflected in the darkened glass of the side window. The vehicle moved off silently and disappeared.

Precisely on the hour the church doors opened and the congregation spilled out onto the pavement, shading their eyes against the sudden light. Melanie emerged from the crowd, crossing herself as she stepped down off the pavement, and with the same seamless gesture waved across at Alex and smiled.

"How was the service?" Alex beckoned to the waiter for more coffee.

"Fine, but I wish I could follow the sermon more closely. My Spanish isn't up to it yet. You must teach me."

"I'll teach you. So long as I don't have to go to church."

"You're not a believer?"

"I could never get past *Genesis.* If you can't take *Genesis* seriously it's hard to swallow the rest."

Melanie frowned, which made her look like a small child.

"Just how serious is your religion?"

"Serious enough. It's what gives the rest of my life meaning."

***

They took the Tarifa road, high into the *sierra,* above the Strait. About twelve kilometres beyond Algeciras where the road runs flat, Alex pulled off the road and parked the car in the shade of an ancient cork tree. He didn't get out of the car right away but sat there waiting to see what the white Mercedes would do. But it continued on towards Tarifa, without so much as a change of gear.

They climbed in silence for about an hour up through the cool cork forest, Bowman leading to find a way through the bracken and ferns, until they emerged at the foot of a great escarpment of rock, the *Peñon del Fraile*.

"This is it? We climbed for over an hour to look at a rock?" Melanie stood looking at the outcrop, her thumbs hooked into the belt loops of her jeans.

"Not *at* a rock, *from* a rock. You'll see when we get to the top."

The final ascent was easy, there were handholds and footholds in abundance and the rock face was firm and dry. Alex reached the top first, forty feet or so ahead of Melanie, and he turned to watch her as she joined him. Her breathing was light and easy, she had taken the climb in her stride. Alex reached for her hand to help her up onto the summit but she waived him away, grabbing at the outcrop instead.

"Wow!" She wiped her cheeks and brow with the back of her hand. "I see what you mean! That's quite a view!" The Strait of Gibraltar from the Rock all the way to Tangier was spread out below them looking like a model of itself. "It feels like I could throw a stone all the way to Africa. Do you know it well, Morocco I mean?"

"Once I took a jeep over the High Atlas and across the dry valley to where the Sahara begins. Up in the Atlas below the snow line everything is lush and green and then when you get past Ouarzazate, where the desert begins, there's this incredible sense of space, of openness."

"Is there always snow in the Atlas? How high does it get over there?"

"High enough." Alex smiled. "The Toubkal is the second highest peak in Africa. Over 7,000 feet."

Melanie looked out to the mountains of Morocco across the narrow stretch of water. Then she stood up, found a stone, and hurled it at Africa with all her strength. It didn't quite reach the line of cork trees below. "I thought you were going back to London, Alex. I thought you said it was important."

He didn't speak. There was no way he could explain, let her get involved, it was far too dangerous for that. Even being seen with him in public put her at risk.

She turned towards him, not smiling. Her jaw was jutting out in a way he knew meant trouble, her cheeks flushed with anger. "Go ahead, Alex. Try me. Explain. I'm an intelligent woman. Explain it to me and I'll understand. I want to understand. And I want to help." She knew it was no good. The man was nothing but a bloody chauvinist and it made her very angry. She decided to give him one last chance. She came and sat next to him, their shoulders almost touching.

"Look Alex, there must be something I can do to help. I'm bored. I don't have any work to do right now and it's getting on my nerves. Why don't you go off to Morocco and do whatever it is you have to do, and I'll go back to

London. I'll work with Ramsay, or whatsisname, Draycott. I'll do anything they say."

Alex didn't even think about it, not for a single second. When he spoke he was talking to a child. "Look Mel, if there were anything you could do I'd ask, I really would. But there isn't, and that's that. Ramsay has the London end covered, you'd only get in his way. As for Draycott, he's a very sick man." He watched her clenching and unclenching her jaw and realised this wasn't going to work. "This is work for professionals."

"Chauvinist! Work for professionals! Work for men is what you mean! Look Alex, I'm a professional too, one of the very best journalists around. Ask Flaherty! I've worked on criminal investigations before, I have contacts, I know people." She stood up and dusted the seat of her jeans, watching him watching her as she did so.

Alex thought about what she said and understood her point of view. She was a bright, active, intelligent woman. That was what made her so attractive. Sitting around with nothing to do must be deeply frustrating for her. "Look Melanie, I know it's difficult, but the answer is no, finally, definitely, irreversibly. No!"

She climbed back down the rock face with an ease and a speed that surprised him. He decided to wait, let her go on, give her all the time she needed to cool down. He watched her disappear among the cork trees before he got up to follow.

He was sure she would be waiting for him by the car, but when he reached it she wasn't there. She must have thumbed a lift back into town. That evening he called her number several times, but she just wouldn't answer the phone.

***

Every once in a while Verity would send off one of the pre-addressed envelopes to the box number in the City with a list of names, dates and times, and the photographs she always managed to take of the people who came to the villa. They all seemed to like posing for her.

On the twentieth day after Verity was installed a white Porsche Carrera turned into the newly surfaced road and immediately swung out to avoid the crew of men digging a hole in it. "Same bloody thing the world over! Why do they always lay a new surface and then decide to dig their bloody holes?" The driver's name was James Fitzroy. He looked like one of those people in the ads in glossy magazines, set against the backdrop of some fabulous country house. James Fitzroy had failed at most things, failed at school, even failed at the bank. His one success was the army, retired with the rank of Captain. The army had taught him to kill. But if he was going to kill he wanted to be well paid, which the army didn't understand. Still, James Fitzroy had three invaluable qualities; breeding, charm, and great good looks. The fourth, the one to make everything else perfect, had eluded him. And that was money.

The Porsche came to a halt in front of the wrought iron gates and James gave the three blasts on the horn, one long and two short, and the gate slid back to admit him. He drove the short distance to the villa and guided the car down the ramp into the garage. As he walked back into the sunshine a man in greasy overalls pressed a button and the heavy metal door dropped back into place.

James walked through the gardens and stopped to admire the bougainvilleas. They were lovely at this time of year and their fantastic mauve and crimson blossoms looked unreal against the stark white wall. He thought of plucking some for his buttonhole but he knew how quickly it would fade if he did, so he passed by on his way to the pool. He found Harvey under the awning, lying in a swing chair with his head in the lap of a gorgeous blond James hadn't seen before. She was stunning.

"James baby! Howyadoin?" Harvey sat up. "Say hello to Verity. Verity say hello to James."

The blond slapped Harvey gently on the wrist. "Come along now Mr Lieberman, make a proper introduction, like I showed you. Miss Verity Fuller, may I introduce Mr. James ....?"

"Fitzroy." James clicked his heels and made a little bow. "Captain James Barrington Fitzroy, at your service m'am. Delighted to meet you Miss Fuller." He took her hand and kissed it. Verity was thrilled.

"Delighted to meet you, Captain James Barrington Fitzroy." Verity repeated the name to fix it in her memory. "And what pray was your regiment, if I might enquire?" She slipped effortlessly into Jane Austin mode.

“Special Air Services, m’am.” He glanced at Harvey. “*He who dares, wins*.”

"James, I tell ya, this broad is something else!" Harvey was laughing. "She wants to make a gentleman out of me! Can you believe that? Harvey Lieberman from the Bronx?" Pride gleamed in Harvey's eyes. Verity was the most precious of all his possessions.

The three of them took a leisurely lunch on the terrace while the mechanics stripped down the body of the Porche. Harvey was obsessed by secrecy and he had found it best if his couriers didn't know precisely what they were carrying, or how much it was worth, or where it was concealed. Innocence is very hard to affect, and the less they knew the better able they were to achieve it.

James was very taken with Verity, and she apparently with him. Harvey was delighted, he loved to see his possessions admired, even coveted, and before James left Harvey took a photograph of the two of them together. They made a very handsome couple, arm in arm, leaning on the Porsche. Verity always seemed to have her camera handy.

At four o'clock in the afternoon Harvey walked James Fitzroy down to the garage. “I didn’t know you were SAS, James. I knew you were army, but not SAS. Might come in handy. You’re the guys who stormed the Iranian Embassy, right? Saw that on TV. Impressive. Maybe I’ll get you to kick a little Colombian ass for me sometime. Whadaya think, James? Interested?“

“Sure. You know me Harvey. Do anything for money!”

"Could you put a team together if we need to? Bunch of guys?"

"Sure, Harvey. Money talks, even when you're having fun."

"Great! I'll let you know if I need you." Harvey placed his hand on Fitzroy's shoulder. "Now this drop, James. It's very important to me. I got a really valuable new customer. Big enough to put us straight into the major leagues. Make sure it goes right."

"Hasn't it always?" James saluted as he climbed into the Porsche. "How valuable?"

"Never mind about how valuable. Just do your job and don't fuck up." Harvey sounded suddenly irritable.

James smiled and waved goodbye. He would be half way to the border by nightfall and in London two days later. He waved again at the men digging the hole in the road and they waved back to him. He didn't notice the one making a note of the time.

When he was gone Verity rode into town in Harvey's chauffeur driven stretched Mercedes to have her hair done and mail the Polaroid of herself and Captain Fitzroy in one of the pre-addressed envelopes the woman in black had provided.

***

Fitzroy left the docks at Dover behind him. He had crossed at the time agreed with his regular contact at customs, so there wasn't any problem. It would cost him five grand, but it was worth the price. The trip had been wonderful. He had travelled on country roads, away from the trucks and tourist traffic and stayed in a couple of his favourite inns. He had eaten the best food, drunk the best wine, done everything he could wish for, except get laid. But best of all he had made money. The trip would pay for the Porsche and a few other things besides.

What made this trip different from the others Fitzroy had made was that he was being watched. He had been watched at the border from Spain into France and again at the channel ports. From Dover into London a succession of cars had interchanged behind and in front of the Porsche in an intricate protracted two-step. George Ramsay had done a deal with Her Majesty's Customs and Excise, his own deal, a private deal, strictly off the record. He was in a very privileged position. Ambrose had passed the information about the Porsche directly back to him, not through the usual channels. So when Ramsay made his offer to the Duty Men they could not possibly refuse.

The drop off point this time was a garage in Wandsworth Fitzroy hadn't been to before. All he had to do was to leave the car over night for an oil change and pick it up again the following morning. The glove compartment would be stuffed full of cash. It was dusk when he pulled into the forecourt in a cul-de-sac in a light industrial backwater of garages and workshops. Most of the labour force had already left by the time he got there, but there were three men in overalls still hanging about, waiting. A large man with his sleeves rolled up over massive tattooed forearms guided Fitzroy as he reversed onto the ramp above the inspection pit. Fitzroy got out of the car and the man pressed a button on a steel girder and the Porsche rose silently into the air. Not a word passed between them. Fitzroy walked to the top of the cul-de-sac to the busy street at the end, and hailed a cab. By the time the taxi reached the end of the street the heavy steel doors were lowered into place. One of the men came out onto the forecourt and fixed a couple of heavy-duty padlocks to each door, bolting the steel curtains to the ground.

George Ramsay stood framed in the doorway of the pub opposite, a pint of Fuller's in his hand. He was the only customer in the place and judging by the charm of the barman it was likely to stay that way

They would know where the stuff was hidden, no point in playing hide-and-seek, so he gave them ten minutes or so to strip the Porsche, time enough to down his pint at leisure. The streetlights had flickered into life by now but the doorway opposite was set back and partially in shadow. Above it Ramsay could see the heat sensitive halogen light and the video camera, linked to a closed circuit monitor somewhere on the inside. A fire escape led from the side of the two-storey building to the flat roof above. He stepped onto the forecourt, out of range of the heat sensitive lamp, and climbed up the fire escape.

Inside, the three men had already recovered eight of the ten half kilo packages, re-assembled the chassis of the Porsche, and let it back down on the ground. The remaining two were easy, sewn into each of the sun visors, and they were half way through unpicking the stitching when Ramsay reached the roof. The skylight ran for almost the complete length of the building. He worked his way along the narrow space till he was directly above the three men. On the front seat of the Porsche he could see the flat, shiny white packages. He watched as they locked the booty in the safe. Then he went back down to the pub and ordered another pint. It went against the grain not to raid the place. But that was what Bowman wanted. "Just make sure the stuff gets through safely, George." Alex had said. "Let Lieberman get himself established."

***

10

Bowman took the direct flight by Royal Air Maroc from Malaga to Marrakech. The flight would take just one hour and twenty minutes. He could have driven it in less than a day, even allowing for the ferry, but he would need four wheel drive to get to the farm, so there really wasn't any point. He checked in, went through passport control and the casual security check and bought a couple of London papers. He sat at the bar and ordered a large single malt. When he boarded the plane, Alex was feeling relaxed. The single malt had worked its minor magic. He fastened his seat belt and grabbed both armrests as the plane surged forward, heading out over the bay. The plane climbed slowly, heading southwest, and banked to the right to give the passengers a view of the great white cliff face on the south side of Gibraltar. Bowman closed his eyes and held on tight. He was listening to the note of the engines when he heard the terrifying words over the PA system. The three words that made him want to die. Clear Air Turbulence. All the way to Marrakech.

Marrakech was not what Bowman wanted. He needed to stay on the Coast, close to where the action was. Close to Lieberman and Ambrose. Close to Melanie. But he had to go where Lieberman sent him now, leaving Ambrose with a free hand, in control of the Spanish end of things.

Marrakech was the only compromise Lieberman would make. He wanted Bowman to live at the farm up in the High Atlas but Alex persuaded him that this was bad security. His presence on a farm in a remote mountain area would draw too much attention and besides, he needed to be in the city for the initial phase of setting up the security systems. The first job was procurement. He needed fence posts, wiring, hand tools and digging equipment. These could be acquired in Marrakech. But there were other things, electronic control gear, sound and movement detectors, video cameras, TV monitors that were simply not obtainable locally. Bowman insisted he had to be free to travel to London and back to Spain if he was going to do a proper job. Lieberman resisted at first but he knew Alex was right, the job had to be done and done to the highest possible standards. Harvey Lieberman wanted nothing but the best.

So Alex moved into Lieberman's penthouse just outside the walled city, on the edge of the European quarter of Gueliz, not far from the Mamounia. It overlooked the Medina and clear across to the distant foothills of the Atlas which rose from the naked rust coloured plain of Haouz. The high peaks of the Toubkal were snow capped even at this time of year, but the dominant colour in the parched landscape was the reddish brown of the desert. From the terrace Alex could take in all the breathtaking magic of the ancient city. The towering minarets of Koutoubia and Bab Doukkala. The formal gardens of the Menara. The stunningly named Djemaa el Fna, the Assembly of the Dead, the fabled central square of Marrakech, part market place, part circus, part open-air theatre. Here were musicians, dancers, storytellers, acrobats, snake charmers, sword swallowers, fire-eaters, jugglers, competing for the attention and the silver of the open mouthed tourists they probably despised.

Marrakech is the capital of the pre-Saharan region, cut off from the desert by the great mountain range of the Atlas. Its character is restless, transitory, veiled, mysterious, its streets narrow and congested, its people stern, withdrawn, hardened, like the desert they had come from.

Finding his way in the *souk* was impossible. So next morning Bowman crossed to the Mamounia for coffee and to find one of the official guides in the white *djellaba* red *fes* and numbered licence disk that is their uniform. There were several waiting in the narrow strip of shade under the canopy of the hotel. Alex picked the one who would get the least work, Ahmed, a stunted boy of about fourteen with the sunken cheeks and hollow eyes of a consumptive. Together they set off to the *souk* to purchase the basic items of equipment Alex would need to carry out the first stage of the project, a rudimentary survey. This kind of work was bread and butter to Bowman. Half the security compounds of the expatriate community on the Costa del Sol had been designed and built by him.

Bowman knew he would be taken for a fool if he didn't haggle, but there was no way he could match the local talent, he didn't have the language and he didn't have the skill. Ahmed was fluent in Berber and Arabic and a couple of European languages, but he was educated on the street, so bargaining came to him quite naturally. He would roll his moist consumptive eyes and turn down the corners of his mouth each time a merchant would reduce the price. Sometimes he would simply walk away with a shrug of his narrow shoulders, leaving the man suspended in mid sentence. Then the merchant would call him back and Ahmed would turn again without so much as a gleam of interest in his eyes. When he felt he had a deal he pounced, concluding the bargain by slapping the palm of his victim's hand.

Ahmed was intrigued by the items Bowman wanted. He never once asked for an explanation, but he took note of everything the Englishman bought, the digging equipment, the hand tools, the barbed wire. In the end he concluded Alex was a farmer or a terrorist, but he couldn't make his mind up between the two.

They spent a good part of each of day together. They became friends. Ahmed liked the Englishman; he was kind and patient, never in a hurry. Whenever he got more than a few yards ahead of the stunted boy, wheezing along behind, he would stop at one of the stalls to examine some item he had no intention of buying, while Ahmed caught him up. Then they would set off again together, Ahmed explaining some detail of local culture, which was the job he had trained for. He had studied hard for two years at the Ministry school before he got his numbered badge.

Ahmed was a trained observer and, lagging behind Bowman as he did, noticed things the Englishman didn’t. He had made a study of Westerners, their facial expressions and body language. He could read them. Interpret their curiosity, their avarice, their fear, their sexual preferences. Ahmed spotted the European watching Bowman, but Alex didn’t. Ahmed quickened his pace to close the gap between himself and his client, brushing past the European. As he did so, he felt the package being thrust into his hand and the friendly touch that meant there was no danger. Ahmed didn't turn but kept his eyes on Bowman who seemed to notice nothing. When at last he looked behind him, there was no one there.

That last evening they ate together at a restaurant in the European quarter not far from the penthouse. It was Ahmed's choice and Alex let him order. It was a banquet, a dozen dishes were brought that Alex barely recognised, *harira, bistila, tajin,* a succulent *mechoui*. Ahmed drank tea but Alex ordered wine, the feast was just too good to eat without it. Ahmed laughed a lot in a high-pitched nervous way. There was something mischievous about him, furtive, as if he possessed some secret he was dying to tell, but telling it would spoil the fun.

They parted in the square at the end of Bowman's street. "Have a good night, Sir!" Ahmed laughed. "Have a *very* good night!"

***

Maybe Alex had too much too drink, maybe it was the rich concoction of spices, but by the time he reached the apartment building he felt like a sailor coming ashore after months at sea. His head was clear but his legs wouldn't hold him. He had the sensation he was floating, that he could move without touching the ground. Somehow his senses seemed enlarged, colours were brighter, sounds more pleasing. When he reached the door of the penthouse it was open. He knew he had left it locked, he was sure of it. He took off his shoes, pushed the door, and went in. He didn't turn on the light. The curtains were drawn back, moonlight flooding the room.

There was a smell he didn't recognise, rich, sweet, intoxicating. There was music, dissonant, rhythmic, exotic. A shadow moved in the darkness. His head was swimming now, his legs unsteady. He sat on the bed, feeling himself drift away, but he didn't want to fight it. He lay down.

She was standing by the bed now, a shadow, an outline. In his dream state Alex didn't understand the mechanics of what happened next. She touched a button at her throat and her dress slipped from her shoulders and cascaded to the floor in a seamless shimmering movement. She was lovely, perfect, her smile was very sweet. She stood in his gaze like Venus Arising and seemed to levitate. She was weightless, they both were. He expected to hear a choir of angels but there was none. She was above him now, floating down on him. When he touched her skin it was silk. She sat astride him, smiling, motionless. Then her hair fell forward over her face and over his as she lowered her mouth to be kissed. He could hear the angels now.

Without a word she undressed him. He didn't resist. She eased off his shirt, pausing to kiss his shoulders and chest, his abdomen. She undid his belt and pulled down his jeans. He lay still, helpless. With her fingertips she traced the line of his shoulder and chest and thigh repeating the same movement over and over. He was letting go, slipping in and out of a dream state, almost on the edge of sleep. He realised he could no longer suppress his erection and tried to think of something else, half hoping it would go away, half hoping it wouldn't. She propped herself on one elbow, surveying the effects of her handiwork and smiled, impressed by his response.

Her touch was soft, gentle, unhurried. The moisture of her lips warmed and soothed and stimulated him till the surging force inside him built up unbearably, demanding release. Judging her moment with care, before the pressures inside him became too explosive for the satisfaction of her own desires, she mounted him, soothing him with soft secretions as she enveloped his member. She sat astride him for a time, not moving, while his eyes explored her body. Her breasts were full, her stomach firm. Her skin was soft and scented. At last she began to move, the slow subtle rhythms of her body modulating gently, till delirious with pleasure she took the full thrust of him inside her, bearing down on him as they lost control, both simultaneously exploding in a single torrent of ecstasy.

The bliss of orgasm attained she lay motionless on top of him, still holding him inside her, their sweating bodies intertwined, till she felt him revive. Then, sighing with pleasure and murmuring his name, she slid off him to lay face down beside him, the line of her back, the curve of her buttocks and thighs inviting the invention of a new delight.

In the street below the stunted boy looked up at the darkened window, smiling. He looked at his watch. It was late. His friend had wanted an early night.

***

When Alex awoke the next morning he lay for a moment in that state between sleeping and waking, trying to recall his dream. As he did so he became erect and turned over to lie on his back. That was when he felt the warm body next to his and heard her light regular breathing. Slowly he raised his head from the pillow so his eyes could confirm what his other senses already knew. *Oh my God! Verity!*

Alex got out of bed as quietly as he could and went to the bathroom. He peed and put his throbbing head under the cold tap. He would have taken a shower but that would certainly have woken her so he stood leaning on the wash basin trying to think through what had happened, how it changed things, how it would affect the project, his relationship with Harvey and with................ *Christ, Verity why did you have to do this!* But whatever he thought of, his erection simply wouldn't go away. There was only one way to get rid of it and that required him to wake her, so he brushed his teeth quickly and returned to the bedroom.

When it was over Verity slept contentedly, the smile of an angel on her face, while Alex showered and shaved. But still he couldn't think through the implications of what had happened and how it might change everything. If Harvey got to know about this it was curtains for both of them. That was the security he needed. Verity couldn't afford to let Harvey find out, any more than Alex could.

Verity woke as Alex was dressing. She pushed back the sheet and lay there expecting him to join her. Alex concentrated on tying his boots.

"Come on Alex, take me again, just once before you go. I can see you want to. It doesn't matter what time you get to the farm."

Alex froze. “You know about the farm?”

“Of course. Harvey tells me stuff.”

“Stuff? What stuff?” She didn’t reply, she just smiled. “What do they grow at the farm?”

Verity looked thoughtful. “Fruit?”

“Right! Fruit! Citrus fruit!” There was no way Harvey would be dumb enough to tell her anything important. “What about Harvey? What if he finds out you’re here?” Alex was concerned enough about himself, Harvey wouldn’t hesitate to have him blown away. But Alex could look after himself. Verity couldn’t.

“Oh Alex! Harvey would be furious! He doesn’t like me talking to the help, let alone.........” She began to giggle. “But who’s going to tell him? You’re not, he’d have you killed. I’m not, what would be the point, I haven’t finished with you yet! When I have, maybe I’ll tell Harvey you seduced me. That should make him good and mad! Bye bye Bowman!” She waved at him. She enjoyed teasing him, teasing him was fun!

Alex swallowed hard. Verity would have to be handled with care. “Aren’t you supposed to be with Harvey now? He’ll notice you’re gone.”

“Alex, don’t be so silly! You don’t think I’m stupid do you? I didn’t just slip away. I knew you were coming to Marrakech, José told me. I knew about the penthouse. I told Harvey I had to go to London for a couple of days to do some shopping. Harvey let's me do what I like. He loves me."

"José? José knows you're here?"

"I shouldn't think so." Verity blushed. "No, of course not. José's stupid!"

"Who drove you to the airport?"

"José did."

"He helped you with your bags? Saw you check in?"

"I just have hand luggage. My night things." She was blushing again. By this time Bowman was seriously behind his self-imposed schedule. Briefly he thought of delaying his departure by one day, there were a hundred reasons he could think of, but he decided against it. Verity was great, but not that great. Not great enough to jeopardise everything. He bent down to kiss her on the cheek. Verity grabbed him, holding him till he began to harden. Then, just as Alex was about to change his mind, she let him go.

"Remember, Alex." Verity smiled her convent smile. "I haven't finished with you yet."

***

Bowman took the Ouarzazate road southeast from Marrakech and followed Lieberman's instructions. The road was bad. It climbed slowly by precarious twists and turns up into the cool green country high above the dusty

Haouz plain. It took two hours to reach the high pass at Tizi n'Tichka at an altitude of over seven thousand feet, where the road begins its long descent to Ouarzazate, on the rim of the great desert region.

At the pass Bowman turned off the main road and headed up to Telouet and beyond, leaving the last of the villages behind. The final stretch was difficult rugged terrain, the road no more than a rutted track. At last he came to a point where he had to ford a swiftly flowing stream, fringed with date palms, and knew from Lieberman's instructions that he was nearly there. He drove on for another mile or so up the canyon and there in front of him were the two promontories of rock that marked the entrance to the farm, just as Lieberman had described them. The stream had cut a deep gorge through the valley floor and the two jagged outcrops made a natural gateway, the only way in or out of the place. Defending it would be easy. A handful of well-supplied men could hold a position like that for weeks if they had to.

Bowman guided the truck through the narrow passage between the two outcrops. A couple of hundred yards ahead was a small collection of derelict mud brick buildings. He pulled up alongside the largest of them where the late afternoon sun permitted a little shade. The place seemed deserted. He knew there were three Europeans at the farm, a chemist and his two assistants who oversaw the production and refining processes, but there was no sign of anyone, just the dogs asleep in the shade at the side of one of the huts. Suddenly he heard a voice and a figure emerged from the largest of the buildings.

"You Bowman?" He had the face of a man in his sixties but he was strong and vigorous and had the meanest eyes Alex had seen in a long time. He was unshaven, and probably unwashed. He called himself O'Malley and claimed to be an Irishman but he had a mid-European accent that made this seem unlikely.

Alex offered his hand, but O'Malley ignored it. "Put your stuff in Lieberman's apartment." He nodded towards the only new building, a modest single storey dwelling set apart from the rest.

"You vant to look around?"

"That's what I'm here for."

"Help yourself." O'Malley spat on the ground between them, turned, and went back inside the building.

Alex dropped his holdall on the porch of Lieberman's apartment and walked up to the top of a low hill behind the group of buildings to get a view of the valley. The farm was big by local standards, three hundred acres or more, but only part of it was under cultivation. Many of the citrus trees still stood but the work of clearing the bulk of the land for replanting with *Erythroxylon Coca* was already under way. The red earth was deep and rich and the stream was full with the waters of the melting snow, cascading down from the high peaks of the Toubkal, which surrounded the farm in a halo of white.

The production facility was housed in the largest of the derelict mud brick buildings. It was crude, but it worked perfectly well. Making cocaine is a very unsophisticated process, no real skill is required, just a few bits of rudimentary equipment, some plastic vats, some tubing. But here things were done on an industrial scale. He saw the drums of kerosene and sulphuric and hydrochloric acid which are used to turn the macerated leaves first to Coca paste and then to cocaine base and finally to cocaine hydrochloride, the deadly finished product. Security was non-existent, there weren't even locks on any of the doors. Nobody in their right mind would touch the stuff, certainly not a trained chemist.

Alex set off up the fertile valley and followed the watercourse. There was a labour force on site that numbered about a hundred, illiterate Berbers recruited from the mountain villages below. They spoke no English, they spoke no Arabic either. They had no idea what crop they were growing, it was a crop they had never seen before. They assumed it was some kind of tea. But they had already been taught how good it was to chew the leaves, how the effect could lighten their labour. They seemed like a very contented bunch of people, chewing and smiling as they sweated in the fields.

Bowman walked the entire perimeter, made a rough map, photographed everything. He hardly spoke to a soul. The Berbers couldn't understand a word he said and O'Malley had warned his two assistants to stay clear of the big Englishman.

When Bowman returned from his trek, it was nearly dark. He went into Lieberman's modestly equipped apartment, took a cold shower and changed his clothes. The room was bare but comfortable. There was a door he hadn't noticed before, that probably led to a sitting room or closet. Bowman crossed the room to open it.

"He keeps that locked." O'Malley stood on the porch. "He calls it his viewing room."

"Viewing room?"

"Sure. Most of the time when he comes up here he doesn't stay over night, goes back to the penthouse in Marrakech. He usually brings a couple of women with him for the trip and they wait for him there. But every once in a while he has to stay up here at the farm. He never brings the women with him. The place is too rough. He gets bored, so he brings a couple of movies. Sometimes he lets me and the boys watch." O'Malley picked at his rotting teeth. "Here, I brought you some food and a bottle of warm beer. I ate already."

Bowman took the dish of stew and the bottle of beer and sat on the wooden porch. "Thanks" he said. "You've got a pretty impressive set-up here." Bowman understood the economics of the cocaine industry. Five acres of well-irrigated land could produce about two thousand kilos of Coca leaf, the primary ingredient. This would produce ten kilos of coca paste, which would be refined into a single kilo of pure cocaine hydrochloride, the world's most valuable commodity. Cultivation, processing and refinement cost peanuts. So if they could harvest three crops annually Lieberman would be making as much as fifteen million dollars a year. Every year. But by the time that innocent looking powder reached London or Amsterdam it would be worth as much double, at the distributor level alone. But the profits didn't end there.

The refining process would now be put into reverse as the white powder was cut, adulterated, added to at every stage of the progression from distributor, to wholesaler, to retailer, to pusher. Anything from dried milk to talcum powder would be added back to the original one kilo package, increasing its weight and its value, until one single kilo of pure cocaine hydrochloride was worth in excess of half a million pounds. Worldwide the trade generated some $400 Billion. About the same as global oil. Except the drugs trade wasn't even taxed.

"Impressive?" said O'Malley. "Sure it's impressive! We're getting three cops a year already. Not as much as they get in Bolivia, but not bad. We made this place. Lieberman and me. Don't fuck with it."

In the dying light Bowman surveyed the *Coca* bushes planted in terraced rows. He saw the primitive processing plant where the deadly white powder was refined, and he knew the enormous, terrifying potential of Lieberman's idea. "I'm not here to fuck with it. I'm here to protect it."

"Protect it from what? From who? Nobody knows about this place. How the fuck would anybody find it? Who would even look? Nobody ever even dreamed of growing cocaine here till we did! Lieberman and me!"

O'Malley was right. That was the beauty of Lieberman's idea, of Tiffany's idea. "The Colombians maybe." said Alex. "If they ever hear about this place they'll wipe you out for sure."

O'Malley spat on the ground and returned to his hut. Bowman finished his beer and thought about Verity.

Harvey's favourite fuck. He could understand that. She would be anybody's favourite fuck. He would have to stay away from Verity. If Verity would stay away from him.

Bowman went inside. He crossed the room and examined the locked door to the viewing room. Nothing special. Just a conventional domestic lock. He leaned on it heavily and it gave way. By the time Lieberman found out it wouldn't matter anyway. He turned on the light and looked around the room. There was a TV, a video recorder, a small bar and several comfortable chairs. On a shelf was a row of videocassettes with hand written labels on the spines. Alex scanned the titles, wondering if Verity had ever put in an appearance in one of Harvey's flicks, but he doubted it. Verity was too good to share, and Harvey too possessive.

Alex found a bottle of scotch on the bar, not single malt but in the circumstances it would do. He sat in one of the chairs, picked up the remote control unit and pressed play. The screen flickered to reveal Lieberman's swimming pool, slightly out of focus. The shot sharpened as it zoomed in on the lone swimmer doing lengths. There was no sound. Alex admired the style before he recognised himself climbing out of the pool as Harvey fetched him a robe. He watched himself drinking coffee with Lieberman and the charade of José awkwardly pulling his gun as Lieberman gestured wildly. Alex thought it was over so he got up to pour himself another scotch when the screen lit up again to reveal himself coming down the terrace steps of the farm house and climbing into the red Ferrari. The shot must have been taken from another car since the next sequence was of the

Ferrari pulling up outside the restaurant in Algeciras and Ben Ambrose brushing the dust from his cowboy boots. The final segment seemed unrelated to the rest. It was a scene of Alex drinking coffee on the terrace of a small café. The camera panned left to the doors of a whitewashed church. The doors opened and the congregation emerged into the light. The camera scanned the crowd and zoomed in on an auburn haired woman. slightly out of focus. She crossed herself as she stepped down off the pavement and with the same seamless gesture waved across at Alex and smiled.

***

Bowman spent three days at the farm, more than he needed, but he thought Harvey would be impressed if he seemed to be thorough. On the day he left he got up early, took a cold shower, packed his things with care, and climbed into the truck. On the passenger seat was a bag that wasn't his. He went over to O'Malley's hut to find out whose it was.

"It's yours." said O'Malley. "The boss vants you to take it. He needs it urgent."

"What is it?" said Alex, knowing exactly what it was.

"Four K."

"Four K." said Alex. "Right. Fine."

He got into the truck and drove back down the ravine. A few miles past Telouet he pulled off the road and dialled Ambrose on his mobile. "Ben, I've got a problem."

"Tell me." said Ambrose.

"I'm on my way back from the farm. I'll be landing at Malaga about three thirty this afternoon."

"So. What's the problem?"

"I'm carrying four kilos of coke. Lieberman sent word to the farm for me to bring it back. I think it's some kind of test."

"Right. And?"

"Can you fix it for me with Customs? Fix it so I can walk through?"

Ambrose didn't speak for a while. Then he said, "No dice, Alex."

"No dice? Whadda you mean, no dice? You fixed it at Ceuta!"

"Ceuta was different. Ceuta was DEA business. The deal was set up in advance. We were only talking Mary Jane. We had the affidavit. This time it's snow and the Spanish boys haven't even been consulted. I don't think they'll play ball. They'll insist on impounding the snow. That makes it official. I'd have to brief Willowby. I'm not ready for that yet Alex. It doesn't suit my game plan. I want the stuff to get through so we can follow the trail."

"And what happens if the brown stuff hits the fan?"

"Duck, Alex." Ambrose chuckled. "Duck!"

"Well, thanks Ben. You've been a real help!" Alex dialled the *Hacienda Blanca* but Harvey wasn't at home, so he tried the film studio number. Harvey was on the sound stage overseeing his latest production, but Alex convinced the assistant that the call was important and the young man got Harvey to come to the phone.

"Harvey? It's me, Alex."

"Alex baby! Howya doin?"

"I'm fine Harvey. I have your package."

"That's great Alex."

"Harvey, I don't think it's a very good idea."

"Oh! And why's that, Alex?" *Was he laughing?*

"Harvey, I'm Head of Security. I shouldn't be carrying a bag. It's too risky."

"Risky? Sure it's risky, Alex! But somebody has to do it. I'm getting a lot of pressure from the UK. They're desperate for supply." He *was* laughing. "Don't worry about it, Alex. There'll be a couple of nursemaids on the flight to keep an eye on you. Standard procedure."

"Well, thanks Harvey."

"Don't thank me, Alex. If you get stopped they'll put a bullet in your back."

***

As Harvey replaced the receiver Hack Bronowski buzzed him on the intercom. "Harv? Can you come by my office? I'm picking up some interesting traffic." Hack Bronowski, a sweaty obese forty year old, worked in a cramped office adjacent to the post-production studio surrounded by a mystifying array of consoles, wires, dials, screens and speakers. When Harvey walked in Hack held up his hand for silence. After a while he muttered "Shit! Lost it." He turned to Harvey. "Never mind. Got everything you need, I think." He pressed the eject button and handed Harvey the cassette. "There you go Harv. The Colombian shipment we've been tracking? That's details of the landing site. Time. Place. Everything you need. Some beach in Wales. Abersomething. Can't pronounce it."

"Thanks Hack" Harvey beamed. "That's great." He put the cassette in his pocket. "Say Hack, there's a new broad on sound stage three. Cute. Ambitious. You can use the couch in my office."

Hack looked in the mirror, licked the palms of his hands and patted down his thinning hair. Next he took a couple of joints from a box in his desk draw. "Thanks Harv. Appreciate it."

***

Alex spotted the minders on the plane. He sat in an aisle seat and they each took a seat in the opposite aisle, one a couple of rows in front, the other a couple of rows behind. The coke was in his hand luggage under his seat. He had no idea what to do if he were stopped. Maybe Ambrose would back him up. Maybe not. It was hard to say.

Alex stood in the customs hall at Malaga airport wondering which exit to go through. The two minders were a few metres behind him. He couldn't see them but he knew they were there. They could probably get off one shot and disappear into the crowd. Alex had set off for the green channel when he felt a hand on his shoulder. He froze and turned slowly to see Raúl Blanco, Head of Airport Security, smiling at him.

"Olá, Alex! Que tal, hombre?"

"Raúl!" Alex was beaming. "I'm fine! You?"

"Muy bien, hombre! Come on up to my office. A friend of yours is up there waiting. Ben Ambrose. You know him?"

"Sure, Raúl. Ben and me go way back!"

***

11

Iberia flight 883 landed at Heathrow Airport punctually at 9.55 a.m. The flight from Malaga had been smooth and uneventful. Melanie Drake stood at the back of the crowd trying to spot her two matching cases come round on the belt. She walked through the green channel, pushing her luggage on a trolley, and out into the crowded concourse. She spotted the chauffeur Flaherty had sent, carrying the card with her name on. He took the trolley from her and they walked together across the walkway to the short-term car park.

She sat in the back of the huge black Mercedes, opened the drinks cabinet and mixed herself a gin and tonic. Sean Flaherty, thank God, still had his uses. She closed her eyes. Alex. Bloody Alex. Whatever he said, she was going to get involved. It wasn't dangerous. That was just Alex making excuses. He needed help. He simply didn't know it.

Her London flat was in an impressive Victorian building just behind the Royal Albert Hall, a stone's throw from Hyde Park. Melanie and Ramsay sat in the drawing room, She had offered him tea, which George thought would come in a mug with a bag suspended over the side, but instead she brought it in a silver pot, on a tray, with cups which looked like they would break when you touched them. There was a taste to the lightly coloured liquid, more a perfume, but Ramsay wouldn't have called it tea.

Melanie mentioned a few buzzwords like Ambrose and Lieberman and Marrakech and explained her background as a journalist. Ramsay could well understand why Alex would want her involved. She was bright and alert and in a word, professional. But George had learned his chauvinism at his father's knee and didn't quite know what to make of her. He had brought along a spare set of the photographs from the funeral to see if she could label any of bright young things he hadn't been able to identify.

"This is very interesting." She flipped through the pile of black and white prints. "What do they have in common? Come on George, you've run them through the computer. What do they all have in common?"

"Not much, I'm afraid. Money obviously. And Oxbridge. Almost all of them were at Oxford or Cambridge, even the ruddy foreigners. But that's about it. They don't come from any particular walk of life. There's no obvious connection."

"Success, George. That's one thing they have in common." She picked up the photographs, moving the tray to the floor to make more room, and counted them out one by one as if she were dealing cards. "Top model, international banker, editor, judge, industrialist. It's like Who's Who in mourning."

"That's what you'd expect surely, they're Berringer's friends after all."

"Wrong George, they're Mary's friends. They're almost all under forty. If Mary were there she'd be the odd one out. She certainly wasn't a success, made a total botch of her life. Even as a journalist she never made it out of the research department. So why was there nobody there like her?" She shuffled the photographs around on the table. "Except if drugs is what they have in common. But that can't be it surely, they can't all be into drugs. This one's a Minister for God's sake, he's practically in the Cabinet!" She pointed to a photograph of Rupert Rutland in conversation with a white haired man who looked like an ageing movie star.

"I don't recognise him George. What a distinguished looking man. Who is he?"

"Marcus Esler, Sir Marcus Esler, but he never uses the title. Career diplomat. Retired early a couple of years ago to run the family shipping business when his elder brother died. Runs a mission in the East End, helping drug addicted kids. Apparently it's very effective."

Melanie re-arranged the photographs and pointed to another shot of Esler and Rutland, this time in conversation with a swarthy younger man with olive skin and tightly curled black hair, and a woman whose back was to the camera.

"Miguel Torres." Ramsay didn't wait to be asked. "Second Secretary at the Colombian Embassy. There's a drugs connection there all right. He was booted out of Ottawa for possession. Christ knows why we let the blighter in here."

"Influence, George. That's why we let him in. But who was pulling the strings? And the woman, who's she?"

"No idea. She appears in a lot of the shots but you never see her face, the camera couldn't get below the rim of her hat."

"Never mind her George. Here we have a Colombian diplomat with a record for possession, in conversation with our former man in Venezuela, at the funeral of a known trafficker! Surely you should pick them up!"

"And charge them with what exactly? Mourning the death of a friend? Besides, Esler and Rutland are pillars of the establishment, their credentials are bloody impeccable." Ramsay could hardly believe he had said it, he knew it was absurd. If Alex had been there he would have laughed out loud.

Melanie liked the look of Ramsay. He was solid, dependable, honest. But there was something else about him, a streak of hardness. He was disillusioned. Maybe he was bitter. Bitter at the way things had turned out, his lack of progress. Somehow he wasn't exactly what she had expected. If she were going to help Alex she would need someone more senior, someone with clout.

"Tell me George, didn't Alex have a mentor? Someone he looked up to? Someone who guided his career in the early days?"

George didn't hesitate, not for a single second. "Peter Draycott. They were very close."

"What sort of a man is Draycott? How senior?"

"Finest policeman of his generation. Everyone admired him. Especially Alex. He was Deputy Commissioner when he retired. He would have been Commissioner by now, if he hadn't had the stroke."

"Would he help Alex? If Alex asked him to?"

"Sure. But in Draycott's condition there's not much he could do."

"Yes, Alex told me about the stroke. Tell me something else George, Alex's wife, did you know her?"

"Only slightly. We never mixed much socially."

"What was she like?"

"American. Pushy. I didn't like her."

"She was an actress, Alex said."

"Not a successful one. You won't have heard of her."

"Did she ever come back from the States?"

"I've no idea. She wouldn't contact me if she did."

"Would she contact Alex?"

"She might. If she knew where he was."

Ramsay made an excuse and left after his second cup of the clear rather tasteless tea. He agreed to leave her with the set of prints so she could go over them with a magnifying glass at her leisure. She showed him out and when he had gone she sat down at the coffee table and picked up the photograph in one hand and the telephone in the other. She hadn't seen him for a year or more but she knew he would remember. She had interviewed him three of four times. He had tried to pick her up, right in front of the cameras. They hadn't had an affair, not exactly, but he had certainly tried hard enough. He really was very persistent.

***

Rupert Rutland was young, tall, good looking, charming. He hadn't got to the top by luck, he had done it by hard work and diligence, and by picking his issues. He had an unfailing instinct for a popular cause and an uncanny knack of making them his own.

"Mel, darling! How are you? You look absolutely fabulous." He'd seemed delighted when she phoned. Delighted, but not in the least surprised. But that was Rupert, she thought. That was his vanity. He kissed her on the cheek and stepped back to look her over, still holding her by the hand. "You look ravishing. Spain obviously suits you. Just look at that tan!"

"You look tired, Rupert. You're working too hard. But then you always did." He had changed, he had lost weight and the zest seemed to have gone out of him. "You should take a rest. Come out to Spain and play some golf. It will do you good."

"Is that an invitation?" He kissed her cheek again, pulling her towards him, an arm around her waist.

"No Rupert, it's a suggestion. But it's for your own good." She pushed him away gently, she didn't want to discourage him too much.

He went upstairs to shower and change. When he came back down he was a different man, bright and lively.

"Come on now, Mel. Relax. Have a drink." He took her by the hand and led her into the drawing room and poured them both champagne. "How are things at the Echo? How's that old war-horse Flaherty? Still hoping for his knighthood?"

"You know Flaherty?"

"Everyone knows Flaherty. He's a very important man, especially to a politician."

She took a sip of champagne. "I'm not at the Echo any more, Rupert. I'm freelance."

He looked surprised. "I didn't know. When did that happen?"

"Just a couple of weeks ago. It's a bit of a risk of course, but it's very exciting, I have to come up with my own ideas now. I have a new project as a matter of fact, maybe you can help me."

"If I can. You know you've only got to ask."

"I'm working on a piece about Alex Bowman. The drugs case? We met on the plane a couple of weeks ago."

"I remember Bowman. He was seconded to the NDIU for a time. That was before the trial of course."

"What is the NDIU, Rupert? How does it work?"

"The National Drugs Intelligence Unit? It's a clearinghouse for information, for intelligence about drugs. It's based at Scotland Yard."

"What does it do?"

"It doesn't actually *do* very much. It's the link between the two enforcement services, the police and customs. They make sure each service knows what the other one is doing."

"It doesn't sound very important."

"Important? I should say it's important! They track major shipments from South America and the Caribbean, carry out surveillance of known traffickers, the big ones, working with their counter-parts in other countries. They process every piece of intelligence we have about drugs. Secret stuff. Highly sensitive. If information like that got into the wrong hands it could be very damaging."

"Do you attend their meetings?"

"Sometimes, if the Home Secretary thinks it's appropriate. And I get all their minutes of course. So I can keep him briefed."

"And what about Bowman, do you think he was guilty? What's the official view?"

"Guilty? Of course he was guilty, otherwise he would have appealed, wouldn't he?"

"I hadn't thought of that!" Melanie blushed, spilling some of the champagne down the front of her dress. "How stupid of me! How very, very stupid" How could she have missed a trick like that? Something that obvious! She couldn't think of what to say next. "You remember Mary Berringer?"

"Mary? Of course. We were almost engaged once. The tabloids thought we were."

"You introduced her to Bowman?"

"Did I? No, I don't think so." He refilled both their glasses. "No, I'm sure I didn't."

"That's odd, I'm sure that's what Alex said." Why would one of them lie about such minor a thing? "I'll have to check my notes."

"This interest in Bowman, it is purely professional, is it?" Rutland was smiling.

"Purely." For some reason the word made her blush. "And yes Rupert, there is something you can do to help." She needed to change the subject. "I want to meet a man called Draycott. I think he can help with background."

"Peter Draycott? That's going to be rather difficult I'm afraid. He's very sick."

"Yes, I know about the stroke."

"I'll see what I can do. I don't promise mind, but for you I'll try." He looked at his watch. "Now what about dinner? *Aubergine* was full I'm afraid, they always are, so it'll have to be *Tante Claire*."

"*Tante Claire* is fine Rupert, but this one's on me. My thanks for fixing things with Peter Draycott." She leaned across and kissed him on the cheek, making a promise she knew she wouldn't keep.

***

Melanie drove into Framlington, following Ramsay's instructions. Through the middle of the village, passed the exquisite little church, along the edge of the common, over the hump back bridge and left along the riverbank. She passed the gatehouse to the great estate looking for the entrance to the narrow lane on the opposite side of the road. She had to break sharply to make the turn.

She pulled up outside the cottage, put the map back in her bag and gathered up her things. The cottage was lovely, a real gem. She guessed it was Queen Anne but she wasn't sure. Two storeys, red brick and white flint stone, partly covered with russet coloured ivy. She loved it. It gave her a real glow.

She walked up the rose lined path to the front door. She was about to knock when it opened. A woman in a nurse's uniform stood in the doorway, quite young, quite pretty, with rather severe features and no smile. If the cottage had a very welcoming feel, the nurse most certainly did not.

"I'm Sister Duncan." she said. "You must be Miss Drake."

"Melanie Drake. I'm here to see Mr. Draycott."

"He's expecting you." She gestured towards an open door leading off the tiny hall. "He's waiting in the lounge. He tires easily. I hope you won't keep him too long."

Melanie walked into a bright cheerful room, which looked out onto the sunny garden. Draycott sat in a wheel chair in the middle of the room. He seemed to be asleep. He must have been handsome once, but now his features lacked definition and the drool which ran from the corner of his mouth onto his collar deprived his countenance of any semblance of nobility. He was a truly pathetic figure. Melanie knocked on the open door. "Mr. Draycott? Mr. Draycott?"

He sat up with a jolt, took the piece of cloth in his hand and dabbed the moisture from his face. "I'm awfully sorry, I must have dozed off. You must be Miss Drake? A friend of Alex? I've been expecting you." He attempted a smile but it didn't really work.

"Melanie. Please call me Melanie."

“Of course. And you must call me Peter. Any friend of Alex.......” His voice trailed away as he dabbed at his face again with the soiled towel. He made a gesture with his limp hand and Melanie sat on an armchair opposite him, facing out into the garden, her back to the door.

“It’s very kind of you to see me, Peter. I mustn’t tire you. The nurse said on the phone how quickly you get tired.”

“Sister Duncan?” he frowned. “She makes such a fuss”.

Maybe, Melanie thought, but the nurse was right, Peter Draycott was a seriously sick man. “I won’t keep you long. Tell me about Alex. You were his mentor when he started out, Alex told me that, how he looked up to you. He looks up to you still.”

“Poor Alex. He should find a better role model.” His eyes smiled but his mouth didn’t move. “Tell me how I can help. If you’re not quick Sister Duncan will come and chase you away.”

Melanie didn’t know where to begin. Not at the beginning, that would take too long. “What went wrong?” she said. “Alex had.......so much promise.”

“He did. He did. So much promise. So many qualities. Except one.”

Melanie was startled. “And what was that?”

“Luck. Alex never had any luck. He never cracked a really big case.”

"He got close, didn't he? Just before the trial?" Her tone was defensive.

"He got close, but he didn't pull it off. It was uncanny. Whatever he did, the other side always stayed one step ahead." He seemed to be smiling. It was hard to tell.

Melanie looked out beyond the garden. Two men with dogs and shotguns were moving across the open field. "He was somebody then. Now he's, what? A nothing. A nobody. Is there nothing you can do to help him?"

"Melanie, look at me! What do you expect me to do?"

"I'm sorry, Peter." she smiled. "Of course, I understand. Tell me, just before he was arrested, he was onto something big?"

"He said so."

"Could the drugs have been planted? The drugs they found in his flat?"

"Planted?" He dabbed at his face again, first at his mouth and then at his moist spaniel eyes. "Planted? Could have been. Yes. Almost certainly were, I'd say. At any rate, that was his defence."

"Didn't he discuss it with you? Confide in you?"

"Not Alex Bowman. Far too independent for that. Far too strong headed." For the first time there was a sense of pride about him.

'But he must have turned to someone? Needed someone?"

'Not me. The girl, maybe. Ramsay. His lawyer. Family. Not me."

'I don't get it." Melanie said. "This was the end of his career, his marriage, everything. It was catastrophic! Why was there nobody there to help him? Not even you, Peter! His hero. His mentor."

'Nothing I could do once he'd been charged. These things are governed by a very strict set of rules. Quite rightly. Alex would agree with that."

"And the same applied to Ramsay."

"To anyone in the force. Anyone in an official position."

He was looking past Melanie, towards the door. She turned and saw the nurse standing there, not smiling. A cigarette hung from the corner of her mouth. It looked incongruous. The smoke caused her partly to close one eye and for a moment Melanie thought she was watching a black and white gangster movie.

"It's time for Mr. Draycott's medication." The cigarette moved as she spoke, ash dropping onto the front of her uniform. Draycott watched her but he didn't speak.

Melanie was almost relieved to see her. "I must go." She gathered up her things. "You're tired, Peter. I've taken too much of your time."

Sister Duncan watched her leave from the doorway. She didn't wave goodbye.

***

Melanie entered the village and parked the car outside the pub opposite the church. She entered the graveyard and found the Berringer family plot without difficulty. The small tombstone was simplicity itself. "Mary Proctor Berringer" and the two dates, just thirty-three years apart. She thought Proctor was a little odd. A family name no doubt. Then she remembered the press articles at the time of Mary's death. They had all said step daughter, every last one of them. Something Alex had never even mentioned. It was impossible he didn't know, so it probably wasn't important. But it was odd.

Melanie turned and walked up to the doors of the church, crossing herself as she entered.

***

James Fitzroy was in the shower when Harvey called. He grabbed a towel and picked up the phone.

"Fitzroy."

"James? It's me, Harvey."

"Hi Harvey! How's things?"

"Fine James, just fine. That project we discussed? Where you'd put a team together? How long would that take?"

"Day. Maybe two. Depends what's involved. What equipment we need."

"Tuesday. Can it be done by Tuesday?"

"Tuesday's days away. Should be fine. Depends what you need us to do."

"Can't go into that on the phone, James. I'll fly over to London. Come by your apartment in the morning. Do this for me James and I'll make you a rich man!"

***

Rupert Rutland's Mayfair house was small and wouldn't accommodate a large party, but it was the quality of the guest list that counted he said, not their number. Melanie had agreed to be his hostess for the evening, a thing she had done once or twice before.

Melanie arrived an hour before the guests were expected, to oversee arrangements with the staff. They sat in the first floor drawing room sipping chilled champagne.

"How was he?"

"Draycott? Fine. No, not fine, he's seriously unwell. He must have been a very impressive man once, Alex certainly thought so, but now he's just a shell. I think he's afraid of his nurse."

"Don't blame him. Nurses can be terrifying. Did he tell you anything useful?"

"Not really. To be honest I got out of there as quickly as I could. Didn't much care for his nurse, either. Reminded me of Mrs Danvers in *Rebecca*." She took a sip of her drink. "Tell me Rupert, if there had been a leak, where would it be, Scotland Yard or the NDIU."

"A leak? What on earth are you talking about?"

"Something Draycott said. Whatever Alex did, the opposition was always one step ahead. Alex said something similar."

"Melanie! Really! A leak at the Yard or the NDIU! It's too preposterous!"

"Really, Rupert. I'm serious! I think there was a leak at a very high level. I just don't know where."

"Melanie! That's just ridiculous. Trust me! I know! I move in these circles all the time!"

The doorbell rang and there were voices in the hall. A moment later the butler announced the first arrivals. The party was small but the guest list was impressive. A full Cabinet Minister, an Ambassador, two bankers, an eminent publisher and their respective wives, and a Bishop who didn't have one. Miguel Torres was there, Second Secretary at the Colombian Embassy, with his latest conquest, a girl of about eighteen who looked like a schoolgirl, except she had the body of starlet.

Marcus Esler arrived late, when the others were already on their second round of drinks. The butler showed him in and he spotted Melanie immediately. Hers was the only face he didn't know and he made straight for her across the crowded room. He couldn't resist a beautiful woman, and as often as not they couldn't resist him either. He took her hand and kissed it.

"Rupert tells me you're my hostess for the evening. I hope I'm sitting next to you, if not I shall complain."

"You're on my right, Sir Marcus. I chose you especially." She blushed, though it wasn't a lie.

"Not Sir Marcus, please. I don't like titles, they're so old fashioned don't you think, so elitist." He was charming, elegant, a perfect English gentleman. Everything about him was understated, effortless, contained. She guessed he was in his fifties but he was fit and lean and vigorous. There was an energy about him that was quite magnetic.

She had placed Esler on her right and Torres on her left. Pleasing them both would be difficult but not impossible. Pleasing men at dinner parties was part of her stock in trade. A professional skill just like any other. Her conversation was animated and her hands expressive, she was hardly able to resist touching them. Her voice was soft, almost inaudible, and they had to lean toward her, shoulder against shoulder, just to hear what she said.

It wasn't till brandy had been served that Rutland began to feel the ache in his joints that was always the first signal. He was afraid he might start sweating. There was no need to panic but he would have to get to the privacy of his bedroom quite quickly now, before it got any worse. He stood up and made his excuses to the rest of the room and went upstairs as slowly as he could. She would know what to say, she was perfect in the role of hostess. Things like that came to her quite naturally.

Rupert locked his bedroom door and took the pouch from its hiding place and went into the bathroom. Sitting on the toilet seat he removed the bandage from his ulcerated forearm. It was difficult now to find somewhere to push the needle into the vein. Soon he would have to start using his thigh, which he knew wasn't as effective. There was no panic but still there was relief as the magic potion entered his blood stream and began to circulate like an elixir. He felt its effect immediately, only a little at first, but building, as it added itself to the toxic brew that already filled his veins. He blacked out for a while and when he came to he was slumped against the tiled wall like a stuffed doll. His mind cleared and he remembered where he was. He felt fine now, absolutely fine. He thought of going back downstairs to join his guests again but he was afraid they might notice the change in him and decided against it. He made it to the bed with an ease that surprised him and lay down. He knew he wouldn't sleep for a while, it didn't affect him that way, it heightened his level of perception wonderfully, even now, after so much abuse.

He didn't recognise the noise at first. It was familiar but he couldn't quite remember what it meant. When he realised it was his door they were knocking on he sat up with a start. He went quickly to the bathroom to check his appearance in the mirror. He saw the bandage lying on the floor and put it back on with a practised hand and dropped his shirtsleeve into place to cover it. Then he went to the door and opened it.

"My, you do sleep soundly." Said Melanie. "I've sent them all away, it's late enough anyway." She was leaning against the door, playing with the buttons of her blouse.

Rutland wondered if she was drunk but she looked too cool for that, so it must be him. His pulse was racing but he was calm, detached, floating above the scene. A participant and an observer at the same time.

"Why do you lock your door?"

"Ministerial papers. They like us to take precautions." He was pleased with his invention and began to laugh.

She knew why he locked his door. She knew why he laughed. She knew why his pupils were dilated, why he was sweating. She had been high herself enough times, high as a kite, but never quite like he was. "What have you been up to Rupert?"

Rutland grinned, pressing his finger to his nose. "Coke! Like some?"

"I don't do coke Rupert, you should know that."

"She doesn't do coke! Such a good catholic girl!" His eyes widened in disbelief. "She works for Flaherty and she doesn't do coke!"

"Not any more, ...something's the matter with your arm, Rupert. Let me see."

"It's nothing, just a superficial burn. It's painful but it's not important. It'll go away."

"Let me see." Her voice was very soothing but he didn't move. Suddenly she grabbed his forearm tight and watched him grimace with the pain. In a second she had his shirt off and held his bandaged forearm in her hand. She could smell the ulceration now. "I knew it! Mainlining! Rupert you must be mad! You're crazy! Absolutely crazy!" She let his forearm drop to his side and stepped back away from him in horror.

He sat on the bed and put his head in his hands. He didn't speak for a while, then he said, "Help me, Mel. For Christ sake help me!" He looked up and saw the expression in her face. At first he thought it was compassion, but then he saw what it really was. Contempt.

"It's medical help you need, Rupert. Don't waste any time. I don't think you've got very long."

***

The following morning Melanie slept late. It was Saturday and she had nothing planned. She took a shower, made herself coffee, and sat on the living room floor flicking through the pile of photographs. She couldn't tell why, but it really didn't look like a funeral, more social gathering, a garden party. She felt she knew them, some of them at least, Esler and Torres and Rutland. She wasn't much interested in Torres, he might be involved, probably was, but he had nothing to do with Alex, with the trial. That left her with Rutland and Esler. Rutland had the right connections, moved in the right circles, but he was an abuser, a victim. Drugs would break him. Which left her with Esler. But Esler worked in

-habilitation, getting kids off the street and sorting them ut. Which left her with nothing. She picked up the one. It rang for ages before he answered.

Rutland."

Rupert, it's me, Mel. I think we should talk. I'm on my ay over."

e went to the bathroom to pee and saw himself in the racked mirror. He wondered how it was possible people adn't noticed the state he was in, the sunken cheeks, the feless eyes, the lethargy in his movements. People were lind, they saw what they wanted to see, saw him as he sed to be, young and vigorous and full of promise. He as flawed, fatally flawed, like the cracked mirror he saw imself in.

e showered and shaved and dressed in casual weekend lothes. He wanted to make an impression. He needed er. She was strong. Someone he could lean on. When lelanie arrived he took her into the kitchen and made offee. He was fine now, absolutely fine. But he knew it ouldn't last. In an hour, two at the most, the whole errifying process would start all over again.

You need help, Rupert. Medical help."

is joints were beginning to ache. The palms of his hands nd his brow were moist with sweat. "I know that Mel. ut it's not just me. A thing like this could bring the overnment down. If the press gets hold of it, it could be igger than Profumo."

"Forget about the press. If you don't get help very soo you're going to die. Is that a better solution?"

He put his head in his hands and she saw his chest heav as he fought back the tears. "Help me, Mel. Fc Christsake help me!"

She couldn't look him in the face, She despised him. Bu she had to stick with him. For Alex's sake she mus "Look Rupert, there may be a way out. Private. Discree No doctors. No publicity. Have you heard c Nightingale?"

"Nightingale?"

"Marcus Esler runs it. It's based in the East End. The look after kids mainly, take them off the streets an straighten them out. There's a file about them at the Echo They have a file on most things."

"You've been speaking to Flaherty?" He panicked. Hi face was contorted, the corners of his mouth pulled bac in a hideous grin.

"I haven't spoken to anyone, Rupert. There's no need. still have access to the computer files. I have a terminal a home. I've been reading up on Esler. He set u Nightingale when he retired from the diplomatic servic about five years ago. Thousands of kids have gon through the system, not just in London, they have centre in Leeds, Sheffield, a dozen other places. Apparently it' very successful. Discipline is very tight."

"Nightingale!" He resisted as long as he could but when felt the onset of nausea he knew he was out of control. He would agree to anything she asked, just as long as she would leave him alone for long enough to get to the bathroom for a fix.

"Look Rupert, all we'll do today is drive out to Stepney and take a look around. We'll talk to Esler and find out how the system works, whether or not they can help you. Take a couple of days to think it over. Then you can either go to Esler and put your cards on the table, or go to a regular doctor and hope it doesn't leak out. It'll be your decision in the end, OK?"

***

They drove through the West End, congested with tourists and shoppers and headed east to the City, the deserted financial district, through Whitechapel and along the Mile End road to Stepney. Here too the pavements were crowded, but the ethnic mix would have rivalled Cairo or Calcutta. The street market was a bazaar. It hardly seemed like England at all.

Rutland parked a couple of streets away from their final destination, a disused Victorian chapel in a street of dilapidated terraced houses. Gentrification hadn't reached this part of town, maybe it never would. There was a feeling of decay, of irreversible decline into deeper and deeper deprivation. This was fertile territory for the pimps, the pushers, the angels of mercy. They climbed the pitted limestone steps and Melanie crossed herself as she entered.

The doorway of Our Lady Of Mercy was crowded. Boys, girls, tall, short, fat, thin, all of them smartly dressed, all of them neat and tidy. There was a sameness about them too, something regimented, well drilled, almost military. They made a very good first impression.

"Mornin' Miss. Mornin' Sir." It was one of the girls who spoke. There was a badge on her blouse that said her name was Mandy. The beautiful boy next to her was Gabriel.

"Good morning, Mandy. I'm Melanie, and this is my friend Rupert. Is Marcus here?" She knew first names would be the thing.

"He's in his office. I'll show you." She looked at Rupert with approval, as if she would like him for lunch. She turned and led the way through the vestibule.

They found Esler in a cramped little office with a bare wood floor, recently scrubbed. He was dressed in casual slacks and an open necked button down shirt. He looked thoroughly at ease, in context. He was going through a bunch of files with a child's name on each. He looked up when they entered and smiled.

"I couldn't resist coming." said Melanie. "I've heard so much about Nightingale, the work you do with the kids. It sounds marvellous. It must be so rewarding."

“Rewarding? Yes, I suppose it is. I never really thought of it that way.” Esler wondered why they had come. “I hope this isn't just a professional interest? We don't much care for publicity. It's no good for the kids. I'm sure you understand.” He’d had trouble with journalists before. Photographers were the worst, always snooping around.

“I’m always looking for a story.” Melanie blushed. “Human interest." She glanced across at Rutland but he seemed to be under control.

"There's lots of human interest here. Generalities or specifics?"

"Oh! Specifics. Specifics every time."

Esler got up and went to the door, opened it, and stuck his head outside. "Mandy." In seconds she had rejoined them in the room. Esler pointed to a chair by the window. She sat down and crossed her hands demurely in her lap.

"Where are you from, Mandy?" said Esler.

"Sheffield, Sir."

"How long have you been in London?"

"About a year, Sir."

"You ran away from home?"

"Yes, Sir."

"Why did you do that, Mandy?"

"My step father..........I'd rather not say, Sir."

Melanie felt a tightening at her throat. She started to blush. The thing was too raw, too wounding. She had almost forgotten why they had come. She felt she was on trial, that Esler was testing her, examining her motives, and of course he was right, she was there under false pretences. She was an intruder.

Esler saw her discomfiture, but went on. "Where did we find you, Mandy?"

"At King's Cross, Sir. In the station."

"What were you doing there?"

"I was on the game, Sir." She was looking at her hands.

"Why were you on the game, Mandy?"

"To buy drugs, Sir."

"What drugs were you using?"

"Crack, Sir. And heroin to help me come down."

There was a matter-of-factness about this exchange that Melanie found disturbing, the child's responses especially. In Esler it was to be expected, he must have helped hundreds of kids like her, possibly thousands. But Mandy was so poised, so controlled, it was chilling.

Esler turned to Melanie. "Is there anything you'd like to ask her yourself?"

It was a challenge. He had made his point. She really shouldn't be there. She was making use of the poor child. She was a parasite. She felt indecent, unclean. "Not now." She spoke directly to the child. "Perhaps I'll come and see you another time Mandy, get to know you better. Perhaps we can be friends?" She knew she was misusing the child but she couldn't think of anything else to say. She glanced at Rutland, hoping he might help. He was slumped forward in his chair now, his forearms crossed on his stomach. She didn't look, but she knew Esler was watching him too.

"Yes, Miss. Thank you, Miss." Mandy had heard it all before. Nice grown-ups were always offering her things. She got up to leave.

"I'd no idea. I'd really no idea." said Melanie as the door closed behind her. "The work you do, Marcus, it's marvellous, truly marvellous." She wanted to leave but didn't feel she could. "How do you cure them?"

"Oh! We don't cure them. There isn't any cure, not in the medical sense, no more than there is with alcohol. Besides, curing them is the last thing we're interested in. Chronologically, that is. If they thought we wanted to cure them, they'd never come to us in the first place. The number one priority, ours and theirs, is to house them, nourish them, and look after their general health. After that we just try to teach them to look after themselves, and after one another. The best thing we can do is give them a sense of purpose, a feeling they belong. Above all that they can lead useful lives. Contribute something. When they're ready we send them back out into the community, to recruit others. They're like a little army.

At one time I thought of putting them in uniform, but of course that wouldn't work."

He watched Rutland take out a handkerchief and wipe his forehead and the palms of his hands. He looked positively ill. This seemed to worry Esler deeply. He glanced back at Melanie to see if she had noticed and realised she had. Esler kept looking at Rutland, staring at him. Rutland was avoiding eye contact, staring at his trembling hands. Suddenly Esler's face cleared. A decision had been made. He turned to Melanie again.

"Would you like me to show you round? You haven't seen the crypt yet, have you? The ones you saw outside have been here for a while. The new arrivals are down in the crypt. I should warn you, they're in a much worse state."

There were fifty or so beds in the crypt, all of them taken, boys and girls randomly mixed in the order of their arrival. The average age was somewhere in the early teens. It was late morning now but most of the kids were still not up. Esler led them down the rows of beds. There was a smell, fetid, stale, unwashed.

Melanie looked at the hopeless staring eyes, the unkempt hair, the acnied faces. There was a lethargy about these children, a lifelessness, no buzz, no conversation. The contrast between them and the group upstairs was total. Esler was achieving miracles. It made her feel ashamed she had come.

***

Fitzroy lay on the cliff top a hundred yards from the beach. There was a good moon and he had watched the launch come into the shallows and a handful of men wade out to unload the cargo. Then the launch had disappeared to re-join the mother ship somewhere over the horizon. He switched on the walkie-talkie. "Hud? Receive me?"

"Loud and clear, James. What's happening?"

"Stuff's ashore. They'll be moving in a few minutes. Target's a Rangerover. Hold on and I'll give you the reg. number." He put down the walkie-talkie and peered through the night glasses. "Hud? V 397 CLR. Dark colour. Probably green. There's a team of minders in a Honda 4x4 but the stuff's definitely in the Rangerover. Pick them up at the main road and I'll follow once they've had time to get clear. Stay well back."

"What if they're not headed for London?"

"Where else would you go with twenty kilos of cocaine?

Fitzroy watched the target struggle up the grassy knoll away from the beach and join the single-track road, the Honda following behind. Ten minutes later he climbed into his own Rangerover to follow. "Hud?" He spoke into the walkie-talkie. "How's things?"

"So far so good. There's no traffic so I can stay well back."

"They'll be headed for the M4. If it looks like they're not, give me a call. Talk to you again once we're over the bridge."

An hour or so later Fitzroy had caught up with Hud Hudson and flashed his lights to let him know he was there. Hud accelerated, moved out in front of the target and disappeared from view.

"James?"

"Hud?"

"How's things?"

"According to plan."

"Did you call Jack?"

"I'll talk to him once we're passed Membury. Just to confirm."

"How's the love life, James?"

"Arabella? Arabella's fine!"

"Rich?"

"Filthy. Absolutely filthy. Can't get my hands on it till she's twenty-one. But what's a couple of years till I take early retirement."

"Good lay?"

"Good enough. But if you were worth twenty-five million Hud, I'd shag you anyway you want it."

They passed the service area at Membury just after 3 a.m. Twenty miles ahead Jack White lay in the long grass above the westbound carriageway facing towards the on-coming target. The walkie-talkie was in his hand and in front of him, supported on its Parker-Hale bipod, lay the PM Super Magnum bolt-action sniper's rifle, loaded with five .388 high velocity cartridges.

"Jack?"

"James?"

"Ready?"

"Yes."

"Should be with you in about ten minutes. Hud will flash his lights three times. Next thing you'll see is a Rangerover and a Honda 4x4 following behind. Take out the Honda. The next thing you'll see is me. But I'll stay well behind so I won't get involved when the Honda crashes. That clear?"

"Quite clear, James." Jack White was a marksman. *The* marksman. He'd been spotted at Bisley, competing for the Ashburton Shield, when he was just seventeen. He had Olympic Gold written all over him but he'd never entered another competition. They wouldn't let him. Talent like that had to be kept under wraps. But what Fitzroy wanted was one hell of a shot. Take out a moving vehicle at a distance of some three hundred yards. In darkness. In daylight he could hit a fixed target with Super Magnum time after time at a distance of a thousand yards. No problem. But at night? And a target moving at a little under seventy miles an hour? So Jack had picked his spot with care where the target would be coming off a long bend and for fifteen seconds or so be moving straight towards him, minimizing any lateral movement.

There was hardly any traffic but it took a while before he spotted Hud coming off the bend below, flashing his lights one two three. Jack shouldered the rifle and peered through the night sight. Next came the Rangerover. Jack took in a gulp of air, pulled the Super Magnum tight into his left shoulder and waited for the Honda. As it came out of the bend, travelling straight towards him, Jack White lowered the rifle down the side of the vehicle till the cross hairs in the night sight centred on the offside tyre. He caressed the trigger and released a single round..

In his rear-view mirror Hud Hudson saw the Honda career into the central barrier, swerve back across the carriageway and disappear into the ditch at the side of the road. He slowed his speed till the Rangerover caught up and a few seconds later Fitzroy moved into position tight on the target's tale.

"Jesus Mary and Joseph!" Paddy O'Brien applied the breaks.

"What?" said Mick Grady, seated beside him.

"The Honda's gone for a Burton! Must have blown a tyre!"

Mick Grady swivelled round in his seat to see Fitzroy sitting on his tale. “Holy mother of God! I think we’ve got company Paddy.”

Fitzroy touched the accelerator and shunted into the target vehicle. Paddy applied the breaks again so as not to crash into the car in front. “Looks like we’re the meat in the sandwich Mick. Are you tooled up?”

“I’m not, Paddy. How about you?”

“Me neither. The armoury was in the Honda.”

Mick Grady turned round in his seat again. “He’s making a sign. I think he wants us to follow the car in front.”

Paddy O’Brien glanced to his right. A third escort had joined the procession, making it impossible for him to pull out into the next lane. “Looks like we have no choice.”

The convoy took the next exit and ten minutes later pulled off the road into the car park of an abandoned motel. Fitzroy Hudson and White dismounted and walked over to the Rangerover. Mick and Paddy sat still and waited. “OK guys. Hand it over.” said Fitzroy as he opened the door.

“And what would that be, Sir?” said Paddy. “If you don’t mind me askin’.”

“That would be the cocaine, old son. Twenty kilos of cocaine.” Fitzroy stepped aside so they could get a clear view of Jack White and the twenty seven-inch barrel of the Super Magnum. “Is this going to be difficult?”

“No Sir, I suppose not.” said Mick. “What do you think, Paddy? Shall we let them take it?”

“That would be best.” Said Paddy. “Better than one of them bullets in the gut.” He and Mick got out of car, opened the rear door and unloaded the twenty one-kilo packages on the ground.”

“Thank you.” Said Fitzroy.

“My pleasure.” Said Paddy. “Will that be all, Sir?”

“Just one more thing.” Said James, unzipping his bomber jacket.

“And what would that be, Sir?”

Fitzroy raised the Beretta and fired two shots at point blank range, hitting each of them square in the middle of the forehead. Mick and Paddy slumped silently to the ground, blood mingling with oil-stained mud. Their bodies twitched in unison and were still.

“Jesus Fitzroy!” screamed Hudson. “Why the fuck did you do that!”

Jack White had gone pale. “You cold-blooded bastard, Fitzroy! You’re crazy! This is the last time I work with you! You’re not real!”

“That goes for me too.” yelled Hud. “Next time you need help, call somebody else!”

Hud Hudson and Jack White climbed into their respective vehicles and drove away fast. Fitzroy opened the door to his Rangerover and started to load the coke. Suddenly blinding lights went on all around the car park. “You had to do it, James. I know that.” It was Harvey. Fitzroy couldn’t see him, he was standing behind one of the lights. “It was cool, James. I’m impressed.”

Fitzroy shaded his eyes with his left hand, the Beretta still in his right.

“Would you mind dropping the shooter, James?” said Harvey. “Makes me a little nervous.”

Fitzroy didn’t move.

“I know you’re tempted, James. Who wouldn’t be? There’s a fortune in snow just lying there between us. Problem is José and a couple of the boys are back here with me. ‘Course they’re not as good as you are James. Not as cool. They don’t have your training, your experience. Difference is they can see you. Drop the piece, James. Then we can all get to bed.”

Fitzroy threw the Beretta onto the ground. “That’s a good boy, James. Now get into your car and go home. I’ll talk to you in the morning.”

Harvey watched them load the snow into the car and smiled. “We’ll keep this little lot off the market for a while." he thought. "Create some tension out there. See what happens."

***

The blue envelope with the words Private & Confidential printed in red in the top left hand corner beneath the Home Office seal reached Ramsay's desk late in the afternoon. There was nothing unusual about the envelope. He would get three or four of them in a normal working week. But he always opened them right away. Every once in a while they contained something really important.

He took out the single piece of notepaper with the ministry seal embossed at the top and stared down and the barely legible scrawl. He could hardly believe what he read. It could be just the breakthrough they needed. He looked at his watch. How on earth was he going to fill the next five hours?

***

Daisy boarded the tube at Waterloo. The evening rush hour was over. The office workers had gone back to their burrows in the suburbs. So the carriage was almost empty. In a far corner sat a girl alone, her coat too short to conceal her nurses uniform. He knew she had glanced at him as he boarded the train but she looked away again immediately, taking no notice of him as she had been told. She would avoid eye contact with him at all costs. He could stare at her as much as he liked, he knew she wouldn't risk a second look. She could describe him accurately of course, even from that one brief glance. She would remember the white hair, the colourless skin, the oddly Negroid features, the eyes. People always remembered an albino.

He got off the train at Green Park and stood on the platform and waited till the doors closed but still she didn't look at him again, though as far as she knew he was harmless.

***

They sat in the first floor sitting room of Rutland's house, overlooking the mews. Melanie had got there early to make sure he was in good shape. She needed a drink. He had offered her one but she refused, so he wouldn't feel obliged to have one too. He seemed fine. She wondered when he had had his last fix. "I wish you'd tell me what you're going to say."

"All in good time, Mel. Ramsay should be here in an hour or so."

Rutland glanced at his watch. He appeared quite calm, at peace with himself. He was about to blow the whole thing wide open, and himself up with it. "I think I'd better make some notes. I don't want to leave anything out." He got up and went down to his study off the landing below, overlooking the patio at the rear of the house. He sat at the desk with his back to the door, looking out at the darkness.

He wondered where he should begin, with his own involvement or the way the organisation was run. He wasn't an insider, just a paid informer providing the intelligence they needed, paid by feeding his habit. So he decided on the organisation first. He knew it inside out. He placed three dots at the top of the sheet of paper, one above and two below, and joined them in a triangle. He labelled each of the dots and began to write.

Daisy walked up Berkeley Street and across the Square to the mews on the other side. It was beginning to rain, a light English drizzle. The uniformed policeman stood outside number 27, single-handedly protecting the minister's house from the terrorist's bomb. Daisy knew he would be there. But he knew that when he turned into the street at the top of the mews he could get up onto the wall that divided the small gardens at the back and work his way along to drop down into the minuscule patio at the back of Rutland's house.

Melanie poured herself a scotch and picked up a magazine. But she couldn't concentrate. She was too tense. She had no idea what he was going to say to Ramsay, or where it would lead. She just hoped it would help Alex, though she didn't see how. Maybe it was too much to hope for. But it was worth a shot. Anything was worth a shot.

Daisy had no trouble with the flimsy lock and at this time of the evening he knew the alarm would not be set. He entered the kitchen and moved silently to the foot of the stairs. He could see the light under the door on the landing, which he knew was Rutland's study. The minister was working late. The stairs creaked slightly but his movements were swift and sure and he reached the door in no time and gave it a push. Rutland sat at the desk with his back to the door but he must have been aware of it opening because he looked up and caught sight of

Daisy's reflection in the window. It was too late. Daisy had the pad ready in his hand. Rutland had no time to recognise the whiff of chloroform as Daisy pressed it to his face. There was a moment's resistance. Then Rutland slumped forward across the desk.

Melanie got up and went to the window to look out. The mews was deserted, a dull sheen on the damp cobbles under the glare of the streetlight. She couldn't see the bobby but she knew he was there, standing in the doorway below. She felt safe. Ramsay should be here soon. She wondered what it was about George she didn't like, something about his manner, his lack of style. He had a great big chip on his shoulder, something Alex hadn't told her about. Maybe Alex hadn't noticed, he wasn't good with details. It was hard to imagine Ramsay and Bowman working together as a team, somehow they just didn't fit. She decided to fix herself another drink.

Daisy had hoped for more of a struggle. He liked people to resist him, to fight back, to hit out. That way he could teach them a lesson. But his instructions tonight were very clear, he must leave no mark on his victim. He took the little bundle from his jacket pocket and placed it on the desk, unwrapping it carefully. Rutland was in his shirtsleeves, which made the procedure easy. In his gloved hand Daisy took the syringe with its highly toxic dose of cocaine, inserted the needle into the vein and watched as the glass phial emptied. Rutland went into a brief spasm and was still. Daisy felt a sudden emptiness fill the room. That was when he heard the noise from the room above. A floorboard creaked. A door opened.

"Rupert? You're out of ice!" Daisy heard her tread on the stair. He tensed. "Rupert?..............never mind, I'll get it myself."

It hadn't occurred to Daisy that Rutland might not be alone. He wondered what he should do. Killing her would be a mistake. The cover for Rutland's death was perfect. Two bodies would blow the whole thing open. But if she pushed the door he would have no choice. His pulse was racing. He felt himself harden. He prayed she would open the door. He heard her light tread on the stairs. Then the noise in the noise from the kitchen below. He wasn't sure he had shut the patio door. A moment later he heard her on the stairs again as she passed the study without a word.

Daisy placed the syringe in Rutland's right hand, making sure he got a good set of prints. He had to remove the pen. Rutland had been writing notes. He had written a couple of pages. Daisy glanced down and realised immediately what it was. He stuffed the papers in his pocket and wondered again what to do about the woman. His instinct was to go up to the sitting room and have a little fun. But he remembered the bobby standing in the street and decided against it.

In less than a minute he was in the street again. The only problem was the forced lock on the kitchen door, but with any nobody would look for signs of an intruder. They would see Rutland's ulcerated forearm and the syringe in his right hand and look no further. The whole thing was neat and tidy and according to instructions. But it wasn't satisfying. Not satisfying at all.

There was a pub at the end of the street and Daisy spent the next hour there building up his courage. It was marvellous what a few good stiff whiskies could do for him. He had promised himself a bit of fun tonight and by God he was going to have it! He kept thinking about the woman in Rutland's house. He didn't even know what she looked like. Then he remembered the girl on the tube who didn't have the guts to look him in the face. She'd be tucked up safe and sound in bed by now, but there would be others, lots of others. But it was the woman he wanted, the woman in Rutland's house. He left a fifty-pound note on the bar. He didn't wait for his change.

"Blimey!" The barman tucked the note into the till. "Funny lookin' geezer, left more than twenty quid in change! Fancy somat on the 'ouse, guv?"

"Why not?" Ramsay wasn't on duty, not in any formal sense. "I'll have a small whisky." He looked at his watch. He was early. In another ten minutes or so he would have to make a move.

The barman poured a double and one for himself, he was still ten quid ahead on the transaction. "Live local, do yer guv?"

Ramsay savoured the scotch. It wasn't his usual tipple, a single malt, something Alex would enjoy. That was the difference between him and Bowman. Alex had acquired polish. "Just visiting."

"Thought so." The barman sniffed, eyeing the frayed cuffs on Ramsay's soiled raincoat. "Copper, aren't yer?"

"Copper." Ramsay confirmed, emptying his glass.

"Takes all sorts." Ramsay heard the barman mutter as he closed the door behind him. He strolled to the end of the street, turned left into the mews and saw the bobby standing guard, one of three who shared the twenty-four hour duty. He approached and flashed his ID.

"I'm expected, sergeant."

The man made a half salute as he pressed the doorbell. He could smell the whisky on his superior's breath but he looked away, pretending not to notice.

"All right, sergeant. It's just a social call." Ramsay put him at his ease. "Try the knocker will you, maybe the bell's not working." A moment later he heard the hurried tread on the stairs and the door was opened.

"Hello, George." Said Melanie. "He's in the study, writing some notes. Why don't you go up?" Melanie pointed to the door on the landing and stepped outside to take a breath of air. The night was chill. She stood in the glare of the streetlight, wrapping her arms around her body against the cold. She sensed a movement in the shadow of the doorway opposite. She could see nothing but she knew he was there. She could feel his eyes watching her. She turned and went back inside.

Ramsay climbed the stairs and pushed open the door to see Rutland slumped forward across the desk. His first reaction was to shake the minister from his sleep, but then he saw the syringe in his right hand and the sleeve rolled up on the ulcerated forearm. The smell was putrid.

The body was still warm. "Check the rear entrance for me, sergeant." Ramsay's voice was flat and without expression.

The sergeant had followed Ramsay up the stairs and stood peering over Ramsay's shoulder. "Suicide?"

"Just check the rear entrance, sergeant." It certainly looked like suicide. Ramsay took a good look at Rutland's bruised and ulcerated forearm. He had been mainlining for a year or more. It must have cost him a fortune.

"There's been a break in all right, Sir." The sergeant called from the kitchen. "Call this security?" He muttered. "It's shocking! Waste of tax payers money!"

Ramsay took the hand written note from his pocket and re-read it for the umpteenth time. He would have to send the silly woman back to Spain. Putting her name to such a thing was lethal. Absolutely lethal.

***

Daisy didn't make it to the tube, he found what he wanted before he got there, standing in front of the brightly light window of the car show room at the corner of Berkeley Street and Piccadilly. The boy was special, a real prize. Two into one will go. He wore make up, discreet, deftly applied. He didn't want to be mistaken for a tart. The dress must have set him back a couple of hundred, the shoes were expensive too but from the way he stood he wasn't used to them yet, hadn't quite mastered the balance.

Daisy clutched the little bottle in his hand, but somehow it seemed inappropriate. The boy looked clean, not addicted, except to himself and to money. The price was fifty, a bargain. Daisy hailed a taxi and they headed off across the Thames and on towards Clapham Common. They hardly spoke in the back of the cab. There was nothing much to say. When they reached the edge of the Common, Daisy took his hand from the boy's silken thigh and tapped on the glass partition. "This'll do." He stood on the pavement and paid the driver, the boy standing next to him, puzzled.

"We'll walk the last bit. Can't be too careful." Daisy didn't explain but set off towards the middle of the Common, the boy teetering on his heels on the soft ground, as he tried to keep up. When he reached a thicket out of range of the street lamps and the lights on the passing cars Daisy waited for the boy, turning towards him, his arms open slightly, pleading. They embraced for the first time. Hands searching, fumbling, grabbing. Mouths joined, open, hungry. Tongues linked, probing, licking. The boy was surprised at Daisy's ardour, feeling him harden, his breathing short, irregular, panting, trembling, coming. Suddenly Daisy released him and stepped back, raising his right arm and striking the boy hard on the side of the mouth. The boy couldn't control his legs and tottered into the undergrowth. Daisy grabbed him from behind as he fell, striking him hard on the nape of the neck. The boy was good. Strong. Desperate. Wild. He fought like hell. Kicking, biting, scratching, digging his nails in deep, tearing at Daisy's hair.

When it was over Daisy realised he had a problem. He should have thought of it sooner. The cabby would remember the boy, the expensive dress, the shoes. No need to panic. He took the scalpel from his pocket and removed each of the fingers in turn, severing them at the first joint, nearest the hand. He was an expert now, a surgeon couldn't have done it any better. There was hardly any blood. He stripped the body, laid the dress out on the ground and placed the severed fingers and the other silken things on top of it, making a tight little bundle, which he placed inside his jacket.

Within an hour he was back at the apartment building. He caught sight of himself in the mirrors in the lobby. The scratch marks down the side of his face were deep and vivid, his shirtfront flecked with blood. The porters were off duty at this hour and he made his way to the basement. He opened the bundle to look again at the boy's silken things, touch them, smell them. That was when he noticed. Two of the fingers were missing. He re-wrapped the bundle and threw it in the furnace.

***

12

Fitzroy lived in an expensive block of flats, just off the Fulham Road. Ramsay waited in the lobby for a couple of hours the following afternoon till Fitzroy came home from what must have been a very good lunch. The girl on his arm was lovely, no more than eighteen, and from the way she was dressed Daddy was loaded. They were both a little tipsy. She kissed Fitzroy's cheek as they entered the lift and Ramsay heard her say, "Not Zermat darling. Zermat's where the wrinklies go. I want my honeymoon in Aspen."

Ramsay decided to give them five minutes. He had forgotten how quickly things could happen when you're in the right frame of mind. He pressed the bell long and hard and when Fitzroy eventually opened the door and peeped round the edge, he shoved against it with his boot and barged into the flat. In a second Fitzroy had him pinned to the wall, one knee rammed into Ramsay's groin, a forearm pressed against his throat, constricting his breathing.

"And who may I ask are you?" Fitzroy was red in the face and furious. "What is the meaning of this? Who are you?" Fitzroy flicked Ramsay's feet from under him, sending Ramsay to the floor face down, one arm pinned behind his back.

The girl was standing near the window, stripped to the waist, a glass of champagne in her hand. Her breasts were small and lovely. She turned towards Ramsay so he could admire her, she liked to be admired. Fitzroy threw her blouse at her across the room and she caught it in mid air with the pretty little movement of a dancer. She seemed reluctant to put it on. James could be such a spoilsport!

"James, don't be so pompous!" Arabella giggled. "He's nice, I like a bit of rough. He's a policeman, can't you tell? Or a tax inspector! James darling, what have you been doing? I can't marry you if you've been up to no good! Daddy would be furious. He'd cut me off completely." Arabella giggled again and sipped her champagne.

The look on Fitzroy's face changed to abject terror. The colour drained from his face. He collapsed into a chair. His legs wouldn't hold him and he felt an almost uncontainable urge to shit. He looked at Ramsay in despair. "Who are you?"

"I'm a friend of Harvey Lieberman." Ramsay croaked as he got to his feet, massaging his throat, trying to swallow. "I'd like a little chat. In private." Ramsay nodded towards the girl.

Fitzroy felt the relief surge through him. He put his head in his hands and took a few deep breaths. Then he got up and went to the drinks cabinet and poured himself a stiff whisky. "Help yourself." he said to Ramsay as he resumed his seat. Arabella came and sat on the arm of Fitzroy's chair and put her arm around him while she took a good long look at Ramsay.

"She really will have to go." It was an effort not to say Sir.

"Arabella darling, please, do you mind most awfully?" Fitzroy looked up at her pleadingly.

"Mind? I should say I fucking mind! You've ruined my whole afternoon! And my weekend! I have to go back to bloody Benenden on Sunday!"

James could see she was upset. He turned to Ramsay. "Look, how long is this going to take?"

"About an hour."

"Arabella, darling." James picked up his jacket and took a handful of notes from his wallet. "Slide over to Harvey Nicks and buy yourself something nice. Pop back in an hour. All right? There's a love!" He kissed her cheek and patted her behind.

Arabella smiled at George on her way out. Shopping was her second favourite thing.

"Nice girl." Ramsay remarked when she had gone.

"Not a girl!" said Fitzroy crossly. "Arabella's my fiancée. Father's worth a bloody fortune!"

***

"Did he bite?" Bowman downed his first pint of the evening.

"Fitzroy? He bit all right. What other option does he have?"

"What sort of bloke is he? Can he handle himself?"

"Physically he's hard as nails. You'd expect that, being ex-SAS. Mentally I'm not so sure. I've never seen anyone so shit scared. When I told the little blighter I really was a policeman he had to go to the bathroom. He was in there so long I thought the poor bastard might have slit his wrists."

"But he'll do it?"

"He'll do it all right." Said Ramsay. "You don't think Lieberman will smell a rat?"

"There's no reason why he should. Fitzroy delivered the first consignment without a problem. It was routine. I'll know for sure in a couple of days. I have to drop in on Harvey on my way back to Marrakech, to give him a progress report."

"He knows you're in London now?"

"Sure he does. I can't make a move without his approval. He runs a very tight ship. As far as Harvey knows, I've been buying a shipment of electronic gear for the security installation up at the farm. Stuff you can't get in Morocco."

Alex got up and went to the bar for two more pints of bitter. The pub crowd had thinned out to a core of real drinkers. The curtain had gone up all over the West End and they would have the place to themselves for a couple of hours. They might even get in a game of darts. From the bar Alex was able to scrutinise Ramsay and was pleased with what he saw. His friend was in better shape than the last time he had seen him. He was leaner and fitter and the old gleam was back in his eye. Best of all his drinking seemed to be under control. Bowman was able to match him pint for pint.

"Any luck with the serial killer thing?"

Ramsay took a drink and wiped the white moustache from his lips with the back of his hand. "We finally had our first break through, at last our boy's done something careless. Dropped two of the fingers near the body. You were right about why he chopped them off. When the lab boys analysed the debris under the fingernails they gave us a good clear description of the killer, narrowed it down to a tiny percentage of the population. A couple of flakes of skin and one precious hair are all it took. Our man's an albino."

"That should make things easy."

"Certainly should." said George. "Aren't too many of them around." He was thinking of the one he had seen in the pub on his way to call on Rutland, but he didn't mention this to Bowman. It hadn't occurred to him right away that it might be the same man but working backwards from the time of death of the boy to the time of death of the minister, left just two hours to be accounted for. He knew from the barman in the pub that the albino had been there for about an hour drinking whisky, tanking himself up. That left an hour for him to pick up the boy and make his way to Clapham Common. Maybe it was too neat a fit. But word had gone out to London's cabbies anyway. It shouldn't take long to get some kind of feedback.

But something else was on George Ramsay's mind, something he wanted to avoid but couldn't. He wasn't sure how to broach the subject. Alex could be very touchy where his women were concerned, but his judgements about women were often flawed, they could be lethal, Mary Berringer was proof enough of that.

"Nice girl, that Melanie Drake. Nice, but not very bright. Never should have let Rutland use her own name. Not in a million years. She was very upset when I told her."

Alex looked at Ramsay in amazement, but his voice was absolutely calm. "Come again, George? What the hell are you talking about?"

Ramsay reached into his pocket and passed Alex Rutland's hand written note. *"Melanie Drake suggested we should talk. I'll be home any time after nine this evening."* It read like an invitation to drinks.

"You've no doubt at all Rutland was murdered?"

"Clear as the spots on my arse, boss. Dressed up of course, but it was murder. I'd stake my pension on it. It's been all over the press. A thing like this could be bigger than Profumo. It could bring the Government down. But it's not being investigated. Not by the Yard at any rate. Apparently the Yanks are furious. Word is the DEA won't talk to our blokes at any level. Can't say I blame 'em."

"So where the hell is the silly woman now?" said Alex. She wasn't safe. Wherever she was, she wasn't safe. *Jesus Christ! Why did she have to be so complicated! Why couldn't all women be as straight forward as Verity*!

"Gone back to Spain as far as I know, she promised me she would. She hasn't been back to her flat, that I do know, not for a couple of days."

They had another hour before the theatre crowd returned to analyse the plot, the characterisation, the accuracy of the translation from the original Russian. Alex got the darts from the fat lady behind the bar and George opened with a double twenty and a pair of triple nineteen's. Alex realised he had been out of the country far too long. Maybe it would be a mistake to come back after all. But his mind wasn't on the game, it was on that stupid woman. He had told her not to get involved, had warned her. And now the silly bitch had let her name be hoist on a ten foot pole and paraded all over London. She was lucky if she was still alive.

Alex didn't sleep that night. He just couldn't get her out of his mind. He tried like hell to be angry with her but it didn't work. Somehow he couldn't help admiring her sheer bloody guts.

***

Lady Berringer sat in the sitting room of her elegant Belgravia home. It was late and time to retire. She had spent the day with Esler at the East End mission, which she found exhausting, and needed a bath and a good night's sleep before driving down to the country to prepare the house for the week-end guests.

Arthur Berringer, Winchester and Cambridge, dedicated capitalist and peer of the realm, dozed in his favourite armchair. He snored in that stop-start way she found so irritating. There was a lot about him she found irritating.

"Shouldn't you be going, dear?" she said.

He looked at his watch and groaned. He got up, said good night without looking at her, and went into his study. He fastened the brass clips on a briefcase, turned the key in both locks and dropped it into the waste paper basket. He put on his jacket, picked up the case, and left the house by the rear door, which gave onto the garden linking the main house to the mews at the rear. He entered the garage and walked through to the cobbled mews, turning left towards the square to hail a cab.

"Where to, Guv?"

Berringer gave the Soho address he had memorised, not knowing where it was.

"Bit over dressed aren't we guv?"

"Sorry driver?"

"Never mind." said the cabby as he turned into the thunder of traffic that was Knightsbridge.

Berringer sat in the back of the cab sweating. He mopped his face with a linen handkerchief. This was the thing he hated most. It wasn't the danger, though that was real enough, it was the lack of dignity, the vulgarity of the whole sordid procedure.

Fifteen minutes later Berringer alighted in Frith Street. He paid the cabby with a twenty-pound note but didn't wait for his change. He looked around and saw the neon sign above the entrance to *Adam's Garden* bedecked in plastic foliage.

He descended into the basement, pushed the door and found himself standing at the edge of small dance floor where two or three couples of the same sex gyrated slowly to music that could only just be heard. Plastic foliage climbed the walls and hung lifeless from the ceiling. The aromas of sweat and pot competed with the drains. He recognised Torres from behind. He was sitting at the bar sipping whiskey with his back to the room trying not to make eye contact with a well dressed middle aged man who sat ogling him from an alcove.

Berringer took the bar stool next to Torres. The middle-aged man looked away in disgust.

"Christ, Berringer!" muttered Torres. "Why do you pick these awful places? Couldn't we meet at the Ritz, or Harry's Bar? We're both members."

Berringer put the case on the floor between the two stools. His legs were too short to reach the ground and he put one foot on top of it, dangling the other in the air. He felt ridiculous. He was sweating and his mouth was dry. "I don't pick them."

"Then who does?" Torres smiled. "Never mind, Arthur. We won't be doing this again for quite a while."

"Fuck's sake! Give me a scotch, a large one, and let me get out of here."

***

13

Alex wasn't expected at *La Hacienda Blanca* till late that afternoon but he took an early plane out of Heathrow so he would have time to see her. He picked up a car at the airport and drove along the coast to Puerto Banus. He got to the tennis club too late to find her, so he went to her flat to see if she was there.

He parked the car in the shade of a bamboo awning and a liveried flunkie appeared to open the swing doors. The lobby was solid marble, white and unveined. The air-conditioned atmosphere was cool, almost clinical. This was an expensive place to live and Bowman wondered just how much a freelance journalist could earn.

It took her a while to answer the door. At last he heard the shuffling footsteps on the marble floor and the bolt being slid back on the other side. He was shocked when her saw her. She was wearing a robe, and her eyes were red and heavy with the lack of sleep. She looked dishevelled, unkempt. He had never seen her like this before.

"Alex, it's you." She didn't smile, but just looked up at him through her sleep filled half closed eyes. "Couldn't you have phoned? I'm not in any state for visitors. What time is it?"

"Mel, what is it? What's the matter?"

"Come in, now you're here. I'll make some coffee." She shuffled off to the kitchen, her hand on the wall to help her find the way. "God forgive me. I feel awful."

When Alex entered the sitting room he smelled the sweet herbal aroma of *cannabis sativa.* His heart sank. A moment later Melanie returned, jangling cups on a silver tray.

"Pour the coffee would you, I really haven't the strength."

When she had drunk her first cup she said, "I had an unexpected visitor last night, someone I haven't seen for years, just turned up out of the blue on her way back to London. We had a heavy night, and now I feel absolutely awful. Do I look a mess?"

"You look wonderful."

"Liar. Look Alex, don't think me rude, but I need to get some sleep. It'll be hours before I'm human again. Why don't you come back this evening about nine and take me out to dinner? Then I want to hear about everything you've been up to, absolutely everything. Promise?"

"I'll be here, but I think you're the one with the explaining to do. I have a few things to take care of in Marbella anyway. I'll pick you up at nine, *hora inglesa."*

***

When Alex reached *La Hacienda Blanca* it was the dead part of the day between *siesta* and drinks. He went to the pool, which he found deserted, so he stripped, dived in and started to do lengths. He wondered if Verity would appear, half hoping she would and half hoping she wouldn't. After a while Harvey came out onto the upper terrace dressed in a towling robe and holding his crotch. He looked like a very contented man.

Lieberman was pleased with Alex, pleased with the way things were going, the progress that was being made. Alex made sure his report was detailed and rich in technical jargon. He discussed dimensions, intervals, frequencies of occurrence, statistical likelihoods, systems and sub-systems and fail-safe devices. Lieberman was greatly impressed with Bowman's professionalism. He was pleased with himself too, with his unerring judgement. He had picked a first class man. But Lieberman still had one major preoccupation.

"How long is all this going to take Alex? How long before the system is up and running?" Sometime soon the woman in black would make contact again. She would have to. Harvey had impounded her supply and she had to be hurting bad. It was important things be ready when she did.

"At least three or four weeks before all the electronic gear even reaches Marrakech. Then I have to get it cleared through customs. I'll have to pay a few people off, just to speed things up. After that we have to finish the perimeter fence, say six weeks if we can divert enough labour from the planting. Then we have to install the generators and the rest of the electrical systems. We're talking maybe three to four months before completion. That allows time for testing and correcting any problems with the installation."

"Good work Alex, you're doing a real fine job." Harvey wanted to hug him. "I guess you'll be going back to the farm tomorrow, right?"

This was what Alex was afraid of. He needed to spend time on the Coast. "No Harvey, I won't be going back just yet, if that's all right with you. There's nothing for me to do there till the equipment arrives from London. Before that I have to recruit a couple of people, people we can trust, people with the right skills, electrical skills mainly. We won't find them in Marrakech. We have to recruit them here on the Coast. Luckily I have the right contacts in the business, but I want to spend time seeing as many candidates as possible. No point in settling for second best."

When Verity appeared on the terrace it was Alex who caught sight of her first, standing just in shadow, looking straight at him. She wore a simple black shift dress, which hugged her breasts and her hips, no make-up or jewellery, no other adornment was needed. She had washed her long blond hair and it fell loose below her shoulders, moving slightly in the gentle evening breeze. She saw Alex looking at her, so she didn't move. She knew the effect her body had on men, and she wanted him to appreciate the value of the offer she was making.

Harvey saw the direction of Bowman's gaze. He didn't need to turn round to know what Alex was looking at, the expression in his eyes was quite enough. Harvey whispered, "Listen Alex, I'm crazy about this broad, really crazy. Just remember that. I'm serious."

Harvey insisted that Alex should join them for dinner. He wanted to show Bowman his appreciation for all the fine work he was doing, and he wanted to show himself that Harvey Lieberman could handle a little competition. Alex resisted for as long as he could, he knew he should stay as far away from Verity as possible, but eventually Lieberman became heated and there was no way out but to accept. They picked Melanie up at her flat in Harvey's chauffeur driven stretched Mercedes and went on to dine at the most expensive night club on the Coast.

Much to Alex's surprise the two girls got on like a house on fire and spent at lot of time in whispered conversation. They were the two best-looking women in the room, and the standard was high. Harvey was very proud. He went out of his way to keep his guests amused and told the most outrageous stories. They all ate too much and laughed too much and had too much to drink.

Alex thought he should ask her to dance, she would expect it. He wasn't good at it, but if the band played something slow and easy and familiar he thought he could just about manage. When he heard the opening bars of *Blue Moon* he decide to take his chance. He touched her hand.

"How about a dance?"

"Oh Alex! Do you mind if we don't?" Melanie whispered. "My head's still throbbing from last night."

Alex smiled, he was off the hook.

"Poor Alex!" Verity grabbed his thigh under the table and gave it a squeeze. "Come on. I'd love to dance."

Alex glanced across at Harvey. "Sure. Why not?" Harvey was a big man. He could stand a little competition.

Verity led him by the hand, out into the centre of the crowded darkened floor.

Blue Moon, you saw me standing alone,
without a dream in my heart,
without a love of my own.

She took his hands and placed them on her buttocks, winding her arms around his neck and pressing her body against his, feeling him harden. Her feet barely moved. She did all the work with her pelvis.

Blue Moon, you knew just what I was there for,
you heard me saying a prayer for,
someone I really could care for.

A hand glided slowly down his side, inserted itself between their clenched bodies and found his erection, holding it firmly. It seemed like the most natural thing in the world.

I heard somebody whisper,
please adore me,
and when I looked,
the moon had turned to gold

She turned her cheek and kissed him, inserting her tongue in his mouth, searching, probing. Alex tried to remember the name of the man who had written the gorgeous lyrics, but somehow his mind wouldn't focus.

“Alex, why haven’t you come to me? You know I want you!” She was pressing against his hard-on, swaying in time to the gentle beat.

"Harvey wouldn't like it."

"Harvey would kill you. But who's going to tell him? Not me. Not you. Come to me tomorrow in the afternoon. Harvey will be out all day, casting one of his movies. He's always out all day when that happens, and he comes home *so* tired. Come to me, Alex. Promise? If not, I may tell Harvey what you did! How you forced yourself on me!"

When Alex felt a hand on his shoulder he was almost relieved. He turned to find the house photographer about to take a picture. She followed them back to the table. Harvey tipped her but waved her away. He seemed displeased about something. It was Melanie who insisted she wanted a souvenir snap-shot; she wanted them all to have copies.

The next day Verity bought a large ornate solid silver frame to put the nightclub picture in. It was the only picture of Alex she had and it was spoiled because it had other people in it, but at least she could have it on display. She decided the sitting room was the best place to keep it. She would have preferred to have it by her bed but she didn't like the idea of Alex being there when Harvey was screwing the arse off her.

***

"Why do they call them bimbos? Girls like Verity I mean."

"Don't knock Verity. There's more to Verity than meets the eye, which is saying a great deal." Alex struggled to suppress a smile.

They sat at a terrace bar, overlooking the harbour. It was nearly 2 am. The place was deserted, except for some couples that were not yet lovers who had come to look at the boats.

"Did you see the way she was looking at you? She could have eaten you with a spoon!" He didn't seem to hear her. She took a sip of her brandy and said quietly, "Alex, why didn't you appeal?"

“Come again?”

“You heard me. Why didn’t you appeal?”

"There wasn't any point." He might have blushed.

They didn't speak for quite a while, there was a silence, but it wasn't awkward the way silence is supposed to be, it was quite natural, unstrained.

"Why won't you let me help you?"

"I've told you, it's too dangerous. Besides, you have no cover now, you blew that arsing about with Rutland and his friends."

"What do you mean, arsing about? Rupert was a friend of mine, he was ill, he needed help, though like you he didn't seem to know it!" She beckoned to the waiter. "*Llame un taxi, por favor.*"

"Mel, please, let me drive you home."

She didn't reply. She simply got up and left him there to pay the bill.

Bowman sat there for some time, savouring his brandy. He drank more than he was used to, more than he had for quite a while. He had forgotten how relaxing alcohol could be, how it could blur the edges. He swirled the *Lepanto* round in his glass and inhaled, still thinking about her. There were points at which their lives touched and points at which they didn't, like a *trompe l'oeil* pattern moving in and out of focus. Then that tune came back to him again, soft, distant, repetitive, and he poured himself another drink.

***

Faraday's practice was one of the most prestigious in London. It puzzled Melanie just why he would have taken the case of a bent copper on a drugs charge with all of the adverse media attention that would entail. The tabloids had covered every detail with front page pictorials almost every day of the trial, though the Echo had given the case very little attention, consigning it to a few column inches lost in the middle pages, and no photographs. Faraday did not come cheap and he was very selective about the cases he chose to handle. Alex had been lucky to get such a prominent barrister to defend him.

Melanie was late. She hated being late. Flaherty had set up the appointment, but Rex Faraday QC had been tied up in court and hadn't been able to arrange a meeting right away. She sat in the high backed chair and caught her breath. She refused a cup of tea, she wanted to get to the point as quickly as she could. "It's good of you to see me at short notice Mr Faraday, I won't take up too much of your time."

"Not at all, Sean Flaherty is an old friend. It's about the Bowman trial I understand?"

"The trial, and what happened after the trial. I'm writing an extended piece, but it isn't clear to me yet what angle it should take. I'm assuming Bowman was innocent, that there was an injustice, and that leads on to how a man like Bowman, a man in that position, picks up the pieces. But if there was no injustice then of course that line won't hold."

"He was found guilty in a court of law. Your assumption he was innocent is just that, an assumption."

"A reasonable assumption?"

"An assumption. Reasonable or unreasonable is a matter of opinion. That he was found guilty by a jury of his peers is a fact."

"But you believed him innocent, otherwise you wouldn't have defended him."

"My duty was to defend him to the best of my ability, whatever I thought. He was entitled to that. As it happens, yes, I do think he was innocent. But I failed to convince the jury. That's the only thing that matters."

"That doesn't happen very often, does it Mr. Faraday? You hardly ever loose a case." He didn't answer, but he reddened slightly. "You're one of the most respected barristers in England, and one of the most expensive. Alex was a senior policeman, but policemen don't make any money, not the honest ones anyway. How come he could afford your fees?"

Faraday shuffled in his seat. "He didn't pay my fees. Mary Berringer paid them."

Melanie looked up from her shorthand pad. "Why would she do that? She of all people!"

"Why not? They were friends. More than friends."

"Yes! But it was she who turned him in! Turning him in and paying his fees makes no sense at all!"

"I think she came to regret it, turning him in I mean. Paying my fees was a way to make amends."

"Maybe. But in court she stuck to her story. That she had found the drugs in his flat."

"She could hardly do otherwise. She was under oath."

"Why didn't Alex appeal? Surely that's what an innocent man would have done?"

"I wanted him to, of course. He said there was no point. And then there was the question of my fees again. An appeal would have been very expensive and it wasn't clear the Berringer girl would continue to provide. The trial was one thing she said, an appeal was quite another."

Melanie decided to take another tack. "You heard about Mary, I suppose? The car accident? It was in all the society pages."

"My word yes! What a tragedy! That wretched girl, perjured herself, I'm sure of it."

"But why? Paying Alex's fees was one thing, they'd been lovers for more than a year. But why tell lies about him? It simply doesn't make sense."

"Alex thought she was under pressure, he must have told you so."

"I don't buy that. I've known women like Mary Berringer. Young, rich, beautiful, privileged. They don't respond to pressure." She folded her pad and put it in her bag. "Tell me something else. How was it that Berringer approached *you* to find Alex for him? It just seems rather odd, in the circumstances, his daughter having been a hostile witness."

Faraday leaned forward over his desk and propped his chin in his hands. "It was a curious business. The appointment had been made in Lord Berringer's name, I recognised it of course, from the trial, but he couldn't come to the meeting himself, he'd been called abroad apparently, so he sent his personal private secretary instead. Rather a daunting woman. I didn't care for her much."

"Had you had dealings with Berringer, before she came to see you? Can you think of any reason why he should have come to you to find Alex for him, rather than the police say, or the prison authorities?"

"No, none. I confess I hadn't thought of that. All I know about Lord Berringer is what I read in the papers, I follow the stock market you see, it's a hobby. I've held shares in his company for years. They've done rather badly I'm afraid. I should have sold them years ago, but I held on too long and now I can't afford to realise the loss."

"I thought his company was very successful?"

"It used to be. But over the last few years he's done a series of very bad deals, selling off assets too cheaply. He seems to have lost his touch."

Melanie looked at her watch. "So when he came here to meet Alex, that was the first time you'd met him?"

"Yes, Melanie, the first time." Faraday was uncomfortable now. He was used to asking the questions, not being cross-examined himself.

Rex Faraday QC went to the window and watched Melanie Drake walk out through the courtyard in front of his chambers. From this angle she looked harmless enough, insignificant even. When she had disappeared from sight Faraday rang for his clerk.

"Dig out the transcript of the Bowman trial for me would you Jenkins, and the other relevant papers. I think I'll take them home for the week-end."

***

Fleet Street didn't exist any more, not as an institution. It had moved east to the man made desert of the docklands. The old bars were almost empty at this time of evening and the atmosphere, the buzz they used to have, was gone.

Melanie had phoned Phillip Hyde, the ageing queer who wrote the gossip column at the Echo. He was delighted when she called, a jar at El Vino's would revive his flagging spirits and with luck under the new licensing laws he could make it last all evening and she could pour him into a taxi and send him home.

He had run the words Mary Berringer and Harvey Lieberman through the computer and come up with a match in one of the Sunday editions of a couple of years ago. It was only a paragraph but it gave Melanie the lead she needed, an item that linked the two of them to a health farm in deepest Surrey.

"Apparently that's where they met." said Phil. "Mary had a problem with the drink poor girl, but the lucky darling could afford the very best treatment and Lakeside Health and Fitness Spa is certainly the best, as well as the most expensive. Also it's very discreet. All sorts of smart people go there. It's the nearest thing we have to Betty Ford." He emptied his glass for the third time and

Melanie wondered if he had ever used the place himself, but on a journalist's pay that wasn't very likely.

"Who owns Lakeside?"

"Some kind of Trust as far as I remember. Not my sort of people darling, the punters like to read about the sinners, not the saints." he smiled. "What's he like, your man Bowman?"

"My man? He's not my man, he's very much his own. Attractive. Infuriating. He never talks about himself, not even if you ask him a direct question. He's a very difficult subject."

“You do fancy him, don’t you?”

“Oh Phil! Don’t be so childish!” As she spoke she wondered what her feelings for him really were. She’d never asked herself before. *Did she? Could she*? No, it was just too silly. She was interested in him certainly, but that was just the project, the article Flaherty was paying her to write. She emptied her glass and looked at her watch. It was almost eleven o'clock. "Do me one more favour, Phil. Come with me to Piccadilly Circus. To the tube station."

"Piccadilly tube? Are you stark raving mad? At this time of night? We'll get mugged, or worse!"

"You won't let me go alone Phil, will you?" She knew very well he wouldn't. He was a gentleman at heart, one of the old fashioned kind.

"What on earth do you want to go there for? Not to buy drugs, is it? I've warned you about that!" He looked aghast.

"No, Phil. I haven't even smoked for weeks." she lied. "It's just that I haven't been there for years, I want to see how it's changed. I've heard the most appalling stories." She was thinking about the kids Marcus Esler was helping. "I'm curious, that's all. Come on Phil, where's your spirit of adventure."

He emptied his glass, she paid the bill, and they went outside to find a cab. They moved through the West End at a crawl, traffic was bumper to bumper. At last they reached the bottom end of Shaftesbury Avenue where the filthy fast food stalls spilled their garbage out onto the pavement. Melanie got out, paid the cab, and led the way down into the concourse. It was crowded before midnight, the last train had not yet gone. There was a crush of people at the ticket barriers, jostling each other, trying to get through. The atmosphere was tense, almost violent.

"Let's get out of here, Mel. This place is awful." He was ill at ease, the crush of people made him nervous. He had seen crowds get out of hand before, knew how things could escalate once they got started, the smallest thing could set them off. Queer bashing, they called it.

"Wait a while, Phil. I want to see what goes on here." She was calm. She knew he wouldn't leave her.

After a while the crowd thinned out, the last train had left, but the kids were still there, some of them would spend the night. The ambience was different now, no longer violent, but threatening still. The two of them were out of place, different from the rest, conspicuous. They did a couple of circuits of the concourse. Suddenly Melanie froze. Fifty feet away, at the entrance to one of the side tunnels, she saw the girl, back half turned, talking to a man in his early twenties. Melanie didn't recognise her right away, but when she did she yelled, "Mandy!"

The girl didn't turn, she ran. She was down the tunnel in an instant. Melanie ran as far as the entrance but when she got there there was no sign of Mandy, or the man. Mel walked back to her companion.

"Sorry, Phil. Someone I know. I thought she might be buying drugs." She felt suddenly depressed. Maybe Esler's cfforts were in vain. This was tragic!

"Selling drugs."

"What do you mean Phil, *selling drugs*?" There was a look of abject terror in her face.

"I saw the trade. It went the other way."

***

Melanie made damn sure she was on time. Mrs Hetherington had told her on the phone that Lord Berringer would give her half an hour and not a minute longer. In the end she was early, ten minutes early. She followed the long legged girl down the short corridor to

Mrs. Hetherington's office, which guarded the access to Berringer's inner sanctum.

Mrs. Hetherington sat behind her desk smoking. "Please take a seat Miss Drake, the Chairman won't keep you a moment." She sat and smoked in silence, while Melanie cast her eye around the sparsely furnished office. All the furniture was the very best quality, but there was surprisingly little of it. It didn't look as if much work got done there, there were no papers on the desk, no filing cabinets, no reference books on any of the shelves. The real work must all get done elsewhere she decided, at the next level down in the hierarchy.

Precisely on the hour a buzzer sounded and Mrs. Hetherington stood up to reveal a neat figure and a very elegant pair of legs. She opened a door so well concealed in the panelling that Melanie hadn't even noticed it was there, and gestured to her to go through.

Lord Berringer stood up and walked round the desk so they could sit together informally in a pair of Hepplewhite chairs next to a large marble fireplace. When he spoke his voice was soft and unassuming.

"I understand you knew my daughter?"

"No, we never actually met. We were at University at the same time, but at different colleges. Though we did have friends in common."

"I must have misunderstood Flaherty, but never mind. How can I help? It's something you're writing about the Bowman case?"

"Not the case. The man. How he came through it in one piece."

"I don't quite see how I can contribute. I never really knew him, and frankly I've no wish to know him." He looked at his watch. "I needed him to find Mary for me, which he did, but too late. The day before the accident."

Melanie wondered how to tell him. She didn't even know if it was true. "Mary didn't have an accident, Lord Berringer. She was killed. Murdered. I felt you ought to know."

Berringer was stunned. "How can that be? It was in every paper, a car accident, on that notorious stretch of road outside Marbella."

"It looked like an accident, was made to look like one. The police may even believe it was one. They'd like to believe it anyway, it would save them an awful lot of trouble."

Berringer had gone pale, his hands trembling slightly. "I suspected all along she was caught up in some unpleasant business. But nothing like this! Nothing to justify murder!"

"What sort of unpleasant business?"

"Mary was a very beautiful girl, Miss Drake. Men took advantage of her. Misused her. I'd rather say no more than that."

"Mary was involved with drugs. She was a user. Had been for years. But she was involved in trafficking too. And I don't mean in a small way. Not just pushing. Somehow your daughter was connected with a very major organisation. When she became unreliable they killed her." This was guesswork, but she was more or less sure she was right.

Lord Berringer closed his eyes in despair. If he was an actor he was a good one. "Please, please, you're talking about my daughter. The poor girl is dead. Can't you let her rest in peace?"

Melanie pitied the old man but there was no tactful way to do this. "You speak of your daughter, but when she died the newspapers all said step daughter, every last one of them."

Berringer hesitated, but only for a second. He seemed suddenly very tired. "Neither one is strictly true. Mary was adopted. But in my heart I never made the distinction. For me she was always my daughter. Does that answer your question?"

Melanie felt almost sorry she had asked. "What was her relationship with her mother?" She probed. "Were they on good terms?"

"Lady Berringer, you mean? Yes, very good terms. Though like me she hadn't seen Mary for some years. But before that they were very close. Almost like sisters. Lady Berringer is my second wife, you see. The age difference between them wasn't very great."

"Did Mary have any contact with her natural mother?"

Another hesitation, no more than a second. "No, none. It was part of the arrangement. As far as I know the mother emigrated. America, I think."

"So Mary never knew her real mother?"

"She never wanted to know. If she had, I wouldn't have told her."

Melanie got up and almost as an after thought she said, "When you decided to approach Alex, why was it necessary to go through Faraday to find him? There must have been other ways you could have tried, the police say, or the prison authorities. Going through Faraday seems, well, a little unorthodox I suppose. Your daughter having been a hostile witness."

"It was an expedient. Faraday knew how to get hold of him quickly. I didn't."

"So you knew Faraday?"

"No, Miss Drake. I knew *of* him."

"And the re-trial?"

"That was my idea. I wanted to give Bowman an incentive. I had to be sure he would take the case. I knew if he did he would find her."

***

The massive wrought iron gateway came into view at the top of the short drive. Beyond it, half a mile away, the facade of Burlington's beautifully proportioned Palladian masterpiece sat on top of a low hill. Melanie slowed the car to take in the colonnaded portico, topped by its dome, and the two identical wings that stretched away on either side. The small hand painted sign by the gate, gold on olive green, announced discreetly "Lakeside Health and Fitness Spa" and below that in a more simple script, "Strictly Private. Keep Out."

She was shown to her room in the east wing by a receptionist. The room was bright and airy and looked out over the sunlit park to the artificial lake, which probably gave the place its name.

Melanie's appointment was not till three in the afternoon so she decided to take a look at the facilities. She walked along the bedroom corridor and down the grand staircase to the marbled lobby. The place was deserted. She saw the sign to the west wing, crossed to the glass door that closed off the end of the corridor, and pushed it to go through. It was locked.

"Can I help you?" The voice came from behind her and Melanie turned to see a desk set back in an alcove, a uniformed male nurse sitting behind it, smiling.

"Excuse me," said Melanie. "It's locked."

"We keep it locked. Some of our patients require absolute privacy."

He didn't offer to open it. Melanie wondered why he said “patients”. She would have expected him to say “guests” or “clients”. After all, Lakeside was a health farm, not a hospital. It must be something to do with his training.

She decided to take a look at the gardens instead. As she approached the main doorway a woman in a doctor's housecoat appeared from nowhere and they nearly bumped into one another. "Do please excuse me!" The woman adjusted her tinted glasses. "We haven't met, have we? I'm Dr. Bligh. I run Lakeside. You must be Melanie Drake? Just arrived from Spain? We have an appointment later on this afternoon."

"Pleased to meet you, Dr. Bligh." They shook hands and smiled at one another. "I was just going out to see the gardens, it's such a lovely day."

"What a good idea! Do you mind if I join you? That way you can tell me what it is you want to talk to me about and I can miss a boring lunch with our resident dietician."

They stepped out into the sunshine and walked round to the back of the great house, taking a path down towards the lake. It was a bright summer's day and there were people in small groups, sitting on park benches and deck chairs, facing into the sun, while others did stretching exercises or jogged up and down in the mistaken belief they were extending their life expectancy.

"So this is where everybody is!" said Melanie. "I thought the place was deserted!"

"Deserted?" Dr. Bligh smiled broadly. "Far from it, I'm glad to say, we're bursting at the seams. This is a health farm, not a hospital, we encourage people to spend as much time out of doors as possible. That's what they're here for after all, the three Rs, rest, relaxation and running about." Her smile was infectious. Melanie liked her immediately.

"I've never been to a health farm before. Are many of them run by women?"

"A few, the best ones I like to think. Lakeside is the best. Is that why you chose us?"

"Yes it is. I'm writing a series of articles about quiet excellence, things that are the absolute best in their field and very, very exclusive. Patek Philipe, Chateau Margaux, the Cipriani, things like that." She was thinking of a couple more items to add to the list when suddenly she stopped. "That man over there, asleep in the wheel chair. I know him."

"Peter Draycott? Poor old boy! He comes here for therapy. He's a neighbour. Would you like to say hello? He's only dozing. I'm sure he wouldn't mind."

"No, really, please. Don't disturb him."

"Then tell me about your project. How fascinating! And how very flattering! Where will the articles be published?"

"They'll be syndicated in the glossies, I expect. American Vogue is interested."

"You've certainly picked the right place in Lakeside." Dr Bligh smiled. "You can't get more exclusive than us." They had reached the lake and were progressing round its edge. "I should warn you though, I may not be able to co-operate. I'd like to very much of course, it would be good for Lakeside, but the trustees are very sensitive about publicity. We avoid it like the plague. I won't be able to talk to you officially without clearance. But I should be able to get an answer by the time we meet this afternoon."

"My God!" said Melanie. "What's that? I've never seen such a beautiful house." They had rounded a bend and a glorious Queen Anne mansion came into view at the top of a rise on the far side of the lake. It was smaller than Lakeside but it was exquisite, a flawless architectural gem of restrained and perfectly proportioned elegance.

"That's Framlington Hall, the neighbouring property. Named after the village I suppose, or would it be the other way around? Beautiful isn't it? I often walk this way just to see it."

"It certainly is. Who owns it? It must be worth an absolute fortune, priceless I would say."

"It was in the Berringer family for generations, but they sold it a couple of years ago. I've no idea who lives there now. I hardly ever see any sign of life, just occasionally at week-ends." They had reached a point where the path divided. "Look, I have to get back to my office now. Why don't you continue on around the lake and I'll cut across here and go back. I'll expect you in my office later, shall we say about four? That will give me time to clear up a few things and I can keep the rest of the afternoon free for you."

Melanie watched Dr. Bligh climb the grassy bank up towards the house. She was impressed by the Doctor, as well as attracted to her. It was good to see a woman, a young, attractive, vibrant woman, at the head of a thoroughly well run operation like Lakeside. Perhaps it was a mistake to approach her obliquely, on the pretext of writing the article. Maybe it would be better to speak to the Doctor frankly. Put all her cards on the table.

***

At four o'clock that afternoon Melanie sat in the lobby waiting to be shown into Dr. Bligh's office. She had brought her shorthand pad and her ballpoint pen and was looking forward to talking to Dr. Bligh as one capable professional woman to another.

“Dr. Bligh won’t keep you long.” The receptionist smiled. “There’s been some kind of crisis.” A moment later the door opened and a male nurse appeared, pushing a stroke victim in a wheel chair, dabbing the side of his mouth with a towel. Melanie tried to look away but Draycott made eye contact with her and held her gaze. “Miss Drake!” he drawled. “How very good to see you!” He didn’t seem at all surprised that she was there.

“Peter! How are you? You *are* looking well!” It was a lie and it made her blush. He looked completely out of sorts. Then Doctor Bligh appeared in the doorway behind him. “I won’t keep you a moment, Miss Drake.” she said and followed the patient and his nurse out into the entrance hall. Melanie watched them say goodbye in a cold rather businesslike way, without any of the warmth she would expect between doctor and patient. Or between neighbours, come to that.

"Disappointing news, I'm afraid." Dr. Bligh sat on the other side of the desk and made a grimace of apology. "The trustees have turned it down flat." She made a gesture towards a photograph on the far wall and Melanie glanced up to see a group of grey suited middle-aged men surrounding the statutory token woman. "No interviews. No articles. No talking to journalists. No publicity. It's maddening. So short-sighted. The right sort of publicity could do us so much good. But there it is I'm afraid, it's out of my hands completely, there's absolutely nothing I can do." She unclasped her hands and clasped them again, in a gesture of finality.

"Damn!" said Melanie. "Damn, damn, damn." She put the top of the ballpoint pen in her mouth and bit it hard. She hadn't come all this way to be turned down flat, go back empty handed. She didn't know precisely what she was looking for, but if she could just get Dr. Bligh to talk, talk about anything, something would come to light. Tiffany Wells had been introduced to drugs at Lakeside, she was sure of that, and it was here that she had first met Lieberman. There simply had to be an angle.

"This is very disappointing, Dr. Bligh. You're a professional woman. I'm sure you understand how annoying it is to come all this way for nothing." Melanie took up her pad again, ballpoint pen at the ready. "Let me tell you about another project I'm working on. I'd like to hear your views. It's about women. Not the usual feminist claptrap about people like you and me who make it to the top and stay there. I want to write about the women who fail to make it, apparently bright, capable, well-educated women who end up in the gutter. Women like Mary Berringer. She was a client of yours I believe? Perhaps you knew her as Tiffany Wells?"

The doctor's face was a total blank, no flicker of recognition. "Mary Berringer was an alcoholic when she came to us. We cured her. She took our detoxification programme. It works very well." Her voice was flat and without expression. It was an answer she had worked out in advance.

"What is the detoxification programme, Dr. Bligh? How does it work?" Melanie was making progress at last.

"Some of our clients are addicted when they come to us. Sometimes it's alcohol, sometimes it's prescription drugs like valium or aspirin, sometimes it's tea or coffee. Whatever it is they need our help. We cure them. We're very good at it. We have a special detoxification wing. Would you like to see?"

"Why not? Since I'm here, I may as well do something useful."

They crossed the hall to the west wing. The male nurse stood up when the Doctor approached, waiting for an instruction. "Hello, Barton." The doctor smiled. "Miss Drake is interested in our detoxification programme. I'm going to show her round. Ask Sister Duncan to join us in the Receiving Room, would you?"

Barton took out a bunch of keys and unlocked the glass door. He watched the two women walk to the end of the corridor and re-locked it. Then he picked up the telephone and dialled the two digit internal number.

***

14

It was a slow news day at the Echo. Flaherty sat at the head of the table and stared out of the window looking bored. “Come on guys! There’s a whole world out there! Something must be going on!” Nobody spoke. “OK. Let’s go round the table one more time. Phil, you go first. What’s happening on the cocktail party scene?” Flaherty wasn’t hopeful Hyde would come up with the goods, but he wanted to get the trivia out of the way first.

Phil Hyde knew he was in the spotlight. He had to contribute something. “The price of coke is rocketing.” He said hopefully. “The streets appear to be dry. Suddenly coke is hard to come by, anywhere in London.”

Derek Fleetwood, city editor, began to take notice. He thought Hyde was commenting on the soft drinks market. He said “Significantly?”

Hyde was pleased he had the room’s attention. I was a novel experience. “Three months ago the price of a rock was £12. Now it’s £15.”

Fleetwood said “That’s a 25% hike in three months. That’s significant.” He looked at Flaherty for approval.

“That tallies with the DEA’s press releases.” Clive Anderson, senior crime reporter, chipped in. “They’re claiming major successes in the Andes. Defoliating half of Bolivia. Price is bound to rise.”

Flaherty sensed they were onto something. “That’s good, Clive. Now, can anybody tie something in to that? Phil gave you the hook. Who’s got the mackerel?”

“There was something curious on AFP.” Bella Parker ran the Iberia desk. ”Reuters had it too.”

“What’s that?” said Flaherty.

“Suicide of some senior customs official in Southern Spain.”

“What’s the connection?”

“Drugs…..Spain.....Customs......Suicide…….....it’s tenuous, I know. Just trying to be helpful.” Bella sounded apologetic. “It played big in Spain.”

Flaherty got up and paced around the room. Nobody spoke. When Flaherty resumed his seat he said, “OK, here’s what we run with. Front Page Banner.” He drew an imaginary line in the air. “*Cocaine Turf Wars Hit Europe. Market runs out of product. Price rockets.* Hype-up the DEA angle, massage their Yankee egos. Give my friend Frank Willowby a mention. That should be worth a lunch. And it will do our boys a bit of good after the Rutland fiasco.” Flaherty turned to Bella Parker. “Don’t tie in the suicide. The connection is too weak. Sorry Bella. But run it as a separate item on the same page. People will draw their own conclusions.”

“Not even a hint at a connection?” said Bella. “If this thing’s Europe-wide, why not?”

"OK, a hint, but subtle." Flaherty was pleased they'd reached a satisfactory conclusion. He would call Frank Willowby right away to congratulate him on the DEA's success. Maybe he'd be free for lunch. The new restaurant at Claridge's should be worth a try.

***

Marcus Esler was a worried man. The Organisation had practically run out of stock. Torres hadn't made the promised last delivery. And he couldn't explain why. Now good people were beginning to defect in droves. If things went on like this for long the organisation would implode. Years of patient work building the distribution network would be wasted. Esler had made an approach to Torres but the Colombian refused to make more product available. Claimed Medellin were having difficulties of their own, keeping their markets in the States supplied. There was only one thing to do. Offer Lieberman a partnership. Buy up his entire stock. It was risky, Lieberman was still untested. Yes, he had successfully delivered a trial shipment without a single hitch. Quality was excellent. But to put him into such a key position, rely on him as the main source of supply, was something Esler wouldn't countenance unless it were forced on him.

The chauffeur pulled up outside Helen Proctor's Mayfair flat and Esler got out, clutching the newspaper in his hand. He took the lift to the penthouse and Daisy let him in, gesturing towards the sitting room door.

"I know." She said. "I've seen the papers too."

"What are we going to do?"

"About what? The Colombians? Or Lieberman?" Unlike Esler, she was at her best under pressure. Esler tended to panic.

"Forget the Colombians. Torres won't play ball. Says they have a crisis of their own."

"That's been obvious for quite a while Marcus. Lieberman's our only answer. He's been right all along. He predicted this would happen. I think I'll pay him a visit. Offer him a partnership. We've already agreed to that in principle, all three of us. That way we secure supply and the Colombians can go hang themselves. I have the jet on standby. I'll fly down to Marbella in the morning and make Lieberman a proposition."

***

Verity had been doing fine until Alex turned up. But after she met Alex everything changed. For the first time in her life Verity Fuller was in love. Her problem was she had no idea where Alex had gone, where to look for him, when he might come back. So she had no option but to stay put till he did. Asking Harvey where Alex had gone was out of the question, Harvey was as crazy about her as she was about Alex. She let Harvey go on making love to her, she had no alternative, but she hated it now and had to fake every move. She tried to satisfy him in other ways, make him come outside her, without penetrating her, but Harvey wouldn't settle for that. Foreplay was fine he said, but it was a bit like seeing the trailer without being able to enjoy the whole movie. So Verity would fake it, rolling her eyes like a china doll and making little moaning sounds as if she were delirious with pleasure. It was simple, she had done this kind of work a hundred times before and Harvey was easier to convince than most, he needed to believe she really loved him. He was crazy about her, absolutely crazy.

Harvey was by the pool the day he got the call. Verity was lying face down on a sun bed with her head resting on her forearms and he was looking at the line of her gorgeous back, the way the edge of her breast curved out from her body in a beautiful sensuous protrusion. One of the servants appeared on the terrace and made a sign that meant Harvey should come to the phone. Harvey went inside to take the call in his study. He was only away for a couple of minutes but when he returned he was beaming with pleasure like a child who had just been offered a trip to Disney World. He had his wallet in his hand.

"Verity honey, I want you to go shopping. Buy yourself the whole goddamn town if you want." He took out a great wad of notes and stuffed them down the back of her bikini and patted her behind. "Don't come back till six o'clock at the earliest, OK? Get that gorgeous ass of yours out of here, right now."

Verity hesitated. She hadn't seen Harvey as agitated as this before. Something big was going to happen. Someone important was coming to the villa. Verity knew she should stay, find out who it was, take a photograph. But she had no interest in the project any more. She could only think of Alex. So she took the money, wandered into the house, picked up his picture in the ornate silver frame and kissed it. Then she went to her room, showered, put on a pair of tailored shorts and a blouse and went down stairs to find one of the drivers to take her into town.

It wasn't long before Harvey heard the sound of the car's horn at the gate. He came outside onto the terrace to watch the Rolls Royce with the darkened windows glide silently down the slope towards the garage. When it came to a halt the driver dismounted immediately and went to the rear of the vehicle to open the passenger door. Harvey recognised the guardian angel, the evil looking albino with the lifeless pallid eyes. Then he saw the long slender legs swivel out of the car as the woman in black alighted onto the pathway. She wasn't wearing a hat and her hair was brushed back off her face in a severe, rather mannish style. She was smoking a cigarette, which she gave to the albino to dispose of. For the first time Harvey took a good look at the man. There was something not quite human about him with his bull's neck, and the face of an overfed rodent.

"What a lovely villa, Harvey." She said. "Shall we go inside?"

They walked past the pool, up the steps to the terrace and into the house, the albino following behind. He didn't go in, but took up a position just outside the open terrace doors and unbuttoned his jacket. The woman took off her dark glasses to compensate for the light and looked around the room. "My word, what a lovely home you have Harvey. Such taste! It's exquisite!" She pointed at one of the pictures, a still life, with the heavy varnish to make it look antique. "Is that a *Murillo*?"

"Some kinda fruit." said Harvey. "Is that what they're called?"

She sat on the sofa and sighed. “Is there a Mrs. Lieberman, Harvey? I can’t believe you live alone. Shall I get to meet her?”

“There’s a girl, but no wife. She’s out shopping. She loves shopping. She’ll be gone for the rest of the day.”

"Those men digging up the road, how long have they been there?"

"Ain't that something? First they put down a brand new surface and then they dig a f........a hole in it. Same thing the world over, I guess."

"They took a lot of interest in my car."

"Sure they did. Everybody notices a Rolls Royce."

"In Marbella, Harvey? They're two a penny, otherwise I shouldn't have hired one. You should pay more attention to detail. Details are always important. Check with the local authority, find out if they're legitimate. Nothing is ever as simple as it seems in our business. That's what makes it so exciting." She looked out at the albino, his back towards her, waiting and hoping. "But that's not why I've come all this way to talk to you. Sit down Harvey, I've something very important to say."

They talked for two hours but it wasn't a conversation, it was an inquisition. Harvey didn't mind one bit. She was checking him out, making her assessment, testing him to see if he was as good as he said he was. This was fine by Harvey. Christ! It was better than fine! It was goddamn wonderful! Eventually she seemed to be satisfied.

"Harvey, I have good news for you. My partners and I want to make you a proposition, a very attractive proposition. I'm sure you won't refuse. First let me tell you our assessment of the situation. I'll be frank. You may not like some of what I have to say, but be patient, I'll save the good news to the end." She paused to light another cigarette. "You probably know our organisation is the biggest of it's kind in Europe. You are a good local operator, well organised on a modest scale, but without major international connections. Somehow you've come up with an absolutely brilliant concept. I don't know how you did it, but the idea of growing cocaine in the High Atlas is masterly. I confess we never would have dreamed of it ourselves." She inhaled deeply and puffed smoke at Harvey to put him in his place. "The problem is the idea is bigger than you are. You'll never be able to pull it off alone. There are too many pit falls you haven't even thought of, finance, management, political connections. My organisation can supply all those things. Think about it, Harvey. We're a perfect match." She paused again. "The proposal I want you to think about is this. I'll send in a team of auditors to evaluate your business. They'll look at your assets, your liabilities, your profit performance, your cash flow projections. We'll agree a valuation of your business and make you an attractive offer. We'll take a majority stake. Inject new capital. You will become a minority partner. But you'll go on managing the business at the local level, here and in Morocco. You'll be given a precise job description, targets to achieve, incentives. We run a very tight ship

Harvey, I think you'll enjoy working for us." She made it sound like she was doing him a favour. The truth was she had run out of options. She was desperate for product. Harvey knew that. He had her last delivery secreted away somewhere safe, ready to flood the market.

But Harvey knew she was right, right about everything, right about the huge potential of the idea. Tiffany's idea. But right too about his own limitations. For a moment he thought of playing hard to get. Asking what would happen if he refused. But he already knew the answer to that. That was why the rat faced albino was standing just outside the terrace doors with his jacket open and his hands hanging loose at his side.

“In the meantime, Harvey” the woman resumed. “We have a major problem. You were right about the DEA. They’ve had a real impact on supply. Product is very hard to come by. We need you to supply every ounce you can immediately. How much can you muster right away?”

“More than you guys can handle.” Harvey stalled. Now the deal was on the table he wasn’t sure he wanted it. A partnership was what he’d dreamed of. But now it was on offer he wondered if he didn’t value his independence more. “Problem is, most of my stock is warehoused in Morocco. It’ll take a while to get a shipment that big into Spain. Let alone England. It’s not as easy as it used to be. I lost one of my key people a while ago. Give me a week. Then you can have all you want.”

She was disappointed at the flatness of his reply. Harvey didn’t seem to grasp the magnitude of the opportunity she was offering. “Harvey, you should at least offer me a drink, some celebration champagne."

"Sure! Champagne. Let's celebrate!" Harvey raised both hands above his head, clicked his fingers and banged his heels on the marble floor. Then he left the room and returned a few minutes later with a magnum and two glasses. He opened the bottle with a loud explosion and saw the albino stiffen. He poured the golden liquid into the glasses, spilling a little on the silver tray. He took a glass across to the woman and raised his own for a toast. “To life."

"To life." she replied, and took a little sip. It was as she put her glass down on the side table that she saw the photograph. Alex Bowman was looking out at her from the ornate silver frame. He was grinning.

The woman screamed. A loud, piercing, high-pitched scream.

Daisy whirled round, drew his gun, Harvey plainly in its sights. He hesitated for a second, awaiting an instruction that didn’t come. He got off a single round, missing Harvey by inches. Then a shot rang out, from beyond the pool. Daisy dropped to his knees, turning again to face the direction the shot had come from. A second shot knocked the gun from his hand.

An instant later José walked into the room, a Kalashnikov AK74 in his right hand, a telescopic sight attached to the barrel of the rifle. To the woman and the albino, even allowing for the rifle and the telescopic sight, it looked like marksmanship of the very highest order. José and Lieberman both knew it was luck.

Harvey looked from José back to the woman, certain the whole situation was blown apart. But for now he had the upper hand. José had pocketed Daisy's gun. Harvey tried to grasp exactly what options he still had. Daisy was looking at José in a crazed way. There was murder in those colourless empty eyes. The woman was deadly calm, still seated on the sofa. She looked up at Harvey and smiled.

"I like a man who takes precautions. It's really very reassuring." If she had any doubts about Harvey they were totally dispelled now. Underneath his slightly absurd exterior was a highly developed instinct for survival. "I'm sorry, Harvey. The whole thing was my fault, I really shouldn't have screamed like that." She took a calming sip of champagne and picked up the photograph. She carried it to the window and looked at it carefully in the light, to make sure she wasn't mistaken. "This man in the picture Harvey, what is he doing with you?"

"That's Bowman. Alex Bowman. My Chief Security Officer. A nobody. A bent copper down on his luck." Harvey shrugged and glanced at José who stood smiling and listening in the doorway, the Kalachnikov still trained on the albino.

"Where is he now? At this very moment?" She appeared perfectly calm, but the pitch of her voice had risen.

"Right now? He's over in Morocco, up at the farm, completing the security installation. Is there a problem?"

The expression on the woman's face changed suddenly from outward calm to absolute fury. She raised the picture frame above her head and hurled it to the marble floor with all the strength she could muster. The frame buckled and chards of glass scattered across the room. Harvey knew something was wrong. What was it about Bowman? He always seemed to have an affect on women. He had had an affect on Verity too, the dumb bastard. Harvey looked again at José. "I won't be needing you again today, go get laid or something." José deserved his reward.

The woman resumed her seat and didn't speak for a while. Her problem was how much to tell Lieberman. Enough to make him act, but nothing more than that. Nothing that would indicate how dangerous Bowman could be. In the end she opted for simplicity. Getting rid of Bowman was too vital to be left to chance. But after what had just happened she was convinced Lieberman could do it.

"I suppose you know about his background?" She said. "He came very close to breaking our organisation once. Even he doesn't know how close he came. All bets are off Harvey. There'll be no deal. No partnership. Not till you kill Alex Bowman."

Harvey shrugged. "Consider it done. I'll send a couple of the boys up to the farm tomorrow and blow the cocksucker's head right off. I got a feeling there's nothin' José would like better."

"Make sure it's done properly, Harvey. If you screw up on this one you'll find there's more at stake than just the loss of a good deal." She stood up to go and for the first time since the shooting she looked the albino directly in the face. It was impossible to say that he blushed, but he hung his head in shame as he followed her out of the room, like a dog that was going to be whipped.

When Verity returned to the villa that evening she found the shattered picture frame and took the damaged photograph and hid it in a drawer. Harvey must have had a fit of rage, she thought, but he seemed to be over it now. Harvey was on top of the world. That night he was absolutely uncontainable.

***

The Learjet Challenger 604 touched down at Heathrow Airport and taxied to a group of single storey industrial buildings, away from the main passenger terminals. It came to rest with a slight jolt and the high-pitched whine of its twin engines ceased abruptly. A couple of men in uniform came out of the nearby building and waited as the aircraft's steps were lowered to the ground. The passenger appeared in the doorway, her hand held over her skirt to prevent it flying up in the air, and they helped her alight onto the tarmac before boarding the plane. They were customs men and they did a brief search of the interior of the plane before returning to the building. The whole performance was perfectly routine. This particular aircraft was in and out of Heathrow more or less constantly and it was always clean, never so much as a bottle of whisky on board. The pilot handed in his flight plan and signed a couple of official forms. The customs men asked the statutory questions but the sole passenger had nothing to declare. It was all perfectly routine. Outside a uniformed chauffeur was waiting. He opened the rear passenger door of the Daimler. "Where to Miss?"

"Lakeside. And don't call me Miss!" Why could he never get it right?

"Yes Miss. Sorry Miss." He slipped the car smoothly into gear and eased out into the heavy evening traffic.

The woman flicked on the reading light in the rear compartment and read once more the decoded message she had received mid-flight. She sank down in her seat, crumpling the paper in her hand. What could it possibly mean?

The M25 was hell as usual but they made good time once they hit the A3, heading south away from the capital. They were at Lakeside in under an hour. The car came to a halt in front of the main entrance. The woman didn't wait for the chauffeur to open the door but got out and strode into the marble hall and through into Dr. Bligh's office.

Dr. Bligh stood up when the woman entered. "I wasn't expecting you so soon."

"Who is she?" The woman brandished the crumpled paper in her hand. She was on the very edge of panic. She had lost control of the pitch of her voice.

"The new patient?" Dr. Bligh was determined to stay calm. "Her name's Melanie Drake. She says she's a journalist. She lives in Spain, somewhere near Marbella. That's all we know. She wanted to interview me about Lakeside. I referred the matter to Security and they told me to stonewall her, which I did. Then she started on a different tack, asking about Mary Berringer and the detoxification programme. I knew something was wrong. I put the emergency procedure into action and sent the message through to your office. Everything worked perfectly. She'll be sleeping now. Would you like to take a look?"

Melanie was kept sedated in a windowless cell two floors beneath the detoxification wing. The cell was twelve feet square and painted white. In a corner were a washbasin and a toilet bowl with no seat. There was a single electric light set into the wall, high up out of reach, no flex leading to it. It was kept on twenty-four hours a day. The only furniture was a metal bed and a single straight-backed wooden chair, both bolted to the floor.

Dr. Bligh looked through the spy hole, unlocked the door and pushed it open for the woman to enter first. Melanie lay on the bed in a drugged sleep, face to the wall. The woman sat on the bed, took Melanie by the shoulders and turned her bodily to face into the room. She took Melanie's head in her hands and lifted it towards her. After a moment she whispered, "I know this face." She brushed the hair from Melanie's forehead in a way that was almost tender. "Let me see, where did I.......?" It took a moment for the realisation to dawn but then her puzzled look gave way to outright panic. "My God! Oh my God!

It's the woman in the photograph with Bowman!" She turned to Dr. Bligh. "What are you giving her?"

"Diazepam. 10 milligrams. Twice a day, by intramuscular injection."

"Don't be technical with me! I'm not a doctor!" The voice was strident now, almost a scream.

"It's just something to make her sleep."

"Is it addictive, damn you!"

"Not normally. Not unless it's misused."

"I want her on heroin right away." She stood up, ready to leave.

Dr. Bligh hesitated. "I can't do that. I was trained to………"

"You're already in too deep to think of that Dr. Bligh. You know the consequences if you refuse. It's up to you. If you don't do it somebody else will." She shrugged. "How long before she can't survive without it?"

"Without endangering her health? I'll have to start her off with a small dose. Build it up gradually. Say a couple of weeks. Ten days, if there are no complications." She wanted to resist, but how could she?

"Start now! I want her hooked. As hooked as you can make her. But whatever you do, keep her alive. This little beauty is my insurance policy. Yours too, come to that."

Melanie's eyes fluttered, opened, and closed again. The woman looked at her again, brushing the hair from her face. She realised then how pretty she was, in her excitement she hadn't noticed it at first. She turned to Dr. Bligh, her voice calm now, almost soothing.

"You can leave us. Give me the keys. I'll lock up myself later. And send Daisy to me. I have a little present for him. Something he'll really enjoy." When the doctor had gone the woman turned again to Melanie, still coming out of her deep sleep. She undid the first few buttons of Melanie's blouse and stopped, leaving that part for Daisy.

"Well now, my dear." The woman murmured. "I wonder what interesting games we can teach you to play. You won't be able to resist, you know. Not when the heroin takes over. But you must resist all you want to now. That's what Daisy likes. A little resistance."

***

15

When Bowman returned to Marrakech with the two electronics experts from the Spanish Narcotics Bureau he went to the customs clearance agents to check how much of the equipment had arrived. Most of it had. He paid the customs officials generously, rented a couple of trucks and the three of them drove up to the farm to make a start on the installation. So by the time Lieberman dispatched his team of hit men a certain amount of work had already been completed.

Lieberman decided on a team of three, less would be too few and more would look like a posse. He chose José to head the team. José had hated Bowman ever since he went to San Roque that night to pick him up. Since Lieberman had made him draw his weapon but not allowed him to fire. Since Lieberman had given Alex the top security job. Harvey knew José wasn't the quickest with the gun, nor the best shot, but he was the cleverest of the bunch and the meanest, and he wouldn't let the Englishman out smart him.

The three hit men flew into Marrakech, rented a vehicle with four-wheel drive and followed Lieberman's instructions. It took longer than they expected and by the time they got to the farm it was late in the afternoon. They drove the final stretch of rugged terrain up the floor of the canyon and there, jutting out of the hillsides just as Lieberman had said, were the two outcrops of rock, which marked the entrance to the farm. But it wasn't quite as Harvey had described it. There, across the narrow gap between the outcrops, was a maximum gauge security fence with a gate in it.

José stopped the jeep, dismounted, and went to open the gate. It was locked. There was a button mounted next to the lock, with electric wires running from it, so José pressed it and the gate swung open, leaving a gap of a couple of feet, and stopped dead in its metal tracks. The three of them walked through and immediately the gate closed behind them. José looked up when he heard the voice and saw the video camera and the loudspeaker, fixed to a boom above the gate. The voice was Bowman's.

"Well, if it isn't my old friend José, come to pay us a visit. Welcome to Happy Dust Farm, José. We're just carrying out a training exercise, so your timing's perfect. Come forward to the second gate."

José and his men walked forward a few yards to a point where the gully through the rocks made a sharp turn, and came to a second gate, identical to the first, and above it another camera and a loudspeaker.

"José, I'm sending a couple of men in to frisk you. It's a procedure they haven't carried out before, so just be patient with them, OK?"

José saw two men appear and the gate was opened and closed again by remote control. A new voice came on the loudspeaker and spoke in the Berber language. The two men frisked José and his companions. Each of them had a weapon the Berbers removed and placed in a cavity cut into the rock. José was impressed with the thoroughness of the search.

"Thanks, José." It was Bowman's voice again. "I appreciate your patience. I'm going to open the gate now." José went to the cavity where the guns were and picked them up. He heard Bowman say, "Sorry, José. We have to stick to the proper procedure. Only designated security personnel are allowed to carry weapons inside the perimeter. If we start to make exceptions these guys will never understand. You'll get your weapons back when you leave."

José knew there was no point arguing with a loudspeaker and he didn't need a gun to do the job anyway. He had a much better weapon. The best one of all. The element of surprise. So he shrugged, put the weapons down and went back to the gate to wait for it to open.

"Thanks, José." said Bowman. "Come on up to the hut, I'd like to show you round."

When José reached the newly built hut, perched on top of a piece of high ground just inside the gate, it was crowded. Bowman was there with the two Spaniards he had recruited in Marbella, and a couple of the Berbers who were learning how to handle the equipment. And there was O'Malley, the fake Irishman who ran the processing side of things.

There was no pattern to life on the farm, no formal meal times, people ate and slept when they felt like it provided they weren't on duty. There were no bonds of friendship between the men, nobody really liked or trusted anybody else. But when O'Malley invited José to come up to his cabin, Alex didn't find it strange at all. They were old friends. They had both worked for Lieberman for years

"You vant to do some coke?" said O'Malley as he pushed open the door.

"*Una cerveza por favor.*" José wiped his mouth with the back of his dusty hand.

O'Malley poured them both a warm beer and they sat on the wooden deck looking across at he communications bunker. Suddenly Bowman appeared, framed in the doorway. "I hate that bastard." O'Malley's eyes narrowed. The chemist was indifferent to everybody else he had to deal with, but Bowman really got up his fake Irish nose. "Before he got here I ran this place, ran it properly. *Alles in ordnung.*" He liked being in charge. That was what nature intended. He was a professional man, a trained chemist, a graduate of Leipzig University. The Englishman was nothing. "Chief Security Officer." O'Malley spat on the ground. "Bullshit! One day I kill him."

"Wrong, O'Malley." José sipped beer from the bottle. "*Lo mato yo*! That's why I'm here. The bastard took my gun. *Muy bien.* I split his head with a rock."

The fake Irishman could not conceal his joy. He ran to his bunk and pulled it away from the wall. He took out a pocketknife, prised up a floorboard and rummaged between the joists. Then he pulled out a package of old newspapers and undid the bundle to reveal the Walther P38, wrapped in a well-oiled cloth. It had been his pride and joy for years. He'd nursed it all the way from the Western Desert to the Eastern Front. It wasn't the prettiest weapon ever made but, aside from its one idiosyncrasy, it was probably the most reliable. The magazine held eight rounds. More than enough for José's purpose.

"I let the Englishman take the Luger." O'Malley's eyes were full of malice. "A glamorous toy for spoiled rich kids, for officers. The Walther is a work-horse, never let me down." O'Malley ran his fingers lovingly along the gleaming black barrel and passed the weapon to José. "Bowman is a careful man. You better be careful too. Shoot him in the back. Who cares about honour any more?"

José smiled. He didn't care about honour any more, he never really had. José cared about *machismo*, his *machismo*.

***

The following morning José asked Bowman to show him round. Alex was glad to, he was proud of everything that had been done, even in so short a time. They started in the hut where the electrical installation was that eventually would control the whole security system. Only the gate at the entrance was functioning properly and the main task in hand was the erection of the perimeter fence that would eventually encircle the entire property. The fence would be electrified and support a system of sound and movement detectors, heat sensitive floodlights and video cameras, linked to the central control room.

Alex wore his side arm like a badge of office. He didn't use his favourite weapon at the farm, the compact Browning GP35FA. It wasn't flashy enough. At the farm a big part of the job was to impress, so he wore the long barrelled Colt .44 Magnum in a shoulder holster, hitched high where everybody could see it. This is the most powerful handgun in the world and its eight-inch barrel makes it by far the most accurate for long-range outdoor use. At ten paces it could lift a man's head clear off his shoulders.

José wanted to see everything, even the remote parts of the farm where the vegetation ceased abruptly and gave way to bare red earth, out of reach of the primitive irrigation system. They stuck to the watercourse, full with the melting snow, and followed the bed of the canyon for the best part of a mile, Alex leading and José following behind. At a point where the stream was dammed to form a pool the men used for bathing, Alex climbed away from the valley floor, up to a high escarpment of rock from the top of which the entire farm could be surveyed. Bowman was fitter and faster than José and used to the rough terrain, so he reached the summit two or three minutes ahead of the Spaniard. The top of the outcrop was a plateau about half the size of a football pitch, strewn with stones and loose boulders, like a piece of the moon fallen down to earth. It was joined to the mountain on one side only and the rest of its perimeter fell away steeply to the valley floor. Alex wandered to the far edge and looked down, waiting for the José to join him. Below he could see the farmhouse and the collection of huts clustered around the entrance. His eyes followed the line of the fence and the groups of men working at intervals along it. Alex took great satisfaction in his work, though it had no ultimate purpose. In the end the authorities would get to know about the farm and send a plane up to spray the place with Agent Orange. He almost regretted it. Especially after so much hard work.

Alex heard José's footstep behind him. Then he felt the barrel of the gun in the small of his back. The tone of José's voice was one of total command. "Take out the Colt and put it on the ground. Slowly. No rapid movements. Or I'll blow a hole right through you."

Alex bent down, put the Colt on the ground and straightened back up. José pushed at the Colt with the side of his foot and shoved it away hard. It travelled thirty or forty feet, skimming across the rocky surface, and came to rest against a stone a couple of yards from the edge. José walked back to a large boulder a few yards away and sat down. He took a good long look at Bowman and smiled his ferocious smile. Then the twitching started. It came in spasms, three at a time, like an eccentric clock.

Alex could see José's weapon clearly. He recognised the distinctive shape of the Walther semi-automatic. Standard issue to German troops in World War II. An outstandingly reliable gun with the same defect as all semi-automatics of its vintage. The trigger pressure required to release the first round is much greater than for the second and subsequent shots, when the hammer is re-cocked by the semi-automatic action. So the gun will pivot more with the first shot than the second. It wasn't a problem in a practised hand, but if José didn't expect it he would aim the first shot low as he pulled hard on the trigger, and the second one high, as he over-corrected his aim.

Bowman knew he would have to take his chance between the first shot and the second. His options were to grab José, moving toward the weapon, narrowing the angle and presenting a bigger target. Or he could risk the greater distance sideways, giving José more time, to where the Colt lay glinting in the sunlight. He decided to go for the Colt.

Alex kept his eyes on José, expecting him to speak. But the Spaniard just looked blankly Bowman, waiting for an instruction from someone who wasn't there. They looked at one another for a full minute while José got the twitching under control. There must be some preamble he wants to go through, thought Alex. Some fantasy he has to fulfil. He is as an actor, playing a role.

"Hey, Alex." José spoke at last. "You been fucking with Verity, *verdad*? That's very very naughty! *Muy malo!"*

"Verity? Come on José, Harvey would go ballistic!"

"Why you think Harvey send me here? Just to see you're alright?" José shifted his weight to the other foot. "Who is she, Alex? This other woman giving Harvey orders now? Why she want you killed?"

Alex had no idea what the Spaniard was talking about. But he kept his eyes on José and the Walther. Not blinking. *What woman?* But he had to put that thought out of his mind right now. Concentrate on here and now. On José and the Walther.

José didn't want to kill Bowman right away, blow him away with a single shot. He wanted to have a little fun, make the Englishman suffer, demean him, un-man him. Yes, that was it, un-man him. José stood up and spread his feet apart, the right slightly forward of the left. He raised the Walther in both hands. He had Bowman's head in his sights. He lowered the gun slowly down the target, to the chest and then the abdomen.

"Christ!" thought Alex, "He's going to shoot my balls off!"

The first shot landed a yard in front of the target. When the second was fired Bowman had already hit the ground a few yards short of the Colt. He rolled, grabbing the gun. The third round grazed his left shoulder but the Colt was in his grasp now and he rolled again and got off a sighting shot. The long barrelled Magnum was far more accurate than the Walther at this range and the shot came close to the target. The second struck José in the middle of the chest, lifting him clear of the ground, blood spurting from him. He went into a short violent spasm and was still. Bowman walked across and prodded the corpse with his boot. "Shit!" he murmured. "Didn't mean to kill the bastard!" There were things he needed to know. Questions José could have answered.

Alex went to the edge of the plateau and looked down. The men working on the fence were toiling undisturbed. The sound of gunshot was an everyday occurrence at the farm. People would shoot anything that moved in the undergrowth, a game bird, a rabbit. The Berbers were especially partial to a particular kind of lizard.

Bowman left José where he lay and clambered back down the canyon. He had to figure out what his next move should be. His cover was blown for sure, but how? And who was this woman giving Harvey orders? He realised now that killing José was a very big mistake. He should have kept him alive, worked him over. As he approached the huts he came across the two Spaniards he had brought with him and together they rounded up first José's two companions, then O'Malley and his assistants. They locked them in one of the huts and told the Berbers to shoot any man who tried to leave. Then they went to the store house and took out a couple of cans of the kerosene that was used in the refining process and set light first to the processing plant and the stock of partly finished product, then the hut which housed the communications equipment. Lastly they went to all the vehicles, bar the one they needed, ripped out the wiring and threw it on the burning buildings.

Bowman and his companions piled into the only functioning vehicle, knowing they would have a head start of at least a day, two if the Berbers had enough patience. Bowman turned the key in the ignition. The explosion was deafening, shaking the ground beneath them. The red and black plume of the fireball filled the sky as the main kerosene storage tank exploded.

***

The room wasn't guarded, not any more. There was no need. The heroin was the chain that bound her to them. The room was large and bright and airy, not like a prison at all. She was free to wander if she chose, she had the run of the house and grounds, but she never did. She couldn't summon the energy. Melanie stood at the window looking out across the vast expanse of lawn, holding on to the curtain to steady herself against the dizziness that never left her. On the terrace below stood one of the guards and a pair of Dobermans. The dogs were beautiful. Their coats glistened in the morning light. In the distance, on the far bank of the river, she could see the village clearly and the squat tower of the Norman church on top of the low rise. She had tried once to walk to the village, she hoped to get to a phone, but they wouldn't let her out of the estate. If only she could get to a phone she could call Flaherty and he could get hold of Alex. Alex would come for her. She was sure he would.

They looked after her very well. Almost spoiled her. She could eat whatever she wanted and the linen was changed every day, more often if it was needed. She was losing weight but up to a point it suited her. Her face was more sculpted now, but her breasts and hips were still full. They wanted to keep her looking good, so they could enjoy her.

She knew it was nearly time. Knew it by the ache in her joints. The nausea. No need to panic. She had control. But the woman liked to play games. Tease her. Make her squirm. On a good day Melanie could take it. But today was a bad day. A very bad day. She needed a fix right away.

There was a knock and the woman entered, dressed as always in black, as always smoking. One day it would kill her. If Bowman didn't get there first. "Well now." she smiled, "Have you remembered anything more interesting today?"

"I've told you everything. Everything I know. He told me practically nothing. He didn't want me involved." She crossed her arms over her stomach and held them tight.

"This farm, you must know where it is? Surely he must have told you?"

"It's in Morocco. Near Marrakech. South east of there. Somewhere in the High Atlas. I just don't know where it is! He never told me!" She was cold. She wiped the sweat from her face with the palm of her hand and tried to get the shaking under control, the tremor that went from her shoulders down to her legs in uncontrollable spasms of nausea.

"How big is it?"

"Stop doing this! Give it to me! Now! For Christsake I need it! Please!"

"How big is the farm? How much can it produce?

"For Christsake I don't know! Do you think I wouldn't tell you if I could? I've told you everything for Christsake. Everything I know." She started to wretch but her belly was empty.

"How much can the farm produce?"

"Please! I'll do anything, damn you! Bitch! Motherfucker!" Her head was splitting and the ache in her joints was torture. Her stomach was in knots. Then the awful formication started, the terrifying sensation of armies of ants crawling all over her body, gnawing at her skin. They were everywhere, on the backs of her hands, in her mouth, feeding on her eyes. "Who are you? Why are you doing this to me?"

The woman sat on the chair by the window, smiling. She knew if she made her wait any longer Melanie would crack. So he put the package on the table and watched her scurry off to the bathroom.

Melanie pushed open the door of the cubicle and bolted it behind her. She took off her blouse and dropped it on the damp floor, revealing her already bruised and ulcerated forearm. She sat on the seat and opened up the package with shaking hands. The syringe was already loaded but in her panic she had to jab the needle several times into her arm before she hit a vein. She watched the magic liquid disappear from the phial as she pressed down on the syringe. Then she leaned back against the wall of the cubicle and slowly, beautifully, everything changed and the pain and the nausea receded. She was calm. Serene. The elixir pumped through her veins and worked its magic. Its marvellous, necessary, indispensable magic. The magic she could no longer live without. The magic that turned her, fleetingly, into a God.

The woman was amazed at the effect the drug had, and had so quickly. The way Melanie's faculties returned immediately. Her confidence. Her self-control. But the woman knew it was only a conjuring trick. An illusion. The drug was both the affliction and the cure. But only the affliction was real and lasting and irreversible.

Melanie lay on the bed, waiting. Words could not describe the feeling it gave her. It was good beyond description. She was calm, at peace, floating free. She soared. There was nothing she wouldn't do to achieve this state. Nothing. She wished it could last forever.

Then he came to her, the fair angel with the pale skin and the lifeless pallid eyes. At first she had hated him, loathed his touch, his coarse animal brutality. She had fought him. Hitting and scratching and gouging and biting. It only excited him more. But she couldn't resist him any longer. Not now. She hadn't the strength. This seemed to disappoint him, but he enjoyed her still. She knew he did, she could tell. She did her very best to please him. It seemed only fair. It was the only way she had to pay them back.

The woman had enjoyed her too at first, but now she would only watch. She would sit on the chair by the window smoking, puffing smoke rings in the air. Sometimes she looked bored and would make a suggestion and Daisy would take her a different way. Something he hadn't tried before, nor had the wit to imagine for himself. He seemed to like that. To be told what to do. He was only a servant after all.

***

Bowman took the Royal Air Maroc flight to Malaga, picked up his car and drove along the coast. At Marbella he turned off the main road and headed inland into the hills. By the time he reached *La Hacienda Blanca* it was dark. He switched off the headlights at the entrance to the private road, cut the engine and drifted silently down the incline, passed the gate, to where the wall took a sharp right angle to run along the back of the property. He parked close to the wall, took a length of rope from the boot and clambered onto the car roof. He threw one end of the rope over the iron spikes and hoisted himself to the top of the wall. The problem would be getting out in a hurry if he had to. The drop on the other side was over fifteen feet. He paid out the rope and descended rapidly into the darkness. He took the Browning from his belt and checked the clip. He waited, watching and listening, but there was no sound and no movement. He moved quickly to the shadows at the rear of the house. He knew the windows weren't alarmed, and soon found one that had been left ajar. He climbed inside, closing the window behind him. There were movement detectors all over the ground floor but Alex knew where they were and the areas they covered. With his back to the wall he was able to make his way to the foot of the main stairway and began to climb. There was no security system on the bedroom floor. When Harvey gave one of his famous parties he liked people to be able to move about freely up there. Bowman moved along the corridor to the master bedroom and pushed open the door. The room was in darkness but he could hear the breathing of two people, one light and even, the other deep, nasal, irregular. Harvey had gone to bed drunk. Alex crossed to the window and opened the curtain a few inches to let in a little light. Down by the pool he could see two figures standing partly in shadow, moonlight glinting off the weapons in their shoulder holsters.

Alex returned to the bed and looked down on Verity's long silken back. He hadn't had a woman since

Marrakech. And it was a long time since he had had one as gorgeous as she was. Her blond hair fell loose across her shoulders. She was uncovered to below the waist, the cleavage of her buttocks just clear of the black satin sheet. Her slender back had a deep tan but below the line of her bikini the flesh was a startling luminescent white. As he watched she turned in her sleep to face towards the door and away from Harvey, whose breathing ceased for a moment and then resumed its deep nasal monotone. Verity sighed with yearning or dissatisfaction, he couldn't tell which, he wasn't listening he was looking, looking down on her gorgeous body, the fullness of her lovely breasts, the line of her long legs visible beneath the black satin sheet. *Blue Moon, you knew just what I was there for, you heard me saying a prayer for, someone I really could care for.*

His pulse was racing as she moved again into the foetal position, her slender arms crossing her breasts in a gesture of the purest virtue.

Alex put the Browning in his belt and placed a hand gently over her mouth. She didn't wake at once so he put his hand over her nostrils to restrict her breathing. Her eyes opened suddenly as she turned towards him with a jerk and choked back the sound she was about to make. Her eyes looked startled, then pleased and then delighted as she worked out what was happening. Alex had come for her at last!

Verity turned to look at Harvey. She saw he was asleep and knew he wouldn't waken, he never did. She slipped silently from the bed, took Alex by the hand, and led him into the corridor. She closed the door, pushed Alex against the wall and wrapped herself around him. She kissed him urgently, pressing her body against his, moving, sighing, wanting, pleading, feeling him grow, feeling him harden. She unbuttoned his shirt. She kissed his neck, his chest, his abdomen. She knelt before him, fumbling hands on the buckle of his belt. It was then that she found the Browning. It wasn't what she expected. She touched him again, just to make sure, and led him into the adjacent room. She took a robe from behind the door and put it on.

"It's Harvey, isn't it? You've come to kill him!" The idea clearly startled her.

"Not unless I have to. I need him alive."

"He won't wake for hours. He never wakes till day light."

Alex wanted Verity, wanted her badly, wanted her now. He took the belt around her robe and pulled her towards him. As he let go of the belt the robe fell slightly open and he pushed it back all the way to the edge of her shoulders and watched it slide slowly to the floor. She was lovely, a silken statue. He cupped her breasts in his hands and kissed her mouth. She unbuckled his belt, feeling his raw hardness. They moved together onto the bed. She was beneath him now, her thighs enfolding him. She took his penis and guided him inside her, sighing, moaning, feeling him move, pushing back on him, responding. She wrapped her legs around his body, rising against him, holding him close. She took his head in her hands and kissed him urgently, wanting, yearning, almost coming, not now, not yet, too soon, more slowly, make it last, slow, easy, gentle, good, harder now, harder, almost hurting, flowing, thrusting, deeper, deeper, ah!, make it last, not yet, no, *NO*! slowly now, easy, gentle, good, good, flowing, thrusting, *FUCKING*, harder now, harder, yes, *YES*! Coming, coming, now! Now! Now! *NOW! NOW*! She released him, holding his head in her hands, kissing him softly as he rode her, plundered her, made her whole.

***

Verity didn't notice how the light changed from the silver of moonlight, to the pink blush of dawn, to the bright gold of morning. She just lay there waiting for Alex to wake up and take her again, as she knew he would. It was the sudden noise from below that brought her back to reality.

"Hey Verity! Where the fuck are you?"

It was Harvey, calling from the sitting room below. She looked at her watch. It was past nine o'clock. She shook Alex awake, wanting him, wanting him badly. "Harvey's downstairs. What shall I do?"

Alex sat up with a start. "Go down and distract him. Give me a couple of minutes."

"What will I tell him? I'm supposed to be there when he wakes up. Harvey's a morning person." She began to blush.

Alex kissed her cheek. "You'll think of something."

"I certainly hope so." She slipped into the robe and opened the door. As she went down the stairs she saw Harvey was already dressed, standing in the middle of the room. He saw where she had come from.

"Where the fuck have you been, Verity? What the hell is going on?"

"Nothing is going on Harvey, I just couldn't sleep that's all. I've told you before how your snoring keeps me awake. Last night was worse than ever, so I slept in the guest room. There's absolutely nothing to get excited about."

"Gee babe, I'm sorry, I missed you. I woke up so goddamn horny."

"So did I, Harvey." said Verity with feeling. "So did I." She stretched and yawned in a way that Harvey took to be an invitation.

Harvey moved towards her and put his hands inside her robe. It surprised him when she backed away. But not as much as the sight of Bowman standing at the head of the stairs, brandishing a pistol.

"You fucking bitch!" Harvey raised his hand to strike her.

"Don't, Harvey." Bowman's voice was calm. "I may kill you anyway. Don't give me one more reason."

"Bowman! Alex fucking Bowman! You're supposed to be dead! Don't you know that? You'd better get the fuck out of here. Take the bitch with you. They're on to you

Bowman. You're dead already. You're just too dumb to lie down!"

"Who's on to me Harvey? Besides you and José that is."

"The big guys! The Organisation! You poor dumb clutz! Christ Alex, you still can't figure it out, can you? The woman in black! She came here. She saw your fucking picture. She recognised you." Harvey was grinning all over his face.

Verity knew immediately it must be the same woman. The woman who had sent her here in the first place. But Verity had enough sense to keep quiet in front of Harvey. She would tell Alex, she would have to, she wanted to, but not now, not with Harvey standing there.

"Picture? What picture?" Alex was saying.

"The picture in the night club, dumbo. The picture your girlfriend wanted. The cold assed English broad." Harvey looked at Verity and rejoiced at her reaction. Her face reddened and she made a tight little fist with each hand. Verity was jealous, jealous as hell. She looked at Alex as though she could kill him.

"What sort of a fuck was she anyway, Bowman?" Harvey continued, pressing his advantage. "A touch of the ice maiden, eh? Maybe not. Maybe she likes it up her ass." Harvey grinned. Bowman showed no reaction. Perhaps he didn't care about her after all. But Verity cared. Verity cared like hell.

"Sit down, Harvey." said Bowman. "There's a few questions I want to ask you. If you co-operate, I may decide to let you live." His tone was casual, but it was the casual tone that convinced Harvey he was serious. "Describe her to me."

"The woman? Sure, but it won't help. She has no distinguishing features. Nothing to make her stand out. Medium height. Medium build. Medium age. Medium dark complexion. Short straight hair. Probably dyke. Dresses well, but always in black, every time I've seen her. She wears a hat most of the time, and sometimes she puts on an American accent. She does it well, I have to admit. I think it's when she's taking the piss."

Verity followed this exchange intently. She knew who the woman was, not her name, but how to find her. She had the envelopes, pre-addressed to a box number in the City. She couldn't say so. Not now, with Harvey sitting there. She would save it for Alex. Alex would be so grateful!"

"Was she alone?" said Alex.

"She had a driver."

"Local?"

"Brit. I saw him once before, at our original meeting. The one Tiffany set up. He carries a heater. Not much of a shot though." Harvey smiled.

"What do you mean, not much of a shot?"

“The woman screamed when she saw your ugly mug. He took a shot at me. The whole thing was a misunderstanding. The slug’s still there, over in that cabinet.”

Alex walked across to the drinks cabinet and ran his finger across the centre panel. He took out a penknife, eased the bullet out of the woodwork and put it in his pocket.

“Describe him.”

“Sure. This one’s easy. Albino. Meanest looking sonofabitch you ever did see!”

“Albino?” Alex was stunned. “Albino? You’re sure he was albino

“Sure I’m sure! How could I be mistaken about a thing like that?”

"Why did she come here?" said Alex after a pause.

"To buy a piece of my business, asshole." Foul language helped Harvey keep his spirits up.

"How come she saw my picture?"

"It was on display, Verity kept it in a nice bright silver frame. Now I understand why." Harvey turned towards her. “I’ll kill you, you bitch. I’ll fuckin’ kill you!”

"What happened when she saw it?"

"She went bananas. Absolutely bananas. She smashed it on the floor, frame and all. There was glass all over the place."

"So you decided to kill me, sent José up to the farm?"

"Not me, cocksucker. She decided." Harvey looked at the Browning, which Alex nursed in his lap. The idea that he was in deep deep trouble had dawned only slowly but the message was getting through to him now. It was time to start talking. Talking counted more than thinking when your life was on the line.

"It had nothing to do with me, Alex. I like you. Always have. She was giving me orders. Can you believe that?" Harvey chuckled at the absurdity of the idea. "You and me should stick together Alex. Like old times. Partners."

"Partners." Alex repeated. It was something he had thought about before.

"I'll raise your salary. One hundred grand a year. No deductions. Salary! Shit, I'll give you part of the action."

"Shut up Harvey. I need time to think." Alex looked across at Verity, following every word. She was gorgeous. Absolutely gorgeous. And she screwed like an absolute dream. Alex sat in silence, as an idea took shape in his mind.

"How will she know, Harvey? How will she know I'm dead? Are you supposed to make contact?"

"That woman is amazing, Alex. I still don't know who she is. I have to sit and wait till she gets back in touch. I've never known anyone so goddamn cautious."

"That's good, Harvey. Play ball with me and you might even save your skin." Alex went to the phone and dialled the Algeciras number. "Ben? This is Alex. I'm at the *Hacienda Blanca*. Come on over. Things are moving along pretty quickly now. It's time we had a chat." Bringing Ambrose back into the picture at this stage could be a mistake. But it had to be done to secure the Spanish end.

"Who's Ben?" Harvey looked suspicious.

"Benjamin Ambrose. I think you'll like him. He's with the DEA."

"The *schwartze?* The cowboy in the red Ferrari?" Harvey went completely white. It was clear to him now just how much trouble he was really in. He watched as Alex went outside, stripped, and dived into the pool. Verity came to the window to watch him too.

"You know, it's a funny thing," said Harvey. "I could have sworn Alex had the hots for the ice maiden. Still, he's a big guy. I'm sure he can service you both." He watched Verity biting her lip. It surprised him how hard she bit. Verity was bleeding.

Harvey came a step closer and put his mouth to her ear. "I'll kill you, you fuckin' bitch." he whispered. "I'll fuckin' kill you."

***

Early that afternoon the whole of Harvey's establishment was rounded up and replaced by officers of the Spanish Narcotics Bureau. The hole in the road was filled in for the last time and the gang of men went off to celebrate the end of a very boring assignment. Ben Ambrose went over in detail the best deal he could get for Harvey in exchange for his co-operation. Harvey was shitless all the same. He had never done time anywhere, not in the States, not in England, not anywhere. There had always been some other poor dumb *clutz* to take the rap for Harvey Lieberman. But Harvey had heard stories of what happened to people who went to jail, the beatings, the overcrowded unsanitary conditions, the homosexual advances of the other inmates, the drugs. Ambrose explained that those conditions need not apply to Harvey. Ben could arrange for him to be shipped back to the States to face charges. The Spanish people would be glad to get rid of him and avoid the publicity of an extended trial. The Americans had special jails for prisoners who co-operated with the authorities, whose testimony could lead to the arrest of some really important people. Harvey would have to serve his time, as much as four or five years, but it would be in *Club Fed*, almost a country club. After a year or two with good behaviour he could even get out for weekends.

The installation of the listening device took hardly any time and no real expertise. They fixed it up in Harvey's study so they could monitor and record every call that was made. After that it was a question of time and patience till the right call came through. It came at six o'clock precisely, that very first evening. They set the tapes running and Harvey and one of the operatives picked up their phones in unison as they had practised doing.

"Let me speak to Mr. Lieberman." Harvey recognised the voice and nodded to Alex.

"Mr. Lieberman is resting at this hour." The Spanish operative adjusted the recording level on the machine as he spoke.

"I'm calling from London. Please tell him. It's very important."

"Who may I say is calling?"

"Just tell him it's London. He's expecting my call."

The operative put the phone down on the wooden table with a thump, waited for about a minute and then picked it up again, signalling Harvey to speak.

"Harvey Lieberman on the line, who am I speaking to?"

"You know who this is Harvey, don't be cute with me." The American accent was there, just below the surface. "That little project we discussed, has it been completed?"

"Yes mam. Just like I said. The very next day."

"How can I be sure of that, Harvey?"

"Whadaya want me to do? Cut off his ear and send it to you in the mail?" Harvey looked across at Alex and had a better idea. "Or his dick maybe?"

"No Harvey, that won't be necessary. I've seen how you perform." There was silence at the other end, she seemed to be conferring with some one. It was a while before she spoke again. "Harvey, now Bowman's out of the way we need to put the shipment back on track. We need supply within the next four or five days."

"What about payment? I need half up front or there's no deal!" Harvey's outrage was completely genuine.

"Look Harvey, we're partners now. We have to trust one another."

“Sure. We're partners now.” He seemed to be speaking to Alex. “No problem. Where should I have it delivered?" He saw Alex cross his fingers and lift his eyes to heaven.

"Just have your courier make his way back to the UK. I'll confirm the final destination once he gets here."

"Right." Harvey looked at Alex for his next cue. There was more silence at the other end.

"What's his name, Harvey?" she said suddenly, sounding impatient. "I need to know the courier's name."

"His name?" Harvey repeated. Alex grabbed a piece of paper and scribbled a single word. Harvey picked it up and looked across at Alex. "Bastard."

"What was that Harvey? I didn't catch the name."

"His name's Fitzroy. Captain Fitzroy. He's good. I've used him before a dozen times or more." Harvey wanted to go on, spin the conversation out as they had told, but the line went suddenly dead.

Alex looked at his watch. "A little under two minutes. No chance of a trace, not even if we'd been in the same country."

"What about a voice print, Alex?" said Ambrose.

"We have the technology, but there's no data bank to speak of. The chances are one in a million. Fitzroy is our only real hope."

"How come you know about Fitzroy?" said Harvey.

"We've been watching you for weeks, Harvey. You should pay more attention to details. We dug the same hole in your road three or four times."

“You mean you really plan to use this guy?” Ambrose broke in. “A mule for Christsake? Why not put an agent in place? The other side can't know anything about this guy, whatsisname, Fitzroy. Not even what he looks like. An agent would be better, more reliable. I'd do it myself if it wasn't for the accent.”

Verity was twisting in her seat, making tight little fists with both hands. She looked across at Harvey then back to Alex, but she didn't speak. *Of course they know what he looks like! They have his photograph!*

"Maybe you're right, Ben. Maybe we should put an agent in place. I'll discuss it with George. See what he thinks. He'll be running the London end." Things were moving in Bowman's direction now, which was just the way he wanted it.

"Like I said Ben, I'll talk to George, see what he thinks. But there's a bigger issue we have to decide. Do we ship the real thing, or a placebo?"

"A placebo? Jesus, I hadn't thought of that!" Ambrose's brow was furrowed. "Look, Alex, it's about time I came clean with Willowby. This thing is getting really scary. I'd rather have Willowby's ass on the line than mine. I have to put him in the picture now anyway. So let me consult him about the placebo. Right? It'll make him feel good. And that way, if this thing goes pear shaped, me and you don't have to carry the can!"

Harvey went to his room. They posted a guard in the corridor, another on the balcony outside the window, and sent him up a tray of food. Ambrose told him he would have to get used to confinement, and he might as well start right away. Verity went upstairs to move her things into the guest bedroom, so she could be with Alex.

"Do something for me, Ben" said Alex when they were alone. "Keep an eye on Verity for me. Harvey will kill her if he gets the chance."

"Sure, Alex." Ambrose looked surprise. "No problem. Harvey won't even leave his room."

When Verity came back downstairs she was surprised to find Bowman was leaving. "Alex, where are you going?" She was terrified of the answer. "You're going to her, aren't you? Why Alex? Why are you going to her?" She had an envelope in her hand.

Alex didn't know the answer. "I just want to check she's OK, that's all. I'll be back."

Verity felt suddenly threatened. "Alex, there's something I have to show you. I think it could be important." She tried to show him the envelope but Alex had the door open now and was going down the terrace steps. "Alex, I know it's important. I know it is." She raised her voice and lowered it again as he climbed into the car. "It's to do with the woman Alex, the woman in black. I think I know how to find…........" Her voice trailed away to silence as she watched him drive off into the darkness.

"You bastard! Oh Alex! You bastard!" She crossed the room, tore the envelope in tiny pieces and threw it on the fire.

***

Ambrose was left alone with the Spanish operatives and their monitoring equipment. He checked the available space on the hard drive and loaded the DEA's encryption software onto Harvey's PC. It took forty minutes to compile a detailed account, claiming the credit for himself. He didn't even mention Bowman's name. He reckoned there was a promotion in the offing. And a pay rise. When he had finished his report he passed the big decision to his boss. The real thing? Or a placebo?.

***

Willowby read Ben's decoded message in a state of shock. It was the biggest thing that had come across his desk in the whole of his career. Ambrose's report had implications that were truly global. Willowby wasn't sure how to handle it. He decided to stall. He sent a brief reply. "Excellent work Agent Ambrose. I'll have to consult about the placebo. Will call you at your apartment on the secure line in a couple of hours."

Willowby left the Embassy by a side door and went to the pay phone on the corner of South Audley Street. He dialled the Colombian Embassy. "Miguel? We have a problem. A big problem. Get over to my apartment as quickly as you can." It was when he replaced the receiver that the penny dropped. It wasn't a problem. It was a godamn opportunity!

***

Alex parked the car under the canopy in front of the apartment building and walked up to the porter's desk. The uniformed figure stood up as Alex approached and smiled in recognition. "*Buenas noches*, Señor Bowman."

"Is Miss Drake at home?" Alex wasn't in the mood for pleasantries.

"Miss Drake? Why no, Señor. Miss Drake returned to England several days ago."

Alex wasn't surprised. "Did she leave any message?"

"Miss Drake? No Señor. But a package was delivered in your name." He searched the shelves below the desk and placed a parcel on the counter in front of Alex.

"Who brought this?"

"A courier."

"That's it? Just the package? No message?"

"No, Señor Bowman. No message." The porter watched as Alex went back to the car and drove away. Then he picked up the phone and dialled the twelve-digit London number.

Alex was tired, exhausted, he needed to sleep. Most of all he wanted to be alone for a while and to think. He had had enough for now, enough of Harvey and José, enough of Ambrose and Ramsay, even enough of Verity. He decided to go back to San Roque that night, to get some rest. But first he would look at the tape. He loaded the cassette into the recorder, and watched the screen flicker into life. There was no sound and it took a moment for the picture to become clear. When it did he saw a dimly lit room, quite small but comfortably furnished. The camera panned the room and settled on a bed where a woman lay naked and apparently asleep. Her face was to the wall but Alex knew who she was. She began to twitch violently, then the spasm ceased and she was still. In a while she sat up with a jerk and swung her legs over the side of the bed. She was thinner than he remembered and her movements were slow and lethargic. Suddenly she placed both forearms across her stomach and bent forward, head between her knees as if she were about to vomit. She wretched several times but her stomach was empty. Then the camera closed in on her forearms. Alex saw the tell tale signs of bruising, the tiny marks where the needle had punctured the skin. Then the camera panned to the door. Melanie seemed to have heard a noise outside. She went to thc door and beat on it with her fists and scratched it with her fingernails till they bled. The noise must have ceased and she sat on the bed again, crossing herself repeatedly, muttering a silent prayer. As her head fell back Alex saw her eyes, wide staring eyes, looking straight at him, full of despair. She was screaming now in utter silence. He watched her muted mouth forming the words and tried in vain to decipher their desperate message. Then the picture went suddenly dead and Alex was left alone with the pain. He could still see her mouth in front of him now as he sat in the darkness, and the words were suddenly clear. "ALEX! ALEX! ALEX!"

He went to the cabinet where he kept the booze and took out a bottle of brandy. He poured four fingers of the fiery liquid, emptied the glass at a single throw, and filled it again. Then he rewound the tape and played it again from the beginning, trying as best he could to keep his eyes from Melanie and concentrate on the detail. In a little while he heard the sound of a vehicle at the top of the gravelled drive and a moment later the footsteps on the terrace steps. He took the tape from the machine and put it back in its packaging. That was when he found the note. "Here's the deal. We get the shipment. You get the girl."

"Jesus Christ!" Alex muttered. "If Willowby opts for the placebo, Melanie's as good as dead!" He left silently through the rear door and walked across the fields to the village. He still had time to catch the last London flight.

***

Willowby's call came through at eight o'clock that evening on the secure line in Ambrose's apartment.

"Agent Ambrose?"

"Yes, Sir."

"So what the fuck is going on, Ambrose? How come you've been sitting on this for weeks without putting me in the picture? Don't you realise how big this is?"

"It's only just come to a head, Sir. I wasn't sure it was real, till I sent you the email. At first it seemed so unlikely. I didn't take it seriously." Ambrose lied. It was hard to explain without giving Bowman credit.

"OK! OK! We'll go over everything when this is over. But right now we have to make plans. Here's the deal. There's a brace of Rangerovers on the overnight ferry to Bilbao. Should be with you tomorrow night. One will transport the dope. It's fitted with satellite tracking. There's a team of minders in second car."

Ambrose frowned. "I thought I'd be running things from this end, Sir."

"You've done enough, Agent Ambrose. I'm taking control now. This isn't just a local Spanish matter any more. It's European."

"So the Brits are in the frame, Sir?"

"The Brits! Are you kidding? The NDIU is a sieve! You heard about Rutland? A Minister for Christsake! Till this thing's over, if you see a Brit don't talk to him. Listen to me, Ambrose. Here's what I want you to do. When the Rangerover turns up, pack it tight with every ounce of snow you can find."

"Snow?" Ambrose interrupted. "Not a placebo?"

"We decided to ship the snow. It's a risk if we do, and a risk if we don't. So that's the deal. We can impound the stuff here in the UK, once we see where it leads us. Agent in charge of transportation's a guy called Richter. Know him?"

"No Sir."

"Do whatever he says. He'll go over the details with you and instruct you how to brief the courier, whatsisname, Fitzroy?"

"Fitzroy."

"That's it. Richter takes over. You can take a well-earned rest." Willowby's tone became suddenly softer, more friendly. "By the way Ben, this farm where Lieberman's growing the stuff, any idea where it is?"

“Not exactly. But I’ll know for sure in a day or two. Harvey’s keen to co-operate.”

“That’s good, Ben. Get as much information as you can. Squeeze him dry. When that’s done, take a few days off. Don’t want you getting in Richter’s way. Make your own way back to London. Stop by the Embassy and make a full report. Verbally. Nothing in writing. Nothing the Brits can get a hold of. Then we’ll talk about your new assignment.” The line went suddenly dead.

“What new assignment?” said Ambrose to himself. “I haven’t requested a new assignment!”

***

16

George Ramsay lived in a grubby little flat in a converted Edwardian terrace house, just off the Wandsworth Bridge road. He had promised himself for years that he would move to something better in the suburbs but he had two kids to bring up and an estranged wife to support, and somehow had never got enough capital together.

When the doorbell rang at half past one in the morning. George thought it must be one of the kids, too drunk to go back to their mother's house. It happened about once a month. When he opened the door and saw Alex standing there he was pleased on two counts, pleased to see his friend and pleased he wouldn't have to clean up after the kid in the morning. But when Ramsay saw the expression on Bowman's face under the naked light in the hall, he knew it was no time for small talk. Alex's face was empty, drained, all life gone out of it. He seemed to be wearing a mask. It was the expression he had worn in the dock when the judge had sent him down. Alex handed George the videotape and followed him into the sitting room.

George sat on the sofa and Alex on an armchair in the corner where he couldn't see the screen. He watched the expression on Ramsay's face in the grey light of the television and saw how moved he was by what he saw. Ramsay didn't speak, but when the tape came to its sudden end he picked up the remote control and rewound it to watch it through a second time, just as Alex had done. They sat in darkness for a time, not speaking. Then

Ramsay said, “I don’t get it, Boss. Aren’t they supposed to think you’re dead?”

“Maybe they do. Maybe they don’t. This is just their insurance.” Alex got up to help himself to a Scotch. “They offered me a deal, George.”

“What deal?”

“They get the shipment. I get the girl.”

“Jesus! What’ll you do Alex?”

“She got herself into this, George. No one invited her in. She’ll have to take her chances. We’ll just have to do the best we can.” Alex stayed silent for a while, then he said, "OK, detective sergeant, where are they holding her?"

"Christ knows. There's some detail in the background but not much, and the picture quality is poor. I'll take it to the lab in the morning and get them to enhance it, maybe there's something there we can use, but I doubt it." He got up and switched on a light. "Why did they send it to you, boss? What's the bloody point?"

"To flush me out, George. Make sure I go after her." He put his head in his hands and closed his eyes. "Christ George! Why did she do it? Why did the silly bitch have to get herself involved?"

Ramsay got up to go to the kitchen. He wanted to give Alex something else to think about so he took the photographs from the drawer and put them on the table. "Take another look at that lot boss, the pictures of Mary's funeral. Now we know we're looking for a woman you might spot something new, something we'd missed before."

"Just look at them!" said Alex, when Ramsay returned with the bottle of scotch. "You'd think they were at the races, this one might as well be at Ascot." He had picked up a photograph of Rutland smiling at a woman with her back to the camera wearing a broad brimmed hat. He re-arranged the photographs on the floor in front of him and there she was again, sideways on to the camera this time, surrounded by a group of men. "Melanie saw all of these? She went through the whole lot?"

"That's right boss, she recognised quite a few."

"Did she know any of them personally? Anyone besides Rutland?"

"She didn't say so. She didn't even tell me she knew Rutland, not till it was too late."

Alex assembled all the photographs into a pile and began to deal them out in front of him, rapidly, like a gambler. When he had dealt the whole deck he picked them up again and went through the same procedure a second time, looking for one particular card that wasn't there, the missing joker. He stopped at a shot of the woman in the hat talking to Miguel Torres. "This is her George, I can smell it. Just because black is what you'd expect her to be wearing at a funeral I didn't spot it right away. Look at them George! They all know her for Christsake! Esler knows her! Torres knows her! You can bet your pension

Berringer knows her too, otherwise why would she be there?"

"So let's pick one of them up Alex, sweat it out of the bastard. Any pretext would do."

"How can we George? As long as they're holding Melanie!" He could hear it clearly now, the silent sound that never left him, calling out his name, over and over and over. “Except maybe .... maybe........”

“Maybe who?”

“Maybe Torres. He’s not part of the organisation. We could take him out and they wouldn’t even notice he was gone.” The more he thought about it the more he liked the idea. Torres the supplier. Torres the outsider.

“Take him out?”

“If we have to.”

“If *you* have to Alex. If it comes to killing count me out.” There were limits to what even Ramsay would do, which was something Bowman should have known.

Alex stood up and stretched himself to his full impressive height, waiting for the scotch to do its work. “Don’t worry George, he’d be no use to anybody dead. What about Fitzroy, did you make contact with him yet?"

"He'll be here at nine in the morning, he's booked out on an afternoon flight. You can brief him yourself if you like, while I take the tape to the lab."

"You think we're right to use him? You don't think an agent in place would be better, more reliable. Ambrose was keen to do it himself."

"Best leave Ambrose out of it, boss. Keep this to ourselves. Like old times. At least we know where we are with Fitzroy and surveillance will be watertight. He'll be watched every inch of the way."

"OK George, you're the boss. Captain Fitzroy it is. But you brief him. He already knows you. No point showing myself if I don't have to."

***

Punctually at nine o'clock the next morning James Fitzroy rang the bell. He looked uncomfortable in the seedy little flat, with the stained carpets and damp showing through the wallpaper. He refused the mug of instant coffee the clumsy copper offered him and took out a cigarette instead. He didn't offer one to Ramsay, it might have made the plodder feel like his social equal.

"It's that simple." Ramsay said in conclusion. "You just pick up the consignment in Marbella and follow Ambrose's directions. When it's over you'll be given a new identity, birth certificate, passport, and a ticket to any destination in the world. One way, I'm afraid, but then you won't want to come back. No money, but you probably have enough stashed away by now anyway."

Fitzroy accepted, what other choice did he have? It was a pity about the money, it went against the grain to do something for nothing, there was a principle involved, a creed. But the plod was right, he had over four hundred thousand in his numbered account in Zurich, enough to make a fresh start somewhere where the sun always shone and the exchange rate was favourable. The whole thing should be over in a week, less if he was lucky.

Fitzroy took a cab back to his flat off the Fulham road. It was only minutes away, but it was another world. He had ample time to pack his bag and take a second shower to wash off the odour of Ramsay's nasty little flat. He noticed the strange looking couple as he entered the lobby. They seemed to be waiting for someone. The woman was elegantly dressed in black, the man a total contrast, hair white, skin as pale as could be. The albino was massive, a brute. He came up to Fitzroy as he waited for the lift.

"Excuse me, Captain Fitzroy. I wonder if we might have a word?"

"I'm in a bit of a hurry I'm afraid, and anyway who are.......?" By this time the albino had Fitzroy's arm in a tight grip and guided him to where the woman sat on a sofa. She gestured to Fitzroy to sit between them.

"We're friends of Harvey Lieberman." she smiled. "There's something we'd like you to do."

"Harvey who?" Fitzroy couldn't resist the temptation to be clever.

“Oh James!” the woman sighed, turning to Daisy. "Show him the photograph." The albino took a photograph from his pocket and placed it on the table. It was the Polaroid of Fitzroy and Verity leaning on the Porsche at the *Hacienda Blanca*, the mauve and crimson bougainvilleas in full bloom behind them. "You can't see Harvey of course" she said. "He's the one taking the picture. Look James, we haven't got much time, let me show you something else." She nodded to the albino who produced a black leather briefcase from beside the sofa and put it on the table in front of her. When she opened it Fitzroy saw that it was full of used £50 notes in tight little bundles, as if they had come straight from the bank. He couldn't tell exactly how much was there, but it might have been as much as fifty thousand pounds.

"Now, James." She touched him gently on the knee. "Why don't we go upstairs and have a little chat in private? It will only take a couple of minutes."

Daisy did a sweep of the room, pronouncing it clean. The woman sat in an armchair by the window. "Now James, we've arranged a delivery with Harvey. A very large amount of coke. We know Harvey has asked you to do the run for him. But Harvey doesn't realise we've made contact. Or how. It's important he doesn't find out. Do you follow me so far?"

"Perfectly. Miss.........?"

"If he does find out we've been in contact, I'm afraid it's curtains for you, James. Daisy will take care of you personally. Got that?"

"Got that." Fitzroy looked across at the albino. Daisy didn't look so tough. He was over weight and muscle bound. Probably slow on his feet.

"So what I want is for you to go to Spain and follow Harvey's instructions to the letter. This is your reward." She patted the briefcase. "There'll be another one just like it for you once we have the coke. OK?"

"Very much so. Rather." James grinned.

"There's a couple of other chores we want you to do. You remember Verity? The girl in the photo?"

"My word, yes!"

"Once you have possession of the coke, kill her. Then Harvey. It's for your own protection, James. They can both identify you. Any problem with that?"

Fitzroy went white but he didn't speak.

"You've killed before. In the army. In Ulster. We've done our research, James. We know what you're capable of."

"That was different."

"Of course. You didn't know the victims. This will be much tougher. But it's you or them, James. So who's it to be?"

"Them." Fitzroy eyed the briefcase.

The woman followed Fitzroy's gaze. "You'll find what you need in the briefcase. Also a mobile phone. Don't use it to make calls but have it switched on all the time, so we can stay in touch. Once you're safely back in the UK, I'll let you know your final destination. Is everything clear so far?"

"Perfectly."

"Harvey will certainly have arranged to have you followed. He's like that. Cautious. There's no way he'll let you swan across Europe with a few million pound's worth of coke unattended. Keep you eyes peeled and try to spot the tail. That way we can take care of them."

"Fine."

The woman made ready to go. "One last thing, James. An old colleague of mine, Alex Bowman, used to work for Harvey. Ever come across him?"

"Bowman? No." Fitzroy didn't recognise the name.

"You're sure?"

"Quite sure. I always deal direct with Harvey."

"Tall, good-looking man. Athletic." She paused. "I heard he'd been killed in an accident. But I think there may be some mistake. I'd like to be sure. I wouldn't want to send flowers to his widow if he's still alive."

"Why not check with Harvey?"

“It isn’t important. Just thought you might have heard something.”

“No. Nothing I’m afraid.”

“If you do hear anything, be sure to let me know. If he knows what’s going on he may decide to tail you himself. He could be dangerous.”

When the woman left Fitzroy poured himself a drink and tried to grasp the implications of the position he was in. Ramsay had promised a new identity, new passport, new life. And now the woman had put money on the table. This could be a very tricky situation, fraught with danger. But there had to be a way to garner both prizes. He would have time to work out the strategy later. Once he had control of the coke.

***

It was a dream or a nightmare, she couldn't tell which, so perhaps it was both. Melanie wondered how long she had been there. At first she had tried to count the days, made scratch marks on the wall when she woke each morning. But after a while she realised there was no point. She had no conception of time any longer. Night and day were the same, blurred together in the same seamless continuum. There was no such thing as reality. Just a sense of aimlessly drifting between one injection and the next. The injections were the one fixed point of reference she had left, the sunrise and sunset of her days.

She stood naked in front of the mirror and hardly recognised herself. There were still times when she was lucid and understood precisely what was happening, and why. At others she was in a different realm, a state of total unreality between torment and joy, as the craving for the drug that made life possible at all built up to the terrible pitch where she lost control and the nurse would come like an angel of death to inject the deadly life-giving elixir into her veins.

She had fought it at first, she still did sometimes, but the nurse was always there to oblige when the time came. The nurse was kind. She seemed to have a mild regret about what she was doing, treated her patient with a care that was sometimes quite touching.

Melanie's self-esteem had been the first thing to desert her. She had hung on as long as she fought it, fought them. But once she gave herself more or less willingly to Daisy it had left her. She was broken. She wanted to die. Only the craving for the injections kept her going, and it was killing her. Her appetite went next. She couldn't summon the energy to eat. She couldn't summon the energy to think, not any more. She even gave up on prayer. She lay on the bed simply being, not thinking or doing. As long as she was high, it was enough. More than enough.

Melanie looked at her emaciated body with indifference. Her collarbone and ribs were visible now. The breasts she had once been so proud of had almost disappeared. Her hair was matted and lifeless, cheeks hollow, eyes sunken and without expression. The nurse encouraged her to bathe daily but the effort was too great and she thought she probably stank. Daisy didn't come to see her any more. The fair angel no longer enjoyed her.

What would Alex think of her now? She had kept herself for Alex like a good girl should, making him wait, saving herself for later. He wouldn't want her now. She had nothing left to give. She was a whore. Daisy's whore. It didn't matter. Alex would never come. Wouldn't find her even if he tried. And if he did come he wouldn't be able to save her. She no longer wanted to be saved.

She looked at the silent clock on the wall. In a few minutes the nurse would come with her injection. They didn't torment her now. There was no point. She had told them what little she knew, the house in San Roque and all the names, Lieberman, Ambrose, Draycott, Ramsay, the trips to Morocco. They seemed to know most of it anyway.

Sister Duncan came in with the syringe on a silver tray with a white cloth as if it were a dry martini. Melanie felt fine. The ache in the joints was still some way off. She was pleased the nurse had time to talk.

"There's still no sign, he hasn't come for you yet?"

"There's no point any more. Just look at me. It doesn't matter. This is my lover now." She put her hand on top of the tray and caressed the syringe, knowing it was nearly time. He wouldn't come. Why should he? They had never been lovers. Barely even friends.

It was time. Melanie lay on the bed, waiting. Her breath came in gasps, a little at a time. She saw the outline of the nurse only dimly now, it was hard to focus. She felt the hands on her arm as the nurse swabbed the place above her wrist that was still unmarked. She didn't feel the needle. Just the sudden surge of toxin through her veins. She blacked out.

The nurse felt a short sharp spasm. She searched for a pulse but in her panic she couldn't find one. She ran to the door, screaming.

"Get Dr. Bligh! For Christsake get Dr. Bligh!"

***

Bowman's taxi dropped him at the offices of The Echo, an elongated box of steel and glass set in the desert of the docklands. He paid the driver, walked through the revolving doors and across the marble lobby to the reception desk. The security guard wore a uniform lifted from "B" movies of the fifties, gunmetal buttons, epaulets, gold braid. The man was an asthmatic, seriously overweight. A half consumed cigarette balanced on his lower lip, ash ready to drop. When he spoke he wheezed.

"You don't got no appointment then?" The cough started in his stomach, spraying ash over his barrel chest.

"I'm sure he'll see me."

"Most irregular." He would have to consult. He picked up the phone and dialled Flaherty's personal private secretary. "Bloke here wants a word with the boss, name of Bowman." A pause, then he put his hand over the mouthpiece and whispered, "She says what's it about?"

Alex took the instrument and said, "Tell him it's Alex Bowman. And tell him it's bloody urgent." He slammed the phone back in its cradle. Five seconds later she rang back and Alex rode the lift to the top floor.

She was waiting by the lift when the doors opened, a mature woman, in an elegant black suit. She seemed to be under some kind of stress. "I'm sorry, Mr. Bowman, I didn't recognise the name. Mr. Flaherty will see you right away." She led him down the corridor and into Flaherty's spacious office overlooking a bend in the river and downstream toward the Isle of Dogs.

Flaherty stood by the window, his features blurred by the glare. He was on the phone but he barely spoke. Now and then a monosyllable, sure, right, fine, OK. He motioned Alex to an armchair. He barely glanced at his assistant as he put down the phone. Bowman wondered what made her so nervous. She was avoiding eye contact with him and with her boss. Perhaps she was new to the job.

"Bring us some coffee, would you?" Flaherty's tone was brusque. When she had gone he turned to Alex, "I'm sorry, would you have preferred tea?"

"Coffee will be fine. It's good of you to see me right away."

She returned in seconds, jangling cups on a metal tray. Flaherty said, "No calls. And cancel my three o'clock with the City desk, OK?" His voice was calm as he came to join Alex at the table. "What can I do for you, Alex? You don't mind if I call you Alex, do you? I almost feel we've met."

"We haven't, have we?"

"Met? No, we haven't, but Melanie talks a lot about you. It's about her you wanted to see me? Not being a nuisance, is she? I know how persistent she can be. That's what makes her such a bloody good reporter. I miss her, we all do."

"When did you last hear from her?" Alex watched Flaherty stir his coffee. He hadn't added any sugar but he stirred it just the same.

"Must be three or four weeks at least. She was doing a piece for me. About you as a matter of fact. Bent Copper Badly Wronged. That's why I recognised the name. Last time I saw her she asked me to set up a couple of meetings for her. With Berringer. And your QC. Faraday,"

“Faraday?” Alex looked surprised “Why Faraday?”

“Search me. But that’s what she wanted. I haven’t heard from her since. Looks like you haven't either. I did hear she’d taken time off to go to a health farm for a couple of days."

"She left Spain in a hurry. While I was out of the country. We seem to have lost track of one another." Alex wondered if he should tell him about the tape but decided against it. "Tell me Sean, if she needed help, who would she talk to? If she wasn't talking to you?"

“Help with her project, you mean?” Flaherty thought for a second. "Harriet, I suppose."

"Can I speak to Harriet?"

"Not easy. Harriet's a computer. You would have to know the protocols."

The intercom buzzed on his desk. The assistant’s voice was shrill, “I have Phillip Hyde on the line. You wanted to speak to him urgently.”

“I said no calls.” Flaherty interrupted. “That means no calls, damn it!”

Flaherty saw Alex hadn't understood. "Melanie has a terminal at home, and a modem. She would have had a password. Normally we would cancel access if someone left the paper but with Melanie it's unlikely anybody bothered. She was too senior, too well liked. She could dial Harriet, using the modem, and ask her anything she liked. Harriet houses the data bank. Carries a copy of everything we print, going back ten years or more. Harriet’s unique. Best archive in the country. We're very proud of her."

"So she could read anything that's on the files. What else?"

Flaherty got up, went to the window and stood with his back to Bowman, watching a tugboat manoeuvre onto its mooring. "She could look for matches."

"Matches?"

"Pick any number of random items. South Africa. Israel. Chemical weapons. Harriet will search the files and come up with anything we ever ran where the three inputs occur. Where they match."

"Do you keep a log? Can you track the matches she was looking for?"

"Not any more. We used to, but there wasn't any point. Most of the time people are looking for connections that don't exist. It was a waste of time."

"That thing on your desk, it's a terminal, right?"

Flaherty nodded. The tug was secure now, straining on its hawser.

"Do you know how to ask the questions?"

"Sure."

"OK, lets try one." Alex stood over Flaherty to watch the sequence in which he pressed the keys.

"Let's see." Alex thought for a moment. "Try Berringer, Torres, Esler." He watched Flaherty's face for a reaction. There was none. "How long will that take?"

"Maybe a minute, a minute and a half. Depends how many terminals are accessing data at the same time." The screen flashed back its answer. "No match found."

"OK." said Alex. "Let's try another way. Delete Torres."

Flaherty re-typed the two remaining names. "*Adios,* Miguel." he said as he pressed the keys.

"*Adios* Miguel?" said Alex. "You know Torres?"

"Sure I know him."

"How come?"

"I run a newspaper. Knowing people is my trade. You want to meet him?"

"Why would I want to meet him?"

"No reason." said Flaherty as an article appeared on the screen from an edition that was six years old, about the time of the trial. *"Berringer Takes A Bath."* It wasn't very flattering. Berringer had sold a tanker fleet to Esler's shipping company. There was a suggestion Berringer had done another very bad deal, sold assets for less than they were worth.

"Mean anything?" said Flaherty.

"Not to me it doesn't." There was a lot of technical financial detail. "Who writes this stuff?"

"The financial editor. Or someone on his staff. You want to speak to him? He's just down the corridor."

"Why not?"

Flaherty buzzed his assistant on the intercom. "Ask Fleetwood to pop in. And bring us more coffee and another cup." He pressed a key and the printer rolled off a hard copy of the article.

Derek Fleetwood was a very young man to be running the financial desk on a major newspaper. He had the air of an academic, tall, slightly distracted. Flaherty didn't bother with introductions but put the article on the table in front of the young man.

"You wrote this yourself?" said Flaherty.

"I wrote it. You cut it."

Flaherty reddened. "Nonsense, Derek. I never cut anything, you know that. Not without good legal grounds. Not unless it's libel."

Fleetwood shrugged. "Maybe it was libel. Maybe it was worth it. It's about time someone blew the whistle on Berringer. The man's a total incompetent. Or worse"

"What do you mean?" said Alex.. "I thought he was very successful."

"He's done a string of very bad deals. Selling off assets too cheaply. If I were a shareholder I'd be asking questions. Maybe I'll buy a few shares. Turn up at his Annual General Meeting."

"You'll do no such thing, my lad. Not if you value your job." Flaherty was angry.

Alex looked across at the arrogant young man. "You're a qualified accountant?"

Fleetwood's lips curled up at the corners. "Good Lord no! I read Classics."

"Let me try something on you anyway. Suppose you're running a large business. A very large business."

"As big as Berringer's?" Fleetwood was into games.

"As big as Berringer's."

"A public company?"

"A public company. You want to siphon money out of the business. Very large sums. Millions. But it has to be legal. It has to get past your auditors."

"Blackmail?" Fleetwood was warming to the challenge. He enjoyed puzzles.

"If you like. How would you do it?"

Fleetwood put his hands behind his head, leaned back in his chair and closed his eyes. After a while he said, "Immateriality."

"Immateriality?" Alex repeated.

"I'd need an accomplice on the other side of the deal. Preferably offshore. I'd sell him an asset for less than it's true worth. He'd sell it on to a third party for its real value, making a profit. We'd split the difference.

"And where does immateriality come in?" Alex wanted to be sure he understood.

"It's a public company, right? In theory if there's a loss against book value I should report it to the shareholders in the annual accounts. But if the loss is small in the context of the overall size of the business, it's immaterial. I don't have to show it as a separate item in the accounts."

"And that would be legal? Your auditors would go along with it?"

"Of course they would. The auditor's real job is to bury bad news. Keep everything tidy. Think of Maxwell. Think of Enron. Auditors have to keep their clients happy, just like everybody else. Otherwise they'd go out of business. If the deal makes them nervous I could always re-value some other asset and report the net position. They'd always go along with that."

"And you reckon that's what Berringer's been doing?" Fleetwood didn't answer. Bowman turned to Flaherty. "Is that where the libel came in? Is that why you cut the article?"

Flaherty returned to the window and looked out at the river. "Derek's just guessing. There isn't any proof. If Berringer took us to court we would loose."

"OK, there's no proof." said Alex. "But assuming Fleetwood is right, how long has it been going on?"

"At least ten years." said Fleetwood. "He must have processed millions."

Alex was making ready to leave when Flaherty's assistant came on the speaker phone. "Sorry to interrupt. There's a Dr Bligh on the phone."

"Bligh?" Flaherty interjected. "Never heard of her!"

"She says it's about Melanie Drake."

"Put her on." said Flaherty, eying Bowman.

"Mr Flaherty?" Dr Bligh sobbed into the phone. "You must get a message to Alex Bowman. It's vital! Tell him she has only days to ...." The line went suddenly dead.

***

Verity lay by the pool. Looking back at the house she could see Harvey leaning over the balcony of his room observing her. He was losing weight, which suited him, and losing his tan, which didn't. She waved, to make sure she had his attention. Then she removed the top of her bikini. Taunting Harvey had become an obsession. Ambrose had warned her not to. He said Harvey could still be dangerous. On the upper terrace stood three of the Spanish personnel who were there to keep an eye on her, which they certainly did. She waived at them and there was a ripple of appreciation through the group.

She was thinking about Alex, and why he hadn't returned. She couldn't understand it. Nor why he had gone away in the first place. It was Verity he loved. She was sure of that. She thought about the woman in black. She was the key to getting Alex back. Only Verity knew how to find her. Knowledge was power. Alex would have to come back to her, make love to her, earn his reward. When Ambrose appeared on the terrace she beckoned to him to join her.

“Cover up.” said Ambrose, looking back at the house. “Too much exposure will upset the help.” Ambrose knew everything there was to know about Verity. Nobody had told him a thing. He just knew. Knew how she earned her living. Knew what she had done for Harvey. And as likely as not done for Bowman too. Ambrose liked her. Any man would.

“What can I do for you, sweetheart?”

“I need to speak to Alex. I have something for him.”

“I bet you do.” thought Ambrose. But what he said was “Alex isn’t here, sweetheart. He flew back to London in a hurry. Don’t ask me why. He hasn’t been in touch. Didn’t even say goodbye.” Ambrose was as concerned as she was. What the fuck was Bowman up to?

“It’s very important. Really it is.” Verity smiled her convent smile.

“Sure it is, sweetheart. Why don’t you tell me what it is and I’ll pass it on to Alex when he calls. He’s bound to phone soon.”

"No." said Verity. "This is just for Alex. Let me know when he phones. Then I can speak to him direct. Tell him it's very important.."

Ambrose climbed the terrace steps on his way back to the house. "OK you guys!" he shouted at the group of guards. "Give the lady some air willya! Nobody within twenty metres! And you Harvey!" he gestured to the balcony. "Get your friggin' ass inside and close those shutters! What do you think this is? A fuckin' peep show!"

***

Fitzroy arrived at *La Hacienda Blanca* late that afternoon. The taxi deposited him in front of the wrought iron gates and he rang the bell. The guard closed the gate behind him and checked his name off on a list. He was expected. He was an hour early for his appointment and Ambrose wasn't back yet, but the guard let him through anyway and watched him wander up the terrace steps towards the pool, briefcase in hand.

Fitzroy wanted to say goodbye to Harvey. He was fond of Harvey. Grateful for the money he had made working for him over the years. Harvey had set him up. Given him his start. The financial freedom he enjoyed. If Harvey's time had come, at least the messenger was a friend. Fitzroy entered the sitting room and paused while his eyes became accustomed to the light. He opened the briefcase, took out the Beretta and screwed the silencer in place.

Harvey was supposed to be under guard but the Spanish took their duties lightly and were far more interested in looking after Verity down by the pool. So Fitzroy climbed the stairs unnoticed and went up to find Harvey resting in his room.

A little later Fitzroy appeared on the balcony outside Harvey's bedroom. An acute observer would have noticed he was trembling slightly. He saw the knot of guards surrounding Verity on the lower terrace by the pool. She couldn't have had more protection if she'd been a visiting Head of State She looked as gorgeous as ever, demure in a one piece bathing suit that set off her tan and figure to perfection. Fitzroy had never known a woman like her. He'd known girls of course, lots of them. But Verity was all woman. He wanted her. Wanted her badly. And the thought he was about to kill her gave him an unexpected edge. An edge he'd never experienced before. He didn't think he could control it.

Fitzroy went down to the terrace and called out, "Hey Verity. Come on into the house. I'd like to say goodbye."

"James! I didn't know you were here!" Verity put on her robe and rushed to him, the guards watching her every movement as she bounced up the terrace steps. James had disappeared back inside and she followed him into the dark room. She didn't see him till her eyes became accustomed to the light. Then he was there, standing behind her, taking her breasts in his hands, kissing her neck. *Fondling her*. She could feel his pathetic little hard-on ramming against her buttocks. "No, James! For Christ sake! Stop it!" She turned and slapped him across the face with all the force she could muster. Fitzroy ejaculated.

"It's Harvey." James whispered, holding the side of his face. "I don't think he's very well. I think he could be having a heart attack." *You bitch! You fucking whoring bitch!*

Without thinking, Verity rushed upstairs to the bedroom, Fitzroy following behind. When she entered the room she saw Harvey lying on the floor. She knelt down beside him and took his head in her hands. As she lifted it she saw the pool of blood and what was left of the back of his head, splattered against the wall. Verity turned to Fitzroy in panic as he picked up the silenced Beretta from the table. It coughed once as he pumped a single shot into her heart. Verity slumped to the floor, her arms intertwined with Harvey's.

Fitzroy wiped the weapon clean on the satin sheet and pressed it into Harvey's palm, making sure he got a good impression of the index finger on the trigger mechanism. Then he lay on the bed and quickly relieved himself of his hard-on.

Five minutes later the Ambrose arrived in the Rangerover, packed tight with two hundred half-kilo envelopes of fine white powder, concealed in every possible nook and cranny. The briefing took no time at all, there was nothing much to add to what Ramsay had already said. Ambrose placed a map on the table. "Here's the route you must take, highlighted in yellow. You'll spend tonight here, at Chinchón, just outside Madrid. Tomorrow you cross into France here, at Irun, and spend the night at Biarritz. Tuesday you head for Calais and spend the last night at Montreuil. It should be a leisurely trip. There are some arrangements we need to put in place before you hit the UK. At Dover, go through the green channel. They'll be expecting you." Ambrose lied. The Brits weren't even in the frame. "Don't try anything cute, James. The Rangerover's fitted with satellite tracking. So if you deviate one inch from the designated route, a carload of tooled-up heavies will be on your ass before you know what's hit you. And be sure to wear a seat belt. Don't want you hauled over for some minor traffic violation, do we?"

"Can I see Harvey before I leave? I'd like to say goodbye."

"Sure, why not? He's resting up in his room."

A moment later Fitzroy's scream pierced the air. "Ambrose! Get a doctor, fast! He's shot himself. Verity too! Oh my God! This is awful!"

Ambrose bounded up the stairs, ran down the corridor and entered the bedroom to see the two corpses lying on the floor. "Holy Shit! What a mess!" He bent over Verity and touched her cheek. It was still warm. This was just what Bowman had predicted! "Jesus! Must have happened while we were downstairs talking. I've heard him threaten her often enough, but I never thought he'd do it!" He took a corner of the sheet and removed the weapon from Harvey's grasp. "Beretta 92F." he recited automatically. "Heavy duty silencer. I wonder why he bothered with that?" He didn't really consider the question for more than a second, he was too grateful to Harvey for taking the clean way out.

Suddenly Verity groaned and her eyes flickered for an instant. Ambrose cradled her head in his hands. “Jesus, sweetheart.” he whispered. “Jesus loves you!” He didn’t know what else to say. Her lips were moving, but made no sound. Red bubbles formed at the corners of her mouth. She raised a hand and seemed to be pointing at Fitzroy. Then she took a massive intake of breath and her eyes widened. “Tell Alex.............tell Alex.......” Then she closed her eyes and was gone.

Ambrose kissed her lightly on the forehead and laid her down to rest. He was silent for a while, then he looked up from the floor and said "You know what I think, James? Harvey's idea was brilliant. He just wasn't big enough to bring it off on his own, the idea was bigger than he was. But someone other than Harvey, someone with real international experience, someone connected, might just have made it work."

Fitzroy shrugged. He had no idea what Ambrose was talking about, or why he was telling him this. He looked at his watch. He would have to move fast if he was going to reach Chinchón before dark.

Ambrose called an ambulance and the police and spent the next couple of hours on tedious formalities. Then he went to Harvey’s study and sent a coded email to the London Embassy, confirming Fitzroy was on his way, so Willowby could monitor the satellite tracking device without leaving his desk. He didn’t mention he hadn’t managed to de-brief Harvey. Get details of his operation.

The location of the farm. How much it could produce. Who ran it. These were all things Bowman would know. But Bowman was out of the loop.

Ambrose knew that the Spanish phase was over. The centre of action was moving to London, and the centre of action was where he intended to be. Bowman's turf. Pity. But it had to be.

***

Fitzroy was about an hour from Marbella, high in the *sierra*, when the woman called on the mobile. He had spotted the heavies ten minutes out of the *Hacienda Blanca.* They were fifty or so metres behind him now and didn't notice Fitzroy drop his speed slightly when he took the call.

"Fitzroy." he said into the phone.

"Where are you, James."

"About an hour out of Marbella, heading north on the Madrid road."

"Do you have company?"

"There's a Rangerover behind me now. It's been there for a while."

"That'll be Harvey's people. He'll have set it up before you came to call. Or it could be my friend Bowman. What colour is it?"

“Dark green”.

“Can you read the registration?”

“Not unless I slow down. Narrow the gap”.

“No, James. Don’t do anything to attract attention. Try to have the number for me next time we speak. Don’t want to blow the wrong people away, do we? What route do you plan to take?”

“I should make Madrid tonight and cross into France tomorrow at Irun. I plan to spend tomorrow night near Biarritz and be at Dover Wednesday morning. What happens after Dover?”

“All in good time, James. Did you take care of Harvey?”

“Harvey got your message. Verity too.”

“And Bowman? Did you see any sign of Alex Bowman?”

“Bowman? No. I told you. I never heard of Bowman.”

“If you do hear anything, be sure to let me know. Otherwise everything seems to be going to plan. I’ll phone you once or twice a day, just to stay in touch.

***

Fitzroy arrived at Chinchón too late to eat, so he went to the bar, ordered beer and sandwiches, and thanked the gods that somebody, somewhere, had had the good taste to lodge him in a *Parador*. He began to sort through his options. In the far corner were two of Ambrose's heavies. Two more would be in the car park, baby-sitting the coke. The fifth would be resting, waiting his turn on the roster. But they were a problem the woman had promised to take care of.

Fitzroy had two offers to consider. There was the woman and her measly £50,000. There was Ramsay and his air-ticket, new identity, new life. But no cash. And outside, in a Rangerover to which he had the key, was approximately seven million pounds worth of coke. Give or take the odd million, one way or the other. So if the woman managed to dispatch the heavies he could find himself in pole position. In control of the cocaine. He regretted now he'd blown Mick and Paddy away. That had cost him his relationship with Hud Hudson and Jack White. They'd both vowed never to work with him again. Otherwise maybe they could have put a deal together.

Next morning Fitzroy was in the shower when he got the call. He grabbed a towel, rushed to the bedroom and snatched the mobile from the bedside table.

"Fitzroy." He sat on the bed and caught his breath.

"James? I'm sorry to call so early. I have meetings all morning so I thought I'd just touch base. Do you have that vehicle registration for me?"

"Y 592 COR"

"English plates? That's odd. Who are the heavies? How many?"

"Five of them. Yanks. No sign of your friend Bowman."

"Harvey's people. Otherwise everything's OK?"

"Everything's fine." Fitzroy cleared his throat. "Just one small problem."

"Oh? And what's that, James?" she sounded nervous.

"£50,000 isn't enough. A million would be better."

"I see. And if I say yes to a million James, what'll it be tomorrow? Two million? Five million?"

Fitzroy didn't answer. He had the car keys in his hand.

"Hold the line for a minute, James. There's someone here would like a word."

"James?" A new voice. Young. Female.

"Arabella?"

"James! Who are these people? What do they want?"

Then the old voice came back on the line. "What a lovely girl, James. So young. So attractive. Such a rich Daddy. I don't think she's done coke before, has she? I'm sure she'll enjoy it. Now be a good boy, James. Make your delivery, just as we agreed. Then you can marry Arabella in the spring, the way you planned. Live happily ever after."

"Shit!" said Fitzroy as he put down the phone. "Shit! Shit! Shit!" Arabella was worth more than the coke!

***

Torres hadn't reported Willowby's news to Medellin. There was no way they could have known about it, or even dreamed a thing like that could happen. But for Torres and Willowby it was the opportunity for a little private enterprise. The opportunity of a lifetime. That didn't stop Torres being mad at Helen and Esler for out-smarting him. Tearing up their sole-supply agreement. And then there was the heist on the M4. He didn't believe Helen and Esler were responsible, didn't think they were capable of such a thing. But he couldn't be sure. He didn't see who else it could be. He was determined to teach them a lesson. But at first he couldn't work out how. Torres could easily have had them blown away. But he didn't want to decapitate the Organisation. Just blow off its limbs. That way the Organisation would be damaged but intact. It could still function. Still buy the product when more became available. Esler and Helen would get the message and go back to doing what they were told. Torres and Willowby would be left with this massive new opportunity. Take over the farm.

It took Torres three days to put everything in place. He couldn't fly in a team from Medellin, it would give the game away. So he subcontracted the job to the Irish. They had a close working relationship and the Irish had a ready supply of semtex and detonators, right here in London. And more experience of urban terrorism that anybody else in the field.

Torres briefed the team personally. He gave them a map of the location, a detailed plan of the building, and the address where they should pick up the explosive and the van. “As soon as it’s done,” he concluded, “Take a train to Paris or Brussels and lay low for a week or two. Then make your way back to Dublin separately and in your own time.”

The three hit men collected everything they needed from a garage in Hammersmith and made their way back across the centre of town to the East End. Finding the location proved difficult and took more time than it should have. So by the time they pulled into the derelict street it was almost light.

They unloaded the van and struggled up the steps with the two heavy suitcases. They entered the church, unpacked the explosive, and distributed it along the nave, taping a small parcel of inert plastic to each pillar. Then they wired the packages and ran the cables back outside to the top of the steps and connected them to the detonator. The whole operation took about seven minutes. They drove the van to the end of the street and stopped. One of the men stepped onto the pavement, so he would have a clear line of sight back to the church. He aligned the transmitter, extended the aerial, pressed the red button and triggered the detonator. The explosion was deafening as the black and orange fireball filled the sky.

The van was half way to Waterloo Station when the first of the kids emerged bleeding and screaming from the crypt.

***

17

Ambrose took the first available flight, so he would be in London before the coke. He turned up at Ramsay's flat the following afternoon. There was nothing left to do at the Spanish end. Harvey's suicide had seen to that. So Ben had left it to the Spanish boys to tidy up the loose ends and close down what remained of Harvey's operation, leaving him free to concentrate on the coke.

"What's up, Ben?" said Alex when he opened the door. "I thought you were back in Spain nurse-maiding Harvey and the coke."

"You ready for some bad news, Alex old buddy?"

"Tell me." Alex held his gaze.

"Harvey's dead. Topped himself."

"Shit!" said Bowman. "I had a soft spot Harvey. That's bad."

"There's worse. He took Verity with him. Just like you said he would."

"Oh Jesus! No! Not Verity!" Alex collapsed in a chair.

"Afraid so, Alex. I knew you'd be upset."

"Christ, Harvey!" Alex put his head in his hands. "Why did you have to waste her?" Alex was silent for a while as he struggled to put the thought of her out of his mind.

Then he said “So what’s happening with Fitzroy and the coke?”

“I’m off the case. Willowby has taken charge. Fitzroy’s driving the stuff to the UK. There’s a carload of minders on his tail. Willowby’s men. They should hit Dover sometime Wednesday.”

“Willow’s informed the NDIU? Customs? The Yard?”

“He doesn’t trust the Brits, Alex. Not after Rutland. You guys are off limits.”

“Can’t say I blame him. Rutland was a disaster.” Alex took a sip of his scotch. ”So how come you’re still talking to me? If Willowby doesn’t trust the Brits?”

“He doesn’t know about you, Alex. I left certain details out of my report. You know how it is. Besides, you’re not exactly legit. No quite an establishment figure, are you old Buddy?” Ambrose chuckled.

“So where’s Fitzroy and the coke right now?” said Alex

“No idea. Not till I get to a computer. Give me a good PC and I’ll be able to hack into the Embassy system and lock-on to the satellite tracking signal.”

There weren't enough bedrooms for the three of them, so Alex decided to sit up with Ambrose. Ben had bought a bottle of The Balvenie on his way out through Malaga airport and before either of them knew it the bottle was half empty.

Alex was thinking about Verity, about her body, how wonderful she was to make to love to. He shouldn't have left her. He could see that now. But now it was too late. He could understand why Harvey had done what he did. Letting go of Verity would be impossible. But he couldn't forgive Harvey. It was such a waste. He took another sip of the scotch and silently drank to her memory.

"What do you plan to do when this is over, Alex?" said Ambrose. "Go back to being a Costa bum?"

"Haven't thought that much about it, Ben. Maybe I'll go somewhere new. The Philippines or South America. Somewhere my Spanish would be useful. Maybe I'll stay on in San Roque. It's not a bad life. The sun shines most of the time, and I don't pay any taxes."

"Not paying taxes is illegal, Alex. You know that."

"Between me and the law old chap, I reckon I'm in credit." Alex waved his empty glass and Ambrose crossed the room to fill it.

"Right on, Alex. You bet you are." Ambrose's voice was mellow. "You know what we two have in common, Alex? We're both disadvantaged. You because of your record. Me because of the colour of my skin. We're both disadvantaged, but neither one of us is at fault. It makes a bond between us. No matter how good we are, how honest, how hard working, how successful, neither one of us is ever going to make it to the top. Not in the straight man's world. How's that for honkey justice?" His tone was casual but there was an edge of bitterness too.

Alex closed his eyes and raised his glass to toast the truth of what his friend was saying.

"How much money do you make in a year, Alex? In dollars? Thirty grand? Fifty? I make seventy-five. Big deal. And I pay my taxes."

Alex raised his glass again, to honour his friend's achievement.

"You know what we should do Alex? Go for the big bucks! We'd need three years, five at the very most. We'd be billionaires. We should take over Harvey's operation up at the farm. Pick out a couple of broads and live rough up there till we stash enough away to live like kings for the rest of our natural lives. It'd be easy. Growing the stuff is no big deal. We both know our way around the business. We both have the right contacts. We could get the Brits to finance us at the start, same as Harvey had in mind. What d'ya say Alex, you had one bite of the pie, wouldn't you like some more?"

Alex lay back in his chair, feet on a table, sleeping. The American got up and went across and shook him gently by the shoulder to make sure he wasn't faking.

"Only kidding, old buddy. Only kidding. Still, you must admit, it makes some kinda sense. It sure beats what we're doing now. Five years hard work and we'd be in Tit City for the rest of our lives." He tipped the last of the bottle into his glass and raised it slowly towards the sleeping Alex. "Partners."

Alex's eyes fluttered, opened, and closed again. "Sorry Ben, I missed that. Come again?"

***

Next morning Bowman woke early. He took a shower, came back downstairs and made himself breakfast. Ramsay had already left for the Yard and Ambrose was still asleep in the armchair. Alex poured two cups of coffee and went into the sitting room to wake him.

“So what’s the score?” said Alex, when Ben was on his second cup. “You plan to touch base with Willowby?”

“No hurry. I’m on leave for a couple of days.”

“I need to get my hands on the coke.” said Alex.

“You do?” Ambrose beamed. “So would a lot of people, Alex. Myself included.”

“Just for a couple of days. I’ve been offered a deal.”

“A deal? What deal?”

Alex drew the curtains, switched on the television, and played Ambrose the tape. Then he handed him the note.

“Jesus, Alex. That woman is in deep trouble. She looks seriously ill. I were you, I wouldn’t count on her surviving.” Ambrose thought for a moment. “So you need to hi-jack the snow?”

"Borrow it. Just for a couple of days. Then Willowby can have it back."

"Willowby can have it back? You sure of that, Alex? You don't think you'd be tempted..............? Not once you had it under your control............? No, of course not.............of course you wouldn't." Ambrose mused. "So where do I come in?"

"You can lead me to it."

"And then?"

"Like you said. We hi-jack the stuff."

"We?"

"Yes. We. I could use a little help."

"Willowby has a team of heavies on the case."

"How many?"

"Five."

"Armed?"

"Sure they're armed! What do you think this is, Alex? Amateur night?"

"But you'll give me a hand?"

"Sure, Alex. There's nothing I wouldn't do for you, old buddy. There's just one condition."

“What’s that?”

“I keep control of the snow.”

***

Late that morning Ambrose logged-on to Ramsay’s PC and hacked into thc DEA computer at the Embassy in Grosvenor Square. In a minute he had the satellite-tracking image on the screen and zoomed in on Fitzroy, nearing Bordeaux on the autoroute. He was right on schedule. He’d be at Montreuil that night, and Dover the following morning. Before logging-off Ambrose decided to check his email. There was an urgent message from Willowby, instructing him to call. Ambrose dialled the Embassy immediately.

“Agent Ambrose, Sir. You wanted me to call.”

“Ambrose! Where the hell are you?”

“London, Sir. I flew over. So I’d be here before the coke.”

“Have you heard from Richter?”

“Richter? No, Sir. Is there any reason I should?”

“He’s disappeared!”

“Disappeared? What about the snow?”

"As far as I know, the snow is where it should be. I have it on screen all the time. But Richter is supposed to call me every hour on the hour, confirm everything's OK. I haven't heard from him all morning. I keep dialling, but he doesn't answer."

"How come?"

"We're getting garbled reports from our people in France. There's been an explosion on the autoroute, twenty miles north of Biarritz. Maybe a petrol tanker. We're not sure. The situation's very confused. Richter could have been caught in the blast."

"That's terrible."

"Ambrose – get your ass over here right away. We need to make alternative plans. Fast"

***

Willowby sat in his office, transfixed by the slow-moving dot on the map that was now about two hundred kilometres north of Bordeaux on the autoroute travelling at a steady ninety five kilometres an hour.

"What's important now Ambrose, is safeguarding the snow."

"And rounding up the bad guys?"

"That too. But the snow's what really matters. We're talking millions here. I want you to meet this guy Fitzroy off the ferry and bring the coke here to the Embassy. I'll take care of it from then on."

"I thought we were following the snow to the bad guys, Sir. See where it leads us? I thought that was the whole point. We could have kept the snow safe in Spain."

Willowby had no idea how to answer. Ambrose was smarter than he had allowed for, more tenacious. If Willowy said the wrong thing he could blow his own cover. Jeopardise the entire project.

"If we stick to the plan, Sir" Ambrose persisted "We can still keep tabs on the snow. We'll know where it is. Then the Brits can round up the bad guys and we can impound the snow."

"We'll keep the Brits out of this if you don't mind, agent Ambrose. Incompetent bunch! I don't trust 'em. There's nothing the Brits can do for us that we can't do for ourselves." He would explain things to Torres later. Torres could have the place raided, wherever it was, and re-possess the snow before the Brits went in and arrested Esler and the rest. That way Willowby could keep his cover intact. "OK, Ambrose. Have it your way. Meet Fitzroy at Dover. Tail him to wherever he's going. Once delivery's been safely made, report back to me immediately. But remember. No Brits!"

***

It was mid morning and traffic was light in both directions so Ben spotted the BMW immediately it appeared in his rear view mirror. Ambrose was travelling in the outside lane, so he pulled over to see if the beamer would pass but it moved in behind him and stayed tight on his tail. He slowed down to thirty miles an hour, keeping an eye on Fitzroy's Rangerover as the distance between them lengthened, but still the BMW stayed put. Ambrose kicked the accelerator and closed the gap between himself and Fitzroy in seconds, but the beamer was still there, sitting on his tail.

Soon Fitzroy left the main highway and the road narrowed to a lane with hedgerows on either side. There was barely enough room for two vehicles to pass. The lane was heavily wooded on both sides and thick foliage overhead made it feel like a tunnel. After a while the road began to climb steeply, a long straight stretch ahead of them, rising to the top of the hill. Fitzroy was a hundred yards ahead now and Ambrose picked up speed so he wouldn't loose visual contact as Fitzroy went over the top of the rise.

The truck appeared from the opposite direction as Fitzroy reached the crest. It hurtled down the long straight stretch, skidded on the wet surface and jack-knifed, blocking both sides of the narrow lane. Ambrose braked hard and went into a skid, tyres screaming. His car spun out of control as he fumbled with the manual shift. He closed his eyes and hit the truck broadside on. Fitzroy had disappeared over the brow of the hill.

Ben held his breath, waiting for the beamer to smash into the rear. It didn't happen. When he opened his eyes he saw it had come to a halt a few yards back, the driver and passenger running towards him, shouting.

"Christ mate! You all right?" One of them had opened the passenger door and was unfastening the seat belt that had probably saved Ben's life.

"I'm fine, I think. Thank Christ you guys stopped in time! I'd be a pastrami sandwich by now!"

Ambrose sat still. He felt nothing except the cold. He was in shock. He sat like that for a couple of minutes, then struggled out through the passenger door. He stood by the side of the vehicle, leaning against it, making sure his limbs were intact. He was badly bruised down his right side but nothing was broken. He wasn't even cut. He still felt cold, the shock hadn't passed, and his reflexes would be slow. He sat on the bank at the side of the road and put his head between his knees and took a dozen deep slow breaths.

There were three of them. Two from the beamer and the one driving the truck. They were in a huddle, inspecting the damage to car, unsure what their next move should be. They had a yank on their hands, a goddamn nigger at that, and they didn't know what to make of him.

Ambrose stood up as the shock receded. "You guys have a phone? Could you call somebody to give me a tow?" He saw the exchange of glances as the penny dropped and they realised what the next move had to be.

"Yeah, sure. I'll call the AA for you."

Ambrose watched the man go back to the BMW to phone. He got inside the vehicle and closed the door before he dialled the number. Ambrose loosened the zipper on his bomber jacket. He didn't think these guys were armed, but he couldn't tell for sure.

"They say they'll be here in an hour." The man had got out of the vehicle but didn't approach the American. "Look, you're probably still in shock, why don't you come back to the house for coffee. Vinny can wait here for the tow truck and call me when they get here. They say an hour, but it could be two. They have to come out from town. No sense you waiting here, when you could be in the warm." The man smiled, a nice friendly open smile to show he was sincere.

"Could you throw in a shot of brandy?"

"All the brandy you want."

Three of them bundled into the front of the truck, Ambrose sandwiched in the middle. The driver backed up to the crest of the hill to a spot where he could turn. Ambrose saw Vinny standing by the beamer, phoning ahead to say they were on their way.

"You American? Long way off the beaten track, aren't you?" It was the one who had driven the BMW who spoke.

"The name's Ambrose, Ben Ambrose." He would have offered his hand but the space was too tight. "I was lost. I like to get lost, your English countryside is so pretty. I thought I might find a nice country pub. You know any good ones around here?"

The man didn't answer. They had turned off the road, through a massive wrought iron gate, and up a long secluded drive, well wooded on both sides. As they rounded a bend, Ambrose saw before him the most magnificent house he had ever seen. It took his breath away. He had no idea what period it was, he knew nothing about such things, except that it must be very old.

"You live here?" Ambrose said in amazement.

"I work here. We both do."

Ambrose walked between them up a long flight of stone steps and into the great hall. It was cavernous. The floor and walls were stone and above was a vaulted wooden ceiling below which a large minstrels gallery hung suspended. He felt like a tourist about to take the guided tour. They led him to a doorway on the far side and into what he knew must be the library. The room was panelled in unstained oak and book-laden shelves reached almost to the ceiling. Behind the desk sat a woman dressed in black, not young but very attractive. Behind her and slightly to one side stood the meanest looking sonofabitch Ambrose had seen in a long time, a pale-eyed albino built like a wardrobe. *"Jesus!"* thought Ambrose. *"The beast that ate Tokyo!"*

"He says his name is Ambrose, Ben Ambrose." said one of the guides. It wasn't exactly a formal introduction.

"Are you armed, Mr. Ambrose?" This surprised him as an opening line and he didn't answer right away. She sounded almost bored.

Slowly Ambrose lowered the zipper on his jacket and opened it to reveal the Smith & Wesson strapped to his chest. One of the heavies stepped forward and took it from its holster while the other frisked him from behind.

"Wait outside." She said, and the two heavies disappeared. "Who are you, Mr. Ambrose?" She sat erect, taking more interest in him now.

"Agent Benjamin Ambrose. Drug Enforcement Administration."

She stiffened, but she didn't speak. Instead she lit a cigarette and leaned back in her chair to blow smoke rings in the air, watching them expand and disappear into infinity.

"Is it all right if I sit down?" said Ambrose.

She made a gesture towards a high backed leather chair but still she didn't speak. Ambrose sat and watched her as she watched the rings intently, as if they were some kind of experiment to do with the origins of the universe. She seemed totally absorbed in them, forgotten he was there at all.

Ambrose was pleased she seemed so calm. It meant they could discuss things in a rational way. He was playing for very high stakes and didn't want things getting out of hand. "You have a lovely home". he said.

"Framlington? Yes, Framlington is lovely." The child had grown up here, in this very house, played here, laughed here, cried here. The child had thought of Framlington as home, which was why Helen had to have it, had to own it. She couldn't own the child, not any more. It was too late for that.

"I'd like to do a deal." Ambrose spoke softly, not wanting to distract her from the rings. He was seated now and it made him feel more equal. He reached across the desk and took a cigarette from the silver box and lit it. As he did so hc noticed the photograph in a silver frame. It was of her as a much younger woman, devastatingly beautiful, holding a young girl in her arms. Behind her, slightly out of focus, was a man with a fat featureless face and thinning hair.

After a while she said, "What deal?"

"I want to take Lieberman's operation over. Not the Spanish end. That's blown. I want Morocco. You can't run an operation like that from the UK. It has to be done locally. By somebody living on site. I'll need some help to get started. Financial help. Just like Harvey did. In exchange, I'll give you an exclusive on everything I produce."

"This farm, you know where it is?"

"Not exactly. Just that it's in the High Atlas. South east of Marrakech. It can't be that difficult to find. I'll hire a plane and fly over the whole goddamn Atlas if I have to."

She lit another cigarette but didn't smoke it, just watched it burn between her fingers slowly. With Lieberman gone, and the Colombians out of the picture, it was a very tempting offer. "Where's Bowman?"

"Looking for me and Fitzroy, I guess. I just got one step ahead of him. I'd kinda like him for a partner, if that's all right with you. He's a good man. Besides, he knows the location of the farm. He’s the only one who does, now Lieberman is gone."

"He's dangerous."

"That's what makes him a good man."

She sat thinking for a long time, turning the idea over and over in her mind, examining all the angles, till the unsmoked cigarette had burned down almost to her fingers. She stubbed it out in the crystal ashtray. "Bring me the head of Alex Bowman. Then you can have your deal."

***

The phone woke him. He must have nodded off. The curtains were drawn and the television set was on with the sound turned down low so he wouldn't miss the telephone when it rang.

"George?” Bowman yawned.

“He’s on his way." said Ramsay.

Bowman's mind had not yet cleared. He felt drowsy. Maybe he’d had one scotch too many while he waited in the unfamiliar room. "What time is it?"

"Nearly midnight. He must be planning an early night."

"Thank Christ for that. Is he alone?"

"Yes."

"I'll call you when it's over."

Alex replaced the phone in the cradle and went to the window, moving the curtain a fraction of an inch. In a few minutes the sleek black Mercedes pulled up in front of the apartment building and ten floors below he saw the driver open the rear passenger door for Torres to get out. As far as Alex could tell as he watched him cross the road, the spic was sober.

Alex went to the alcove in the hall, switched off the lights and waited for the sound of the key in the door. He had memorised the layout of the flat so Torres wouldn't have too much of an advantage. As he waited in the darkness he heard another sound, feet running, then the high-pitched sound of a woman screaming. "Shit!" he muttered. The television set was still on, a dull light flooding the hallway. Alex heard the key turn in the lock and then the hinge creaking as the door was opened. He could sense Torres standing in the doorway listening to the muffled voices from the TV, not knowing what it was. Then Alex saw the barrel of the Luger glinting in the light from the corridor as Torres stepped silently inside. Alex judged the moment Torres would pass the edge of the door and pushed it with his foot with all the force he could muster, crashing the butt of the Browning down on the spic's head. He mistimed the blow, catching the side of Torres's face, cutting deep into the flesh. The Luger clattered to the floor. Alex grabbed him by the hair and brought his knee up sharply into Torres's face as he dragged his head forcefully downward. The impact made a soft squelching sound as the nose shattered. Torres dropped to the floor unconscious, the Luger by his side.

Alex removed Torres's tie and bound his hands behind his back in a secure knot. Then he picked him up, carried him bodily into the sitting room and dumped him in a high backed chair. Torres slumped forward, blood gushing down his chin. The blow had broken his nose and split his lips wide open. His jaw was ajar so he could breathe. Alex slapped him around the face a little and soon the spic began to make incoherent moaning sounds, as he recovered consciousness.

"Come on Torres. Time to wake up. Time to talk to uncle Alex."

Torres was conscious now but looking decidedly uncomfortable. His nose was beginning to swell and the torn flesh on the left side of his face was oozing blood. Breathing was difficult. The nasal passages were blocked by the swelling and the blood, and his open mouth was dry. He made a movement of his arm as if to wipe the blood away and realised he was tied. He looked at Alex but he didn't speak. There was malice and fury in his eyes. He could feel the broken bone in his face throbbing with a dull persistent pain. But worse than the pain was the thought that he was trapped. He tugged at the binding on his wrists and felt it give a little.

"Who is she, Torres?" Alex pushed the photograph in front of him. There was no answer. Alex sighed. Torres was going to make things difficult. "Let me ask you once again nicely. If you think you're going to hold out on me things will get rough for you, OK? Whichever way you want to play it is fine by me. Here goes. Who is she, Torres? Where do I find her?"

Again there was no answer. Alex was losing patience. He stood over Torres, placed the palm of his right hand over his damaged face and pressed down hard, driving the head back against the chair, flattening the broken nose and grinding it with a slow circular motion. The pain, suddenly needle sharp, shot up into Torres's brain. He didn't scream. He didn't even flinch. But he tugged again at the binding on his wrists, feeling it give a little more. The Luger was still lying on the floor in the hall. He had a clear line to the door.

When Alex took his hand away the nose was twisted out of shape and Torres's eyes were full of tears. The blood was congealing now, its colour dark, almost brown. It flowed more slowly down his chin. Alex knew Torres was hurt. It showed in his eyes.

"Get smart Torres. I can do this all night. You can't. You've seen men crack. They always do. You'll weaken in the end. You know you will. Anybody would." The moist eyes stared back at him, showing nothing. Not even fear. "I can make things easy for you, Miguel. I have connections. They'll charge you with possession. Nothing major. Nobody will ever know." Still there was nothing, not even curiosity, in those tear filled eyes. "Whoever it is you're protecting isn't worth it, Miguel. She's a professional. She'll understand." Now there was something, just the flicker of a smile. "It won't be difficult to get to her now I have you. But if I do all the work, you get none of the credit. They'll throw the book at you. Smarten up Torres. Make it easy for the both of us." Throughout this long tirade Alex never looked away from Torres's eyes. He was looking for the chink, but so far he hadn't found one.

Torres was thinking of the stash of coke at Framlington Hall. The deal he had made with Willowby. The future they planned. Turning in Esler and Helen was a pity. But it wasn't a problem. There were other distributors he and Willowby could use, once they'd set things up at the farm. But he needed to protect the coke. The coke would finance the entire operation in a single hit. And if Framlington was raided, it was lost for sure.

"Suppose I turn you over to the Cartel instead?" Alex resumed. "Save us all a lot of trouble? You've made a pretty big mess of this whole operation. Miguel. Whoever it is you report to isn't going to be pleased."

It did the trick. The malice and fury in Torres's eyes gave way to outright panic. He moved his cut and swollen lips, trying to speak, but the new configuration of the nasal passage made it difficult for him to get out a coherent sound. At last he said "Marcus Esler and Helen Proctor. There's a third partner. The senior partner. Never met him. Don't know who he is."

"Where do I find them?" Alex held his breath. Wherever they were, Melanie would be there too.

"Framlington Hall."

“Framlington?” The name meant something to Alex but he wasn’t sure why. He looked at his hands. There was blood on them. He went to the bathroom and washed them repeatedly, scrubbing and rinsing them several times before he was satisfied. When he came back into the room he looked at the sad and broken figure of Torres. The malice and fury had gone from his eyes and without them he was nothing.

"You want to freshen up?" Alex helped him to his feet and untied his wrists. He put a consoling hand on Torres's shoulder as if they had just gone five rounds in the amateur ring and Torres had put up a good fight and lost.

Alex listened to the sound of running water. Torres had opened both taps full on. He must be running a bath. After a while Alex heard water flooding onto the tiled floor. He went to the bathroom to turn off the taps. Torres hadn't even bothered to undress. The blood draining from his wrists was turning the water pink. Alex tore a towel and quickly tied a tourniquet on both of Torres’ arms. Then he turned off the taps. “Not so fast, old chap. I haven’t finished with you yet. I want you to set up a meeting with Esler, Proctor and whoever it is they report to. Tell them you want to meet at Framlington Hall. The venue is important. Nowhere else will do. Say you want to repair bridges. Make a fresh start. It’s vital they’re all there. I want them all in a single hit. Afterwards I can have someone serve you with a warrant. They'll charge you with possession. Nothing major. You can use diplomatic immunity if you like. Leave the country on the quiet." Medellin would do a better job than any court of law. Quick and easy, and with no appeal.

***

"What the fuck took you so long?" Bowman looked at Ambrose across the kitchen table. He was angry. This was his problem and his territory and Ambrose had no business acting on his own.

"Like I said Alex, I take my instructions from Willowby. What more do you want? I know where the coke is. I know where the bad guys are. I know where your girlfriend's held. That's a pretty impressive list, if you ask me. Like I told you, I had to go through the motions of negotiating a deal. Otherwise I'd never have gotten out of there alive. It couldn't be done over night. Things like that take time. Right now I'm supposed to be on my way to Marrakech. Charter a plane and find the friggin' farm." Ambrose smiled. "'Course it would have been a help if you'd told me where it is in the first place."

Alex had an overwhelming sense of *déjà vu.* Had he thought of doing the very same deal himself? No, it must have been a dream. And yet the whole thing seemed so real. "Was there any sign of Melanie? Where she's being held?" For days he had blocked the thought of her out completely. He struggled now to keep the image from his mind, the painful vision of her mute lips mouthing his name in silence. "Alex! Alex! Alex!"

"Sorry old Buddy. It's a huge house. I couldn't go looking for her obviously. But I guess she's in there somewhere. Assuming she's still alive." It was brutal but it had to be said.

The thought that she might be dead hadn't occurred to Alex. He must have blotted it out. He closed his eyes and felt the spirit go out of him, leaving him empty inside. "Tell us about the house. How big is it? What's it like inside?" Bowman watched Ambrose intently.

"Like you'd expect, it's heavily guarded. The grounds are pretty extensive and densely wooded, so there's lots of cover. Approaching the place would be easy, except for the dogs. The whole property is crawling with Dobermans. Also I'd expect there to be trip-wires and other detection devices. Maybe booby-traps. There's nothing amateurish about this lady. The house itself is surrounded by a gravelled terrace so there's no way you can get close without making a noise. There's a security system. The usual sort of thing. Video cameras. Lights. Heat and movement detectors. Same thing inside. The place is patrolled constantly and the guards are armed. Her Ladyship even has her own personal guardian angel, a real sweetie name of Daisy. Meanest looking sonofabitch I ever did see. Albino."

Ramsay looked up from his mug of tea and frowned, but he didn't speak.

"What do you think, George?" said Bowman. "How do we get inside?"

"It's a Grade I listed building, so getting hold of the plans should be easy. They'll be lodged with the local authority. It shouldn't take long to find out who installed the security system. There's only a handful of companies capable of doing work that complex. With a set of plans and the electrical layout we should be able to find a way."

"Well, Ben." Alex smiled. "You're a maverick. But you've done a great job. Thanks to you we're holding some pretty impressive cards. Best of all, we have the element of surprise. How long would you say before they spot whose side you're really on?"

"A week at least. Maybe longer. I'm supposed to get back in touch once I've found the farm."

***

Dr Bligh sat at the end of Melanie's bed, crying. She wanted to take a pulse but couldn't find one, so she held Melanie's limp hand instead. She remembered the bright young woman who had come to see her, not so very long ago. A vibrant, intelligent, purposeful woman. And now, thanks to Dr Bligh's own intervention, that same woman was teetering on the edge of death. It would be a miracle if she survived. She had days to live at most. But the patient's problems weren't merely physical. Her spirit was broken. She hadn't the will to fight. Dr Bligh had tried to save her. Tried to get a message to Bowman. But in the end her nerve had given out. She hadn't the courage to do it. She knew all too well what would happen if she did.

Dr Bligh held the syringe in her hand. Melanie couldn't live with heroin now. But she couldn't live without it either. She wasn't strong enough to survive withdrawal. A massive dose would be a true release.

***

Bowman spent the best part of the afternoon examining the plans in minute detail. Alex was an expert in this field. He had never done a job this big, but he had done enough smaller highly complex projects to know a loophole when he saw one. Yet, try as he might, he could find none. The security people had done a very thorough job. They had the best reputation in the business and a client for whom money was no object. It was a combination that left no room for careless errors. Even arranging a power cut in the village would serve no purpose. There were stand-by generators that would cut in within seconds. And then there were the armed patrols to think of, and the dogs.

"Shit!" Bowman buried his face in his hands. "Shit! Shit! Shit! There has to be a way in! There simply has to be!"

"Christ, boss!" Ramsay yelled. "That's it! Of course it is! Brilliant! Absolutely brilliant!" Ambrose looked across at the scruffy overweight policeman. He was mystified.

"You don't get it, do you Ben?" Ramsay beamed. "It's so obvious! What Alex just said! The sewage system, for Christsake! Look at the size of the place, it's a palace! Big as a ruddy hotel! Don't you see? The sewage system has to be enormous!" He got up and walked around the room so he could look over Ambrose's shoulder and view the drawings from the other side. He picked up a pencil and used it as a pointer. "There's the main outflow. Straight into the river." He used the pencil to make a rough check of the distance against the scale on the plan. "Looks like about three hundred feet. They built quality in those days Ben, none o'yer Yankee pre-cast concrete. Nice piece o'brick work, you mark my words, six foot diameter or I'm a Dutchman." He threw the pencil down on the table to underline his point.

"What do you think, Alex?" There was a look of hope in Ambrose's eyes. "Do you think it could work?"

Alex smiled up at Ramsay. He wanted to hug him. "'Course it could, couldn't it, George? Even if the diameter isn't really six feet, which heaven knows it might be. I'll crawl up there on my hands and knees if I have to!"

***

18

The river defined the eastern boundary of the Framlington estate. It was about forty feet across at this point and the water slow moving and sluggish. The other bank was common land, belonging to the village as a whole and not to any individual. The villagers had the right to graze sheep or cattle there, but nobody did. They used it mainly for exercising their dogs.

They decided to go in early, just as soon as it was dark. They reached Framlington Common at dusk and spotted the sewage outflow pipe on the far bank with ease. About a third of it was above the water line. It looked as if Ramsay's guess about the diameter might be roughly right.

One or two commuters were still about, throwing old tennis balls for their young Labradors to chase. But it wouldn't be long before nightfall. When the last dog lover had gone home for an early supper they put on their wet suits and folded their clothes into zip-up waterproof bags.

Bowman was first into the water, closely followed by Ambrose. Alex turned on his back, kicking gently, and was across in seconds with Ben not far behind. Ramsay stood on the other bank looking like a beached dolphin. He watched Alex rise out of the water and pull against the centuries old ironwork grid that sealed the end of the outflow. It crumbled in his hands like rotten wood.

Reluctantly, George put his foot in the water. It took him a full minute to pluck up courage and by then Alex and Ambrose had removed half the grid. Ramsay bent his knees slowly and plunged in, the only one to make a wave, and dog-paddled to the other side. He found Alex standing upright inside the massive pipe.

"See what I mean, Ben." said George as he joined them. "Look at that brick work! Beautiful, really beautiful!"

Alex turned, flashlight in hand, and made his way up the tunnel. He could have cut the stench with a knife. It was lethal, but he had to breathe. The footing was treacherous and progress slow. Ramsay had difficulty keeping his mouth above the waterline. But with arms out-stretched he could touch both sides for support. Within minutes they had reached the wall at the far end and stood by the iron steps that led up to the inspection cover.

Alex climbed the steps, jack-knifed under the cover, and heaved. It didn't give. He heaved again. But still there was no movement. He closed his eyes and the image burned into his consciousness. Alex! Alex! Alex! He heaved again and heard a scraping sound above his head as the iron cover moved.

They stood in a vaulted room that must once have been a scullery or a fuel store, but now was empty. They took off the wet suits and changed into dry clothing, leaving the iron cover where it lay.

"What about the alarm system?" Ramsay whispered.

"Forget it." Alex checked the clip on the Browning. "It's only ten o'clock. There'll be too many people moving about. It won't be armed till the last of them have gone to bed." He stuck the Browning in his belt and turned to Ambrose. "OK, Ben. You might as well lead. Let's go."

Ambrose went to the door and opened it. He had no precise idea where he was, it wasn't part of the house he had been in before. But from his memory of the plans he reckoned they were in a sub-basement somewhere below the kitchens. They found a narrow staircase and moved to the floor above. Then to the floor above that. Ambrose thought he knew where he was by now. He had spent a couple of days negotiating his deal and had been in this part of the house before. He pushed open a door and they emerged into a broad corridor.

"The library is that way. She uses it as her office."

"Not yet." Alex grabbed his arm. "Let's try the bedrooms first."

Ambrose moved off towards the main hall but Alex held him back. "Not the main staircase. The servants' stairs." Alex had a clear image of the plans in his mind, had studied them in meticulous detail. Memorised every last doorway and passage. He turned left towards the secondary staircase, leading now.

The three of them climbed silently to the first floor and came to a landing with a door that gave onto the gallery overlooking the main hall. Alex pushed open the door. It was the female voice he heard first.

"We need to process about five million dollars fairly quickly. There's some real estate in Spain we want to buy. Good coastal land. Isolated. We'll use the fruit canning plant in California. I have a buyer at nine million. You sell it to me for three."

Little by little she was bleeding Berringer's company to death. She'd been doing it for years. It started when she re-appeared from the States ten years ago and began to take an interest in the child. After he agreed to do it once, there was no way he could stop. She said if he did what she wanted she would leave the girl alone. But she never did.

"Why did you have to kill her?" Berringer pleaded. "Wasn't she as good as dead anyway?"

"It was an accident."

"It was murder. The police think it was murder."

She was about to stub her cigarette out in the ashtray but her wrist froze in mid-gesture. "How would you know a thing like that?"

"I don't *know* anything."

"Then stop guessing. Guessing could be dangerous. You wouldn't like that Arthur, would you? You've never had the courage of your convictions. Not even for your darling daughter. Except of course she was never really yours." She completed the gesture now, crushing the cigarette firmly in the ashtray. She had taken it from the hotel in Marbella. It had the hotel's name on it and an old

Spanish proverb. *"Si no tienes, no eres."* She had worked out what it meant. "If you have nothing, you are nothing." Nothing. She had started with nothing. Nothing except the child.

A second male voice came from directly below the gallery, out of sight. "What time are you expecting Peter, Helen? Shouldn't he be here already?"

"Any time now." She said. "They're bringing him across from Lakeside in an ambulance."

"Where's Daisy?"

"Upstairs with the girl. He'll be down before long I expect."

Alex let the door close softly and they resumed their upward climb. He went straight to the top floor to what would have been the servants quarters when the house was built, so they could work their way down from there. When he reached the top of the staircase he went left to the end of the corridor, the others following behind. He opened the door to an empty room, then another, then a third. By this time he was back almost to the head of the stairs.

He heard a sound from below and looked down to see the albino emerging from a room, putting on his jacket. He was packing something big and powerful in a shoulder holster slung on his right side. So he would go for the gun with his left hand.

Alex watched the white head disappear down the stairs. He waited no longer than a minute and lead the way silently to the floor below and pushed open the door. She was sleeping, heavily drugged and sleeping. She wore a white towelling robe that wasn't tied and lay on top of the bed, limbs akimbo. She was skeletal. She looked as if she would break if you touched her. There was a dank unpleasant smell in the room, though the window was open. The curtain fluttered gently in the breeze. It was trying to reach her, to be her shroud. Alex couldn't bear to look.

He beckoned to Ramsay and whispered, "Stay with her, George."

Then he turned, signalling Ambrose to follow. Within seconds they were back on the gallery, overlooking the hall below. It was pitch black, well above the level of the lights in the hall below. As he looked down, Alex saw the distinguished grey haired figure of Marcus Esler.

But it wasn't Esler's voice he heard. And it wasn't Berringer's. A new voice. New and not new. Not slurred, but without edges. "Where on earth is Torres? Surely he should be here now?"

Alex leaned forward and saw the moist spaniel eyes, the soiled cloth dabbing at the ill-formed mouth. His heart sank.

"I don't understand it." she said. "He's never been this late before."

There was a movement on the stairs, just outside the gallery door. Alex froze.

"What's the point of bringing him here any way." Said Esler. "There's nothing to discuss. He could have killed scores of people at Our Lady of Mercy. It could have been me!"

"I'm not bringing him here to discuss anything, Marcus." Said Helen. "I'm bringing him here so Daisy can take care of him."

Suddenly there was a noise on the stairs. Loud this time. The sound of feet descending in a hurry. Running. Close to panic. Then a new voice. Screaming. "She's gone! Madame! She's gone!" A woman in a nurse's uniform appeared in the hall and almost bumped into the albino.

"What do you mean? Gone? She can't be! It's impossible! She can barely even walk!"

"I went in to check that she was sleeping, Mrs. Proctor. She's gone. I swear it. I've checked everywhere."

"But she hasn't walked for a week or more! She hasn't had the strength! Daisy, get a couple of the men and search the upper floors. Search the whole goddamn building if you have to."

There was the sound of footsteps running. Half a dozen men entered the hall, all of them armed. Alex decided it was time to make his move. He had waited long enough. He fired a single shot into the hall below, shattering a vase that stood on the centre table.

"Hold it right there, Daisy. One step and I'll blow your fucking head off. I'm coming down. Nobody moves. Or my partner here will blow your fucking brains out." He turned to Ambrose. "Cover me Ben. They can't see you through the glare of the lights."

"Yes, masser." Ambrose fired a shot into the wall, just to let them know he was really there. "Evenin' folks! Goddamn nigger up here, hidin' in de dark."

"Bowman!" She screamed, as Alex entered the hall. She had gone pale. She was trembling. "Ambrose, is that you up there? Kill him!" She pointed a shaking finger at Alex. "We made a deal! Kill him!"

Ambrose moved along the gallery to get a better view and fired a second shot from a different angle, so they wouldn't dare move below. It hit the wall a foot or two from Daisy. The albino froze.

Daisy stood back to the wall, just behind Alex, waiting and watching. Ambrose saw him unbutton his jacket with his left hand and look across at the woman. She nodded. Daisy was quick, amazingly quick. But Ben had the advantage. Both shots rang out at once. The albino slid to the floor, blood from his head staining the wall behind him. Alex fell forward over a chair, blood oozing from his side. Then a salvo of shots was let loose from below as a posse entered the hall. Ambrose threw down his gun. What was the point now, after all? He was alone against so many. Maybe he should have done the deal. Perhaps it could still be done.

"Take them outside! I'll kill them myself!" The woman screamed, pointing at Ambrose and Bowman. She screamed again and there seemed to be an echo. A distant screaming from outside. Suddenly all hell broke loose. Alarm bells went off all over the place. Blinding halogen lamps lit up the grounds. There was the sound of men running, dogs barking. It was bedlam outside. Shots were being fired. She ran to the window and saw the blue light flashing, one at first, then many. A convoy of cars was coming up the drive. There was a voice. A loud amplified voice. Issuing instructions.

"Lay down you arms. It's no use. You're surrounded. We have a hundred men out here." Ambrose recognised the accent, but not the commanding tone. It was George Ramsay, taking charge.

Suddenly the hall was full of uniforms and the sound of feet escaping. Ramsay rushed to Alex who had fallen to the floor, bleeding profusely. George bent down to see if he was breathing.

"So you got her out OK?" Alex's voice was very weak.

"Light as a feather, boss. Light as a bleedin' feather."

***

It was several days before the doctors would allow visitors. For a while it looked as if they might not save him. The bullet had entered the rib cage from behind at an angle, travelling right to left, and shattering the sternum.

Ramsay and Ambrose had travelled together but the nurse suggested they should go in one at a time. He was still very weak and needed all the rest he could get. She would allow them a few minutes each. Ambrose said George should go in first.

"You can come back if you want to, boss. Berringer came good. Queen's evidence. They packed the jury at the trial, paid off the bleedin' lot. Bought the judge too, spent a bloody fortune. The Commissioner is delighted. Over the moon. He's picked up the lot of ‘em, Proctor, Esler, that bastard Draycott! Half of Who's Who was involved. We've broken the bastards Alex! Broken ‘em!"

"How is she?" It was all Bowman could manage.

"She's fine boss, absolutely fine. Considering. Still weak of course. Much too weak for cold turkey. They have her on a substitute, methadone I think. They'll have to keep her on it for a while. They think she'll be all right. As long as she has the will to fight. She's already putting on weight."

Alex eyes closed, opened, and closed again. He seemed to be on the very edge of sleep. Ramsay tiptoed to the door and found Ambrose standing in the corridor outside. "Don't be long Ben, I think he's very tired."

Ambrose sat on the edge of the bed. Alex's eyes were closed now and he didn't want to wake him. "You bastard, Bowman!" He muttered. "Why didn't you tell me what you and George were up to?"

He saw Bowman's lips move but he couldn't make out what he said. He put his ear to Alex's mouth. "What was that, old buddy? Come again?"

"I had a dream." Alex repeated. "I had a dream."

“Sure you did.” said Ambrose, not knowing what he meant. “This is good-bye Alex. For a while anyway. Willowby’s given me a new assignment. I start a language course on Monday. He wants me to learn Arabic.”

***

Bowman joined the A3 at the top of Putney Hill and watched the depressing stretch of cloned suburban houses slip by. The urban sprawl gave way to lush green fields with a suddenness that surprised him. He eased the car into fifth gear and turned off the radio.

He had spoken to the doctor by phone. Her general health was improving slowly and she was still putting on weight. She was taking more interest in herself and her surroundings and was able to go for walks quite frequently now. She was still taking the substitute of course, would have to take it for some time, but the dose was being reduced slowly and signs were that she was becoming less dependent. But the overall prognosis was still unclear. There were deep psychological scars that would have to heal themselves. Something dreadful had happened to the patient. Something beyond the drugs themselves. Something she couldn't bare to think of even now. Everything would depend on her willpower in the end. On her having a reason to survive.

The massive wrought iron gateway came into view at the top of the short drive. Beyond it, half a mile away, the facade of Burlington's beautifully proportioned Palladian masterpiece sat on top of a low hill. Bowman slowed the car for a moment to take in the colonnaded portico, topped by its dome, and the two identical wings that stretched away on either side. The small hand painted sign by the gate, gold on olive green, announced discreetly "Lakeside Health and Fitness Spa" and below that in a more simple script, "Strictly Private. Keep Out." Stapled across it was a temporary legend in large red letters. "Under New Management."

Alex parked the car on the paved terrace opposite the portico and pulled up the canvas hood. It was beginning to rain with that light English drizzle that permeates everything.

He sat on a chair by the window. It was open and the curtain fluttered in the light breeze that blew in from the garden, carrying with it the scent of spring. Outside he could see the artificial lake, which probably gave the place its name.

"She's been through a very harrowing experience." the specialist said.

"The drugs?"

"Not just the drugs, There's something else, ...a complication." He paused, wondering how best to phrase it. “How close are you to the patient, Mr Bowman?"

"Close?" Alex looked out across the lake.

“She’s been seeing a priest.”

“A priest?”

"You see Mr Bowman, I'm afraid she's....,......." He began playing with the pencils on his desk, arranging them in some sort of order. "Perhaps I'd better let her tell you herself."

Melanie was sitting up in bed. She was wearing make up for the very first time. It made her feel good. She hadn't wanted him to come. Not yet. She wasn’t ready. Had told the doctor so. But the doctor seemed to think it would help her in some way and she didn't have the strength to argue. She wasn't strong. She wasn't even clean. Her body was full of chemicals. She couldn't survive without them. Not for a single day. Her body was defiled in other ways too. Ways she couldn't bare to think of even now.

Alex didn't want to tell her all that had happened, she wasn't strong enough, not yet, so they just made small talk instead. There would be time for other things later on as her health slowly improved. The nurse had said no more than half an hour and even in the almost silence it passed very quickly. When it was time to go he went to her side and kissed her gently on the cheek. She took his hand in hers and held it.

"Who was she Alex? This evil, evil woman."

"Mary's mother. Mary's natural mother. Not now. I'll explain it all another time."

"Now Alex. I really need to understand. It helps to know."

Alex sat on the bed. "Mary was adopted. Berringer paid the mother off, gave her a bucket of money provided she lived abroad. She went to the States and ended up in the drugs trade in a pretty big way. But she never forgot about the child. And she never forgave Berringer for taking her. When she'd made her pile she came home and tried to get Mary back. But she couldn't win her affection. So she put her on drugs and started to use her for other things. Mary was helpless once she became addicted. Then Helen started blackmailing Berringer as well. She's been bleeding him for years.

"And where did you come in?"

"We were pretty close to bringing them in, her and her partners. Draycott knew that. But he only knew the big picture. They needed someone close to me. So they could follow developments in detail. Limit the damage to their operation. Mary moved into my flat. I used to tell her everything. So they were always one step ahead. In the end they planted the cocaine, and Mary turned me in. The rest you know."

"Was Faraday involved?"

"No, not Faraday. They wanted me to have the best possible defence so there'd be no chance of a mis-trial. They simply bought the jury."

Melanie made a sharp intake of breath. "Oh my God! Mandy! Alex, there was a girl........."

"We know about the children. They're getting treatment now. Those that weren't killed in the fire. They recruited them as addicts and turned them into pushers. A disciplined army of pushers." He could see she was fading fast. "That's enough now. You need to get some rest."

Melanie took his hand again and held it tight. "My turn now. There's something I must tell you." She was fighting back the tears. "Alex…….Alex…… I'm.........” She started to sob. "I'm pr..........."

"Not now. It's late. I have to go." There was a knock and the nurse came in to tell him it was time.

Melanie held him for a moment longer. "Friends?"

"Friends."

"You'll come again? Promise!"

"Promise."

***

The tiny biplane taxied to the end of the runway. The pilot turned to the sole passenger and put up his thumb to signify they had clearance to take off. Then he opened the throttle and the plane lurched forward to begin its dash to get airborne. As it began its steep climb the ancient walled city with its minarets and vast central square came into view below. The plane banked to the south east to follow the Ouarzazate road and continued its ascent through a patch of clear air turbulence, till it was over the high pass at Tizi n'Tichka where it banked again and headed up towards the snow capped peaks of the Toubkal.

O'Malley heard the distant drone of the engines high above. He wondered what it might be, a sightseeing trip for some rich tourist, or a farmer out spraying his crops. He looked up and raised his hand to shade his eyes from the glare of the noonday sun. From a distance it would have looked as if he were waving.

the end